PRAISE FOR H

This Violent Heart

"*This Violent Heart* follows a woman's struggle with identity, regret, and the unanswered questions she's carried ever since her best friend died as a teenager. Come for the chapters dripping in longing; stay for the sizzling love story and redemption arc."

—Elle Marr, #1 Amazon Charts bestselling author of *The Alone Time* and *Your Dark Secrets*

"A sultry, immersive thriller about the impact of deception: the lies of religious fundamentalism, the lies our loved ones hide behind, and the lies we tell ourselves. Levy deftly explores the complexities of teenage love, burgeoning sexuality, spiritual trauma, and survivor's guilt—with enough suspense to keep you constantly on edge. This one's a scorcher."

—Amy Suiter Clarke, author of *Girl, 11*, and *Lay Your Body Down*

"An utterly unputdownable read that hurts and heals in equal measure. *This Violent Heart* is not just a twisty thriller but also a poignant, nuanced deep dive into identity, sexuality, and belonging. With its dual timeline narrative and cleverly interspersed journal entries, tension and secrets build until the shocking truth is exposed. Powerful, intense, and wholly addictive."

—Laurie Elizabeth Flynn, author of *Till Death Do Us Part* and *The Girls Are All So Nice Here*

"Sexy, addictive, and riveting, *This Violent Heart* is a twisty mystery in which a damaged woman works to solve the mystery of her best friend's death as a teenager, grappling with her own bisexuality as she does . . . This evocative thriller is a sizzling page-turner you won't want to miss!"

—Christina McDonald, *USA Today* bestselling author

"Filled with scenes that will make your heart race one second and break the next. Levy conquers the dual timeline with perfection, which cleverly unfolds as you beg for more. An unmissable story of acceptance, revenge, and redemption."

—Jaime Lynn Hendricks, bestselling author of *A Lovely Lie*

"*This Violent Heart* is the kind of book you can't help staying up all night—maybe even under the covers with a flashlight—to finish. Simultaneously racy and romantic, Heather Levy's latest is the thrilling, twisty story of a young woman trying to embrace her identity and solve the mysteries of her past. Come for the hot sex; stay for the real insight into friendship, forgiveness, and the human heart. I loved it."

—Julia Dahl, author of *I Dreamed of Falling*

Hurt for Me

"*Hurt for Me* is a sensual, suspenseful, and sometimes terrifying walk through the secret chasms between what we tell people we want and what our hearts desire. After you turn the last page, you will be BEGGING for more from Heather Levy, the new voice of erotic thrillers."

—S. A. Cosby, bestselling author of *All the Sinners Bleed*

"Visceral and authentic, *Hurt for Me* is a deliciously kinky thriller that subverts the tired, traditional power dynamics of the genre and centers the kind of women who are too often relegated to a sexy accessory."

—Christa Faust, author of *Hit Me* and the Edgar Award–nominated
Money Shot

"*Hurt for Me* is a sizzling, expertly constructed thriller that doesn't cool down for even a second. Best of all, Levy gives us a main character, Rae, who is wholly original, richly imagined, and hugely appealing."

—Lou Berney, Edgar Award–winning author of *Dark Ride*

"Levy's latest grips you by the throat from page one and never lets up. It's a riveting, sexy, twisty mystery full of beautiful writing and characters you can't help but care about."

—Jess Lourey, Edgar Award–winning author of *Unspeakable Things*

"A damaged woman reclaims her power in this sharp and insightful thriller set in an original (and spicy) world. Heather Levy more than delivers on the intriguing premise of a dominatrix whose client goes missing, leading her into a shadowy world of secrets, cruelty, and corruption. A steamy page-turner."

—Robyn Harding, international bestselling author of *The Drowning Woman*

"*Hurt for Me* is a sexy, nonstop thriller full of kink, fun, and murder. Both provocative and illuminating, Heather Levy nails it, or rather, paddles it. A must-read for anyone who likes their mysteries with a side of bondage."

—Amina Akhtar, author of *Kismet*

"A sweat-inducing dark romance wrapped in a thriller plot tight as bondage restraints, *Hurt for Me* will leave you hot for power couple Rae and Dayton, bothered by the infuriatingly realistic injustices they battle together, and begging for more from Heather Levy's brilliant mind."

—Layne Fargo, author of *Temper* and *They Never Learn*

"*Hurt for Me* is a steamy thrill ride with something for everyone: a dark, sexy romance; an exploration into the world of BDSM; a sharp, twisty thriller; and a hopeful exploration of the joy and power of chosen family. Rae Dixon is a heroine to root for!"

—Halley Sutton, author of *The Hurricane Blonde*

"Heather Levy's latest will have you gasping one minute and hollering the next, thanks to whip-smart prose and a protagonist who will fight like hell to keep the past from threatening her present."

—Kelly J. Ford, Anthony Award–nominated author of
Real Bad Things

"*Hurt for Me* is a raw, visceral, unforgettable novel that honestly and openly portrays the kink community while delivering a knockout of a thriller. Heather Levy's talent seems effortless as she beautifully weaves an emotional, suspenseful, hypnotizing story about a fierce, admirable heroine who has to confront her mistakes when her past and present come face to face. A tale of love, sex, murder, and redemption, this powerhouse of a book needs to be on everyone's must-read list."

—Samantha M. Bailey, *USA Today* and #1 international bestselling
author of *Woman on the Edge* and *Watch Out for Her*

Walking Through Needles

"A spellbinding novel at the nexus of power, desire, and abuse that portends a bright future."

—*New York Times*

"*Walking Through Needles* is a challenging but worthwhile read, a standout for its frank but sensitive exploration of trauma and desire."

—*Los Angeles Times*

"A gripping, disturbing read and, perhaps for some, triggering, but I couldn't turn away."

—*Star Tribune*

"An unflinchingly brutal and beautiful journey through the darkest rivers of desire."

—S. A. Cosby, bestselling author of *All the Sinners Bleed*

"An unflinching and unforgettable look at the darkest side of desire from a fearless new voice in crime fiction. This book will get under your skin and stay there forever."

—Layne Fargo, author of *Temper* and *They Never Learn*

"A stunning, devastating debut. As the story's taut mystery unfolds with beautiful prose across past and present, a deeper, far more monstrous truth awaits readers: nothing's as capable of cruelty quite like the human heart."

—P. J. Vernon, author of *Bath Haus* and *When You Find Me*

"A midnight exercise in noir fiction that is carefully executed and fascinating in a reptilian way . . . a dark success."

—*Booklist*

THIS
VIOLENT
HEART

OTHER TITLES BY HEATHER LEVY

Hurt for Me

Walking Through Needles

THIS VIOLENT HEART

Heather Levy

Ⓜ Montlake

Published by Montlake, Seattle

www.apub.com

Amazon, the Amazon logo, and Montlake are trademarks of Amazon.com, Inc., or its affiliates.

ISBN-13: 9781662524332 (paperback)
ISBN-13: 9781662524325 (digital)

Cover design by Ploy Siripant
Cover Images: © AleksandarGeorgiev / Getty; © Atria Borealis / Shutterstock

Printed in the United States of America

To all the confused still finding themselves and to the brave ones who paved the way

To love another is something like prayer and can't be planned, you just fall into its arms because your belief undoes your disbelief.

—Anne Sexton

AUTHOR'S NOTE

This book contains themes, discussions, and content that includes homophobia, racism, suicide and suicidal ideation, mental health, religion, sexual abuse (off page), and consensual BDSM. Care has been taken to depict these aspects in a sensitive manner.

If you or a loved one is experiencing suicidal thoughts, please reach out to the Suicide and Crisis Lifeline by calling or texting 988. No one is ever alone.

SUMMER'S JOURNAL

August 2012

I promise, I didn't mean for any of this to happen. Soon, everyone is going to hate me. I don't know—maybe you will too. I hate myself for so many things, but I don't hate myself for what I'm about to do.

Remember when you gave me the book by that Neruda guy? You read that poem to me, the one about secretly loving obscure things, and you said how much you loved it. I've read it so many times and thought about how perfect and simple it is, and it scares me that I may never read it again. It's funny—when it comes to love, how much it hurts, Neruda sure knew his shit.

I don't even care that you'll never see this. I just needed to get it out of my head before I do this. I've thought about things so much, and now I know some mistakes stay with you forever, deep in your belly, rotting you from the inside out. I only hope when you find out you'll understand and that you won't hate me.

I could never hate you. I really wish I could.

CHAPTER 1

DEVON

2025

Empathy is a motherfucker—don't allow it to consume you. Devon thought of her graduate school professor's words as she listened to her young client recount the worst day of her life. It was her eighth session with Macayla Perry and the first one where the girl was finally able to give details about what happened to her six months prior.

Macayla sat across from her on the gray love seat, her hands cradling one of the fuzzy white pillows in her lap as tears streamed down her face. At first, her eyes had danced all over Devon's office as she began to slowly rock back and forth. Then she stopped and stared, as if in a trance, at the succulent plant sitting on the low coffee table between them.

She was a pretty girl, even with her huge blue eyes puffy from crying. She had golden brown hair and delicate features that reminded Devon of a book of fairy illustrations she'd been obsessed with when she was younger, the fantastical drawings of various fay, usually nude, so alluring. Or—as her mother had called them before she threw the book in the trash—lurid.

No, Devon thought. *Lurid* described everything this poor teenager in front of her had gone through. She listened and knew the girl's story was the same as so many others. A high school boy, older than Macayla. She, walking home the same way she always did, cutting across the football field. He calls out to her, offers to share a joint under the bleachers. No football practice going on. No one else around. She doesn't know him, but she knows he's on the team, knows he's a big deal at school, so she's surprised he's talking to her. She's only a freshman. He's so cute, so she walks over. They smoke, talk. She feels special. Seen. He kisses her, and she likes it, but she needs to get home. She has to watch her little sister after the bus drops her off. Her mom works late. But the boy kisses her hard when she tries to push away. Then his hand is up her shirt, and she pushes harder. He leans into her until she's on the ground, his hand wrapped around her neck. She can't breathe.

Devon finds herself holding her breath, the sense of being strangled so real she digs her nails into her palm to stay in the moment with her client and away from her own memories.

"I . . . I just let him do it," Macayla said, her voice barely a whisper. "It was my fault. I should've gone straight home."

"Macayla, this was not your fault." Devon waited until the girl's eyes met hers. "None of this was your fault. No one blames you for what he did to you."

Macayla's mouth tightened. "Yes, they do. The kids at school—they send me messages, say I'm destroying Davis's life. They text me all the time and spray-painted my mom's car. They . . . they tell me I should kill myself." More tears roll down her face, and she pulls another tissue from the box on the coffee table.

"The only one destroying Davis's life is him because of what he did to you," Devon said, leaning forward. "And once the hearing takes place, after you speak, everyone will know he's a liar. They'll hear from the police officers who helped you and see the hospital report, and then he'll be punished."

Devon thought of the police report her supervising psychologist had shown her, the photos of Macayla's tiny body covered in deep-purple bruises. She had fought that piece of shit, but the boy had a good hundred pounds on her.

Macayla started rocking again, her golden brown hair half shielding her face. "I don't want to speak at the hearing. I know my parents and the police want me to, but I . . . I can't do it."

"You can. You did such a great job today telling me everything. It will be the same way in the courtroom. All you need to do is tell them what you've told me." She wanted to sit next to her and hold her, to tell her she knew firsthand what she was going through, but she had to keep a professional distance, something she often struggled with. *Empathy is a motherfucker.* "You're stronger than you think you are, Macayla."

After the session, Devon sat at her small corner desk, feeling drained. Something about Macayla nagged at her, reminding her of another golden brown–haired girl from long ago, a girl who had retreated to a place so deep within her own mind Devon could no longer reach her.

Sometimes she wondered if she had chosen the wrong field of work. She'd spent the first few years of her adulthood working various shift jobs until she found sex work. Dominating rich men had paid the bills and a good chunk of her student loans before it all ended with one bad decision. Then came bartender work while she got her master's degree, a requirement to be a therapist in Oklahoma. She had also taken on a side job as a burlesque performer, which was much safer than the dominatrix work but didn't pay nearly as much. She'd learned it could be an expensive line of work, with the cost of extravagant outfits, but she had gotten by with making her own and borrowing costume pieces from other, more seasoned performers.

Now, she was almost done with her practicum and would be able to take on clients without supervision. She always thought becoming a counselor would allow her to understand what drove people to do the most horrendous things to each other. To themselves.

She closed her eyes, and a beautiful girl's sun-soaked face, mouth open wide and laughing, flashed across her mind, threatening to undo her. She swallowed over the fullness in her throat, the tears trying to emerge, but she tucked them away.

She needed to understand. She had to know how to piece someone like Macayla back together after someone else had taken a sledgehammer to them.

"You think she's okay for next week?"

Dr. Paulette Bailey, her supervisor, entered the office, making the intimate space somehow cozier by her calming presence. Like Devon, Paulette had the sensual curves of a woman who didn't skip on desserts, but the older woman's heart-shaped face and smiling brown eyes reminded Devon of her favorite seventh-grade teacher, Mrs. Higgins, whom she'd had a huge crush on, a confusing combination that made Devon sometimes turn shy around her.

"The hearing?" Devon said. "Yeah. I think she'll be okay. She recounted all the way through today."

Paulette sat on the arm of the love seat. "Well, the state has plenty to go on. And with her testimony, he won't walk."

Devon bit her tongue. Macayla's rapist came from a wealthy family, and he had one of the best defense lawyers in Oklahoma. Money just might buy him a slap on the wrist. She knew the defense would do anything possible to grind that fifteen-year-old girl into the ground. Didn't matter that she'd been a virgin; they'd somehow make it seem like she wanted it, like she sought him out. Nothing mattered if a perpetrator had enough money to rewrite history. She'd learned the hard way how society had a high tolerance for the suffering of women.

She'd seen too many sexual predators walk and feared her own would do the same. Memories of the year before came to her uninvited. Memories of taking a job she never should've taken. The job was for a bunch of mostly older rich men seeking a professional dominatrix for a private party at the infamous Coulter mansion. What they really wanted was to imprison and torture . . . and rape. She had survived, and intense trauma therapy had helped her regain control of her life, but she doubted the men involved would ever be prosecuted, not with how their money and connections kept the court case tied up. Still, she wanted her day in court, however long it took. She needed to face the men who'd hurt her, to show them she was no longer afraid of them, and she wanted the same closure for Macayla.

"You okay, Devon?" Paulette's kind eyes turned worried.

"Yeah. Just tired is all." She turned to face her computer to avoid Paulette's analytic gaze. The woman could read body language better than anyone she knew, which she supposed was why Paulette was so good at her job, but it made Devon hyperaware of everything she said or did in front of her. "I'm just going to finish this charting before I head out."

She heard Paulette shift from the edge of the love seat. "Do something fun for yourself this weekend, okay? Decompress."

Without turning away from her computer screen, Devon nodded, her thoughts toggling between Macayla's tear-streaked cheeks and the sun-drenched face of her memories while suppressing thoughts of everything that had happened to her and the other women she was held with the year before. A dread tunneled its way into her stomach, twisting and tightening until she thought she'd double over in front of her supervisor. She had to keep herself together, at least long enough to do her charting and drive home.

The sunset brushed pinks and purples across the expansive sky as she drove to her small apartment on the east side. Rent was cheaper there than in central Oklahoma City, but the neighborhoods were rougher. When she'd first moved in, there was a food desert, and she had to drive far to get any kind of fresh produce or meat. But even the east side was becoming gentrified, driving up housing costs. A beautiful, huge grocery store and new restaurants seemed to sprout up overnight, and then the investors came, flipping the older houses and raising property taxes for the mostly Black and brown area of town. With Oklahoma's overall low cost of living, she knew more out-of-state investors would come. Eventually, if she didn't start earning more, she'd be priced out of her apartment and would likely have to get a roommate.

However expensive living got in the city, Devon knew she'd never move back to Arkana, the rural town she'd called home for most of her life. She would rather live in a shoebox than go back. The thought alone caused her chest to seize, her breath trapped and aching with too many memories.

Someone was parked in her designated spot, so she had to circle around the apartment complex a couple of times before she found another. As she exited her car and entered the furnace of June's heat, that sickening dread squirmed in her stomach again. She told herself it was because of her session with Macayla, but she knew that wasn't the real reason.

No, the dread was because of a completely different girl, a girl Devon had fought for thirteen years to forget.

CHAPTER 2

DEVON

March 2012

Devon sat at her desk in the front row, staring straight ahead at Mrs. Freeman as she explained a math algorithm, but all she could concentrate on was Keaton Harrison sitting behind her. She could hear him scribbling notes, something she should be doing as well. She imagined his large hand gripping his pen, pressing it hard into the notebook paper. The way he wrote in class sounded so assured, with no pause. Almost aggressive in its surety. For a moment, she wanted to be the pen in his hand, to feel his fingers wrapped around her.

She shuddered and shook the image from her mind. Even though she had learned long ago that God wouldn't strike her dead for her fantasies, the thought of her parents somehow reading them on her face when she got home shot fear to her heart.

A hand tapped her shoulder, and she startled hard, causing a few of her classmates to snicker.

"Devon Mayes, pay attention." Mrs. Freeman stared down at her, her dry-erase marker hovering in the air. "Tell me how you would solve this system of equations for x, using the substitution method?"

"Um . . . I—I'm not sure." She looked down at a doodle on her desk a student from long ago had drawn: "FUCK MATH" Sharpied within a penis-shaped balloon. "I'm sorry."

Mrs. Freeman sighed and asked Keaton the question instead. He answered it with ease, as he always did. She was just as good at math as he was, but when a teacher called on her, it was like her brain turned off.

She was relieved when the bell rang, ushering in the end of class. As students filed out of the classroom, Keaton came up beside her, gently nudging her arm with his.

"Hey, what's up with you?" he said. "Been a little spaced out today."

"Nothing."

Devon smiled up at his tall frame, which made her feel petite even though she was of average height. Everything about her felt average next to him—her boring, long dirty-blond hair; her plain complexion, since her parents forbade her to use makeup like other girls her age did; and her clothing, which consisted of the basic, modest outfits her mother bought her on their annual trip to the Walmart Supercenter in Newcastle. The only thing remotely interesting about her was her green eyes, which Summer once said reminded her of the sea glass she and Keaton had found on a beach when they went to Hawaii on vacation as kids.

There was nothing average about Keaton and his twin sister, Summer. When they moved to Arkana two summers before, at the beginning of sophomore year, Devon had watched Principal Morris showing them around the school. She was so completely enamored by their beauty she could hardly catch her breath. Summer, who was a few inches taller than Devon, had tan skin the color of toffee, with freckle-kissed cheeks, her shoulder-length hair as deep golden brown as the spiced pecans Devon's mother made each holiday for the church fundraiser. Keaton had the strong build and bronze skin of the farm laborers in town, his hair the same candied-pecan color as Summer's but with threads of cinnamon that lit up in the sun.

She never understood why they chose to be friends with her. Maybe it was simply because they went the same way home from school. Or maybe it was because most of the other kids had avoided them the first few months after their arrival. They were too different in how they dressed and acted, and different was never good in Arkana. Plus, their family didn't attend church services at Calvary Baptist like most of the town, which meant Devon had to lie to her parents about the depth of her friendship with them. As long as she said she was sharing the word of God with the Harrison twins and trying to convince them to attend church, her parents allowed her to be around them. When Summer had joined the track team with her, it was like winning the lottery to be so close to her during after-school practices.

"Are you still coming over after practice to study?" Keaton asked, strolling next to her down the hallway. "Or we could forget studying and finally watch *Crouching Tiger, Hidden Dragon* instead."

He'd wanted to show her the movie for a long time, but she knew Summer didn't like subtitles. Devon's parents didn't allow her to watch any movies that weren't rated PG or below, and so far she had loved every movie Keaton introduced to her, her favorite being *Eternal Sunshine of the Spotless Mind*.

"Yeah, I'll be over. You helping your dad plant first?"

He grinned at her. "Not unless I can hide out with you."

"Oh, so you want to do laps until your legs fall off? You wouldn't last ten minutes."

"I was thinking more like hiding in the showers until you get done."

Devon turned her head so he wouldn't see her blushing.

"Planting isn't hard," she said, stopping outside the girls' locker room. "It's just putting seeds in the ground. Shouldn't take you long."

"Says the girl who's never worked in a field."

The Harrison family had moved to Arkana after Keaton and Summer's grandfather died, leaving the farm to his two sons. They mostly grew wheat, but in the early spring, they planted Swiss chard and spinach, among other crops they sold at the local farmers' market.

Before they moved to Arkana, Keaton and Summer's father had been a project manager for an energy company in Oklahoma City, their mother a middle school English teacher. Summer once told Devon her mother hated Arkana and had begged her husband to sell off their portion of the farm to Boyd, Summer's uncle. Devon didn't blame her. She couldn't imagine moving to a nothing town after living your whole life in a vibrant big city.

Devon repositioned her backpack and turned to Keaton, a wry smile on her face. "Have I never told you? I worked at my granddaddy's farm every fall harvest until he passed. And I never got paid for it like you do. Go be responsible." Keaton had been saving for a used truck for the last year, and Devon liked to imagine riding with Summer and him on the weekends once he was able to buy one, windows down with music blasting. Real music like Radiohead and Twin Shadow, which Summer and Keaton introduced to her—not the Hillsong Worship music her mother loved.

Keaton sighed. "You're right." He ran a hand through his tousled hair, and she thought about reaching up to move a stray strand away from his forehead. "I think your goodness is rubbing off on me. I might even rescue a few kittens on the way home."

Devon laughed. The thoughts she had about him, about Summer, too, were anything but good. At night, in her bed, she allowed the thoughts to flourish and grow into such vividness she was sure her body would explode into flames. *God is always watching you,* her parents were fond of telling her. Then God had seen her do plenty with her hand under the covers.

She didn't understand how something that felt so good could be bad, could put her soul in jeopardy. After all, it wasn't like she was doing anything in real life. She'd never even held a boy's hand. She had thought of holding Summer's hand many times. She'd walk home from school next to her when the weather was nice, Keaton's long legs carrying him far ahead of them, and she wanted to reach out and touch Summer's fingers, to feel them grip her tight in return. She'd seen girls hold hands in church as they prayed together, though they'd never held hers. So many nights, Devon thought of the warmth of Summer's palm against her own as she stoked pleasure between her legs.

"Hey, asshole, stop blocking the locker room." Summer play-shoved Keaton as she came up to them, and he jostled her backpack in retaliation.

Devon was much better about not flinching whenever Summer cursed. She used to flinch every single time. Keaton cussed, too, but Devon noticed he avoided it around her since he knew she didn't use vulgar language. Not Summer. She said cusswords like they were her second language.

"Dev was just saying how she'd sneak me into the showers so I don't have to plant with Dad," Keaton said, winking at her. "Might even let me wash her hair."

Devon felt her mouth part, her breath caught in her throat at his words.

"Don't be gross," Summer said, looping her arm through Devon's. "You know you can't joke with her like that, or she might spontaneously combust."

Keaton sucked in his lips, fighting a grin. "I'd love to witness that. See y'all later."

Devon was still too shocked at his joke to say goodbye to him.

"He's such an ass," Summer said under her breath as she tugged Devon through the heavy metal doors to the locker room. "Seriously, he needs to get laid."

Devon looked away so Summer wouldn't catch the blush blooming on her cheeks again. She knew Keaton wasn't flirting with her; he just liked to shock her sometimes to see her reaction. There was no way he would be into her, not with how she looked next to him, like an ugly weed in a blooming field of tulips.

Summer let go of her arm. "See you on the field."

Other girls on the track team were already changing into their practice clothes. Devon never felt comfortable changing in front of the other girls, so she took her things to one of the bathroom stalls. On her way, she tried to avert her eyes from her half-naked track mates, their breasts and underwear out as they shimmied into their sports bras and shorts. Out of the corner of her eye, she saw Summer pull her shirt over her head, her small breasts lifting with the movement.

Devon said a silent prayer. Thinking of Keaton was sinful enough, but thinking of Summer in that way . . . it was a straight shot to hell. It's what Pastor Walters said during sermons, how there was a gay agenda and they had to protect themselves and the young children from it. Her parents had never asked her if she had impure thoughts about girls, but they made it clear there was no room for sin in their household. Summer hadn't been the only girl she had thought of in that way, but she was the only one she wanted to think about now. Still, she knew she wasn't a lesbian. She couldn't be because she thought of boys too.

Once inside the bathroom stall, she removed her top and held it against her chest. She closed her eyes tight and said another prayer: *Please, God, take these sinful thoughts from me. Please, remove them from my head forever.* "Amen."

CHAPTER 3

DEVON

2025

The Thursday workday was flying by, and the strange dread plaguing Devon the week prior had died down some once she acknowledged the main cause for it. It was getting closer to the anniversary. The hottest months always felt like a premonition of what was to come.

Summer's death.

She liked to tell herself she didn't go through years of college and hundreds of hours of practicum work because of what had happened with Summer, but there was no other reason. The suicide of someone you love will do that to a person. It makes you obsess over every last exchange you had with them, every word they spoke, all the things you should've told them but were too scared to say. Perhaps one word would've made the difference.

Her mind was just negotiating with her emotions. That's what her training had taught her: separate emotions from facts. Get to the root of where the emotions germinate, and then you can heal the soil and cultivate coping mechanisms.

She didn't force her best friend to overdose next to a pond. For a moment, she could feel the sweltering heat of summertime in Arkana— she, Summer, and Keaton dipping in and out of the cool water where they all used to hang out. No, she didn't tarnish those memories. She wasn't the one who destroyed so many people by killing herself right at the beginning of senior year. She didn't cause it, she reminded herself once again.

But you did, a small voice said in the deepest back corner of her mind.

Devon ignored it, but she couldn't help thinking of Keaton and his parents, the devastation on their faces during the funeral. Summer had parents who loved her, who were supportive of her. *Fam forever.* The phrase popped into her head, unbidden, nauseating her. She absently rubbed the frog tattoo on her inner right wrist with her thumb.

Devon wasn't so lucky. She was sure if her parents found out about her sexuality, her next holiday visit to them would be her last. They'd pack up every childhood memory they kept of hers—her track meet medals, her honor roll certificates, old drawings she did when she was a small girl—and set them on fire in the pit out back, the same pit they had used to burn leaves each fall. They'd pretend she never existed.

After she finished her charting, she took out her cell phone and scoured the local news sites for Macayla's court case. She knew the cross-examinations were supposed to happen the day prior, and she was nervous for the girl. Her eyes scanned article after article until one headline stopped her dead: ASSAULT TRIAL FOR LOCAL FOOTBALL STAR PAUSED.

What the fuck? As she read on, her body went cold:

> The sexual assault trial for Davis Harrington, age 18, of
> Oklahoma City is paused. Harrington's defense attor-
> neys have filed a motion to dismiss all charges against
> the high school football star after his accuser died . . .

Her heart thundered in her ears, a sharp ringing getting louder and louder as she made herself slowly breathe in and out. She couldn't believe what she was reading. She had to know what had happened to Macayla, but she was also scared to find out. The article didn't give the cause, and she didn't know who to ask. Not the girl's parents. It wouldn't be right to call them and ask questions of them right after their only child died. Maybe Paulette knew. She was the supervising psychologist for Macayla.

As Devon stood up from her chair, dizziness overtook her, and she had to hold on to the edge of her desk for a moment. She steadied herself and walked to her supervisor's office.

Paulette looked up from her computer, her expression slightly annoyed at being interrupted when Devon entered unannounced. When she took in Devon's face, her demeanor immediately softened. "So, you've heard the news? Come in and sit down."

Devon sat across from her. "What happened? How did Macayla die?"

Paulette didn't say anything for several seconds. "Before I tell you, I need you to know that things like this happen in our profession. We can't allow it to consume us, or we'd never get up each day to help other people. I need you to understand that."

Devon said nothing, the bottomless dread she'd felt the week prior stretching up from the darkness, choking her.

Paulette blew out a sigh. "Macayla's attorney reached out this morning to inform us of her suicide." She paused, allowing Devon to take it in. "I was planning to tell you at the end of the day."

It's your fault. All your fault. Just like before.

Paulette stared at her, worry in her eyes. "Are you okay?" Her words sounded muffled, like being underwater.

"Yes." Devon's own words were fuzzy and faraway.

"I know it's difficult losing a client, especially one so young and under these circumstances." Paulette reached for her hand, but Devon jerked back. "But it's not your fault, okay?"

"Yeah . . . okay." Devon stood up on shaky legs. "I . . . I just need to get something."

Devon couldn't feel her feet, but they somehow carried her into her office. She grabbed her purse and phone and left. When she exited the building and the warm, muggy early-evening air hit her face, she looked up at the storm clouds off in the distance, the startling rays of the departing sun fighting to break through.

It's all your fault.

All the way home, on repeat, burrowing deeper into every part of her.

She didn't remember driving down the highway or pulling into her parking spot, didn't remember climbing the breezeway stairs to her upper-unit apartment. Didn't even notice the small children playing on the bottom steps who said hello to her.

When she unlocked her door and shut it behind her, it felt like she was shutting herself in for the last time, like entering a cave where she could hibernate forever with those words playing in her head.

She died because of you.

Just like Summer.

CHAPTER 4

DEVON

April 2012

"Spring training sucks ass."

Devon smiled at Summer as they kept a steady pace running next to each other. Summer said those words before, during, and after every track practice, although Devon kind of agreed with her that particular day. It was cold and dreary, with rain drizzling down on them as they ran endless laps on the muddy field.

Her mind kept shifting back to sitting on the old couch next to Keaton in his parents' basement watching *Crouching Tiger, Hidden Dragon*. During a scene where a male character was clearly touching a woman between her legs, Devon had to squeeze her thighs together to suppress the ache she felt, afraid to glance at Keaton to see if he noticed.

"I just want to go home and watch *Glee*," Summer whined. "And eat an entire bag of mini Snickers."

"Well, at least you're preemptively burning calories. I don't know how you can eat that many carbs and stay so thin."

Summer snorted. "Do I look like I give a shit about carbs? The day I ever get like Cara, you have my permission to shoot me."

Cara McKinnon, another track-team member, ate nothing but five baby carrots and one white cheddar rice cake during lunch every day, and almost everyone acted like it was totally normal. Devon didn't know how she wasn't passing out during practice.

"It's easy to say stuff like that when you look the way you do," Devon said. Summer had a model's body with long legs and a butt that could fit the tightest jeans with no muffin top. "I would pay a million dollars to have your body."

"Oh, my God, Dev, shut your face. You're gorgeous."

"Yeah right."

"Guys like curves." She paused, her breath a rhythmic burst in and out as she increased her speed. "A lot of people do."

No guys she knew, but Devon didn't say anything. Sometimes, she'd stand in front of the full-length mirror hanging off the back of her bedroom door and examine every part of her body, trying to see herself as Summer did, but all she saw was too much—her breasts, her hips, her thighs, the slight pooch of her stomach no matter how many crunches she did. Too much to be beautiful.

She couldn't change her body, but there were other things she could change about herself. Many times, she'd asked her mother if she could color her hair like some of the other girls at school did, but her mother always said no, said it was a show of disrespect toward God to change how she was made. So, she was stuck with her boring dark-blond hair. Every time she saw Morgan Miller walking down the hallway with her vibrant red-dyed hair, a part of her wanted to rebel and steal a box of dye from the pharmacy in town. She wanted to be free to make choices for herself like every other seventeen-year-old she knew. She wanted to be free like Summer.

"Okay, girls," Coach Thompson called out to the team, "you can stop now. Come on over."

Devon's lungs burned, her shirt wet and sticking to her chest, making her too aware of the other girls on the team, how their tops clung to them, too, the shapes of their breasts distracting her as she made her way over to their coach by the bleachers.

Coach Shrader Thompson was fairly young. Maybe early thirties—she wasn't sure. Most of the girls were in love with him, and Devon supposed he was attractive, but nowhere close to Keaton. Summer once called the coach an older doppelgänger of Zac Efron, which Devon kind of agreed with after Summer showed her *High School Musical* on her very own TV in her bedroom, something Devon's parents would never allow. Coach Thompson had a new baby boy at home, but he loved to volunteer for the high school to give back to the community. His wife didn't have to work since he came from old money, so she usually stayed home with the baby while he coached the girls' track and cross-country teams during the fall and spring as he had since Devon was in middle school.

The Thompson family, along with the Stinchcombs, had established the town of Arkana during the oil boom of the 1920s. The two families owned most of the major buildings, including Malcolm Thompson High School, but Coach Thompson never acted snobbish around others, not like a lot of the Stinchcombs, including the mayor. Coach even brought the team snacks during practices.

"So, most of you are getting to where you need to be before our meet in two weeks," Coach Thompson said. "But some of you need work. I'm looking at you, Jackie. I don't know what's going on with you, but you need to step up."

Devon looked over at Jackie Byrd, whose face was going beet red, her arms crossed and mouth a straight line like she was fighting back tears. Jackie rarely spoke to anyone on the team, although Devon sometimes saw Summer talking to her after school. All Devon knew about Jackie was that she used to live on a Choctaw reservation before her single mom moved them to Arkana a few years ago. Kids at school said she was kicked off the reservation for being a lesbian, which didn't make sense to Devon, but then she didn't know what rules the reservations followed. One thing she knew for certain was that Jackie was a good runner, so she didn't understand what Coach was talking about. All of them had off days. Maybe Jackie was sick.

"I expect a lot out of you girls because I know you have it in you," Coach continued. "So, make sure you're limiting your caffeine intake and get plenty of sleep each night so you're prepared for practice. I don't want to see any slacking."

Devon elbowed Summer's side, grinning. Summer guzzled a liter of Dr. Pepper every day during lunch.

"All right. You're free to go. Have a good evening, ladies."

As Devon and Summer walked together down the gravel road leading to their houses, the drizzle finally let up some and the crisp spring air made Devon crave her mother's baked-potato soup, which she knew would be waiting for her after she took a warm shower. Her mother was a good cook, but her grandmother had been the best. She missed Mimi, her mother's mom, and her warm hugs. She missed how she'd have Devon blow kisses with her into the mixing bowl when they'd bake cookies together. *Love is the secret ingredient,* she'd say. When her mother baked, it wasn't the same. Without the kisses, cookies were just cookies.

"Did you see Jackie after practice?" Summer asked her.

"No."

"She was crying pretty hard." She let out a loud exhale. "Coach can be such an asshole sometimes. Like, we all get it. We need to do well at the meet, but fucking chill, dude."

"She seems lonely."

"Well, yeah, Dev. Everyone's a bitch to her. Wouldn't you be lonely?"

"Sure, but . . . I don't know." She slowed down a little. "Maybe if she wasn't so out about liking girls, people would be more comfortable talking to her."

Summer stopped and turned to her. "For real? Did you really just say that?" She crossed her arms. "I mean, I know your family's all up Jesus's ass, but I never thought you'd say something like that."

"I—I just meant . . . I don't know. Like, she could try to fit in more."

Summer cocked her hip. "You're right. You don't know because you and everyone else in this stupid town lives in a bubble where you're supposed to be little Bible-thumping robots afraid of rainbows, and if anyone is different, then they're automatically evil. You've never lived in the city, so you think it's normal to think that way, but it's not."

Devon felt her eyes well up at Summer's sudden anger. In the almost two years they'd known each other, they'd never fought. "Look, I'm sorry. I didn't mean it like that. I like Jackie."

"You don't even know her."

"But I want to." Fear creeped up her neck. She felt like Summer was going to somehow slip away from her. "We can all hang out after practice tomorrow, okay?"

"I need to get home." Summer turned away from her. "See you tomorrow."

"See you," Devon said, her voice small and cracking.

Tears sprang into her eyes, and she couldn't make her feet move for a long time. When she finally stepped inside her home, she was soaked through and shivering.

"Devon, honey, what took you so long?" her mother asked, hands on her full hips. "And you're dripping wet. I told you to bring your umbrella if you weren't going to take your bike to school."

"I'm sorry, Mama. Practice ran over."

"You walk back with that Harrison girl?"

Her mother knew she did, so Devon wasn't sure why she was asking. "Yes."

"Watch yourself around girls like that. I doubt she's even been baptized, with parents like hers. *Atheists.*" Her mother said the word like it was an obscenity.

Devon knew better than to argue.

"But you do what you can to save her soul. Her brother's too. It's what we're called to do in His name." Her mother took her numb hands, blanketing them with her own and sending brief warmth into her. "Just like I thought—blocks of ice. Good thing I made soup. Warm you right up, and God willing, you won't catch cold. Now, go on and hurry."

Upstairs in the bathroom, Devon closed her eyes and cried while the shower's hot water sluiced over her nakedness. She thought of Summer's face, the disappointment and anger at her, and she was disappointed and angry with herself too. She wished she could go back and stop her stupid mouth from repeating the same words she'd heard so many times in church. She didn't really think there was anything wrong with being gay. Not for other people. But for herself . . .

Someone knocked on the bathroom door. "Dinner's ready. You need to wrap it up and come down." Her mother's sharp voice went through her.

"Yes, ma'am."

For herself, there was only one way to be, or she wouldn't have a family.

She would never have the same freedom Summer had. The thought lodged in her chest like a splinter too deep to dig out.

CHAPTER 5

DEVON

2025

Devon's cell phone rang again. She looked at the golden light of dusk filtering into her bedroom and let the call go to voicemail. She knew it was likely Paulette trying to reach her again, wanting to know why she hadn't been to work in two days. She didn't know how to tell Paulette she was drowning in memories, both old and new. When she closed her eyes, the despair on Macayla's delicate face bled into Summer's, how she had looked so lost the last time she'd seen her alive.

And now Devon was lost, too, unmoored by the girl's suicide and by Summer's all over again. She could've helped Macayla more. She should've consulted with the girl's attorney, let him know how the court case was impacting her mental health and implored him not to have her testify. With Macayla being fifteen, the defense team legally couldn't force her to testify. But that would've done nothing about the social media attacks and harassment she had faced. Devon hoped to hell Macayla's parents would go after the harassers and make them pay for contributing to her death.

Devon's next-door neighbor was yelling at someone, the paper-thin walls of the apartment allowing her to hear every other word. She wanted to sleep, but it was impossible. Not even her cannabis edibles, something she tried not to take too often for her anxiety, did anything. It was like her psyche was punishing her by withholding rest, and she deserved it.

She dragged her ass up and went to her freezer, where she kept a huge bottle of unopened Grey Goose, a gift from a friend after she had finished grad school. She rarely drank outside of an occasional beer or glass of bourbon—didn't have much head for it—but she needed her racing thoughts to stop, at least for a little bit. So, she opened the bottle and plopped down on her green couch. She turned on *House Hunters*, wrapped herself in her favorite fluffy throw blanket, and chugged the ice-cold vodka. The burn down her throat was soothing, and her limbs went soft. She hadn't eaten all day, and the alcohol hit her fast. Good. She wanted to black out. She'd never passed out from drinking before, but she was willing to learn.

She was two episodes in when someone knocked on her door. The couple on the screen were going over their three home options, all houses Devon could never imagine affording in her lifetime. She was rooting for the English Tudor, but the asshole husband wanted the sterile-looking new build.

Another knock.

Fuck. She couldn't feel her lips, and her arms and legs felt too heavy to move, but she forced herself to stand up and answer the door. Her body swayed as she looked out the peephole first. Paulette stood there, her face full of concern.

"I can hear the TV playing, Devon," she said. "Please, let me in."

Devon cracked open the door. She knew she looked like a mess. Probably smelled horrible from not showering.

"May I come in?" Paulette held a to-go bag from Gorō Ramen, and Devon smelled the enticing aroma of tori paitan. "I thought you might be hungry."

She moved back so Paulette could enter. Her supervisor had never been to her place, and it was jarring seeing her standing in the small living room, like seeing a teacher out in the real world doing mundane tasks like grocery shopping. It didn't feel natural.

Paulette handed her the bag of food. "You should've called me back." Her glance landed on the large bottle of vodka on the coffee table and then back to Devon. "I've been worried about you."

"I'm sorry." Her head swam as she took the food to her U-shaped kitchen. She took down a large bowl from her cabinet and fought the plastic lid off the to-go container.

"Is this response all about Macayla?" Paulette asked.

Devon stopped pouring her ramen into the bowl and looked at her. "What do you mean?"

"I mean last year, when you had to take leave after . . . everything."

Paulette was one of the few people in her life who knew what had happened to her at the Coulter mansion. Devon had been in the middle of her practicum when she was held against her will and sexually assaulted.

"No, it has nothing to do with that," Devon slurred.

Paulette didn't look like she believed her. "I understand Macayla was your client, but you're taking this harder than I expected. This is why we must keep our emotions out of our work."

Devon stared at her supervisor, disbelief and anger bubbling up in her out of nowhere the longer she watched Paulette's calm face. How could she be so calm about a girl's suicide? How could anyone? It was callous. "Oh, I see, Paulette. I didn't know I was supposed to be a cold-hearted bitch about this like you!" She instantly regretted her words as Paulette's mouth grew tight. Even through the alcohol, she knew she'd crossed way over the line.

"Macayla's death is sad, Devon, but she will not be the last suicide you see in this line of work. If you fall apart every time one of your clients dies, you will be a liability to your other clients. And to me. I've been doing this long enough to know when someone has personal issues they haven't resolved, so I suggest you figure that out before you come back to my practice."

It was like she had doused Devon in ice water. "Paulette, I—"

"You're on mandatory leave, effective today."

"Leave? For how long?"

"However long it takes." Paulette took her hand. "I'm not doing this to hurt you. I'm doing this so you have time to heal the wounds you've been burying. You've been highly distracted, even before Macayla. You'll never be an effective therapist if you can't even take care of yourself." She gave Devon's hand a small squeeze before letting go.

She didn't know what to say. Each night as she tried to fall asleep, her mind would inevitably replay every last moment with Summer, every poisoned word spoken, and she'd wake up questioning herself and her ability to counsel others. Paulette was right. Maybe if she had dealt with Summer's death rather than running away from Arkana as soon as she graduated from high school, she could've helped Macayla better. She could've saved her. Instead, she allowed Summer's suicide to cloud every decision she'd made since she was seventeen.

"Do what you need to do, Devon, and then we'll talk. I'll see myself out."

She stared down at her cooling bowl of ramen, at the congealed yoke of the egg swimming next to the menma, and her stomach churned with the alcohol. *Just get it out,* Summer had once commanded her when she'd had too much to drink at Holly Lynch's party at the end of junior year. *You'll feel so much better.* She leaned over the sink and vomited until there was nothing left inside her. *See? I told you so.*

She closed her eyes tight and saw Summer's face, her wide grin so dazzling it had hurt to look at her sometimes.

She knew what she had to do. She needed to go home. To Arkana. To finally face all the ghosts she'd been avoiding for thirteen years.

CHAPTER 6
DEVON

April 2012

It had been almost a week since Summer blew up at Devon after track practice, and everything felt off kilter, like stepping off a merry-go-round and trying to run without falling. Summer was still talking to her, sat with her during lunch like normal, and walked alongside her after school, but Devon sensed the change. It was in how Summer stopped offering her a chug of her Dr. Pepper as they ate cafeteria food. And while kicking up red dust on their way home, she no longer told Devon all the juicy town gossip she'd heard from her mother.

She watched Summer walking down the hallway with Jackie on their way back from algebra, one of the many classes she didn't share with Summer. Devon was in the AP courses with Keaton, but right then she wished she were in the regular classes so she could try to overhear what Summer and Jackie were always chatting about. Had Summer told Jackie what she said about her?

"Hey." Keaton came up next to her at her locker as she dug around for her math book. He followed her eyes darting toward Summer and Jackie again. "My sister still being weird?"

"What? No," she said too fast. "Why do you say that?"

"Dev, I'm not blind. You two have been really strange around each other all week. Why?"

Because she'd said something horribly ignorant about Jackie. The more she replayed her words each night, struggling to fall asleep as she pictured the scene over and over again like a broken movie reel, the more she realized how she must've sounded to Summer. She sounded like her parents, like most of the people in town who regurgitated the anti-LGBTQ sentiments Pastor Walters preached about every Sunday.

"You'd have to ask her, Keat."

"She sure is hanging out with Jackie a lot."

"She's allowed to have other friends."

He nudged her, smirking. "So are you."

She knew her friendship with him was vastly different from the one she had with Summer. With Summer, there was the ease of sameness, of being girls and knowing certain things without having to voice them. Although she sometimes craved deeper conversations with Summer like the ones she had with Keaton, she loved how they could laugh and have fun at the dumbest things. It was so easy to love Summer and her vibrancy. But with Keaton, there was a tension in him, something she recognized in herself too. How he moved, how he spoke, how he looked at people, the tension was there, like a rubber band pulled taut, and he didn't know how to fully relax. He could joke and have fun, too, but the tension never left him completely, at least not from what she could tell. She did notice how he seemed more relaxed around her, though.

"I know I'm only your number two best friend," he said with a gleam in his eyes, "but I can fill in for her. We're basically the same person, genetically speaking. True, I may be missing certain parts, but . . ."

Devon laughed, and it was the first time all week when she felt normal. "Is that right, huh? *Genetically* the same?" She playfully pushed his arm.

"Okay, so not genetically, if you've got to get all technical about it."

Although Summer and Keaton were different in just about every way possible, they did share one thing: their hazel eyes, which shifted with the light like a kaleidoscope moving from a gray blue to a soft copper with flecks of gold at the center. Devon found herself getting lost in them again as Keaton slowly shook his head at her, a smile tugging on his full lips.

"You didn't hear anything I just said, did you?"

"Uh, no."

"I asked if you wanted to grab a coffee. I'm skipping ag club today."

She knew how much he hated agriculture club, which his father had forced him to join. She didn't understand why he stayed in it when he had no interest in carrying on the farming business.

"Does your dad know how much you skip?" she asked.

The familiar tension entered his face, his mouth tightening. "What he doesn't know won't hurt him. Besides, I'd rather hang out with you."

She'd rather hang out with him, too, than gather up her nerves and talk to Summer. There was no track practice after school. Even if she did go with Keaton, she didn't want to have to explain to her parents her reason for being home late since she had no way to call them and didn't want to call them from Keaton's phone. She was the only teenager she knew without a cell phone. Her parents believed cell phones allowed kids direct access to pedophiles through the internet, but when Devon had suggested getting a cheap phone with no internet for emergencies only, they still shot the idea down. The irony wasn't lost on her that she could be in real danger someday and would have no way to call for help.

"Let's do it tomorrow, okay?" she said to him. That would allow her time to make up an excuse for her parents.

His shoulders relaxed a little. "Yeah, sure. See you tomorrow."

She watched as Summer grabbed some things from her locker, shoving them into her backpack with Jackie standing next to her. Devon was too far away to hear what they were saying, but Jackie looked upset, her olive-toned skin flushed like she was embarrassed or mad—Devon couldn't tell which. Summer then looked down like she was pondering something before she gave a quick shake of her head and slammed her locker door shut. Without looking back at Jackie, who now had her arms crossed and looked ready to cry, Summer walked straight to Devon.

"Hey," Summer said with a small smile as if nothing was wrong. "Ready to go?"

"Sure."

As they cut across the track field, Devon knew she couldn't keep acting like everything was normal with Summer. She had to explain why she'd said what she said about Jackie, how she wasn't homophobic like so many others in town. She had to tell her the truth, or at least enough so Summer would understand.

"So," she began, her nerves tightening her throat, "I need to talk to you about something. Can we stop for a minute?" She motioned to the small bleachers.

Summer sucked in her lips. "Sure."

They sat down, and all the words Devon had imagined saying, had practiced countless times in her head each night, suddenly vanished.

"What do you want to talk about?" Summer prompted.

"Um, I . . ." Sweat ran down the back of her neck, her mind frantically searching for the words again. "It's about Jackie."

Summer's expression grew wary, like she was expecting Devon to spout off more homophobic things to her.

She swallowed, hanging on to the words she needed to say. "I'm sorry about what I said about her. I didn't really mean it. It's just, I was scared."

A crease grew between Summer's eyes. "Scared?"

"I've never told anyone before."

Confusion crossed Summer's face. "Dev, what are you trying to say?"

The hint of annoyance in Summer's voice made Devon's throat tighten even more, her lungs barely able to take in shallow breaths as tears threatened to rip through her. She knew she shouldn't be scared, because Summer was her best friend, her family. *Fam forever*—their mantra, the abbreviation they had scribbled on notes and turned into friendship bracelets, into the key chain Devon had made Summer sophomore year, the FAMF letters surrounded by rainbow beads and a single silver frog charm because Summer had been obsessed with them ever since she was a little kid reading the Frog and Toad books. Summer was closer to her than anyone else, but speaking the words would put it out into the world, and she wouldn't be able to take them back.

"I . . . I don't want people to talk about me like they do with Jackie," Devon finally said, the confession coming out in a whisper, and Summer's mouth dropped open a little.

Summer took her hand. "Dev, are you saying you're queer?"

The word was terrifying to hear. Too neon bright.

"You know I wouldn't care, right?" Summer, those same kaleidoscope eyes as Keaton's shifting blue and gold, watched her like she was a frightened rabbit about to dash back into the bushes. "I would never tell anyone."

Tears rolled down Devon's cheeks. "I know."

"So, are you?"

Devon nodded.

"What are you then?" Summer asked.

"I don't know."

Summer fiddled with the rainbow key chain Devon had made her, twisting the FAMF letters round and round. "Do you only like girls or boys too?"

She thought about all the nights she'd touched herself while thinking about Summer and Keaton, and her body flushed. "Um . . . both."

"Then you're bi."

It surprised Devon how easily Summer could say it, like it was the simplest thing to name what had eluded her ever since the seventh grade, when she'd had fantasies of burying her face between Mrs. Higgins's huge, pillowy breasts during class while also wondering if

John Newsom's tongue tasted like the cinnamon Altoids he constantly popped into his mouth.

"Yeah . . . I guess I am." More tears flowed from her, the relief of saying it out loud making her soft crying sound more like low laughter.

Summer squeezed her hand. "It's okay." She paused. "I'm glad you told me. You know you can trust me, right? I won't tell anyone, I promise. We're fam."

Summer held out her pinkie to Devon until she extended hers, too, their fingers linked tight.

"Forever," Summer said.

Devon nodded, her head feeling too light on her neck.

"Forever."

SUMMER'S JOURNAL

April 2012

Dev came out to me today. Guess Jackie was right. She said her gaydar is never wrong, but I thought she was full of shit. I'll never tell Jackie, though. One thing I know for sure is that Dev will never really be out. Not as long as she's living in Arkana. I see how everyone treats Jackie, and I get scared for Dev. She's not as strong. I swear, this town would send every queer kid to conversion camp if they could, like they tried to do with Jackie. Thank God her mom told Pastor Walters to fuck right off. It's like the Dark Ages here. I hate this place so much. It's the one thing Mom and I agree on. I know Keat hates it too, but he's doing what he always does, acting like he's okay with everything, doing everything Dad wants him to do. Like it will somehow stop Mom and Dad from fighting all the time if he's Dad's little slave. If he's not careful, he'll end up as fucked up as me. Ha!

Seriously, why did Papa have to leave this place to Dad and Uncle Boyd? Mom says we should just sell our part of the land to Uncle Boyd, but Dad says he wants it passed down to us when he dies. I don't want it, though. I don't even want to live in Oklahoma. I want to live in LA or maybe Portland. Someplace where there aren't a bunch of racists and misogynistic assholes. Maybe I can convince Dev to come with me when we graduate from college. Then she can finally be herself. Sometimes, I'm not sure if I even know her. How can you really know someone if they can't be themselves? But then, I guess she doesn't really know me either.

CHAPTER 7

DEVON

2025

As Devon drove into Arkana for the first time in almost two years, the gray sky opened its mouth, raining sheets down on her old black Toyota Prius, the cracks of thunder sounding too close for comfort. Puddles quickly appeared on the red dirt road like pools of blood as she turned onto the lane leading to her parents' house.

She slowed down as she passed the Harrison farm on her left, the white farmhouse standing tall and bright in the gloominess of the June storm. Although she knew Keaton didn't live on the farm like his mother and uncle, she still looked for his blue Ford truck, if that was even what he still drove. During her last visit home, she had seen him from afar when she drove through town. He was getting out of his truck at the local feed shop, and her heart pounded in her chest at the small glimpse of him. She hadn't been in the same room with him since his father's funeral ten years earlier. Even then, she had stayed at the back of the funeral home where the service was held, her eyes darting away from his whenever he'd look her way. The thought of running into him again scared the hell out of her. What could she possibly say to him after everything that had happened? She could apologize to him for leaving without so much as a goodbye after senior year, but it wouldn't matter. If he knew the real reason for why she'd left, he'd never speak to her again anyway, so it was easier to avoid him.

She looked away from the Harrison house and increased her speed down the road, guilt weighing heavy as lead in her ribs.

She pulled up to the old dark-blue two-story craftsman, the front porch sagging a bit with age. For so many summers during her childhood, she'd sat with Mimi on that porch, shelling peas or cracking pecans for her grandmother's famous pie she made every holiday. Devon's heart pinched with the memories.

Devon knew her parents wouldn't ask too many questions about her visiting them for an extended time, not after she skipped the prior three years' holidays to get through her licensure test to become a counselor and deal with the aftermath of her assault, something she never planned to tell her parents since it would involve them knowing about her past sex work. Really, she could've driven the two hours to visit them anytime she wanted, but then she'd see her mother sharing posts on Facebook, like one about banning LGBTQ books in schools or how drag performers are pedophiles, and she'd lose the mental energy to be around her. Her father, thankfully, didn't have a Facebook account, although she knew his views likely fell in line with others' in Arkana. Living in Arkana meant you'd always have neighbors to look out for you, to bring you food if you fell ill or help you harvest crops if your tractor broke down. But it also meant you couldn't deviate too far from what was deemed acceptable.

Devon flipped her car visor down and checked her appearance. She certainly didn't fit the bill of what was acceptable in town, not with long cherry red hair and tattoos running down her arms. She braced herself for whatever judgmental comments her mother would toss at her like tiny bombs.

Before she was even out of her car, her mother was standing on the porch, her father trudging toward her holding an umbrella. He handed it to Devon, and she did her best to hold it over them both.

"Hey, honey. It's so good to see you," he said, giving her a side hug. "Why don't you go on inside out of this storm, and I'll get your bags. Take the umbrella so you don't get soaked."

"Okay, Dad. You sure you can get them with your back?" She looked at the two large suitcases in the back seat of her car and then again at her father, who was pushing sixty.

He smiled at her. "I'm not that old, missy. Hurry on now before your mother scolds us both for lingering in the rain."

Devon was too conscious of her appearance as she walked up to the house to her mother. Her old jeans suddenly felt too tight against her curves, her green V-neck T-shirt too low cut, and her tattooed arms too exposed. Her mother scanned her head to foot, and Devon imagined her checking off a list of everything wrong with her.

"Hey, Mama."

"Hope you didn't hit too much traffic on your way. This weather has been relentless, hasn't it? It's gotten so cold I had to turn on the heat."

Her mother would never admit the crazy weather was due to climate change. Oklahoma had seen a week straight of endless rain, a perfect backdrop for how Devon felt, with memories of Summer and Keaton constantly floating to the surface of her thoughts.

"It wasn't too bad," Devon said.

Her mother reached out and pushed a strand of hair back from her face. "Still red, huh? I sure wish you'd go back to your natural color. It's so pretty blond."

"I like the red, Mama." Devon loved how it set off her fair skin and green eyes.

"Well, I hope it doesn't damage your hair too much. Mary Wilson's granddaughter had to cut off all her hair after she bleached it so she could dye it orange. Her hair was falling out in clumps. Can you believe that?" Her mother shook her head. "Orange hair. It's like kids these days are trying their best to look ugly."

Devon flinched inside. Before she had gone red, she'd dyed her hair a sunset orange, and she was positive her mother remembered.

"I'm careful about it," she said, keeping the hurt from her voice.

She followed her mother inside the house, the burst of warm air feeling good against her chilled skin but also slightly suffocating. This was the only home she'd ever known, yet she was so removed from it now, like a stranger walking into the wrong house.

"Since it's been so cold," her mother said, "I decided to make some chili and corn bread. That sound good?"

Her mother's famous chili was one of Devon's favorite meals. She knew her mother's go-to method of communicating was through food, and this was her way of offering comfort. She'd told her parents nothing about why she was visiting, but her mother knew something was eating at her.

Maybe this time back home would be good for her. Maybe she could finally find some kind of common ground with her parents and come out to them. The idea always sent electric panic throughout her body. She wasn't even out with most of her friends, although they probably assumed she was bisexual given her dating history. One of her closest friends back in Oklahoma City once asked her why she never dated anyone seriously, and Devon didn't have an easy answer. It was difficult to explain her fear of getting too close to others without thinking about Summer, and now she had the added fear of having sex again after her assault. She knew Summer was always at the heart of her relationship issues, and she also knew deep down this visit to Arkana would force everything to a head.

"Chili sounds amazing, Mama." She trailed her mother toward the kitchen just as her father entered the house with her suitcases. "You need any help?" She knew her mother hated chopping peppers.

"Only if you're not too tired from driving."

"I'll take your bags up to your room," she heard her father calling from the entryway.

"Thanks, Dad."

"Your father's back is getting worse." Her mother went to the sink to wash her hands. "Dr. Cooper says he might need surgery."

"Maybe I should help him with my bags first."

"No, no." Her mother dried her hands on a dish towel hanging off the oven handle and turned to her. "He'll be fine. You know how he gets—doesn't want to admit he's no longer a spring chicken."

"Okay, Mama."

Devon eyed the wood prep table in the center of the kitchen, the various peppers sitting on the cutting board as if waiting for her. She washed her hands and got to work chopping, her eyes quickly tearing up from the capsaicin fumes. The peppers came from her mother's huge garden, and Devon recalled the time she and Summer had stolen strawberries and pedaled their bikes out to the grove near Chullusa Pond, where wild black-eyed Susans and milkweed grew tall and the spicy fragrance of blue moon phlox surrounded them, making the secluded spot feel touched by fairy magic. Chullusa, the Choctaw word for being serene, that's what the grove was to them—a place away from town where they could relax and be themselves without eyes watching them, judging how they looked, what they said or didn't say. They had gorged themselves on the strawberries, their fingers sticky with the juices, and Devon had wanted to kiss Summer's full lips, to taste the sweetness on her.

"I ran into Keaton Harrison the other day when I was getting milk at Braum's," her mother said, an unspoken question in her tone.

"Oh, yeah?"

"He looked good, but he was always a handsome young man. Polite, too, though I do wish he attended church." Her mother paused, the rhythm of their chopping the only sound for several moments. "He asked about you."

Devon stopped chopping, heat searing her face. "What did you tell him?"

"Just that you would be home for a bit." Her mother cleared her throat, and Devon went over to the window above the kitchen sink, cracking it before they both went into a full-on coughing fit from the pepper fumes. "I invited him to the Fourth of July potluck next week. Pastor Walters and Mayor Stinchcomb have really outdone themselves this year with the fireworks display they've got planned. It's going to be the biggest one yet. You came at a perfect time."

If Devon survived that long being under her parents' roof. She hadn't been to the big town fireworks display since she was a teenager. The thought of Keaton showing up to the event sent a sharp wave of anxiety mixed with excitement through her rumbling stomach.

"Everyone at church is looking forward to seeing you on Sunday."

She loved how her mother didn't even ask her if she wanted to attend service. It was an unspoken requirement for her to stay with them, and she didn't have enough money to stay at the lone motel near the outskirts of town. With her small savings, she really couldn't afford to be off from work longer than three weeks, and Paulette had made it clear not to return to the practice until she had worked out her shit. Arkana contained every bit of shit weighing her down, and she hoped three weeks would be enough time to work it out.

"Looking forward to it, Mama."

While the chili simmered and the corn bread baked, Devon went up to her old room to unpack her things. Her twin bed looked too small to hold her now, or maybe it only felt that way given everything she'd experienced since the last time she'd slept in it. She realized this would be her first time sleeping in the bed as a woman who'd had sex, who'd done some of the most perverse things possible with others, which would give her parents a heart attack if they found out.

She sat on her bed and pressed her face into her pillow, sucking in the familiar scent of lavender. She glanced around her room, every surface free from dust. Her mother had cleaned for her visit, had made sure her bedding with the T-shirt quilt her Mimi made was freshly laundered. Another way her mother showed love. Devon tried not to psychoanalyze her family and friends, but it was difficult to avoid it. It was so much easier trying to figure out others and their idiosyncrasies than to dig into her own behaviors and reactions. She thought of Paulette's words to her: *You'll never be an effective therapist if you can't even take care of yourself.*

Devon rose from her bed and went to her large window. The rain had slowed, the green fields in the distance draped in a low fog. She stood at the window for a long time watching the gray sky darken with dusk, wondering if she had gone through all the years of schooling and the hard work to pay down her student loans for nothing. The past decade of her life had been solely focused on getting her therapy license, and now she couldn't stop questioning her ability to do the job. If she failed yet another person . . .

Bright headlights flashed through the mist, pulling her away from her troubling thoughts. A truck was passing by her parents' house, slowing down for a moment before driving on. She was sure it was only wishful thinking, but for a moment she allowed herself to believe the truck belonged to Keaton.

CHAPTER 8

DEVON

April 2012

After Devon had revealed her big secret to Summer, their friendship seemed to change overnight. And she'd had no idea there was this invisible divide between them until it no longer existed. It was like Summer had been scratching at the protective layers Devon had shielded herself with, and now every part of her was exposed and accepted. She never wanted to keep anything from Summer again.

Well, almost anything. Sometimes, like now as they ate lunch in the cafeteria, Devon had to look away so Summer wouldn't think too hard about why her best friend was staring at her. Summer was certainly more open minded than anyone else Devon had known, besides Keaton, but she was positive Summer would freak out if she knew Devon lusted after her, had pleasured herself countless nights in bed to thoughts of kissing and touching her.

The night before, Devon had sparked an explosion in her body with her hand, the most powerful one she'd ever felt, the amount of wetness shocking her. Afterward, she had sucked her fingers and imagined she was tasting Summer.

Something pinged off Devon's head and landed on her lunch tray. She looked down and saw a Tater Tot chilling on top of her slice of cheese pizza.

"Yo, earth to Dev," Summer said, getting ready to fire another of her Tater Tots with her fork.

"What?"

"Trey's party Saturday night. We're going."

Trey Weaver's parties were notorious for having tons of alcohol, sometimes drugs, so the kids in town had to devise sneaky plans so their parents wouldn't catch them. Devon never even attempted to go to one because she knew she'd somehow get caught. "Uh, I can't."

Summer's tight expression said no wasn't an option. "Tell your parents you're spending the night at my place." She laughed. "Say you're working on converting my heathen ways."

"Seriously, I can't."

"You just don't want to." Summer sulked as Devon expected her to do, dissecting her remaining Tater Tots with her fork and stabbing them until they were scattered all over her tray. "You *never* go to parties. I'm starting to think you're embarrassed to be seen with us."

"Come on," Keaton said next to Summer. "Stop being a dick about it. If she can't come, she can't come."

Devon gave him a tiny smile of gratitude.

"I mean, if you want to be lame, then stay home, but everyone's going to skinny-dip in the pond by Trey's house, so you're going to miss seeing all the tits and ass." Summer smirked at her, and Devon's face went red. "Keaton's stripping down too. Balls out, right bro?"

"Maybe your crazy ass is, but not me," Keaton said. "It's like sixty degrees outside."

"Good thing we ladies don't have to worry about shrinkage, do we, Dev?"

Devon's face grew redder thinking about Keaton naked. She'd seen him shirtless many times during the summer prior when they'd gone swimming at Chullusa Pond. His chest had grown more muscular, his abs more defined, from helping his father and uncle at the farm.

"Come on, Dev. Do this for me. Please," Summer begged, her hands clasped under her pouting face. "I promise you won't go to hell for having a good time."

"Don't let her bully you into going." Keaton nudged Summer as he looked across the table at Devon. "Though it would be nice to have a sane person to talk to there."

"Please, please, please, Dev. I'll let you borrow anything you want. Just come with us. No one's going to say shit about you going."

Most of the kids who would be at the party went to the same church as her. Going to one of Trey's parties meant no ratting out others or you'd never be invited to anything ever again.

Devon bit her lip and grinned. "Okay, fine. I'll go. But I get to wear your black dress."

◆ ◆ ◆

The rest of the week had been so busy with three AP-prep tests that Devon didn't have time to be anxious until Saturday arrived. She followed the plan and lied to her parents, telling them she was spending the night with Holly Lynch. Devon's mother loved comparing her to Holly, who was the niece of Pastor Walters and was apparently perfect in every way. Devon wondered what her mother would think of Holly now, standing in the middle of Summer's bedroom, prancing around in a tight blue minidress with black ankle boots and a smear of raspberry-colored lip gloss on her mouth, her long dark hair falling in waves around her face.

"Devon, oh, my God, you look so hot!" Holly slurred out the words as she tugged on Devon's hands. "You should dress like this all the time."

Devon was certain Holly and Summer had done what Summer once called pregaming. She pulled her hands from Holly's grasp and went over to Summer's full-length mirror. Summer came up behind her, and Devon could feel the heat radiating from her body, caressing the bare parts of her skin.

"You do look fuckable, Dev." She smiled at Devon's reflection, Summer's thick electric-blue eyeliner making her hazel eyes that much more mesmerizing. "Aren't you glad I talked you out of the black dress? The green is perfect with your eyes."

It was true. The long-sleeved olive green dress with a back cutout did bring out her eye color, as did the gold eye shadow and copper eyeliner Summer had applied on her. Summer's dark-brown booties were a little tight, but Devon would suffer through any pain because they looked good on her. Besides, she liked the pain. It was another secret she kept from Summer, how she frequently hurt herself to stop her impure thoughts. Her mother had thought it strange when Devon asked for a prayer candle to keep in her bedroom. *We're not Catholic,* she'd said, but she bought her one anyway. Night after night, Devon would light it and pour the hot wax on her inner thighs as she prayed for purity. But then she grew to desire the pain, and her prayers turned to fantasies of Summer or Keaton pouring the wax on her, sometimes holding her down as they did it.

"All right, bitches," Summer said, "let's get the fuck out of here." She pounded on her wall. "Keat—we're leaving!"

The night wasn't as chilly as Keaton had predicted while they waited for Keaton's best friend to show up, but Devon saw Summer and Holly shivering in their more revealing outfits. Mason Turner arrived in his beat-up Honda Accord, and the girls all crammed into the back, Mason making a lewd comment to Summer about helping him with his stick shift before Keaton punched him in the shoulder at the exact same time Summer kicked his seat.

Summer, being the slimmest of the girls, was squished in the middle seat, and Devon couldn't focus on anything else during the short drive but the soft floral scent of Summer's perfume, the same she had sprayed on her, and the skin of their cold thighs pressed tight.

When they pulled up to Trey Weaver's house, the white vinyl siding bright against the dark sky, Summer pulled her close and whispered, "Don't be nervous, okay. I'll watch out for you."

This was it. She was going to an actual party, and not some tame one thrown by the church with popcorn and snow cones. A real party where she could be someone different, someone cooler.

They all got out of Mason's Honda and followed the thin gravel trail leading to the back of Trey's house, where the bonfire shot embers into the air and the deep bass of rap music thump-thumped so loud it vibrated the ground up into Devon's chest. The moment she saw the large group of people, an older guy shoved a drink into her hand.

"Hey," he said, scanning her body. "Haven't seen you before."

Summer immediately took the drink from Devon and dumped it onto the ground. "Always get your own drinks unless you want to wake up face down with your pussy out."

Devon looked over to where Keaton was standing with Mason, both waiting their turn at a beer keg. She pointed to them and asked, "Is it okay to drink that?"

"Sure, if you like drinking piss water. I'm getting a real drink if you want one."

She shadowed Summer to a card table laden with liquor bottles, liters of soda, and red Solo cups. Summer immediately started mixing them drinks—a healthy amount of something clear with a splash of Dr. Pepper. She seemed so comfortable, like this was something she had done a million times. She handed Devon the drink.

Devon took a cautious sip and stopped herself from gagging. She'd never had alcohol before, and she never imagined it tasting so repulsive with how kids at school talked it up.

"Good, huh? You have to drink it fast," Summer said before she chugged her entire cup. "Like that. Now you do it."

If Devon tasted it again, she knew she'd throw up, so she pinched her nose as she drank it down. The liquid sat in her stomach with a sickly warmth.

"See?" Summer wrapped her arms around her, squeezing her tight. "You *do* know how to have fun. I'll make you another."

She started mixing two more cocktails, and Devon's gut rumbled in protest.

"Hey, sis," Keaton said, sidling up next to Devon. "Go easy tonight, okay?"

"Fuck you." Summer downed one of the new cocktails she had mixed and sneered at him.

"Here." He handed Devon a cup of foamy beer. "This is safer."

"Thanks." She took a sip, and it tasted foul, but it was much better than the concoction Summer had made.

"We don't want your shitty piss water, Keat. Go away!"

"I don't mind it," Devon said.

"Let's go to the pond." Summer pulled Devon away from Keaton. "I dare you to skinny-dip with me."

"Um . . . I don't really want to skinny-dip, but I'll make sure you don't drown," she tried to joke.

"So, you just want to watch?" Summer smirked. "Such a naughty little voyeur."

Devon didn't know what she meant, but she didn't like her mocking tone.

Summer drank from the cup she had mixed for Devon. "Okay, bro. You babysit her while I go find the fun people."

The comment felt like a hot poker being shoved into the center of Devon's chest. Like Summer was calling her a burden, a little kid to be watched over. Anger rushed through her, burning her eyes. She hadn't even wanted to go to this stupid party, and now Summer was just going to ditch her?

"Stop being such a bitch, Summer!"

She'd never cursed at anyone before, and it felt a little good. Without knowing where she was going, she took her cup of beer and went over to where Holly was smoking with Jenna Long, the skunky cloud haloing their heads making them look like strange angels.

"Hey," Jenna said, passing the joint to Holly. "Summer being a cunt again?"

"Yeah."

"It's not you," Holly said, being oddly nice and holding the joint out to Devon. "She's just pissed because Coach made her run extra laps for being late again."

It was true Coach Thompson was hardcore about practice, but that didn't give Summer an excuse to take it out on her. Everyone, including herself, had done extra laps before as punishment.

She looked to the other side of the bonfire to see if Summer was going to come over and apologize, but instead she saw Keaton staring at her, the flames casting dancing shadows across his face. Something in his expression made her conscious of her movements, of how her borrowed dress clung to her curves. Like Summer, was he waiting for her to trip up and prove to everyone she didn't belong at the party? That she wasn't cool enough? *Let him watch,* her mind whispered, and she took the joint.

SUMMER'S JOURNAL

April 2012

I fucking hate myself. Why am I doing these things? I feel infected, like I'm being eaten from the inside out by some parasite with rows and rows of jagged teeth, and there's no way I'll ever get rid of it because the parasite is me. I feel so alone, even when I'm around Dev. I want to tell her things, but I don't know if I can trust her. I want to.

Please, let me disappear so this feeling will go away. I don't think I can take it anymore.

CHAPTER 9

DEVON

2025

Devon stood, politely listening to Mary Wilson ramble about her grand-daughter's unfortunate orange-hair disaster, wishing she was a child again, free to enjoy the Fourth of July celebration without the obliga-tion of making small talk with the elderly church members. When she was a child, she'd loved the Fourth of July in Arkana—the live music and cornucopia of food throughout the entire day; the bicycle races with other kids, their bikes decorated in red, white, and blue streamers; a Bomb Pop dripping over her fist while she ran barefoot through the cool grass; the sparklers streaking through the night. Then she'd watch the night light up with blinding colors next to her family, her dad covering her ears for her so she could continue eating one last Popsicle.

As Mary moved on to complaining about her granddaughter's choice of clothing, Devon tried not to think about Macayla and what her parents must be going through. That morning, she'd made the mis-take of looking up Macayla's obituary. She'd ended up in a fetal position on her childhood bed, crying for over an hour.

"Oh, really?" she said to Mary, who continued to talk about everything wrong with her grandchild. She imagined her own mother talking about her, going down a list of her failures, starting with not being married with kids.

Devon searched the crowd of townspeople again. She didn't want to admit it, but she was disappointed when she didn't see Keaton anywhere. She did see his mother, Annie, talking to a gaggle of old church ladies. Annie's silver-streaked chestnut hair was pulled back into a low ponytail like Devon's, her figure still tall and lean, making Devon wonder if this was how Summer would've looked if she had lived long enough to grow older. Annie Harrison was the type of person who could talk to anyone, just like Keaton. But Annie surely realized those sweet little old ladies she was chatting with said the vilest shit about her family even as they flashed their dentures and asked how the farm was doing.

"Devon, honey," her mother said, popping up next to her. "You should go catch up with Holly. You know her twins are almost three now? They are just darling."

"Are you seeing anyone, dear?" Mary asked, her rheumy eyes falling on Devon's tattoo-covered arms.

Before Devon could answer, her mother piped in. "I don't know how she could find anyone decent in the city, but she might have a chance if she put some effort into her appearance."

"I'm right here, Mama."

"All I'm saying is you're such a pretty girl, but you do these things to yourself." Her mother seemed to motion to every part of her. "And your clothes. Always in jeans and T-shirts. You know Holly sells LuLaRoe. You should buy some while you're here."

Devon held her tongue, but God, she wanted to tell her mother to shove perfect Holly and her perfect twins and LuLaRoe leggings up her ass.

"I sure do wish Keaton could've come," her mother continued. "I heard he had to take care of some things at the farm."

So, he wasn't even out of town. He had chosen not to come, knowing she was here.

"Terrible thing, what happened with his sister," Mary said. "Not a surprise, though. Bad things happen when you turn away from God."

Devon's head shot toward the older woman. "What do you mean, exactly?"

Mary shrugged. "She hung out with that Indian girl. The *lesbo*." She whispered the word like it was a curse to speak it out loud.

She meant Jackie Byrd. Devon hadn't thought of her since senior year, when Summer died and her world fell apart.

Mary tittered, her bluish-gray helmet of hair unmoving in the warm breeze. "Probably best that girl killed herself before that Indian turned her into one too."

Devon felt blood rushing to her head as Mary benignly smiled back at her as if she hadn't just spouted the shittiest thing possible. How could she look her in the eye and say Summer's death was a good thing when it tormented Devon every night? She tried so hard, but she couldn't keep the words in. "Better to be a lesbo than a horrible old bitch like you!"

"Devon Marie Mayes!" Her mother's face was a mask of horror. "Apologize to Mrs. Wilson right now."

She couldn't rein in the fury flowing through her veins hot as lava, not with her mother staring at her like she was a wayward child. "Hell no. How are you okay with her talking about Summer like that? My *best friend*."

"I can't believe you're acting like this." Her mother actually looked on the verge of crying. "If you don't apologize . . . well, then you're not welcome to stay at the house."

Devon bit her bottom lip hard, her tongue aching to spew more vitriol at Mary, at anyone in the world for thinking Summer's death meant nothing.

Her mother's eyes darted between Mary and her, but Devon already knew how this was going to go. Mary was a church elder, and she stood there with smug triumph on her face even before any words were spoken. "I'm serious, Devon. You need to find someplace else to stay if you don't say sorry for your rudeness."

"Fine."

Devon was too angry to cry. She turned to walk away and saw Annie standing at a nearby drink station, her mouth slightly parted. It was clear she'd heard what went down. Devon wanted to walk past her all the way back to her parents' house so she could pack her shit and leave. She didn't need this. She didn't need this bigoted town that would always look at people like her with hatred.

She ended up heading straight to Annie, to one of the people she had hoped to avoid during her visit, and she embraced her. "I'm so sorry."

Annie seemed stunned for a moment, but then she hugged her back. "You can stay with me at the farm if you want, hon."

"I'm so sorry," Devon said again, knowing it would never be enough.

◆ ◆ ◆

After getting her things from her parents' house, Devon considered driving back to Oklahoma City and calling Paulette to say her shit was as worked out as it was going to get. She knew her supervisor well enough to know it wasn't going to be that simple. Paulette held the power to sign off on her practicum hours, and if Devon couldn't prove she knew how to compartmentalize her personal life from her job, all the years of hard work would be down the drain.

When she pulled up to the Harrison farm, she was struck by how little had changed about the two-story house. It was over a hundred years old, and it looked like it from the outside. Inside, it smelled like apple-cinnamon air freshener with a faint hint of wheat. As Annie walked with her upstairs to where she'd be staying, Devon glanced at the family photos hanging on the wall above the wooden handrail. A young Summer and Keaton, dressed in identical clothes, though gender specific—the requisite pink and blue. A photo of them at a white-sand beach bordering crystalline blue water, something Oklahoma didn't have. And a family portrait, John Harrison standing tall and strong at the center.

They said he'd died from a massive heart attack, a widow maker, as they called them, and only three years after his daughter had killed herself. She couldn't imagine what Annie and Keaton must've gone through, and she felt a wave of guilt. She should've called or stopped by. Something. But she'd been a coward, tucked away at college, only making a brief appearance at the funeral without saying a word.

Devon followed Annie down the hallway, past what used to be Summer's bedroom and toward Keaton's room.

"Figured you could stay in Keaton's old bedroom. I'll have to get a fresh change of sheets for the bed. We don't get many guests."

Devon assumed by *we* she meant Boyd, Keaton's uncle. He owned half the farm, so she figured he still lived there. Keaton, she knew, owned his own house somewhere else near town.

Annie opened the door to the bedroom and yelped in surprise. "God dammit, Boyd."

The bedroom was filled with fifty-pound bags of wheat seed, with no bed in sight.

"What in the hell was he thinking moving the bed?" Annie asked as if Devon could explain it. "And I have no idea why he'd put these bags in the house when we have a perfectly good barn. Oh, Devon, I'm sorry."

"It's okay. I can take the couch."

"No, no. That couch is likely to break your back." She paused, hands on her narrow hips. "I don't know how you'd feel about staying in Summer's room."

How did she feel? Like it would be a messed-up form of immersion therapy. "That'd be fine."

"All right. I'll go grab some fresh bedding for you."

Devon felt awkward standing in the hallway, so she sucked up her nerves and entered the room she had been inside innumerous times, splayed across Summer's bed, covered in her collection of stuffed animal frogs, including her favorite Build-A-Bear her uncle had bought her one birthday.

She flipped on the light and almost gasped. It was all the same, even the stuffed animals on the green bedspread, like stepping inside a time warp, like how her mother kept her room, too, as if she was trying to memorialize the innocent girl who no longer existed, who probably never existed.

She picked up Summer's favorite stuffed animal frog from the bed, squeezing it against her chest for a moment before gently setting it back against the pillow.

Devon slowly moved over to Summer's white vanity, where photos were taped around the mirror's border. She remembered when Summer was obsessed with having a Polaroid camera, bugging her parents until they bought her one for Christmas. Summer had taken dozens of photos, until she ran out of the special film and couldn't afford to buy more. Devon's eyes went to one she remembered Annie taking of them— Devon in the middle, flanked by Summer and Keaton. A tightness pulled and tugged in her chest.

In the mirror's reflection, something caught her attention—a book sitting on an old sewing table Summer had used as a desk. Devon went to the desk and saw it was their yearbook from junior year. She opened it, flipping the pages until she got to the juniors and her photo, a heart around it in red ink. But then there, toward the top of one page, Jackie Byrd's class photo was scribbled out in black pen with the word *LIAR* written over her head, followed by several exclamation points. What the hell?

It was so strange, she got out her cell phone and snapped a photo of it. She closed the yearbook and was about to place it on the bookcase next to the vanity when she noticed a thin book of poetry she had given to Summer. She pulled it from the shelf and opened it, and a folded piece of paper fell out. It appeared as if it had been torn from a journal. Immediately, she recognized Summer's large loping handwriting, how her letters looked like plump dancers leaping across the page. At first, she didn't grasp what she was reading, so she read it again, slower, and an awful dread dug its fingers deep into her skull, making her face go numb.

CHAPTER 10
DEVON

April 2012

Devon stared at Mrs. Bartles, her AP Language teacher, talking about their next book assignment over *Wuthering Heights*, but she couldn't get her brain to connect to pay attention. She was still stuck on what had happened at Trey Weaver's party over the weekend and what she had witnessed.

After she had smoked the joint with Holly and Jenna, her lungs burning from coughing a ton, her memory got fuzzy. She remembered drinking another beer someone handed her, and then she felt like she was going to throw up, so she walked toward the woods and heard splashing at the pond. She went to the edge of the shoreline and saw bodies bobbing in and out of the water, the moonlight giving glowing glimpses of breasts and backsides as laughter echoed up into the sky.

Then moans behind her, like a chorus of Sodom and Gomorrah that made her hips go weak. A single word among the pleasure sounds so clear—NO. She followed it into the woods—NO—and there, against a tree half shadowed by night, she saw her: Summer, her tight dress pushed up, a boy—Mason Turner?—hunched over her like Satan himself. Summer's mouth open, her eyes closed tight.

"Leave her alone!" Devon tried to scream, but her voice croaked out instead. Something was wrong with her. Why couldn't she speak? She closed her eyes, her head swimming in the cool air, and someone tugged on her arm, pulling her down to the ground. Sharp rocks stabbed her back, rough hands on her chest, and her words wouldn't come out—no. *NO.*

"Get the fuck away from her!"

Her eyes fluttered open enough to see a shadowy figure over her.

"Dev?" Keaton's voice, right in her ear, but she couldn't open her eyes again. "Are you okay?" She tried to answer him, but only a strangled whimper came out, and then a black nothing overtook her.

That was all her mind could remember.

The next morning, she woke up in Keaton's bed, bonfire smoke in her hair and her throat raw. She didn't know where he was, but Summer was asleep in her bedroom, dead to the world. Devon had checked on her before sneaking out, stumbling her way home in the blue light of dawn and barely making it through the front door before her parents got up. If her parents noticed the smoky stench coming off her during church that Sunday morning, they said nothing to her.

Then Summer ran up to her before first hour Monday, asking to borrow her history notes as if the party had never happened.

If it hadn't been for Keaton, Devon would've thought she'd imagined the entire night. Before the first-period bell rang, he had rushed into AP Language, face flushed from running. His eyes glanced her way, and she saw concern etched in them.

After class, he came up to her desk. "Hey. You wanna ditch next hour?"

He clearly wanted to talk, but she was nervous about what he might say. "Sure."

The April morning was overcast and chilly, and Devon shoved her hands into her blue hoodie as she walked with Keaton to the metal bleachers. They sat, and the cold went straight through her jeans, sending a shiver through her.

Keaton gazed at her for a moment, his hazel eyes getting that troubled look again. "So . . . Saturday, when that guy was on you, did he hurt you? Like, did he . . . do anything?"

Devon knew what he meant by the apprehension on his face. "No. I mean, I don't remember a whole lot afterward, but I don't think he did anything before you got to him."

"Dev, you were really messed up. Summer was wasted, again." He blew out an annoyed sigh. "She could at least walk. But you were like *out* out. I had to carry you to Mason's car. I heard you screaming, and that older guy was on you."

"Where was Mason?" she asked.

He looked confused at her question. "With us. He had too much to drink, so I drove his car to my house. He crashed out in his back seat until the morning."

"Wasn't he with Summer?"

"I don't think so. Summer was throwing up on the shore when I found her."

Had she imagined it, Mason's hand up Summer's dress, the bell-clear *NO*? "Did she seem okay? Like on the drive back."

"You mean besides almost vomiting in Mason's car? Yeah, I guess."

Maybe she'd been more out of it than she thought. She remembered Summer's warning about always getting her own drinks, and she had failed that simple rule. She didn't want to think about what might've happened if Keaton hadn't heard her.

"Where did you sleep that night?" she asked. He could've carried her to Summer's room, but he didn't.

He looked a little sheepish. "On the floor. I was going to put you on Summer's bed with her, but I was afraid she might throw up on you." He grinned. "And then I moved to the couch because I didn't want you to wake up and, you know, like get weirded out seeing me."

The thought of him watching over her while she was passed out in his bed did sort of weird her out, but it also excited her. She recalled the way his room smelled—a strange, not unpleasant muskiness mixed with something citrusy that was the opposite of Summer's bedroom, which smelled like her Bath & Body Works Japanese Cherry Blossom lotion—and knew she would now think of the scent whenever she touched herself at night.

"Well, thanks for looking out for me," she said, suddenly feeling shy around him. "I think I'm good on parties for the rest of my life."

He smiled. "Nah, you just had one bad night. If people didn't party around here, they'd probably kill themselves." He ran his hand through his wavy hair, his expression turning serious again.

The tension she always felt in him seemed to stretch out to her, making her suddenly anxious. His moods weren't as mercurial as Summer's, but he did have times when he'd get quiet for long periods, making Devon worry if he kept certain things hidden from her because he either didn't trust her enough to tell her or didn't think she'd understand.

"But, hey, I've actually been meaning to ask you something." He clasped his hands, his thumbs digging as he looked at her. "Has Summer talked to you about anything, I don't know, bothering her?"

Devon didn't know why, but she was disappointed by his question. "Um, I can't think of anything. Why?"

He stared down at the ground and shook his head. "Never mind. It's nothing."

He was keeping his thoughts from her, and it bugged her more than she wanted to admit. Out of both twins, he was more open with her, whereas Summer was like a ripe pecan that didn't want to crack. Sometimes, Devon wished she could combine the two of them into one person so she wouldn't feel so confused about being attracted to the different parts of them.

She didn't like the awkwardness hanging in the cool air between them. "Why don't you use your psychic twin connection to find out what's going on with her?" She leaned into him. "Y'all have one, right?"

A smile tried to emerge on his face, but it didn't quite make it. "I wish."

CHAPTER 11
DEVON

2025

Devon didn't want to drive to Oklahoma City the day after the Fourth of July, but she'd already planned on going back to perform in a burlesque fundraising show Saturday evening for one of her friends. During the two-hour drive through the heat without A/C, she could think of nothing else but the torn journal page she'd found in the poetry book, the frantic, loopy handwriting almost undoing her: *I know you don't want to talk to me after everything that's happened, but I have to tell you something important. Meet me at our spot after school. Please. I'm scared and I need your help. You're supposed to be my fam forever, remember?*

She knew Summer had written it to her, but she didn't know why she never gave it to her. Since Devon had been the freak at school without a cell phone, Summer always left notes in her locker in lieu of text messages when she wanted to meet somewhere after class or to invite Devon over to her house. But this note was different. She sensed the fear behind it, and she knew the note had been written after one of the worst days for them both. A day Devon wished she could erase from her memory. It made her think of that Jim Carrey and Kate Winslet movie she once watched with Summer and Keaton one fall evening, the mugs of apple cider Annie had made them warm in their hands as she pondered how romantic it was to fight to hold on to the memories of someone you loved. But was it really? So many times, Devon thought her life would be easier if she could forget Summer and Keaton.

What had Summer been scared of? It was bothering the hell out of Devon. Her gut told her it had something to do with why she'd killed herself. And then there was Jackie Byrd's yearbook photo blacked out in ink, the accusatory *LIAR* above her name. They had been good friends at one point, but something obviously happened between them. Devon vaguely recalled the time she'd seen Jackie at Summer's locker and how upset Jackie had seemed. She made a note to herself to pay Jackie a visit when she got back to Arkana.

For now, she needed to focus on getting ready for her performance at Ponyboy, an Oklahoma City bar that frequently hosted burlesque and drag shows. One of her friends, Derek Lane, a burlesque drag queen who went by ChaCha Wylde onstage, had been the target of a hate crime after a recent Drag Story Hour. Devon was relieved to hear he was now out of the hospital, but he was still suffering from his injuries—a few broken ribs and a cracked jaw—and would miss another week of work. Like a lot of people in Oklahoma, he was uninsured, so the hospital bills were going to be insane. Devon hadn't performed burlesque in months, but if it meant raising money for her friend, she was ready to glue on pasties and shake her ass.

Most of the other performers were already in the small backstage area when Devon arrived. She scanned through the feather boas and fans, looking for the bright-orange wig of her friend Neko, a.k.a. Viva St. Claire. Neko had been her burlesque mother, showing her the ropes and teaching her how to tease the audience. She also pushed Devon to use kink as her niche onstage. Working as a sex worker had always been like playacting for Devon, something she'd done most of her life in Arkana, pretending to be a perfect, God-fearing girl who never dreamed about sex and certainly never fantasized about being tied up and hit with a riding crop. When she used to work as a dominatrix, she could pretend to be dominant when she'd always known her kink ran more on the submissive, masochistic side. Burlesque dancing was no different. It was all an illusion people were willing to pay for, and Devon was good at putting on whatever mask the audience desired.

"Dev!" Neko screamed, bouncing up to Devon in her six-inch strappy heels, her glittery orange pasties already glued in place. "Girl, you are so late. You don't even have your face on. And your hair!"

"Shit, I know." Devon had hit traffic after stopping by her apartment for her costume and makeup. "I'll be quick. I'm just doing a high pony. But will you pretty please help me with the extension? It's so fucking tangled."

Neko rolled her gray eyes. "You're lucky I love you. Need any help with gluing on your nips? Been a while since I've had the pleasure."

"Tempting." Devon grinned at her before grabbing a chair in front of the long mirror. "But I'm just using tape tonight." Neko flirted with everyone during performance nights, like most of the women surrounding her, tapping into their inner Bettie Page.

Neko poked around in Devon's bag and pulled out a pair of black elbow-length latex gloves and red candles. "Yay—you're doing the wax routine! Haven't seen that one since the Tulsa festival last fall."

"And it's taken me that long to clean the wax from my hair," Devon joked as she leaned closer to the poorly lit mirror to perfect her cat eye with her black liner so she could glue on her eyelashes next.

After she'd finished her makeup, she smiled at herself in the mirror, her lips bloodred and her dimples showing. Her black corset was cinched tight, pushing her ample breasts up so much she could see the edge of the black tape X she had placed over each nipple to stay Oklahoma-law compliant. For a moment, she didn't recognize herself, especially with her long red ponytail extension that went down her back, grazing her ass.

"Hey, Dev, you're up," another performer said.

Devon squeezed the leather crop in her hand hard and listened for her stage name to be called, her nerves trying to get the better of her until she heard the emcee announce: "Get ready for some hot, kinky action with our next performer, who will have you on your knees begging for more. Give it up for Mistress Maven!"

The first few notes of the Deftones' "Change" started as she came onto the small stage, her low-temperature candles and a square of black plastic tarp already laid out for her by the helpers, also known as the stage kittens. Within seconds, the heat from the bright lights caused a trickle of sweat to run between her breasts and down her spine, and she prayed the tape covering her nipples would hold up.

She held eye contact with some of the audience members in the front row, teasing them by running her tongue along the tip of her leather crop before striking her ass with it. The pain sent pleasure through her body, warming all her senses as she licked her lips and hit herself again and again. She gave the audience a coquettish smile as she waved the crop close to an older man in the front row, motioning for him to stand up and turn around, which he happily did. She lightly hit his ass with the crop a couple of times before tossing it to the side. The wealthy-looking middle-aged woman sitting next to the man appeared hypnotized as Devon slowly rolled one latex glove down her arm until it was dangling from her fingertips. She soaked up the audience's growing desire as she stretched out the glove and stroked it up and down like it was a lengthy erection, before letting it snap off into the crowded bar to an uproar of cheers.

She used her teeth to pull off her other glove and slapped her ass with it. As she began untying the back of her corset, the heavy, distorted guitars of the song throbbing excitement through her, she remembered why she enjoyed doing this. It was the power to make others want her without repercussions.

She timed removing her corset perfectly with the chorus of the song, her breath hitching as she turned around and revealed her breasts, the X's over her hardened nipples holding strong while she dragged her red nails down the center of her chest to between her legs, closing her eyes as she did it. She got lost in the music, in the feel of her fingers sliding into her latex shorts and near the edge of her thong, so close to touching the needful ache at her center. She made herself stop before she went too far onstage and positioned herself over the plastic tarp, the roar of the audience getting louder as she picked up one of the burning red candles from the front of the stage. Before she began dripping the wax over her breasts, she looked out into the crowd, all the way to the back where it was standing room only, and she nearly dropped the candle when her eyes landed on a tall man.

Even after so many years, she instantly recognized him, how he carried his strong frame fully erect, never slouching. She couldn't believe it, but there he was, eyes piercing and paralyzing her.

Keaton.

CHAPTER 12

DEVON

May 2012

It had been almost a week since Trey Weaver's party, and Summer was still acting as if nothing had happened by the pond with Mason, so Devon decided not to say anything about it. But in her gut, she knew she hadn't imagined it. She might've been high and probably drugged by whoever Keaton had seen with her, but what she saw and heard was burned in her mind like a nightmare she couldn't escape.

If there was one thing Devon now knew about Summer, it was that she was good at putting on a happy mask. Almost as good as her. And Keaton obviously felt it, too, how something was off when he had asked her about Summer. During the week, Summer was late to nearly every track practice, and Coach Thompson wasn't happy about it. It was like she was asking for extra laps and burpees. Devon missed walking home with her, and she wondered if Summer was getting punished on purpose to avoid her for some reason.

She watched as Summer finished her stretches before track practice began, her long legs golden from never putting on sunblock like Devon did.

She glanced over at Devon and smiled. "What's with the serious face?"

"Nothing. Just stressing about an essay due tomorrow."

"Sure you're not stressing over something else?"

Devon got down into a quad stretch. "Like what?"

A wicked grin spread across Summer's face. "Like . . . a crush."

A blush raced up Devon's neck to her cheeks. "I don't have a crush. Why do you think that?"

Summer's smile dropped a little. "My mom saw you asleep in Keat's bed. After Trey's party. She apparently heard moaning and checked his bedroom."

"It's not like what you're thinking. Like not at all." Devon let out a nervous laugh. "I don't even remember how I got to your house. Keat said I was passed out when he took us home, and he slept on the couch downstairs."

Summer stared at her for a few beats. "Then why didn't you two tell me you stayed over?"

She didn't know why Keaton hadn't said anything to his sister about it. But the longer she gazed back at Summer's expectant face, the more Devon realized she had kept it a secret. It's not like it would've hurt Summer, but she didn't want her to think she was into Keaton. And that was exactly what Summer now thought.

"I didn't think it was a big deal," Devon said. "It's not like I had any control over anything that night. I was drugged."

Summer's eyes got huge. "What? Are you serious?"

"Yeah. I had a drink and felt really weird, and then some guy was trying to touch me." Whenever she thought about it, it felt like worms were crawling around in her stomach and she wanted to vomit. "Keat stopped him, though."

She saw hurt in Summer's eyes. "I can't believe you guys didn't tell me this."

"I—I'm sorry. I should've told you, but I didn't want you to worry or feel guilty about it since you basically forced me to go to the party."

Summer looked like she had been slapped, and Devon immediately regretted saying those words.

"Shit, I didn't mean that. You didn't force me. I wanted to go and have fun with you, but everything got messed up. I'm sorry."

A tiny smirk emerged on Summer's face. "Um, did Miss Goody Two-shoes just cuss?"

Devon grinned. One curse word and she was somehow forgiven. Summer apparently didn't remember Devon calling her a bitch at Trey's party. She would do anything to keep seeing Summer smile. "I sure fucking did."

Summer's mouth dropped open. "Oh, my God, I feel like lightning's about to strike you."

"Ladies!" Coach called out. "Pay attention and get over here."

Devon and Summer jogged over to where the rest of the team stood around Coach Thompson. He looked tired. Probably because of his baby boy. When she'd seen his wife at church the prior Sunday, she looked exhausted, too, as she cradled their fussy infant. Devon sometimes wondered how he had time for coaching. Seemed like every adult she knew had a million different things going on, which made her want to stay young forever. Her parents were already bugging her about what Christian colleges she should apply to, but she wanted to go to a public college, same as Summer and Keaton.

"There are some things we need to go over before the meet tomorrow." Coach reached up to massage his shoulder, his chest muscles flexing with the movement, and Devon imagined the girls around her were drooling. "As some of you might've heard, Jackie is no longer on the team."

Devon looked around at the other girls, and all of them looked surprised. Not Summer. Her arms were crossed, mouth tight.

"Why, Coach?" Devon asked, thoroughly confused. "Jackie is our strongest sprinter."

He sighed. "I know, and that's what made it a hard decision, but she broke the rules."

Jackie had never been late to practice, which meant she'd been kicked off for a different reason.

"Did she get caught in the locker room munching on some girl's cooch?" Jenna said, and a bunch of the girls laughed.

"That's enough, Jenna." Coach crossed his arms, his hard expression mirroring Summer's. "Tomorrow is going to be a challenge for us. Every single one of you needs to step up and come prepared. No partying tonight and no late-night cuddles with your boyfriends."

A few of the girls giggled at that.

"Be on time. The bus is leaving at seven a.m.—sharp—and we *will* leave without you. Okay, on the track, and make this practice count."

As the girls made their way to the track, everyone was buzzing about why Jackie had been kicked off.

"I heard she was caught doing meth by the dumpsters," Holly said with that supercilious smirk she always wore, like she was somehow privy to special knowledge.

"Laura Smith said Jackie's trailer park was raided by the cops last week, and that's when they found Jackie all strung out on crack with all the other red-skinned trash out there," said Kinzy, a short girl who was forever trying to get into Holly's clique.

"Thought it was meth," Summer spit back at them. "At least get your lies straight before you start spreading them all over this stupid-ass town."

Holly stopped in her tracks and whipped around so fast she almost smacked herself in the face with her long dark ponytail. Her good little minions halted behind her like they were programed robots. "You're friends with her, aren't you?" She sneered. "Maybe you're a cunt muncher too. Here, let me smell your breath."

The other girls laughed as if on cue. Devon didn't.

Summer glanced at Devon before looking at Holly dead-on. "Someday, I'll be out of this fucking place, living it up in LA while you bitches will be stuck here, popping out future neo-Nazis. So, say whatever you want. I don't give a shit."

Holly only grinned and kept walking toward the track, her minions following behind.

Devon stayed with Summer, who turned to her, arms crossed again. "When are you ever going to speak up, Dev?"

All she could do was guess why Summer sounded angry with her. "I know, I should've had your back. I'm sorry."

"I'm not talking about me." Summer dropped her arms to her sides, her face strained. "When they say shit like that about Jackie, they're saying it about you too. They're saying it about all queer people. At least Jackie isn't afraid to be hated. She'd rather be hated than be a coward."

Summer hit the track and started running while Devon stood there, her face burning with the truth of Summer's words. But Summer didn't understand the risks coming out would mean for her, how Devon would lose her family and the only community she's ever known, so it was easy for Summer to say what she did. Maybe someday she could be out like Jackie, but it felt like a life she could only touch with her eyes closed while nestled in her bed.

CHAPTER 13

DEVON

2025

Seeing Keaton in the back of Ponyboy made her feel like a flashing sign in the dark, her pale skin so exposed and lit up for him, and all she wanted to do was run off the stage. But she couldn't. She didn't want to ruin the fundraising show, and she knew her kinky routine would raise a lot of money in tips, something her friend desperately needed for his hospital bills.

So, she continued pouring the red wax over her breasts, the heat and slight pain forcing her to focus on the act and not on Keaton. After she'd slowly removed each fishnet stocking, she poured more wax over each thigh. She teased the audience some more before sliding down her latex booty shorts, revealing her tiny black thong. As she poured more wax down her back and onto her ass, she tried not to find Keaton in the crowd as she made eye contact with people sitting in the front row.

When her song had ended and she blew out the candles, she had to stop herself from rushing backstage.

"You okay?" Neko asked her. "You look like you've seen a ghost."

"Yeah, I'm fine. You mind if I head out early?" She wanted to slip out while it was still crowded to avoid Keaton. She wasn't ready to see him. Not like this.

"Sure, but you'll miss the final bow, and you know people will pay to see your ass again."

"Sorry, just feeling off. Might be coming down with something."

"Okay." Neko gave her a big hug. "Hey, don't be such a stranger. I miss you, lady."

"Miss you too. I'll call you soon."

Devon quickly scraped off the wax from her body with some help, got out of her costume, and removed her ponytail extension. She changed into her gray T-shirt and jeans and threw her long red hair into a messy bun. She kept her stage makeup on and grabbed her things, stuffing them into her tote bag.

The only feasible exit out of the makeshift changing room was through the back side of the bar. She cracked the heavy door and didn't see Keaton, so she took the opportunity to slip out.

She'd almost made it to the narrow stairs leading to the lower bar area when someone touched her shoulder.

"Dev?"

Hearing her name spoken by that deep voice was like a phantom dragging her into the past, her own voice trapped in her throat. She put on what she hoped was a semi-normal face and turned around. Keaton stood tall in front of her, his expression questioning. He was dressed casually in a plaid button-up, the sleeves rolled up, and slim-fitting jeans that looked sexy as hell on his lean, labor-hard body, his work boots the only indication he was no longer a city boy.

He smiled a little. "Trying to escape me?"

"Oh, my God, no! I, uh . . . just didn't see you." The dumbass words left her mouth before she could stop them. Of course, he knew she had seen him. "What are you doing here?"

"My friend invited me since I was in town."

"Did you know I was performing tonight?" She couldn't help asking.

He paused before saying "No."

"Well, I hope the performance didn't disappoint."

He grinned in that unguarded, charming way she always loved, where the skin around his eyes crinkled. "I have no complaints." He looked nervous. Maybe as nervous as she was. "It's been . . . a long time."

"Too long."

He eyed her tote and purse slung over her shoulder. "Do you have time to get a drink? Maybe catch up?"

Catch up. The way he said it, so breezy but also with a hint of apprehension. He knew as well as she did there was no easy way to bridge the thirteen years since they'd last spoken to each other, since she'd left him with his grief when he needed her the most. And here he was extending an olive branch. How could she not take it?

"Sure. But let's go to the bar downstairs." She didn't want Neko and the other performers to see her chatting it up with him after she'd skirted out early.

"Okay. Let me tell my friend where I'm going since I came with him."

She watched him make his way over to the other side of the bar to a Black man she recognized as Kingston Allen, the owner of Subspace, a BDSM club she used to go to on occasion when she worked as a dominatrix. The kink community was a fairly tight-knit group, and she was curious how Keaton knew Kingston, who was now looking her way and grinning like the Cheshire cat. She nodded to him.

Keaton came back over to her, and they made their way downstairs, Devon in front of him. Her nerves were making her hands shake as she replayed everything she'd done onstage just minutes before. For a moment, she had the stupid fear that he'd go back to Arkana and tell her parents what he had witnessed.

The downstairs bar was a little less packed since most customers were upstairs for the second half of the burlesque show, and Keaton was able to snag them a two-top.

"What can I get you?" he asked.

"Um, any hazy IPA is good if they've got it. Thanks."

Devon attempted to get herself together while he bought their drinks. She thought about the note Summer had written to her, and she knew she should've shown it to Annie. Instead, she had tucked the torn journal page into her purse, afraid to let it out of her sight, lest she start to think she'd imagined it. Showing Keaton the note now when she hadn't spoken to him for so long would probably make her look insane. But she also needed to know she wasn't alone in thinking something didn't feel right about it. Summer had feared something, and then she killed herself. It didn't make sense to her. She couldn't help but hope she had been wrong all these years, that she maybe wasn't the catalyst of her best friend's death after all.

Keaton placed a pint of beer in front of her before sitting down, and she saw he'd ordered the same for himself. He took a healthy swig before he studied her for a moment.

"You look good," he said. "I like the hair. It's different, but it suits you."

"Thanks. My mother almost died the first time she saw it."

He chuckled. "I bet."

She drank some of her beer, her nerves trying to take hold of her again. "You look good too." If it was possible, he was even more attractive than he'd been as a teen. "Farming life treating you right?"

"Not really, but I'd rather not talk about it right now." He leaned forward, crossing his arms on the table. "I'd rather talk about why you've been avoiding me all these years."

Wow. He was going to jump right into it. "Um . . . shit." She stared down at her hands resting on the tabletop, away from the intensity of his hazel eyes, which appeared almost black in the darkness of the bar. "I don't know what to say."

"Try. I think you'd agree you owe me that much."

She looked up to see his eyes trained on her, waiting for her response. "I was afraid."

"Afraid? Of what?"

"Of you hating me."

"I've never hated you, Dev. Why would you think that?"

He didn't know about the day in the grove with Summer; no one did. If he had, he wouldn't be saying these words to her. "Because . . . I was her best friend, Keat. I should've done more to help her."

Keaton closed his eyes and breathed in and out slowly a few times, as if it were something he did often, like a reset button. When he opened his eyes again, they appeared glassy under the dim lights. He placed his large hand over hers and squeezed, his touch electric against her skin. "No. You can't blame yourself. It wasn't your fault." He huffed out a sharp laugh. "Took me four years of therapy to say that: 'It wasn't my fault.'" He let go of her hand, the warmth of his touch lingering. "Speaking of which, I heard you're a therapist now, right?"

Her mother certainly caught him up on her life. "Not quite. I'm training to be a licensed counselor. That is, when I'm not stripping in front of strangers." She smiled.

Even in the shadows, she could sense his face reddening. "You, uh, definitely put on a . . . visually stunning show. I had heard through the grapevine about your other, *other* work."

"By 'grapevine,' you mean Kingston?"

"Maybe," he said with a hint of coyness.

"How do you know him? He's pretty big in the kink community."

He took another drink of his pint, shifting a bit in his chair. "I guess you could say he's a customer."

"Customer?"

"I, uh, I make toys as a side hustle. I like doing it, and it helps pay for my mom's medications."

She cocked her head in disbelief. "Toys as in kink toys?"

"Yeah," he said, looking a bit shy about it. "Crops and floggers mostly."

A tiny flurry of excitement went up her back. Was the sweet boy she once knew so well into kink like her? "And do you use your toys too?"

"What do you think?" He gave her a lazy grin, absently rubbing a finger over his bottom lip. "So, how was it beating on rich men for money?"

"Empowering." Her stomach tightened. Yes, it was empowering, until it wasn't.

He smirked. "I always thought you were at the other end of the spectrum. Good little Christian girl and all. *Submissive.*"

If only he knew how often she had hurt herself while masturbating about him, about Summer. "I can be both." Although he was right; she had learned over the years how much she enjoyed being submissive to her partners.

"And how exactly did you get into that kind of work?" he asked.

"A friend introduced me to it when I was desperate to make fast money." She had lost her low-paying office job and was behind on her rent, only a week away from being evicted. Her first job as a dominatrix had been grinding her stiletto heel into a middle-aged man's groin; he'd paid her a cool grand. "And I kept doing it because I enjoyed it. I was really good at it, but . . ."

"But what?"

She swallowed over the thorny memories of her assault trying to push up her throat. "Nothing. It just wasn't . . . sustainable. What about you? How did you get into kink?"

He leaned back against his chair, his arms crossed. "I had an ex who liked impact play, and I don't know, I enjoyed how it made me feel. I liked being trusted on that kind of level by someone, to experience something beyond sex. It's almost humbling in a way, to hold someone's desires and trust like that. You know what I mean?"

She knew exactly what he meant. Her first kinky experience with another person had been with an extremely sadistic lesbian who had humbled her on all levels, opening her mind and body to what true submission and trust meant. And when she got into dominatrix work, she went full force, knowing what it felt like being on the other end. In a way, she always thought that had made her better at her work, being more empathetic to her customers and their desires because she shared them too.

"Yeah," she said. "I know what you mean."

Keaton gazed at her, a slight smile playing on his full lips, sending flutters to her pelvis. "You know, I've missed you. You should've called or come by."

Sudden guilt twisted her gut. "Keat . . . I'm sorry I wasn't there for you. I really am. It was such a shitty thing to do. And then when your dad died . . ." She brushed tears from her eyes, positive her black eye makeup was now in full raccoon mode. "I've missed you too."

He reached out and took her hand again. "It was shitty, but I'm still your friend."

Would he still want to be friends if she showed him Summer's note? If she was any kind of friend to him, she wouldn't hide something so important.

"I need to show you something," she said as she dug into her purse. She handed him the folded journal page.

"What is this?" He opened it, and his face dropped. "Where did you get this?"

"Read it. I found it at your mom's place last night in a book. I got into a fight with my mother, and your mom invited me to stay over."

"What the fuck?" he whispered to himself as he read it. "Was this written to you?"

"Yes, but last night was the first time I've seen it." Then she pulled out her cell phone from her purse and showed him the pic she'd taken of Jackie Byrd's yearbook photo. "It's strange, isn't it? What was Summer scared of? And what happened between her and Jackie?"

Keaton didn't move. He kept staring at the note, his hand shaking the longer he held it. "I . . . I have to go." He dropped the note and stood up. "I'm sorry."

What the hell? "Keat, wait. We need to talk about this."

But he was already beelining for the exit.

CHAPTER 14
DEVON

May 2012

Devon kept looking up at the Saturday-morning sky, hoping to see a bit of sun through the billowing gray clouds, the slight green tinge making her stomach go queasy. Oklahoma weather during May meant peak tornado season, and she hated storms. Mimi had loved them. Devon's grandmother would sit on the front porch for hours with her glass of sweet tea and portable radio, volume blasting so she could hear Gary England giving the play-by-plays. She once told Devon the famous weatherman had asked her out on a date, but she refused because she was already dating Devon's grandfather, who had died a few years before Mimi.

"Don't worry." A heavy hand landed on her shoulder. She looked up to see Coach. "They're not going to cancel the meet. It's going to stay southwest of us."

Devon doubted it. Storms that started southwest of Arkana almost always found their way through town. The summer before, they'd been hit by an F1, the weakest tornado there was, and it still peeled off a few roofs.

"I'm going to need you to be one of my stars today," he said.

She hadn't been able to stop thinking about how angry Summer was at her for not speaking up about Jackie. "Coach, why did you kick Jackie off the team?"

"I didn't." He stroked the stubble on his jaw, his expression serious. "This is not for others to know, Devon, but the school did a random locker check and found drugs in Jackie's. She's been expelled."

She couldn't believe it. She never knew the school did random checks, not that she'd have anything to worry about. It seemed like an invasion of privacy to not let students know there was the possibility of locker searches.

"I trust you to keep that to yourself." He gave her a smile. "I know you're not a gossip."

She nodded, her head feeling disconnected from her body. Jackie expelled. Devon had never known anyone to be expelled from the school. She wondered how Summer would react to the news. She looked around the parking lot; it was almost seven, and Summer was nowhere to be seen.

The bus would leave without Summer for their last and biggest track meet, and Devon would be stuck sitting next to girls who had made fun of her for most of her life. When Summer and Keaton had befriended her, their popularity among the cool kids had somehow extended a little bit to Devon, giving her a sense of protection from the mean girls at school. Without Summer or Keaton next to her, she always felt vulnerable.

A few kids were starting to board the bus, and Devon's heart fell.

She was about to go ahead and board, too, when she heard the screeching of car tires and turned to see an old red Mazda pull into the parking lot, right in front of the idling bus. A petite woman with a tawny complexion and dark hair threw open her car door, not bothering to close it as she rushed up to Coach Thompson.

"Where's Principal Morris?" she yelled. "I want to speak to him right now!"

"Ma'am, he's not here. Is there something I can help you with?" Coach's voice was calm, like he was talking to a small child.

"I know he's going to the meet," the woman continued to yell. "I've seen his fat ass at every school event."

"I think he had something else going on, ma'am, but maybe I can help you."

Devon was impressed with how cool Coach was, given the woman looked ready to claw someone's eyes out.

The woman laughed. "You know how you can help me? You can tell that son of a bitch my daughter doesn't do drugs. Someone planted them, and I'm going to find out who. You tell him Dove Byrd is going to sue his ass and this whole racist school system!"

Then she got back into her Mazda, slammed her door shut, and peeled out.

"What a crazy bitch," Holly said, coming up next to Devon. "Coach, that was Jackie's mom, wasn't it?"

Coach didn't look amused, his mouth a tight line. "Get on the bus, Holly. You, too, Devon."

As Devon waited for Holly and her minions to get on, her hope of Summer making the bus died. But then she heard feet pounding against the pavement behind her.

"Oh, my God, I'm dying," Summer said, grabbing Devon's arm, her breathing ragged. "My dad's truck wouldn't start, so I had to run all the way here."

Devon was so relieved Summer made it she thought her heart would burst. "Why couldn't your mom drive you?"

Summer looked lost for a second. "Um, she had to do something."

It seemed too early on a Saturday morning for her mom to have plans. If they weren't traveling two hours for their track meet in the city, Devon would still be asleep in bed.

"Girls," Coach shouted. "On the bus, now! We're behind."

Devon hurried up the bus steps, but Summer took her time, like she was trying to make Coach more pissed than he already was.

All the prized seats in the back were taken, so Summer and Devon had to grab seats near the middle. No one sat up front by Coach, who was talking to the old bus driver.

There was a furious buzzing about the bus as the girls not-so-quietly whispered about what had happened.

Summer's head shot in the direction of Holly's voice. "What are they saying about Jackie's mom?"

Devon told her about the confrontation, and Summer got quiet.

"He asked me not to tell, but Coach said the school did a random locker check and found drugs, so they expelled Jackie."

Summer looked at her, and her hazel eyes appeared more gray blue today, like the brewing storm hovering over them. "And you believe that?"

"I mean . . . I don't know." Although she had never witnessed Jackie doing drugs, it was hard to ignore what the school had found.

"I'm sure they didn't even bother to drug test her." Summer hugged her arms tight across her chest like she was cold. "Because if they did, they'd see it'd be negative. And then they'd have to figure out which one of these homophobic bitches set her up."

"Maybe her mom can get one of those drug tests at the pharmacy and prove Jackie wasn't taking anything."

Summer looked at her like she was an idiot. "You still believe this town gives a shit about people like Jackie?" She lowered her voice. "Like you?"

Anger boiled up in Devon. Summer had only lived in Arkana for two years, yet she lumped everyone into the stereotype people seemed to have of rural towns. "Not everyone here is racist or homophobic. There are good people here too."

"Like who?"

"Like people you would be able to name yourself if you gave them a chance. For one, Pastor Carter."

"The youth pastor? Seriously?" Summer rolled her eyes.

Pastor Stinchcomb, or Pastor Carter, as Devon and the other youth group members called him, had always been nice and not at all judgmental. During Bible studies, he went out of his way to discuss sinners and how most of the time they were only misunderstood people. And he had started a book drive for inmates at the prison where he led Bible studies and an adult literacy program.

"He's always helped me anytime I've had a problem," Devon said, still feeling defensive of her town. "Maybe you should visit him."

Summer's expression turned flat. "I don't have any problems."

"If you say so."

Summer looked away from her, and Devon pressed her forehead against the cold bus window. She watched the darkening clouds galloping across the morning sky like a herd of bison, the first drops of rain hitting the glass with the force of the inevitable.

The storm was here.

SUMMER'S JOURNAL

May 2012

I can't believe I actually went to church. Well, not church exactly, but Pastor Carter. He was surprised to see me. I guess he thinks I'm a heathen like other people in this town. But he was nice. Nicer than I thought he'd be. He's kind of a nerd. I could tell by the Star Trek stuff all over his office. Sort of weird seeing a picture of Spock next to Jesus. We talked about how school's going and his new baby, who's super cute. God, I fucking love fat babies, and his is super chunky. I could tell he was trying to get me to open up, just like that lady my parents sent me to when we lived in Oklahoma City. Fucking Dr. Elizabeth. All she did was put me on pills that make me feel crazy. Sometimes, I think maybe I am crazy. All the things I do, the people I hurt. I don't know how to stop myself. How can I tell a stranger like Pastor Carter these things? How can he help me? So, I didn't tell him much. Then I gave him my number in case he ever needed a babysitter and left. He told me to come by anytime I wanted to talk.

Keat keeps asking if I'm okay. As if he cares. He has his own secrets too. Like when we still lived in the city and Paul's 19-year-old cousin made Keat her fuck toy for the summer. Maybe it's the twin thing, but I always know. I see him clearer than he sees himself. I always have.

CHAPTER 15

DEVON

2025

After talking to Keaton the night before and seeing his reaction to Summer's note, Devon didn't know how to feel. In some ways, she knew she was reopening a wound within him by questioning Summer's death, but she had no choice. In her therapy training, truth was paramount. There was no healing without it, as Paulette had preached to her. But Devon also knew the mind shielded itself from pain by withholding certain facts, and she didn't look at it as lying to yourself so much as a necessity to move forward. But the note changed everything. It unlocked a new possibility, and she had to explore it the same way she'd work with a client, peeling back each layer of their protective mechanisms until the core truth revealed itself.

She never wanted to hurt Keaton further than she already had by distancing herself, but he deserved to know the truth as much as she did. Still, she decided to give him some space, let him process what she'd told him. Besides, she needed more information to support her suspicions. Summer's note wasn't the only clue something bad had happened before her death. There was Jackie Byrd's yearbook photo marked out with a pen. Devon wanted to know why Summer had called her a liar.

Sunday mornings after church in Arkana meant brunch at Nancy's, the diner at the heart of Main Street, right across from the town center, where Calvary Baptist loomed and all the big holiday events were held. Devon heard Jackie Byrd worked as a server at Nancy's, so she headed there early, before church let out.

As soon as she stepped into the diner, the few customers—mostly older farmworkers, who always seemed exempt from attending church services—looked up at her, guardedness in their squinting eyes. Once again, her brightly dyed hair and tattoos othered her to the people she had grown up around. It was like they didn't recognize her at all.

Devon seated herself at one of the open booths and glanced around the diner until she caught sight of Jackie's petite frame. Being one of the few people of color in Arkana, Jackie stuck out with her deep-olive complexion. Devon was surprised how little Jackie had changed. Her long hair, shiny and dark as crude oil, was pulled back into a low ponytail, and her face still had the soft roundness of a teen.

She watched Jackie pour more coffee for an old man strongly resembling a dried-up piece of beef jerky. She was a good server, offering a smile when she would receive none in return. Working hard for tips she probably wouldn't get. It didn't matter that Arkana was within spitting distance of Choctaw land, where Jackie and her single mom used to live and where people within her tribe brought billions of dollars to Oklahoma's economy. To some people in Arkana, being indigenous meant you'd always be looked at as an outsider trying to steal jobs from the white folks. It was ridiculous. And here Jackie was serving these old assholes who complained about the same Choctaw casinos where they gladly wasted away their monthly Social Security checks.

When Jackie finally noticed Devon, her smile dropped right off her pretty face. Unlike the old geezers, Jackie clearly recognized her. She never understood why Jackie didn't like her when they had never really interacted outside of a handful of words during high school. Maybe she had been jealous of how much time Devon spent with Summer.

There were no other servers in the place, and Jackie went out of her way to check on every other table before coming to Devon's booth.

"What can I get you?" she said, her husky voice annoyed.

"A coffee with cream, please."

Jackie swiftly moved behind the long counter to get a mug. Just as fast, she was back, setting the mug, now brimming with hot coffee, down in front of Devon, along with a couple of creamers and a spoon.

"Anything else?" she asked, arms crossed. "Our brunch special is biscuits and sausage gravy with two eggs any way you want 'em."

"I need to ask you a question." She paused, holding Jackie's baffled gaze. "About Summer."

"What?"

Devon held up her cell phone. "That's your photo. I was at the Harrison farm, and I was looking through Summer's yearbook."

Jackie narrowed her dark eyes. "So?"

"So, why did she call you a liar? I thought you two were close."

"Then you thought wrong."

"You know, I saw you two arguing at school one day. By Summer's locker." The time Jackie had been near tears for some reason. "Why did you two stop talking?"

For a moment, Jackie's hard demeanor slipped, and an emotion difficult to decipher—perhaps regret—flashed in her eyes before she slid on her waitress smile again. "I'd heard about you, about why you're back. All the little church ladies chatting in here, saying how you must've had a mental breakdown and had to come running home to your parents." Her grin widened. "Maybe chasing white rabbits isn't the healthiest thing for you to do right now."

So, there were rabbits to chase. "Why did Summer call you a liar?" she asked again. She knew the look of someone hiding something. Her clients deflected all the time during sessions, and she had to keep peeling, removing the husk of deceit layer by layer until she found the kernels of truth.

Jackie leaned down closer to her, and Devon could smell the woman's sweat mixed with whatever vanilla-scented perfume she was wearing. "You should go. Church just let out."

Devon looked out the diner window, and, sure enough, folks were pouring out of Calvary Baptist's huge wooden doors. She could just make out her mother's favorite blue church dress billowing in the wind among the mass of churchgoers, half of whom were heading to the diner. Jackie was already behind the counter preparing for the influx when Devon turned back to face her. She pulled out a five-dollar bill from her wallet and left the diner.

Thankfully, she had parked her car farther down on Main Street in front of Bill's Pharmacy so she didn't have to worry about her parents seeing her. She half jogged to her car to avoid the crowd crossing the road, which was a mistake. Julys in Oklahoma, even in the morning hours, were blazing hot. Sweat ran down her front and back, soaking her bra and plastering her blue T-shirt against her skin. She didn't look forward to driving back to the Harrison farm in her car with a dead A/C. She decided to grab a bottle of water from the pharmacy first.

"Why, hey there, stranger," Margie, Bill Johnson's wife, said from her post at the front of the pharmacy, which, like most pharmacies in big cities, carried just about anything a person in town could need.

"Hi, Mrs. Johnson."

"I'd heard you were back in town, but I almost didn't recognize you with the hair."

Devon tugged the ends of her red strands. "My mother hates it."

"Well, I like it. Brightens your beautiful face. Come here and give me a hug, girl." Margie had lost her right foot to diabetes, so she had trouble getting around. Working the cash register allowed her to sit while she chatted up customers.

Devon embraced the curvy woman, a pang of wishing her mother would be as accepting piercing through her chest.

"Oh, dang, honey, you are *wet*. It's that hot already?"

"Sorry," Devon said as she pulled away. She looked down and saw the front of her T-shirt was soaked through just below her breasts.

Margie smiled and whispered, "I get the boob sweat too." She motioned to her ample chest. "I swear, these girls are a blessing and a curse, but Bill's never complained." She giggled, and Devon couldn't help but laugh too. "Go get yourself a drink before you pass out."

Devon had just turned to go toward the cooler aisle when she ran into someone coming into the store. She was about to apologize, but words escaped her once she saw who it was. She was face to face with Keaton, and she couldn't tell if he was happy to see her.

"Sorry," she quickly said, immediately embarrassed by how she probably looked to him, boob sweat and all. "I didn't see you."

"That's becoming a habit," he said with a cocky grin.

"Morning, Keaton," Margie called from the register. "You see our girl's back in town?"

Keaton smiled at Margie. "I do, indeed."

"Isn't she looking good?"

Keaton met Devon's eyes. "She is."

His words sent a thrill up her spine. Seeing him up close in the daytime was almost too much. He was beautiful, and it made her wonder again what Summer would've looked like now, all grown up.

She sucked in a breath. "By the way, I closed out your tab at Ponyboy."

His cockiness melted as his face reddened. "Uh, thanks."

"I might've added a couple more drinks first." She smirked. "Top shelf."

"I guess I deserve that." He ran a hand through his hair. "But you blindsided me."

She touched his forearm and lowered her voice. "Can we talk about it?"

He looked down at her feet. "I don't know, Dev." When his eyes traveled back to her face, the pain she saw in them almost made her regret pushing the issue.

"Please. You know something is off about that note."

Keaton blew out a sigh. "I don't want you talking to my mom about any of this. I'm serious."

"Okay, I won't."

"I've got to get back to the farm." He paused. "Meet me at Lucky's around nine."

Lucky's was a tiny bar just outside Arkana on a stretch of road leading to a casino. If you drove a little farther on southeast, you'd hit Little Dixie, a place someone like Devon, a queer person, could get tied up and dragged behind a truck.

She nodded. "It's a date."

CHAPTER 16

DEVON

May 2012

Despite Coach Thompson's assurances the storm wouldn't affect the last track meet of the season, the downpour muddied the track so much the meet was canceled. They had driven all the way to Oklahoma City for nothing. At least Coach treated them to Braum's before they headed back.

Monday rolled in, and the rumors about Jackie swirled through the school hallways like a virus seeking to infect. Devon noticed a few classmates discreetly removing items from their lockers. Probably drugs or other things they didn't want discovered during a random locker check.

Summer's sour mood had altered as swiftly as the weather, both now sunny and warm. Devon couldn't keep up with her shifting attitudes. There was a month left of school, and she hoped Summer's good mood would hold up long enough for them to enjoy Ryan Nelson's pool party in June. Every year, Ryan, who was one of the wealthiest kids at school, since his parents owned Nelson Tractor Supply, threw a huge party to celebrate the end of the school year. He only invited the cool kids, and Devon definitely didn't fall under that category. But this year,

Ryan had invited her, or that's what Summer had told her. She knew it was only because of her friendship with Summer and Keaton, but she didn't care. For the first time, she was included in the upper echelons of Malcolm Thompson High School, and she couldn't stop thinking about being around so many beautiful people in the sad one-piece bathing suit she owned, which looked like something a grandmother would wear, with ruching over the stomach and an attached skirt that completely covered her butt.

There was nothing she could do, though. She was just thankful her parents had given her permission to go, but of course they would since the Nelsons were well respected at church. Money always bought respect at Calvary Baptist, Devon noticed, while the poorer parishioners had to sit in the back pews and were forced to the end of the line during church potlucks. Devon's parents weren't rich, her father working as a bank manager in town and her mother doing part-time work as a cashier at the Shop 'n Save, but they tithed enough to earn a spot four pews down from the pulpit.

Devon tried to shake thoughts of her one-piece from her mind as she watched Summer coming down the hallway from her last class. Before she made it to her locker, Mason Turner stopped her. His hand gripped Summer's arm, and jealousy speared heat through Devon's chest like a glowing metal poker left in a fire for too long. What was worse was how Summer didn't instantly push him away. Mason whispered something in her ear, and Summer nodded, smiling. She caught Devon watching them, and her grin fell. She backed away from Mason, saying something to him Devon strained to hear but couldn't, before going to her locker.

Devon slowly walked over to Summer, the burning in her chest making her dizzy. She knew she had no right to be jealous of Mason or anyone else interested in Summer, but the memory of seeing them at Trey Weaver's party was so clear she didn't see how she could've imagined it, though she told herself she had. The pleading *no* calling from the woods, how Mason had pressed Summer against a tree, the moonlight providing glimpses of his hand up her skirt. Why would Summer say no to him if he wasn't forcing himself on her?

She thought of Dinah and Shechem. Pastor Walters had said the Bible made it clear Dinah was a party girl, that she had spent so much time with the Shechemite pagans that she had invited Shechem to rape her, and this was why girls needed to be mindful of how they dressed and spoke around boys. It was true Summer had drunk a lot at Trey's party, but Devon didn't understand how that invited anyone to assault her. But once again, she questioned her recollections of that night.

"You've got your serious face on again," Summer teased her as she closed her locker. "You don't like Mason, do you?"

"Not particularly."

"Why?"

Devon carefully pieced together her response as they made their way down the hallway. "I saw you with him in the woods by the pond. At Trey Weaver's party."

Summer said nothing as they exited the school and walked across the track field toward the road.

"Did he hurt you, Summer?"

They hit the red dirt road as Summer said, "Of course not."

"But I heard you telling him no, and he . . . he was touching you."

Summer stopped walking. "Dev, I think you were confused by that drugged drink you had."

"But I remember it so clearly."

"Well, your memory is wrong." Summer's voice was flat as she said it.

Devon didn't know what else to say, but she made herself ask the thing still smoldering in her ribs. "Do you like him?"

"Mason?" Summer laughed. "Oh, my God, no. He's a total fuckboy."

Devon didn't know what that meant, but she felt relief. If she had to see Summer with someone else, Mason would be at the bottom of the list.

Summer took her hand. "Okay, your turn for confessions." She grinned. "Who does Miss Innocent want to fuck?"

Devon felt a blush reach every part of her body. She could tell Summer right now what she'd been holding on to for so long. *I want you. I want to know what you taste like.* But if she said it out loud, she knew she'd lose the person she cared about most. Summer would be weirded out and stop talking to her forever.

"Don't be scared," Summer urged, her hand squeezing tighter. "I won't tell anyone."

The words were there on her lips, but she couldn't get them to leave her mouth. "No one."

Summer cocked her head. "You don't like anyone? Like no one at all?"

"I mean . . . I do, but . . . it's too embarrassing to talk about."

Summer let go of her hand and spun in a circle. "Holy shit! That church has you so messed up." She stopped turning, her eyes pinning Devon. "Sex is not a big deal. Trust me. Once you do it, you'll be like, 'That was it?'"

Devon had guessed Summer had sex before, but hearing her talk about it made her feel a little ill.

"You know Keat likes you."

A strange exhilaration shot through her stomach at those unexpected words. "Did he tell you that?"

Summer bit her bottom lip. "No, but my twin spidey sense told me, and it's never wrong."

Except Summer had to be wrong this time. Sure, Keaton had joked around with Devon, but she never saw it as flirting, but then she wasn't exactly sure what flirting looked like. She thought about him at night in her bed the same way she did with Summer, though it was different for reasons she couldn't explain. In her fantasies, Keaton was always the one touching her, but her thoughts about Summer were always her exploring her friend's body, running her fingers through her golden molasses locks and kissing her soft skin.

"So, do you like him?"

"No," Devon said too fast. "I mean, not like that. We're just friends."

Summer's expression was indecipherable for a moment. "Well, someone's going to pop your cherry someday."

Devon laughed. "Stop!"

"The fun thing about being bi is that you have twice as many people to choose from. And Ryan Nelson's pool party is the perfect place to lose your precious virginity. His McMansion has so many rooms to hide away in."

"You've been there before?" She'd gone to school with Ryan her whole life and had never been to his house.

"Of course." Summer scrunched up her nose. "It wasn't that impressive. Pretty gaudy, actually. Looks like Hobby Lobby vomited on their walls, but his parents let his friends drink, so that's cool."

Devon pushed down her envy. Everything was easier for people like Summer, people who could talk easily with others without constantly worrying about how they appeared or if they'd sounded stupid. Others naturally gravitated to people like that.

Summer placed her hands on Devon's shoulders. "Don't freak out about the party. You have plenty of time to get bathing suit ready. We can wax you this weekend. I'm really good at it."

"Uh . . ."

"Can't say no. Bushes and bikinis don't mix."

"Fine."

Preparing for Ryan Nelson's party, like Trey Weaver's, felt like another test she had to pass to go into her senior year as someone new, someone more confident. She felt like she was trapped inside a cocoon, and she didn't know how to break out of it, but she knew if she didn't she'd suffocate.

CHAPTER 17
DEVON

2025

Lucky's wasn't like the array of hip bars in Oklahoma City, with their local craft brews and signature cocktails. It was the definition of a hole-in-the-wall bar, where you could get a bucket of six PBRs on ice for five bucks served alongside french fries swimming in nacho cheese.

Keaton was already there, munching on an order of okra, when Devon arrived. Two draft beers with orange slices sat on the table, and she was dying to drink one. Even for a Sunday night, the bar was full of men, mostly young to middle aged, who were likely seasonal farm laborers since Devon didn't recognize many of them. The summer-evening warmth had seeped inside the bar, making sweat run down her chest and back. The jeans and T-shirt she'd worn earlier in the day were so soaked from the heat she'd changed into one of the few light cotton dresses she had packed.

Keaton's eyes trailed over her body when she approached the small booth he was sitting at, and heat zapped straight to her lower belly as if she'd had a heating pad thrown on her.

"Got you a Blue Moon. Best they have." He paused. "You look nice."

"Thanks." She sat across from him, taking in how good his muscular arms and chest looked in his green T-shirt. "It's hot as fuck in here. Don't they have A/C?"

His mouth quirked. "I thought you loved the summer."

"No, I've always been a fall girl. I just loved to swim." As soon as she said it, she thought of Ryan Nelson's big pool party all those years ago, and her face burned with the memories flooding her. "I used to anyway." She gave him a knowing smile. "You know I'm not much on pool parties."

Keaton's expression turned thoughtful, making her nervous about what he was going to say. "Do you regret going? To Ryan's?"

She took a pull of her beer, not sure what to say to him. Finally, she said, "No, I don't regret it."

He smiled a little. "So, are you dating anyone?"

The question made her palms sweat. "Uh, not now. I was a year ago, but she moved to Colorado." Right after her assault, when she'd needed her partner the most, but she didn't tell him that.

Keaton didn't appear surprised, and she wondered if he had asked around about her, maybe talked to Kingston and found out about her bisexuality. It made her feel a bit exposed with him knowing, but another part of her felt relief in not having to hide something so integral to who she was from him.

"What about you?" she said.

"I dated someone for about five years, the person who got me into kink. She worked at the Pepsi plant, but she took a job in Tulsa during the pandemic, and we ended things."

Five years. None of her relationships had lasted that long, maybe six months at most, and she knew she was the common denominator. She looked at Keaton, wondering how he would be as a boyfriend, as a lover . . . as a dominant.

His gaze lingered on her eyes, then her lips, and the center of her pulsed with a need she hadn't felt in many years. She didn't know what to do with the sudden rapid-fire emotions stirring in her. They needed to talk about Summer's note and what to do about it, but she also wanted to fall into this sensation of being entranced, of not having to think about anything else but how he was now looking at her, like he could bring her to her knees with one word.

"Open your mouth," he said, his deep voice going right through her chest.

A trapped breath escaped her at his level, commanding tone, and it felt like her brain stopped working for a second. She blinked hard. "What?"

He motioned to the basket of deep-fried okra in front of him. "You need to try these. Best in the state."

A weak chuckle dribbled out of her, her mind still flustered. "I doubt that." Her Mimi had made the best okra, and no bar food would be able to compare.

"You always loved being wrong." He held up a piece. "Open your mouth," he said again, and his voice seemed to go to the base of her skull, somehow alerting every nerve in her body while lulling her at the same time. Was this how he sounded when he topped someone? Without a thought, she parted her lips as if she were taking communion, and he placed the okra in her mouth, the tips of his long fingers lightly grazing her tongue as he did it. It felt like he was grazing other parts of her as well, and she shuddered.

She bit into the rich nuttiness of the okra, which was well done and crunchy, just how she loved it, and she released a tiny moan, setting her face on fire.

Keaton smirked. "I told you so."

They stared at each other as she chewed, the charged moment making her heart speed up. She swallowed, willing herself to break the trance.

"Keat, we need to talk about Summer's note. My gut is telling me something bad happened. And maybe . . ." She forced herself to say the words she knew he wouldn't like. "Maybe her death wasn't by suicide."

His slight smile faltered before it fizzled away altogether. He leaned back into the booth, crossing his arms. "Why do you want to make this note into something it's not?"

"Is that why you ran out of Ponyboy? Because it's nothing?"

Keaton's jaw tensed. He drank down the remainder of his beer, then set the pint glass on the table a little too hard. "She committed suicide. End of story."

"But what if it wasn't? What if someone gave her something, and she accidentally overdosed? What if the sheriff's office only assumed her death was a suicide."

"Dev," he sighed. "I don't think the police would make that kind of assumption."

"Well, did you even see the toxicology report to know what kind of drug was in her system?"

"No, but I'm sure my parents did. The sheriff said her death was an obvious suicide."

She stared at him. "Weren't you curious to know?"

He looked away from her.

She herself had always wanted to know more, but it wouldn't have changed anything then. It wouldn't have brought Summer back. But now after reading the ominous note Summer had left, every detail of her death felt vital. How could she tell him she needed the doubt? She needed the reason for Summer's death to be anything else but suicide. She needed absolution.

"I spoke to Jackie Byrd," she said, changing gears.

Keaton turned back to her, shaking his head. "And what? You're going to harass her because of a yearbook photo?"

She didn't like his mocking tone. "Something happened between them. She refused to talk about it with me, but I know she's hiding something important, something that could maybe explain what happened with Summer."

"Are you hearing yourself?" He pinched the bridge of his nose, his eyes shut tight for a moment. "Listen, a lot was going on before Summer died. Things she clearly didn't want you to know about." He looked her in the eye. "I guess I didn't want you to know either."

Devon's head suddenly felt fuzzy. "What things?"

He leaned forward, his arms crossed on the table. She noticed his fingers were digging into his forearms. Maybe an anxious tic. "Things weren't good between my parents. The farm was really struggling back then, even more so than now, and my mom wanted to go back to Oklahoma City. She left and went to stay with my aunt in Texas for a couple of weeks. And we didn't know if she'd come back."

Devon had no idea.

"My dad drank a lot back then, too, and he . . . he didn't always know how to control his temper." He paused. "I wanted to go to college like you, but I couldn't leave my mom here."

He lowered his eyes to the tabletop, his hands squeezed into tight fists, and Devon read between the lines. His father had been abusive to his mom.

"I think my dad was mostly angry that he couldn't make this dream happen for us after my grandfather died. He always talked about legacies and wanting us to be our own bosses. He thought he could run things better than my grandfather had, than my uncle. Thought his master's degree would give him a leg up." He finally looked up at her, his pained laughter hitting her in the heart. "He was a joke. He didn't know what he was doing. He wasn't meant for farming life any more than I am. Or my mom. And now we're trapped because everything we own is tied to the farm." His mouth grew tight. "I think Summer knew she was trapped too."

Devon didn't buy the idea of Summer killing herself because of everything going on with her family. Summer had plans to move away from Oklahoma as soon as she graduated from college; she'd said so to Devon many times.

"Why don't you and your mom just sell the land and be done with it?" she asked before sneaking another okra into her mouth.

"Because my uncle owns half, and he has no interest in buying the other half my mom and I own."

"But can't you just sell your half to someone else?"

He shook his head. "We can't. It's how my grandfather's will was written up. The land can't go to anyone outside of the Harrison family unless both parties agree to sell. So, we're in this limbo."

He was still digging at his forearm. She reached out and placed her hand over his to stop him. "I'm sorry you're going through all this. You and your mom shouldn't be stuck here. But, Keat, I don't think Summer would've killed herself because of your parents' issues. You know how she was. She didn't take shit from anyone. She was strong."

Keaton's hand twitched under her own. "She wasn't as strong as you think she was. Obviously. She had secrets. She only told people what she wanted them to know."

Devon sat up straighter in the booth. "Then tell me what I'm missing."

Keaton slipped his hand out from under hers. "Please leave this alone. All you're going to do is cause pain—for my mom . . . for yourself."

"For you?" she said.

"It won't end well." His gaze was heavy on her. "What happened at Ryan's party and afterward . . ."

Don't, her mind hissed. She sank back into the booth's cushion, a weight growing heavy in the center of her chest, making it hard for her to breathe.

His eyes held her hostage. "What happened . . . *that's* what we should be talking about."

Memories tried to rise up and devour her, but she kicked them back down. "I can't, Keat. And I'm sorry, but I can't leave this alone."

He gave her an incredulous look. "Maybe instead of chasing fantasies you should ask yourself why you willingly came back here. I'm guessing the reason's not good."

His words stung, and she couldn't shake it off because he was right. "I don't want to talk about it."

"Fine," he said. "Let's not talk. We're wasting perfectly good beer and okra."

She glared down at her sweating pint. She now understood why fate had brought her back to Arkana, and it wasn't to fix herself. She was going to find out the real reason why Summer died. Someone or something had frightened Summer enough to make her reach out and write a note to the person who had hurt her the most.

And that person was Devon herself.

CHAPTER 18

DEVON

May 2012

Devon couldn't believe she was going to let Summer give her a bikini wax. No one other than her pediatrician had seen her *down there* since she'd entered teendom. The night before, she'd sneaked onto her parents' computer, the one she was only allowed to use for school purposes, so she could look up videos on the internet about what waxing entailed. But after entering *bikini wax*, the first video she pulled up shocked her so much she had trouble falling asleep.

As she walked up the driveway to the Harrisons' house, she felt her hands go slick with sweat. She thought about going back home and calling Summer. Tell her she was sick or something.

She balled her hands into tight fists. No. She was being stupid. Girls did this all the time; it wasn't a big deal. She didn't want to be the only girl at Ryan Nelson's party with pubes hanging out of her bathing suit.

She jogged the rest of the way up the long gravel drive and rang the doorbell. Keaton answered the door, shirtless, his golden brown hair messy as if he'd just woken up when it was noon on a Saturday.

"Hey, Dev." He gave her a lopsided grin. "You here to get pruned?"

She couldn't believe Summer had told him. Right then, she would've given anything for a frackquake to open the ground and swallow her whole.

"Uh . . . yeah."

He opened the door wider to let her inside. "She's still setting up her torture chamber. You want some coffee? I just made some."

"Sure."

She followed him to the small kitchen. Summer complained about how old everything in her house was, but Devon loved it. She especially admired the original cast-iron sink and 1950s mint green stove. It was almost strange to see the modern coffee maker on the counter.

Keaton poured her a cup, adding a little cream.

She was surprised he remembered how she took her coffee, but then she knew how he took his, too—way too much sugar and cream—since they often went to Nancy's diner after school to get their caffeine fix.

He stirred her coffee and handed her the mug. "Are you really going to let her rip hair from your body?"

"Gotta be swimsuit ready, right?" She took a sip and hoped the coffee wouldn't rattle her nerves more.

He shrugged. "I don't get what's bad about having hair. But if someone's going to do it, seems like there'd be an easier option."

Devon had said the same thing to Summer, but then Summer told her about the horrors of razor burn.

"Guys have it so easy," she said, trying not to notice the light trail of golden hair on his lower stomach, the V of his hips disappearing into his shorts. "You can literally flop out of bed and look good."

He squinted at her. "Thanks?"

She remembered what Summer had told her about Keaton liking her, and she blushed. If he did like her, wasn't she only encouraging him by talking about things like waxing?

She smiled. "I should, uh, go get tortured now."

He raised his mug. "Good luck."

She climbed the stairs to Summer's bedroom. Grizzly Bear blasted from Summer's Bluetooth speakers, a band Devon recognized only because Summer listened to them so much and had been upset when her parents refused to drive her to Dallas to see them in concert.

"About time." Summer spied the coffee mug in her hands with slight annoyance on her face. "Been waiting forever."

"Sorry. My mom kept bugging me about where I was going." Devon set the mug down on Summer's vanity. "I told her I was going to weed Mrs. Cummings's garden."

Summer laughed. "Well, someone's garden *is* about to be weeded." She paused, taking in Devon's sheepish expression. "Oh, my God, you actually weeded that old lady's garden, didn't you?"

"Yeah. I had to." Devon saw little strips of cloth laid out next to a Crock-Pot of wax Summer was stirring, and her entire body started sweating. "Okay, what do you need me to do?"

"Just take off your jeans and lie on my bed."

It sounded like such an easy thing to do—lie on a bed—but Devon froze. Summer had seen her in her sad swimsuit many times, but being in her underwear around her felt different. "Okay."

Slowly, she unbuttoned her jeans and slid them down her legs. She had worn her best pair of underwear—bikini-cut pink cotton with tiny red polka dots. When she had showered the night before, she spent a long time shaving her legs, being careful not to nick herself with the cheap razors her mother bought.

She lay back on Summer's green bedspread, almost squishing Sir Croaks-a-lot, Summer's favorite stuffed animal frog.

"You can borrow him." Summer motioned to the frog. "Might help to squeeze him. You know, for the pain."

"Oh, Lord, help me," Devon whispered as she scooped up Sir Croaks-a-lot.

Summer stared down at her. "Uh, Dev, you're going to need to spread your legs."

Devon forced her legs to unlock.

"Now, don't move." Summer dipped what looked like a wooden Popsicle stick into the Crock-Pot of wax. Then she pushed Devon's underwear aside and slathered the wax on.

"Oh," she gasped, surprised by how hot it was on her skin and how close Summer's fingers were to the most sensitive part of her.

Summer's hand was on her again, smoothing a strip of the cloth against the wax. She paused. "This is going to hurt like a motherfucker."

"Wai—"

Summer yanked off the cloth, and a scream like none ever heard ripped from Devon's lungs. She squeezed the hell out of Sir Croaks-a-lot, but it did nothing for the pain throbbing between her legs.

"Damn, girl, you almost blew out my eardrums!"

Someone banged on Summer's door. "Do you need rescuing, Dev?"

"Fuck off, Keat!"

After the initial pain subsided, a sereneness washed over Devon. It was the same sensation she'd had whenever she poured hot wax on herself from her prayer candle but even better. It felt so good.

"Do you want me to stop?" Summer asked, concern on her face.

Devon grinned, her body dewed in sweat. "No. Keep going."

◆ ◆ ◆

Devon stood in front of Summer's full-length mirror examining the smooth, angry-red skin of her bikini area. She replayed each time Summer had touched her skin, how the throb of pain had transformed, spiraling into a rapid pulse at the center of her with each press and pull of wax-covered cloth. She'd closed her eyes, reeling every time her hair was ripped out, the need in her expanding bigger and wider, until she could no longer wield it. Her body had tightened, the center of her contracting so strongly, almost violently, to where she couldn't contain the sounds coming from her mouth.

Summer had stopped, confusion in her eyes. "Um . . . all done. I, uh . . . I'll go get us some drinks."

Devon knew she should be mortified, but she wasn't, not completely. It was the best feeling she'd ever experienced in her life—Summer's touch and imagining Keaton on the other side of the bedroom door, listening to her cries of pain morphing into pleasure. It was everything all at once crashing into her, and she didn't want to think about how sinful it was.

She heard a buzzing next to her. Summer's cell phone on the vanity. The phone buzzed again. And again. Devon moved over to it and caught *UNKNOWN* flashing on the screen, the words of the text transfixing her, the blood in her head pounding louder: i want to lick every part of your sweet cunt. i know you want it too. meet me now.

SUMMER'S JOURNAL

May 2012

I think Dev had an orgasm on my bed. WTAF.

CHAPTER 19

DEVON

2025

Devon knew it was a long shot calling her detective friend in Oklahoma City the next day, but she needed his help on doing some digging for her. Dayton Clearwater was her good friend Rae's boyfriend at the OKCPD, and all three of them had become closer over the last year after the Coulter-mansion incident, when they all thought they might die. Sometimes, though, she couldn't be around them without memories from that time paralyzing her thoughts. She knew her triggers well, and her close friends being one of them was like the universe playing a sick trick on her.

"Hey, bestie," she said once Dayton answered his cell phone. "How's life treating you?"

"Hello, Devon. Why do I get the feeling you want something from me?"

"Because I do?"

He paused on the line, and she heard his heavy sigh. "Is this about your speeding tickets again? For the last time, I can't erase them from your record."

"What? No. It's about something else." She took a deep breath. "I need you to look up the toxicology report for someone who died."

There was dead silence for a moment. "I can't do that."

"I know you can, Dayton. Listen, it's about my high school best friend. She supposedly died by suicide, but I found something. Something that's making me question it. I just want to know what drug was in her system."

She had gone by the Arkana police station to speak with Sheriff Wright that morning. As soon as she showed him Summer's note, he quickly dismissed her concerns. When she pushed him, he became irritated and told her there were other circumstances proving Summer's overdose was a suicide, and then he batted her out of his office like she was a fly.

"Please," she said. "Will you check so I can stop feeling like I'm going insane?"

He was so quiet she thought her cell phone had dropped the call.

"Text me the information. Date of birth, death—all that. I'll see what I can do."

"Really?" Her chest suddenly felt lighter than it had in days. "Thank you so much. I owe you all the drinks when I'm back in the city."

"I'll let you know if I find anything."

Devon stared at her cell phone after she'd hung up. Her heart told her to call her parents and make amends for calling Mrs. Wilson a bitch during the Fourth of July celebration. It was the easy thing to do, to fall back in line with how she was raised. Never speak against your elders and certainly not your parents, and keep your thoughts pure because God is always listening. But her mind said fuck all that.

She sat down on a bench at the town square in the heart of Arkana, where an old water fountain now stood dry. As far as she knew, it had stopped working years ago. When she was younger and the fountain still worked, she and other kids used to toss coins into it, their eyes shut tight as they whispered their deepest wishes. She remembered Holly Lynch making fun of her for only having a penny to toss. Holly had held up her shiny quarter and said with a sneer how it gave her more wishes, and Devon had believed her. A few years later, when thoughts about girls infiltrated her daydreams, she had stolen four quarters from her mother's purse and thrown them into the fountain, her eyes closed so tight, tears down her cheeks as she wished and prayed to be normal.

Devon looked at the flower beds surrounding the fountain, every leaf and petal desiccated by the relentless sun. She took a few deep breaths, in and out, as she imagined slowly squeezing a lemon, a trick she'd learned during her trauma therapy, the same trick she now taught to her own patients. Then she stood up and pulled out a tarnished penny from the bottom of her purse. She tossed it into the bronze fountain, listening to its hollow ping as she closed her eyes. *I wish to know what really happened to you.*

Her phone buzzed in her hand. It was a text from Paulette: I hope you're finding the healing you deserve. Thinking of you.

She hearted the message but didn't reply.

She looked up to see Mason Turner across the road near a little coffee shop that used to be a clothing boutique when she was in her teens. He had been staring at her but quickly looked away when she spotted him. She watched him rush into the café, and she decided now was a good time for caffeine.

When she entered the cozy café, which was filled with teens trying to escape the summer heat, Mason glanced her way, but he gave no indication he knew her.

"Hi, Mason," she said behind him in line.

He turned his head, and a nervous smile spread on his face. He looked nearly the same as he had in high school, with his stocky frame, dirty-blond hair, and ruddy complexion.

"Oh, hey, Devon, didn't recognize you."

"I keep hearing that. Do I really look that different?"

He shrugged. "Been a long time since high school. Sure I look different too."

"Nah, you look the same." She smiled. "You still keep in touch with Keaton and them?"

Mason frowned a little. "Not as much now. Got a couple of kids and a wife, and my trucking job takes me out of town a lot."

She already knew this. She had looked him up on Facebook before and saw he had married some pretty girl from Tishomingo. His young kids were cute, but most of the photos of them were absent their father.

"I get that," she said. "A lot's changed since high school. No more keg parties, huh?"

He gave her a quizzical look. Everyone knew she hadn't been one to attend a lot of keg parties like the other kids, and the few she had gone to were only because of Summer and Keaton.

"Remember Trey's party—the one in junior year?" The one where Devon had watched Mason's hand snake up Summer's dress as he pressed her against a tree, the echoes of pleasure sounds and laughter coming from the pond's shoreline. "It was pretty wild."

Mason's eyes roved toward the one barista working, a teenage girl who looked fourteen, and then at his feet. "No, I don't recall that one."

"Really? You and Summer were going at it by the pond that night."

His eyes shot up to her. "I never messed with Summer."

"You sure about that?"

He feigned checking his cell phone. "Look, I gotta go. Wife just texted and needs me to get some milk for the kids. You take care."

"You, too, Mason. Hope to see you around again soon."

He didn't seem to share her sentiment as he got out of the line and dashed toward the exit.

Later, after a damn good iced latte, Devon was back at the Harrison farm, stretched out on Summer's bed and replaying Mason's reaction at the café. She wasn't losing her mind; he had acted oddly at her mention of Trey's party. Ever since that night, she had known something happened between Mason and Summer. Something not quite right. Her memories were so scattered after Summer's death, but some things were as bright as a candle in the dark. Trey's party was one such memory.

Just as she was dozing off, the afternoon heat in the old house hugging her into placidity, her phone rang. It was Dayton.

"Hey, Devon. I found the toxicology report on your friend. No major drugs in her system, just trace amounts of THC."

She held her breath, her heart trying to pound out of her chest.

"Whatever your friend died from, it wasn't by an illicit drug overdose."

CHAPTER 20
DEVON

May 2012

The school was buzzing louder than cicadas in the dead heat of summer. Holly Lynch was throwing a party on Friday. Her parents were going to Mexico for their wedding anniversary, so there'd be no adults around. Unlike Trey Weaver's parties, where his parents stayed in their cramped living room watching TV, fully aware their underage son was drinking and doing whatever drugs he could find, Holly's church-leader parents would most definitely care about their only daughter throwing a house party.

When Holly had stopped by their table during lunch, she looked reluctant to invite Summer after the last fight they'd had over Jackie, but Holly was smart enough to know Keaton wouldn't come unless Summer was invited. Keaton was too popular with the cool kids not to include him. Plus, Devon suspected Holly was crushing on him.

Summer had smirked and told Holly she'd "try" to make it. Devon, as usual, was invited by default.

"Are you going?" Devon asked Summer after Holly had left their table.

"Free liquor's free liquor." She drank some of her Dr. Pepper as she eyed Keaton. "You should absolutely go, bro. Guaranteed BJ from Holly."

Keaton rolled his eyes. "Not interested."

She grinned at him and turned to Devon next to her. "Maybe Dev will get lucky. Did you know she's never been kissed, Keat?"

Devon's mouth dropped open. She'd told Summer that in confidence, and she didn't need anyone around them overhearing and having yet another reason to believe she was an inexperienced loser.

"I think that's cool," Keaton said. "A first kiss should mean something. Kind of wish I could take mine back."

Summer nudged her. "His friends dared him to kiss this girl Halley Simon in sixth grade, and he did it." She threw a baby carrot at Keaton's chest. "Such a people pleaser."

Devon had to disagree. It was true Keaton tended to avoid getting into arguments with others, but when he did, he usually won by calmly laying down logic in a way she admired. If anything, Devon felt she was the people pleaser, especially with Summer. Many times, she wanted to say no to her best friend, but she never wanted to see Summer's disappointment. Same as with her parents. It was so much easier to lie to them, although it made her stomach churn with anxiety each time she did it.

"You're coming, Dev," Summer said.

Devon swallowed her bite of apple. "Can't wait."

◆　◆　◆

Like with Ryan Nelson, Devon had never been inside Holly Lynch's house. It was in the same wealthy neighborhood where Ryan, Coach Thompson, and half the Stinchcomb family lived, where all the brick houses looked like a variation of the same design, with the only distinguishing feature being the door color. Even the manicured shrubbery and flower beds were virtually identical. And the inside looked like how Summer had described Ryan's house, with its thick-framed Hobby Lobbyish decor devoid of any personality.

The party vibe was vastly different from Trey's backyard bonfire by the pond with red Solo cups and foamy beer kegs. At the center of Holly's massive kitchen was a huge marble-topped island filled with charcuterie boards, various bowls of chips and dips, and a line of liquor bottles and mixers next to clear plastic cups. Devon couldn't help being impressed as she sampled the various cheeses and cured meats, her body feeling too curvy in the tight black dress she'd borrowed from Summer.

"Drink up!" Summer said, handing Keaton and Devon a bright-green cocktail. "Jenna made it. It's called a mind bender."

Keaton looked at his cup with aversion. "What's in it?"

"Who cares. Just drink it and try not to be a buzzkill."

They all downed it at the same time. It wasn't so bad. Sickly sweet, with some kind of juice, maybe pineapple, but Devon didn't feel the need to gag.

Within thirty minutes of being at the party, she'd had two more mind benders, same as Keaton. She'd lost count of how much Summer was drinking.

Feeling a bit dizzy, Devon plopped down on one of the cushy chairs in the living room, which opened up to the kitchen, and watched as Holly tried to insert herself into the group of people Keaton was chatting with. She kept touching his arm and loudly laughing whenever he said anything remotely funny. He'd shift away from her, but she'd be right back at his side again like a puppy begging to be petted.

She could see Summer tucked in a corner by the kitchen from where she sat. Summer kept texting someone on her phone, her face screwed up in what looked like frustration. Then she stopped texting and poured herself a shot of vodka, which she downed without a single wince. Summer glanced at Keaton, who was still batting away Holly's attention, and headed for the front door. Devon followed her, worried Summer was hurrying out the door because she was going to get sick.

When she stepped outside into the warm evening, she didn't see Summer, but she heard her. Something in her friend's voice made her stop.

"I told you not to come here. What if someone sees you?"

Devon couldn't hear the other person's response.

"I bet you'd love that," Summer said, her voice slurring. "You're obsessed, and it's fucking sick." She laughed until she snorted. "What did you think was going to happen?"

Devon wanted to see who Summer was talking to, but she was too afraid to move from the front patio and get caught eavesdropping.

"How about this," Summer continued. "You want to touch me? To put your fingers up my wet pussy?" Summer snort-laughed again. "I'll let you, but only because I feel sorry for you."

A burning sensation started deep in Devon's belly at hearing those vulgar words, the alcohol in her no longer making her feel pleasantly disconnected. Was Summer talking to the mystery person who kept texting her after she had waxed Devon? Was it Mason, who was oddly not at Holly's party?

The thought of someone, anyone, touching Summer made her want to scream. She wanted to be that person, to know how it felt touching the soft parts of Summer, to give her pleasure in whatever way she could, but she would never be the person Summer wanted.

Saliva filled her mouth, and she swallowed hard and kept swallowing until her stomach roiled and pushed hot acid up her throat. She tried to swallow it down, but she couldn't, and she doubled over. The green-tinged vomit narrowly missed her knockoff Vans.

A hand swept over her head, pulling her hair back from her face.

"It's okay, Dev. Just get it out. You'll feel so much better."

Summer's voice above her, so cool and commanding.

Devon kept throwing up until she was as hollowed out as the dead elm tree behind the high school, where kids pushed their used gum into the bark. When her stomach stopped cramping and she was sure she was done, she looked up into Summer's smiling face.

"See? I told you so."

CHAPTER 21
DEVON

2025

Devon's cell phone vibrated, and she read her mother's text message: You should come home. People are starting to talk. If there was one thing her mother feared most in the world, it was people in town talking about their family. But Devon didn't care if people talked, because all she could focus on was what she had learned about Summer's death.

Summer hadn't died from an overdose. Either the toxicology report was incorrect, or Sheriff Wright had somehow read the report wrong and passed on the information to the Harrison family and, by extension, everyone else in town.

After her call with Dayton, she drove over to the police station, the heat drenching her underarms and back with sweat.

"Back again so soon?" Suzanne, the station's perpetually sunny receptionist, said as Devon entered.

"I hate to be a bother, but is the sheriff free?"

"Let me check, sweetie." Suzanne picked up her phone and pushed an extension. "Sheriff, Devon Mayes is here to see you again . . . yes, I know . . . oh, all right." Suzanne hung up the phone and smiled. "You can go on back. Mind you, he's been in a mood all day."

Devon went down the short hallway to Sheriff Wright's tiny office, with its blocky wood desk and filing cabinets from the '70s. The entire building still smelled like the leftover water damage from a tornado that hit ten years prior, and Devon tried not to breathe in the musty air too deeply.

"Why, Devon, I wasn't expecting to see you again until Sunday's service," Sheriff Wright said, motioning to the worn cushioned chair across from his desk. He stroked his graying mustache. Something about him always reminded her of a catfish, how his thin, scraggly facial hair drooped down on either side of his wide mouth. His small dark eyes scrutinized her. "Didn't see you at church. The city hasn't turned you into some libtard afraid of God, has it?"

Devon smiled uncomfortably. Being labeled a *libtard* in Arkana was akin to being called a Satanist. "No, sir, the city has its challenges, but I still know where to find God." And it wasn't at Calvary Baptist.

"Amen to that." He crossed his arms and leaned back in his chair so far Devon worried he might tip over. "So, what do you need? I hope no more questions about Summer Harrison, because that book is done written already."

"Actually, sir, I do have a couple more questions."

He shook his head. "Go ahead then."

"When Summer died, weren't you pretty new as sheriff?" She already knew the answer, but she wanted to set the tone for what she was going to ask next. Sheriff Wright's predecessor, Sheriff Handcock, had dropped dead of a heart attack at age fifty-five, and the undersheriff, Ronald Wright, had won in the special election, in good part due to his anti-immigration stance, since the surrounding factories were hiring so many migrant workers. And for fourteen years, he'd run unopposed during election season.

"I've been with the county for twenty-five years, Devon. But, yes, I was about a year in as sheriff at the time."

"That's a long time." Devon couldn't keep her legs from shaking. With the exception of Dayton, she hated talking to male authority figures, even ones she'd known her whole life. After her sexual assault, she'd had to recount everything in a room full of male detectives, and it was one of the hardest things she'd ever done. "Sir, do you think it's possible something was missed during the investigation of her death?"

Sheriff Wright uncrossed his arms and leaned forward on his desk, his eyes drilling into her. "No, I don't. And I don't appreciate the suggestion of such."

"I—I wasn't trying to suggest anything, sir," she quickly said, hating how her voice wavered under his glare. "It's just . . . maybe the toxicology report was wrong. Or it was . . . interpreted wrong. Maybe she died from something else."

Instead of getting angry again, Sheriff Wright chuckled. "One little note got this into your pretty head?" His face softened. "Listen, Devon, Summer was a troubled girl. That was no secret. Drug paraphernalia was found near her body, and with the amount of heroin she had on her, there was no doubt about her intentions."

"Heroin? That's ridiculous." She didn't mean to raise her voice to him, but there was no way in hell Summer died by heroin. She might've believed him if he'd said oxy, but heroin was never a problem in Arkana. Summer would've had to somehow travel several towns over to get something like that. "She only drank and smoked a little weed, like most of the kids around here." As she said it, she knew that wasn't exactly true, but she pushed the thought down.

"Do you care about the Harrison family?" he said.

The question took her off guard. Did she care about Keaton and Annie? Of course she did. And they deserved to know the truth. Everyone did.

"Yes, sir. I care about them a lot."

"Then I suggest you let their loved one rest in peace and stop stirring up trouble." His steely eyes hardened. "You catch my drift?"

She wanted to yell at him, to tell him she knew about the toxicology-report results, but she didn't want to get Dayton in trouble in case there was some way to track who looked up the information. She felt like she was pounding against a wall that wouldn't break with the sheriff.

"Yes, sir. I understand."

"I'll tell you what." Sheriff Wright stroked his stringy mustache again. "I'll look into the autopsy report again, make sure we didn't miss anything from back then. Would that make you feel easier about it?" He spoke to her like she was a whining child begging for a toy.

She forced herself to smile. "I'd appreciate that very much, sir."

Devon left the police station with a cramp in her stomach and more questions crowding her mind. It was clear to her the sheriff's office had fucked up. She trusted the information Dayton gave her. He was a homicide detective with a lot of experience under his belt in Oklahoma's largest city. As far as she knew, the last murder in Arkana had occurred when Devon was little. Two farm laborers had gotten into a bar fight over some woman, and one of the men shot the other right in the chest.

Sheriff Wright and his department had looked at Summer's death at face value instead of seeing all the pieces of the puzzle that were questionable. Like Jackie, and how Summer's apparent beef with her played into things. Or Mason Turner. Devon needed more information, more evidence for the sheriff's office to take her concerns seriously.

But first she needed to tell Keaton what she'd found out. He didn't want her talking to his mom, which she completely understood, but she wouldn't allow him to keep his head buried in the hay.

She texted him: I found something out. Meet me at your mom's house. We need to talk.

A few moments passed before he texted back: I told you to leave it alone.

I can't. You know that. Just meet with me.

I'm fixing a tractor.

So, take a break.

No.

Why don't you care about this?

She watched the ellipses on her screen stutter a few times before they disappeared.

Fine. She'd like to see Keaton try to ignore her when she was standing right in front of him. Since their meeting at Lucky's, he'd been good at avoiding her by keeping busy harvesting in the fields and then, she presumed, going straight to his house a couple of miles away from the farmhouse.

She got into her dinged-up Prius, the late-afternoon heat nearly unbearable as she threw her long hair into a ponytail. She rolled down her windows, praying it would provide enough relief so she wouldn't pass out before she got to the farm.

CHAPTER 22
DEVON

May 2012

Whoever Summer was talking to outside Holly's house was now gone, and Devon felt too sick to ask about it. Jenna's mind-bender cocktail earned its name because she could barely keep her head up without wanting to throw up again. She took several deep breaths while Summer disappeared inside. She reappeared with Keaton, who seemed tipsy too.

"We'll have to walk back," he said. "I don't know where Jenna went."

Last Devon saw Jenna, she was in no shape to drive them anyway. "It's not that far."

But it was far, and they took several wrong turns, all of them stumbling in the dark on the gravel roads. Summer kept laughing every time they got turned around, which made Devon think she had smoked some weed at the party. Or maybe she'd taken one of the blue pills a kid was selling. She was loopy on something for sure, so Devon relied on Keaton to get them home safe. By some miracle, he did.

Before Devon went inside her house, Summer clasped on to her hard, her breath sour as she said, "You're my favorite person ever. You know that, right? You're my fam. Forever."

"Forever," Devon whispered back, wanting the hug to continue.

Keaton stood there awkwardly, and Devon felt the impulse to hug him good night, too, so she did, perhaps a little too aggressively since he seemed surprised. She pressed her face into the hardness of his chest, so unlike the softness of Summer's breasts squeezing against her own when they hugged.

"Don't get caught," he said before she raced up the driveway to her house.

As quietly as she could, she unlocked the front door and slowly pushed it open so it wouldn't creak like it always did in the warmer months. All she wanted to do was wrap herself in her favorite patchwork quilt her Mimi had made and fall asleep.

"God almighty, girl, it's two o'clock in the morning. Where in the world have you been?"

Devon froze in the small entryway. She made out her mother's curvy figure as she rose from the old recliner in the living room, her paleness moving toward her like a ghost.

"Answer me."

"I, uh . . . I was . . ." She didn't have a lie ready. Sneaking out had been the easy part. She had acted like she was going to bed early and then slipped out the back door while her parents were in the living room watching TV.

Her mother came right up to her, her face almost touching her own. "I can smell what you were doing. Were you out drinking with some boy?"

Words were trapped in her throat, but she managed to say, "No, ma'am. I . . . I was by myself."

The slap across her face was hard, stunning her. Her mother had never struck her before, although Pastor Walters frequently encouraged parents at church not to spare the rod and spoil the child in the literal sense.

"Don't you dare lie to me again. Who were you with?"

She staggered back from her mother, heart racing. She couldn't give Summer and Keaton away, or she'd never be allowed to see them again. "I . . . I was by myself. I . . . stole some of the special wine from church, and I drank it by the school and fell asleep." She knew she had made a huge mistake with her stupid lie when her mother started breathing hard through her nose like a bull about to charge.

"Tomorrow you will atone for your sins in front of the congregation. You will tell everyone what you have done, and you will apologize. We'll see how Pastor Walters wishes to punish you. You will not leave this house outside of going to school and church for the next three weeks. Do you understand?"

She wiped the tears from her burning eyes. "Yes, ma'am."

"Clean yourself up. You look like a whore with all that makeup."

Devon ascended the stairs as quickly as her tired legs allowed her. She couldn't stop crying as she took a fast shower and brushed her teeth.

Why couldn't she have thought of some other lie? Stealing was bad enough, but stealing from the church was a sin she would never dream of committing. And now she'd have to stand in front of half the town, including Holly, and apologize for something she hadn't done. She could picture Holly's arrogant face in the front pew next to her parents, who would be back in town and none the wiser that their precious daughter had hosted a Friday-night party under their roof.

Her damp hair wet her pillow, making sleep difficult as she fought a growing chill reaching down to her marrow. She pulled her grandmother's quilt up to her chin and tried to think about anything else but Sunday. Thoughts of Summer floated into her mind, how she had held on to Devon like she was afraid she'd evaporate. For that brief moment, she'd believed Summer when she said they were family. But then more thoughts intruded, ones about what she'd overheard Summer say outside at the party. *You want to touch me? To put your fingers up my wet pussy?*

She shifted her thoughts to how it felt hugging Keaton, his large hands touching the middle of her back, the scent of citrus and cedar coming from his T-shirt and how solid he was, like a tree born from the earth hundreds of years ago, unyielding to storms. She nestled deeper into the quilt and held on to the idea of him sheltering her, protecting her from what was to come.

◆　◆　◆

Pastor Walters looked out to the congregation, his expression grave as if he were giving a eulogy. It almost felt like a funeral, and Devon was a spirit watching herself from afar as she stood at the front by the pulpit, on full display. Her eyes dared to glance at her parents four pews back. Her mother's normally full mouth was pulled into a tight grimace, like she was the one being punished, and her father sat staring straight ahead, his neutral face looking no different than if he were watching any other sermon.

"Forgiveness comes to those who throw themselves before the Lord and repent of their sinful ways." Pastor Walters's baritone voice rumbled in her chest. "Our sister, Devon Mayes, has committed a grave sin, not only toward God but toward every member of this church." His hand rested heavy on her shoulder. "Tell them what you have done."

Devon licked her dry lips; it seemed every drop of moisture in her body was going to her eyes. She told herself to speak the lie clearly and loudly. "I . . . I stole some of the special Communion wine used for Easter and Christmas, and I drank it." Every other monthly Communion, they used grape juice like most Baptists, but wine was used for the most holy of days, at least for the adults.

Gasps and murmurs erupted, and Devon caught her mother slumping down a little in the pew when people looked her way. Of course, they weren't looking at her father. It was the mothers who held responsibility for their children's actions, and Devon had shamed her mother right into the wood pew beneath her backside.

Devon swiped at her tears. "I'm very sorry. To my parents. To everyone."

Pastor Walters pressed her shoulder harder, so much that it hurt, and she looked up at him. "And to God."

"And to God."

"Devon, you will spend each Sunday for the next month polishing every pew and helping with collections. You will also meet with Pastor Stinchcomb after services for private Bible studies so that you may learn from your sins." He smiled at her, but his gray eyes were steel and held no warmth. "The Lord still loves you. He loves all sinners. You may sit down now."

She slowly made her way toward her parents, but not before glimpsing Holly's smirk as she passed.

After she sat down next to her father, he whispered to her, "I can come get you after you're done with your punishment."

Her mother leaned over her father, her eyes dead center on Devon. "I think it's best she walk so she can think on her actions."

Her father said nothing. Normally, his word was final, but he must've felt the embarrassment and anger rolling off her mother.

Devon swallowed over the lump in her throat and looked up, over the pulpit, where Pastor Walters spoke, his thick neck red, to the steeple window, where dark clouds swelled, promising rain.

CHAPTER 23
DEVON

2025

It was nearing dusk when Devon pulled up to the fields of flaxen winter wheat stretching for thousands of acres. Soon, Keaton and his uncle Boyd would be out in the fields with whatever laborers they could find to harvest the rest of the wheat crop before it got too late in the season. She remembered how Keaton's father once let her climb up into the huge green John Deere combine; now it would most likely be Keaton operating it.

She drove up the dirt road to the large worn wooden barn abutting the southern part of the fields, close to Annie's house; the woods and Chullusa Pond sat just north of the home. From what Devon could remember, they stored equipment and seed for their crops in the building, which made her think about the bags of seed in Keaton's old bedroom at the farmhouse. Annie was right; it was odd of his uncle to store them there, but she supposed they had run out of space in the barn.

Devon got out of her car and spotted Keaton working on a tractor that appeared well past its prime. He looked up at her, squinting against the setting sun, and her heart flittered a little at how the golden light made him appear unearthly, like a modern Adonis.

"Before you say anything," she said, "I come bearing gifts." She held up a paper bag in one hand and a six-pack of PBR in the other.

"Barney's Burgers?"

"You know it."

"Well, shit." He hopped down from the tractor and wiped his hands on his thighs. "You know I can't resist."

Barney's had the best fried-onion burgers in the state.

Devon handed him the bag. "Remember when Mrs. Tate was teaching about the Great Depression and how Oklahomans invented the onion burger to stretch the meat they had? Then she let us all walk over to Barney's during lunch hour?"

Keaton smiled. "That day was the beginning of a bad addiction for me. And you know, I've tried onion burgers all over—Bunny's, Nic's, Tucker's—and none have a thing on Barney's."

"I don't know. Tucker's is pretty damn good." She popped a beer can and took a long swig before handing one to Keaton. They both sat on the edge of the tractor. "This heat. It's like we don't have spring or fall anymore. Just hot as fuck, followed by cold as fuck."

Keaton laughed a little. "Don't jinx us. Last winter's ice storm nearly killed everything." He drank his beer. "Crop insurance barely kept us afloat."

"Sorry. I had no idea."

He paused, digging a hamburger out of the paper bag, and looked at her. "When you left this place, you really never looked back, did you?"

She didn't know what to say to that. Yes, she had left Arkana behind, but leaving didn't erase memories, no matter how much she had hoped it would.

"It's not like that," she said, her voice lowered. She took a bite of her burger and drank some of the beer, wishing the memories would quit popping up. They were like weeds trying to choke anything beautiful she was trying to grow in her life.

"Your mother called my mom the other day," Keaton said.

Her head snapped up. "Why?"

"She was worried about you. Said you came home because of something at your work, that you had a breakdown and had to take leave." He held her gaze. "Is that true?"

How in the hell did her mother know that? She hadn't told her parents about what happened with her client. Macayla's delicate, fairylike face haunted her dreams along with Summer, like they had become phantasmal friends simply to taunt her every night.

"Uh, yeah. It's true." She hoped the fading sunset shielded him from seeing the tears forming in her eyes. "My client committed suicide. She was only fifteen. She was raped and was going to speak at her perpetrator's trial." She watched realization cross Keaton's face, a crease growing on his forehead. "But my client's suicide has nothing to do with why I'm looking at Summer's death. I'm not crazy, Keat."

"I don't think you're crazy." He placed a hand over hers. "That's a lot to deal with, though. Don't you think it would be better to talk with someone about it rather than focusing on the note you found?"

Paulette would probably suggest the same thing. But instead of going back to her therapist like she should have, Devon had crawled into a bottle of vodka. It'd been easier than admitting she had failed someone again.

She swallowed hard, worried how Keaton would take what she was about to say. "Summer didn't die from an overdose, Keat. And I can't . . ." She held in the tears wanting to emerge. "I can't move forward until I know what happened to her."

He inhaled deeply, and she could tell he was attempting to be patient with her. "Okay. I'm listening. What did you find out?"

She told him about the toxicology report Dayton had looked up, and his face remained calm for a few moments before the placidness slowly melted away into confusion.

"How can that be?" he said. "I dug up her death certificate at my mom's house over the weekend, and it clearly says her death was related to hypoxic brain injury. She had no trauma to her head, so she obviously died from an overdose. It can cause seizures and cut off oxygen to the brain."

"I'm just telling you what Dayton told me, and I trust him. He's a homicide detective, and—"

"Oh, my God, Dev, seriously? Murder? Is that where this is going?"

"No, I'm not saying that." Although it was absolutely in the back of her mind. "I'm just saying it's pretty fucking weird there were no traceable drugs in her system besides cannabis."

Keaton drank the remainder of his beer and stood up to grab another from the six-pack.

"I know this is hard to hear, Keat, but something is not right. I can't ignore this, and you shouldn't either."

She watched him pace back and forth as he tossed back the second beer. He finally stopped pacing and stared at her with wild eyes, and her chest ached seeing the wound reopening in him.

"I don't think I can do this," he said more to himself than to her. "It's . . . it's too much."

She stood up and went to him, wrapped her arms around him tight. "I'm not trying to hurt you. I just want to do right by her." She held him close to her, and she could smell the earth and sweat on him.

"It won't help," he said, his breath warm against the top of her head.

She squeezed him tighter. She had no choice but to pursue this. It felt like Summer was at her back, whispering in her ear: *You did this. You owe me. You owe me everything.*

CHAPTER 24
DEVON

May 2012

After Pastor Walters had finished his sermon, Devon helped collect the little envelopes filled with cash and checks. She never understood how tithing more meant someone had closer access to God, like Pastor Walters often preached. Supposedly, being wealthier meant someone was especially blessed by the Lord, but she never associated God with money. Nature was where she felt closest to a higher power; whether it was God or not, she didn't know.

She thought of swimming at Chullusa Pond with Summer and Keaton as she polished the pews, her hands aching from the work. Chullusa was her happy place, where she could be silly and free without judgment from others. She could splash and do cannonballs off the rickety fishing platform with her best friends, and she didn't have to hear her mother reminding her to act like a lady.

"You can be done now, Devon."

She looked up to see Pastor Stinchcomb, or Pastor Carter as most of the younger people called him. He didn't look like most of the Stinchcomb family, who were tall and imposing. Pastor Carter was of average height, with a slightly pudgy physique, and his dark hair always appeared a bit unruly.

"But I'm not finished, sir. I still have six more."

"They look polished enough for me. Meet me in my office."

She took the polish and rag to the janitor's closet and made her way down the stairs to the basement of the church. It was the place where people went if there was a tornado if they didn't have an underground shelter of their own. Pastor Carter's office was one of a few in the basement, and she wondered how it felt to him working in the part of the church with no windows.

"Go ahead and sit down, Devon," he said when she entered his cramped office with its old wood paneling and overly large desk.

Behind him on a massive built-in bookcase, there were a lot of pictures of his wife and new baby and tons of books, mostly of theology but some secular books as well, including some based on *Star Trek*. His love of *Star Trek* was no secret, and it sort of endeared him to her. But it didn't make her any less nervous being in his office as a form of punishment.

"Should I get one of the Bibles from the pews, sir?"

"No, that's not necessary."

She twisted the bottom of her pink blouse, her long skirt making the backs of her legs sweat. "But I thought we were going to do a Bible study."

"We are. What can you tell me about Jeremiah chapter five, verses one through three and twelve through seventeen?"

Her brain immediately clicked on to recite what she'd been taught since she was a toddler. "Scripture states that God brought enemies down upon the city of Jerusalem, destroying everything and everyone because there were no honest people to be found."

"Very good," he said. "And how would you interpret Jeremiah's story?"

Devon shifted in her seat. "Um, that God punishes liars."

Pastor Carter clasped his hands on his desk. "And what do you think God would make of people who lie about lying?"

"Sir?"

He adjusted his thick black-rimmed glasses and sighed. "You're a bright girl, Devon. You've always asked intelligent questions during youth group discussions, so please explain to me why you lied in front of the congregation today."

She attempted to keep the surprise from her face, but she knew she was failing. "I, uh . . . how did you know, sir?"

"I keep stock of the sacramental wine, and where it's kept is always locked." He paused, his eyes heavy on her. "There was no missing wine. So, again, please explain why you lied."

Her heart pounded against her ribs. "Do my parents know that? And Pastor Walters?"

"No. I didn't see the need to tell them. I'm more curious why a good girl like yourself would tell such a blatant lie."

Devon looked down at her lap. Pastor Carter always told the youth group that whatever they told him in confidence stayed in his office, but she was scared to trust him. Most of the adults she knew, including her parents, would immediately turn on a kid and spill their secrets to shame them into obedience.

"I lied because I didn't want my parents to forbid me from seeing my best friends. We went to a party together, and I drank there."

"And who are your best friends?"

She looked up at him. "The Harrison twins."

He slightly nodded. "I'm familiar with Summer but not her brother. By all accounts, he's a good student like you who stays out of trouble, but his sister . . ."

"Has she come to see you?" She thought back to when she suggested that Summer see him.

He frowned a little as he let out a sigh. "Let's just say I've heard rumors."

"What rumors, sir?" She didn't like the idea of people talking about Summer behind her back, but gossip was the favorite pastime in Arkana.

"It's not important. What's important is that you mind the company you keep. Friendships are like crops; we reap what we sow. Perhaps you can support Summer, be a good influence for her and show her a better way through the love of Christ."

She wasn't sure how to be a good influence for herself, much less to someone as strong willed as Summer. "I could try."

Pastor Carter leaned back in his chair. "'Without followers, evil cannot spread.' Do you know who said that?"

"I don't know, sir."

He pointed to the framed photo of Spock behind him on the wall, the one next to the painting of Jesus. "This guy. I'll add an addendum to his words by saying without followers, love and understanding cannot spread. Be careful who you follow, Devon, and be the sort of leader who doesn't spread evil."

Devon smiled a little. "I'm not a leader, sir."

"Yes, you are. We're all leaders of ourselves." He sat up straighter in his chair, his face serious again. "That's also why it's vital that we never lie to ourselves. I'd like you to think about that before our next meeting."

On her long walk home in the rain, her clothes and hair soaked through, she did think about it. She wasn't sure if she was lying to herself by not telling Summer how she felt about her. Maybe she could hint to her without actually saying it so she could see her reaction. By the time she made it home dripping wet, she knew what she would do.

SUMMER'S JOURNAL

May 2012

I saw Carter again today. After Holly's party, I felt like I was drowning, just like before, and it fucking scared me. I had to talk to someone. Mom and Dad were fighting again. They didn't even notice Keat and I were gone. I still don't know how we got home that night. Poor Dev was so drunk.

Carter wanted me to talk about my relationships and what I considered to be healthy ones.

I told him I don't know what that looks like. When I look at my parents, I see Mom and how Dad always takes from her. The job she loved, the home she made for us, all her friends in the city. Take, take, take. All for his own dream. And now he takes from Keat. When I asked Keat about our plan to go to college and get out of Arkana, he said he had to stay on at the farm and help Dad and Uncle Boyd. He's so afraid of disappointing Dad that he doesn't see how he's losing himself. We're supposed to go to the University of Central Oklahoma together—me for occupational therapy if I can get my grades up and Keat in engineering. He's so fucking smart in math and fixing things, but what good is being smart if he's going to waste his life in this place he hates?

If he won't leave, at least Dev will. I know she secretly dreams about leaving Arkana forever, and she's just as smart as Keat. She could do anything she wanted, but she's scared. She's so closed tight. She reminds me of the butterflies we studied in fifth grade back in the city. Keat and I had watched the fat caterpillars form chrysalises on the sticks in the aquarium Mr. Norton set up in the classroom. The whole class was so excited to watch them split open, the butterflies emerging with slick, new wings. But there was one that remained closed. We waited a week and then another. And eventually Mr. Norton told us the butterfly was dead.

That will be Dev if she stays here. That will be me.

Unhatched.

CHAPTER 25
DEVON

2025

Devon had kicked herself for forgetting her old, cheap laptop when she had gone by her apartment for the burlesque fundraiser. Thank God for libraries. She'd spent the last two hours parked at one of the three computers with internet access at Stinchcomb Library.

First, she looked up Summer's obituary, something she had always avoided. There were no clues for her to find. The obituary didn't even state her death as by suicide, instead saying Summer's *life ended too soon.* Devon supposed that was easier for people to read than to hear about how Summer's body was found cold and blue.

Next, she researched other forms of death that wouldn't necessarily show up on a toxicology report. What she didn't want to admit to herself was how she was looking up ways Summer might've been murdered without the police discovering it. There were only two possibilities that looked promising: injecting air into someone to induce an embolism, which would be difficult to do and would show up on an autopsy, and antifreeze poisoning, a better option since it wasn't something routinely checked. Summer did drink a shit ton of Dr. Pepper. It would've been easy for someone to poison her with her favorite drink, but it would've been just as easy for Summer to kill herself with the same method. It would explain why drugs weren't found in her system, but it wouldn't explain how the sheriff's office royally messed up by calling her death a drug overdose.

When Devon hit a wall, she closed out her searches and checked her phone. Annie had invited her to eat dinner with her, Keaton, and Boyd at the farmhouse. She shot her a text saying she'd be there.

"Devon?" a familiar voice said behind her. "Devon Mayes?"

She looked up to see Shrader Thompson, her old track coach, holding a couple of books. There was some graying at his temples, but he looked remarkably the same as he had when he would bark orders to push herself harder, go faster, and ignore any pain. Though now that she was older, she had to disagree with Summer thinking he looked like Zac Efron. There was a puckishness in Efron that Shrader Thompson, with his sharp jaw and piercing blue eyes, never shared.

"Hi, Coach Thompson," she said, standing up.

"Please, call me Shrader." He smiled at her. "Man, you're all grown up. It's always strange seeing my former students. So many have kids of their own now, and here I am coaching them."

There was something comforting about the thought of him still coaching. With how rich his family was, Shrader could've left the town a long time ago with his wife and kid and built a mansion somewhere in north Oklahoma City, spending his days lounging by a sparkling pool, but he stayed in this tiny town doing something useful with his life by volunteering. Maybe it was better to stay a big fish in a small pond. Even Devon felt somewhat exotic in Arkana now.

She grinned at him. "And I'm sure you're coaching your son too. Braden's what—fourteen now?"

"Yes, and full of more venom than a rattlesnake with a toothache."

"I loved watching him when he was itty bitty. I think the entire track team fought to watch him, especially Summer. She was obsessed with his chubby cheeks."

"Oh, wow, yeah. She did watch him a few times." His brow furrowed. "That was, uh, a hard time for the town, what happened to her. I'm sorry. I know you two were good friends."

"I'm glad I ran into you. I'm trying to figure out what was going on in her life before she died. Just trying to piece some things together." She paused, chewing on her bottom lip as she tried to phrase it so she wouldn't sound nuts. "Remember when she started coming to practice late during junior year?"

"Yeah, I remember. She wasn't a fan of being disciplined for her lateness. None of you girls were."

"Did she ever try to talk to you? Like about anything bothering her that was causing her to be late?"

He seemed to be in thought for a moment. "I did try to talk to her a few times, to find out why she was slacking off. She'd been one of my strongest runners, like you. I didn't want to see her going down the same path as Jackie."

"So, you thought she was getting into drugs like Jackie?" she asked, shifting her stance to stretch out her stiff legs.

"I really don't know, Devon. I know she had a falling-out with Jackie, but I don't know if that's why she was struggling. She was a troubled girl. I know that much, but she didn't want to talk to her track coach about it."

So even Shrader had noticed the rift between Summer and Jackie. "I appreciate your thoughts. Being back here is bringing up a lot, you know?"

"I understand." His gaze fell on the computer she had been logged on to moments before. "Internet down at your parents' house?"

"No, I'm actually staying at the Harrison farm right now."

He raised his eyebrows. "And do they know you're asking people about Summer?"

She felt the color rush to her face at his question. "Not exactly. I, um, didn't want them to see the things I wanted to look up."

"Now you've got me curious," he said with a crooked grin. "It's nothing that would make Mrs. Sturgis blush, right?"

Devon glanced over at the elderly librarian sorting books at the counter and smiled back at him. "Nothing like that. More like research involving causes of death."

He frowned. "Oh, I see." He looked down at the books in his hands. "Listen, I hope I'm not prying, but I heard you're going through a difficult time. That you lost a patient?"

She sucked in a deep breath. Her mother strikes again, and she needed to find out how the hell she'd learned about Macayla. "Yes, a client. I'm still completing my practicum to get my license, but the client was under my care. And, yes, it's been a difficult time."

His eyes turned sympathetic. "Well, you know where I live. I'm here anytime if you ever want to talk."

"Thank you, Coa—uh, Shrader. I appreciate it."

"See you on Sunday?"

She'd already skipped one Sunday, and she knew her mother would probably have an aneurysm if she missed another. "Unless the world ends before then, I'll be there."

After she left the library and got to her car parked under a shady tree, she finally called her mother, who picked up after the first ring like she always did. "Who told you about my client, Mama?"

"Well, hello to you too," her mother huffed out.

"Really, Mama, how did you know?"

"Your boss called the house. Doctor Paulette something. She said she'd been trying to reach you, but you weren't responding, so she got concerned and called your emergency contact."

Fuck. Paulette had texted her a couple more times and then called her, but Devon hadn't had the energy to get back to her. "What did she tell you?"

"Only that you had lost someone under your treatment and needed time off." The line went quiet. "I wish you would've told us. We could've prayed with you about it."

"I'm sorry, Mama. I . . . I just . . ." *Didn't trust you.* "I didn't want to burden you and Daddy."

"Honey, that is what praying is for. To unburden yourself and rely on the Lord. You'll be at church Sunday." Not a question.

"Yes, ma'am."

Sunday, she'd put on the one decent dress she had packed and slap on a happy mask for morning service. But, first, she'd put on a different kind of mask for Annie when she ate dinner at her place later, a mask to hide the fact that she'd been looking up various ways her daughter could've been murdered.

She was about to pull out of her parking spot when she noticed a note stuck under her windshield wiper. She removed it and read it, her heart rapid in her chest at seeing the unfamiliar handwriting: *No one wants you here. Leave if you know what's good for you.*

CHAPTER 26

DEVON

May 2012

"It's so fucking perfect today!" Summer yelled, spinning around like a kid, her short skirt flying up enough to show flashes of her pink thong.

Devon laughed from where she sat on an old log by the water's edge. It was a perfect Saturday afternoon, the weather balmy and clear, with the gentle breeze stirring up the sweet scents of the spring blossoms—wild jasmine, bergamot, and milkweed. And it was the perfect place, Chullusa Pond, to give Summer the gift she had carefully picked out. She'd lied to her parents and said she was going to help in Mrs. Cummings's garden again to get out of the house, since she was still grounded, but it was worth it.

"Come sit down," Devon said as she took the gift from her backpack. It was so nice out, they had decided to have a little picnic, so Devon had secretly made them peanut-butter-and-honey sandwiches with chips and hidden them in her backpack, and Summer had brought them soda—Dr. Pepper, of course—which they had passed back and forth while they ate. "I got you something."

Summer stopped spinning, her expression puzzled. "Got me something? Like a gift?"

"Maybe."

"You know my birthday isn't until October, right? What is it?" Summer plopped herself down on the grass next to the log, and her eyes lit up when she saw the package in Devon's hand. "Ooh, gimme, gimme!"

Devon playfully held it back before handing it over to her. Summer tore into the newspaper wrapping like a child on Christmas morning. When she saw it was a book, she looked more confused than disappointed.

"Pablo Neruda?" Summer stumbled over the name.

"He's my favorite poet." When the library had its annual book swap, Devon had snatched it up as soon as she saw Mrs. Sturgis place it on the fifty-cent table. "And I think you would love it." She could see Summer's doubt. "He writes really steamy stuff."

"Well, shit, let's get to reading!" Summer began flipping through the pages.

"Want me to read you my favorite poem of his?"

"Sure." Summer handed the book back to her and lay back on the thick grass, her hands cradling her head. "Entertain me, peasant."

Devon laughed. "Okay, this is the seventeenth sonnet." She cleared her throat, her nerves sprouting shoots of uncertainty throughout her chest as she spoke the words about loving certain obscure things between the "shadow and the soul." She swallowed back her fear and continued reading, watching the afternoon sun bathe Summer's face in gold. As she reached the end of the poem, a smile played on Summer's lips, her eyes closed.

After a few moments, she sat up. "I wouldn't call that steamy."

Devon grinned. "You should read the eleventh sonnet."

Summer grabbed the book back and searched through the pages until she found the poem. Her eyes scanned the words, a grin spreading on her face. "Okay, I'm liking this one." She stood up and recited the poem as if she were a Shakespearean actor, full of bravado and exaggerated hand motions. As she talked about craving mouths and eating skin like an almond, Devon felt warmth travel between her thighs.

When Summer finished, Devon clapped with enthusiasm, trying to hide how heated the poem had gotten her.

Summer sat back down, legs crossed with the book on her lap. "Why did you give me this?"

This was supposed to be the part when Devon told her how she felt. *Because I love you.* The words were right there on her tongue. *Because you make me feel the same way these poems do.* All she had to do was open her mouth and speak them out loud. *Because you make me feel alive.*

"Dev?"

"I . . . I guess I just wanted you to have a copy. His poems speak to me, and I thought they might speak to you too." She gazed at Summer, hoping she would be able to read on her face the words she was too afraid to say. "Plus, you said there was no such thing as good poetry."

"When did I say that?"

"Last year in Mrs. Laynard's class when you were doing the section over poetry."

Summer stared down at the book, her fingers caressing the spine. "Well, I guess you proved me wrong." She looked back up at Devon and smiled. "Thank you."

"Welcome."

Summer grabbed the two-liter of Dr. Pepper, chugging the rest of it. She let out a loud belch, and they both laughed. "I can't believe school ends next week. So fucking ready."

Devon took the soda Summer passed to her. "Then we'll be official seniors."

"Hell yeah. One year closer to getting out of this shithole."

"When are you going to submit your application to UCO?"

"I don't know." Summer began plucking the yellow petals from a dandelion. She scattered them across the book, then blew them off. "I think I might go to my aunt's place in Austin for a while this summer. And maybe after graduation. It's pretty cool there."

Austin? They had always talked about going to school in the city and renting an apartment together. It felt like a buffalo had just sat on her chest, crushing her and making it hard to breathe. "You should still submit, though. I'm going to apply when they start taking them in August."

Summer tossed the bald stem of the flower. "You still going to do literature so you can teach or whatever?"

"I think so." Really, she'd only said it because she was tired of saying she didn't know when people asked her what she'd study in college.

"Well, Keat decided he's staying here, or at least that's what he told me."

This surprised her. Keaton always talked about going into mechanical engineering. "Why?"

"I guess he wants to be a redneck farmer after all."

The crushing feeling was getting worse. If Summer went to live in Austin and Keaton stayed in Arkana, she would have no one with her in the city. The thought of being alone in an unfamiliar place was overwhelming, and her head went cold, as if crushed ice had been poured into her skull.

"Don't look so sad," Summer said, jumping up and startling Devon. "I have a great idea. So, Trey's cousin is growing shrooms. He's like an expert on them."

"Shrooms."

"You know—the fun kind."

"I know what they are." Sometimes Summer assumed Devon knew nothing about the world simply because her parents were religious. "So, what? Do you want to do some?"

Summer took her hands and pulled her up from the log. "I want *us* to do some. Together. Just us, no one else. Trey said they should be ready next month."

"Summer."

"Please. I've never done them before, and I want my first time to be with you. I've read about it, and they say you should do it with people you trust. People you care about who will have your back."

The ice cubes in her head slowly melted. Summer trusted her.

"Please, Dev. Do this with me. To celebrate being seniors."

If Devon didn't do it with her, Summer might do it with some random person, someone who wouldn't care if something bad happened to her. Someone like Mason.

"Okay, yeah. I'll do it."

Summer kept ahold of her hands as she jumped up and down, forcing Devon to bounce with her. "Oh, my God, this is going to be fucking amazing!"

Devon laughed with her, but her voice sounded too high pitched and frantic.

"Yes," she agreed, jumping with Summer, "this is going to be fucking amazing!"

CHAPTER 27
DEVON

2025

Devon's mother was a good cook, but Annie Harrison might give her a run for her money. She took another bite of pork chop with some of the fried cabbage, nice and caramelized with bacon, just how she loved it. She drank down some sweet tea, a luxury she never allowed in her apartment fridge, lest her curvy figure tip into the unhealthy range, and her sweet tooth was bad enough as it was.

She didn't want to think about the ominous note left under her windshield wiper. It could be as simple as someone seeing the Human Rights Campaign sticker on her car bumper and recognizing it as being associated with LGBTQ rights. Being openly supportive of something like that was dangerous in places like Arkana.

"Thank you for cooking all this, Annie," she said after she'd cleaned her plate. "It was absolutely delicious."

Annie's blue-gray eyes brightened with the compliment as she tucked a strand of her graying hair behind her ear. "It was my pleasure." She stood up and started collecting plates. "I hope you saved some room for my lemon-cloud pie and coffee."

"Ooh, my favorite!" Devon got up and attempted to take the licked-clean plates from Keaton and his uncle Boyd, but Annie shooed her away. "Want some help serving?"

"No, thank you, hon. You just sit and make room in your pretty little figure."

Devon could've kissed her for those words. She had never been little, and it took her well into adulthood to love and appreciate her curves.

Keaton pushed back his chair as if he was going to help before his mom shot him a warning look. "You can do the dishes after dessert, son." Then she sashayed toward the kitchen carrying an armful of dishes with ease.

"What about Uncle Boyd?" Keaton called out to her playfully. "He get kitchen duty too?"

"I'm old," his uncle said from the head of the small dining table. "My duty is not to die so I can keep a roof over your mama's head."

Devon caught a sour look cross Keaton's face.

"And here I thought that was my job," he said.

Boyd grunted and drank some of his beer. Devon noticed it was his fourth one since she'd arrived for dinner.

"So, how's this year's crop looking?" Devon said to break up the sudden tension.

"Well, Devon," Boyd said, leaning back in his chair and crossing his arms, "I'd say we're going up shit's creek without a paddle and the water's high."

Keaton shifted in his seat. "We've had worse. A lot worse."

"You've been doing this for two seconds, and you think you know what worse looks like?"

"Over thirteen years." Keaton's tone was sharp enough to cut through Boyd's beer bottle. "And this year wouldn't be as bad as it is if we had diversified the crops more like I had suggested."

"Diversify," Boyd spit out like it was a dirty word. "You go on and do that. I'm going home."

Devon watched Boyd get up and leave the house on unsteady feet. "He staying above the garage now?" she asked Keaton.

"Mom won't let him stay in the house anymore. Not after he came home drunk and broke her favorite tea set. You know that blue Wedgwood one she had."

Annie collected porcelain tea sets she picked up at estate sales and antique shops. "Damn, that was a nice one."

He looked like he was about to say more when Annie came back with slices of pie and fresh coffee.

"Keaton, why don't you grab the other slice and a cup for yourself." Annie sat next to her and patted her hand. After Keaton left the room, she said in a lowered voice, "It's so nice having you here. I've missed you." She squeezed her hand. "Keaton's missed you too. More than he's probably willing to say."

Emotion rose in her, making her throat feel full. "I've missed you all too."

When Keaton came back, they all fell into easy, light conversation, especially with Boyd's caustic presence gone. She'd never known Boyd well, but she didn't remember him being so antagonistic. Perhaps the loss of his niece followed by his only sibling had done that to him.

Annie was over sixty, and Devon couldn't picture her continuing to do farmwork. Boyd either. There was no money in it, and she saw why Keaton was so adamant about getting Boyd to sell so they could all move on.

Once they finished their pie and coffee, Annie slowly got up. "You both keep talking. I'm feeling a bit tired, so I'm going to do the dishes and hit the hay."

"No, Mom," Keaton said, getting up, "I'll do them."

"I'll help," Devon added.

Annie smiled at them. "Thank you. Don't keep her up too late, son." She winked and headed to her bedroom.

Devon helped carry the dishes to the kitchen. Keaton rolled up the sleeves on his plaid button-up shirt and ran hot water in the sink, filling it and squirting dish soap.

"You want to dry?" he asked her.

"Sure."

They were silent as they washed and dried plate after plate. She started to think about her conversation with Shrader, how he had noticed Summer's erratic behavior, and she wondered how many others noticed but did nothing. People just like her.

She reached for a coffee mug Keaton passed to her, and their hands touched, his lingering on hers. She studied his face, the shadow of stubble lining his jaw and the growing crease on his brow, but she couldn't interpret his expression. He ran his finger over her inner wrist, his eyes glued to the frog tattoo she'd gotten so many years ago.

"Was this for her?" he asked, and she knew he was referring to Summer.

"Yeah."

He looked away from her, his eyes on the sink. "I've been thinking a lot about everything." He dropped the sponge, and a little water splashed, wetting his shirt. "I don't want you to be right. I don't want there to be a new cause for her death because it's taken me this long to accept the first one." He leaned over the farm sink, his hands gripping the edge. "But I can't ignore what you found."

She set the mug down on the counter, the urge to rub his back strong, but she refrained.

"She was hiding something," he said. "I know you're right about that, but it's not like she ever told me her secrets."

She debated telling him about her research at the library and the possibility of someone poisoning Summer, but she decided against it. "I ran into Shrader Thompson at the library today, and he mentioned the falling-out between Summer and Jackie. I remember they stopped hanging out before senior year. Did Summer ever say anything about it to you?"

Keaton turned to her, and she saw the same raw emotion in his eyes she'd seen the day of Summer's funeral, how he had clung to his mother like he was going to collapse at any second. "When we were little,

Summer and I had our own language. A language only we understood. It's called cryptophasia. Supposed to be common with twins. We used it so much that our regular speech was delayed, and we had to go to therapy throughout elementary school. We kept speaking it, though, but less and less as we got older. Then the end of junior year . . ." He rubbed his eyes with his thumb and forefinger. "It was like she completely shut herself off from me. Or maybe we both closed ourselves off. So, whatever was going on with Jackie, I had no clue about it."

Once again, the ghost of Summer seemed to be whispering in her ear: *Tell him, Dev. Tell him what you did.*

The intensity of Keaton's stare arrested her. "But I did always wonder about you and Summer."

"What do you mean?"

He paused a beat. "What happened between you two during that summer? When you stopped talking to each other for a while."

The summer before senior year. The best and worst time of her life.

"Nothing. We just had a little fight."

He held her with his hazel eyes, and she wanted to look away so he wouldn't see the secrets buried in her. "About what?"

She couldn't talk about this with him. Any thread holding him together would break. "It was nothing. Just stupid girl stuff and we made up."

He didn't look satisfied with her answer. "So, what now? Go to Jackie again and hope she talks this time?"

"I don't know. It's a start."

"Okay." He paused. "I'll go with you."

"You can meet me at the diner after church."

He took her hand, and his was still warm from the hot dishwater. "Promise me you won't keep anything from me on this. Even if it's the worst thing, I don't want to be kept in the dark."

She'd lost count of how many lies she'd told in her life, to her parents, to Summer. To herself. What was one more?

"I promise."

SUMMER'S JOURNAL

May 2012

He's texting me all the time now. I thought he would stop after the first time at his house, but I was wrong. He told me to bike out to his grandfather's old barn. I didn't want to because I knew what he wanted to do there, but he said he'd have his uncle give my parents an extension on their farm loan if I did. His uncle owns the bank. I thought my family owned the farm, but he said we don't, that we rent it from the bank. He said my parents are behind on their payments, and we could lose everything and be homeless, so I did it. I felt so sick. I can still taste him. He took pictures of me with a Polaroid camera and some with one of those old flip phones. He said if I don't go to him whenever he tells me to, he won't help my family and he'll post the pictures online and everyone at school will see them.

I don't know how to make this stop. What's so fucking sick is that I miss talking to him.

CHAPTER 28
DEVON

June 2012

Pastor Carter sat across from Devon, his face calm and patient. He asked her if she had thought about the topic he'd posed to her prior about not lying to yourself.

Instead of answering, her mind wandered back to the pond and how Summer had looked when she read the Pablo Neruda poem to her. She knew it was stupid to think her best friend would suddenly confess hidden feelings for her. Then she thought about the last day of school and how Summer had clung to Mason Turner's side when all the juniors had a party at Casey McIntire's house. Devon wanted to drink the spiked Hawaiian Punch until she couldn't see straight. She didn't care if her parents found her drunk again.

Keaton had forced water into her hands, then put his strong arms around her, holding her up when she faltered. "Drink this," he said. "Let me walk you home, okay?"

She nodded numbly, feeling half-aware of her feet.

"Are Summer and Mason dating?" she asked him as they walked down the dark road.

"No. Why?"

"He's always chasing her."

"He chases a lot of girls. It doesn't mean anything. Lots of guys are like that."

Devon stopped walking, her calves and feet aching. "I wouldn't know. I've never had anyone chase me."

"Maybe you have, but you didn't know it."

She tried to make out his features in the weak moonlight, but all she could see was the glint of his eyes, like two glowing orbs floating in front of her.

"Who do you chase, Keat?"

He'd turned quiet for a long time. "No one. No point in chasing what you can't have."

"But how do you know if you don't try?"

"Sometimes you just know."

Then he dropped her at her house, her head filled with questions. She couldn't keep lying to herself, chasing after something that could never happen with Summer, but she didn't know how to extinguish her longing. She crawled into her bed, feeling lucky she hadn't been caught by her mother again. She'd left the back door unlocked this time when she sneaked out.

She closed her eyes and tried to dream about anything other than Summer, the flash of her thong and smooth backside when she was spinning around at the pond. She thought about Ryan Nelson's party the next weekend, but it only made her nervous. Keaton was safe to think about, so she forced her mind to shift to him, to imagining his large hands moving over her body and down between her legs, his mouth on hers. She had worked her fingers until she came hard, her face pressed into her pillow to muffle her moans.

If Keaton chased her, she would let him. But she knew he wouldn't. If he really liked her like Summer thought, he would've made some kind of move by now. When he'd walked her home, they'd hugged, the same kind they always had. Like friends, though her body buzzed from feeling his warmth.

"Devon?" Pastor Carter said, pulling her back from her meandering thoughts. "Do you feel you are being truthful to yourself and to God?"

She looked past him to the *Star Trek* figurines behind him on his bookshelf, a photo of his baby boy next to them. "Not always, sir."

"Would you like to talk about it?"

"I don't think it would help."

"Whatever we discuss here never leaves this office."

Her eyes moved to Pastor Carter's passive face. "I know."

He leaned forward, resting his forearms on his desk. "You know, you're at a pivotal age. An age where desires can easily turn to sin. Is the lie in your heart one to do with desire?"

It was like he had pried open her head and poured out her graphic fantasies onto his desk. "Maybe," she muttered.

"There's nothing wrong with having desires, Devon." He adjusted his glasses. "But some desires you must keep hidden from others. Do you understand what I mean?"

Did he know what was in her heart? He couldn't, but the way he was looking at her made her feel naked, her sins exposed. "Yes, sir. I understand."

"We all have desires we have to keep hidden, and we must find strength in the Lord to stay on the virtuous path. I know you are a kind person, Devon. I hear of the good deeds you do for others, especially for your elders. This lie you have in your heart, this desire, is your test to overcome."

She didn't know how to overcome herself. Before Summer, before she understood the meaning of being bisexual, she knew this part of her existed, had always existed. If her test was to ignore those desires, she feared she would fail.

After an hour of Bible study, she walked over to Dotty's Ice Cream Parlor for a treat. She was surprised to see Jackie behind the counter scooping ice cream. When she spotted Devon, Jackie grew rigid.

"I didn't know you worked here," Devon said.

"Just started." Jackie adjusted her hairnet. "What do you want?"

"One scoop of buttered pecan in a cup, please."

Jackie moved over to the huge tub of ice cream and began digging at it with the metal scoop like she was digging a grave.

"So, where are you going to school now?" Devon asked.

Jackie looked up, her eyes narrowed. "What do you care? You and your friends were happy I was kicked out. Y'all never wanted someone like me dirtying up your tighty-whitey school anyway."

"I wasn't happy about it." But she had been. Without Jackie around, she had more of Summer's attention. "They should've warned students they were going to do random locker checks."

Jackie sneered at her like she was stupid. "As if that would've mattered."

Devon recalled how Jackie's mom had screamed at Coach Thompson, saying how drugs were planted in her daughter's locker and she was going to sue the school. As far as she knew, the woman never did. Devon looked at Jackie now, and she didn't seem like a drug addict, but she wasn't sure what a drug addict looked like, other than what she had seen on TV shows.

"Well, I'm sorry," Devon said, taking the cup of ice cream Jackie handed to her. "We miss you on the team."

Jackie took the cash Devon paid her and leaned over the counter, getting close enough to kiss her. "Fuck you." She pulled back, a bright smile on her face. "Have a great day! Come see us again soon."

Devon left her change and hurried out before Jackie could see her tearing up.

As she walked home, the ice cream turning into soup on the warm day, she began to think Pastor Carter was right. Everyone had desires they had to keep hidden, and Jackie was caught for hers and swiftly punished. She knew one thing for sure now: once people knew the things you kept hidden away in your heart, they could use them against you.

They could destroy you.

SUMMER'S JOURNAL

June 2012

I thought I could stop this, but I don't know how. I almost told Dev again, but I don't want her to hate me. I already know what her face would look like if I told her. I wish I could tell Keat, but he feels so distant, like I'm just another random person in his life he has to deal with.

Sometimes, I miss our special language, the one we used to speak to each other and no one else could understand. It used to drive Mom and Dad crazy. It made them scared, too, I think. That maybe if we were too close, we'd never learn to make friends. I guess we proved them wrong.

I tried to say something in our language to Keat the other day, and his eyes were totally blank. It fucking killed me because it was something we'd said a million times before when we wanted to say I love you without actually saying it. He'd saved me the last bagel for breakfast, so I said it. Elephant shoe. He came up with it, said the two words looked like a person was saying I love you when you mouthed it. He'd sometimes hold me and say it over and over when Mom and Dad would be fighting, their yelling so loud all I could do was turn myself into a ball and cry. Elephant shoe. Maybe he didn't hear me? Or maybe he didn't want to.

CHAPTER 29

DEVON

2025

Devon was trapped under an army of hands and chanted prayers. She never would've agreed to come to church had she known her mother was going to ask Pastor Walters to have the elders lay hands on her. They said it was to heal her heart after the loss of her client.

When she was younger, she used to think the practice was magical. To have so many people caring about your well-being at once, their prayers uniting to comfort and heal. But now, being in the middle of it, it felt like being smothered. These same people touching the top of her head would spit in her face if they knew she slept with women.

She spotted Shrader Thompson and Pastor Carter in the front pews watching her. Shrader gave her a little smirk, telling her he likely recognized the spectacle for what it was, and it had nothing to do with healing her heart.

Her mother seemed mollified by the theater of it all, and Devon didn't want to take that away from her, so she smiled after the parade of prayers was finished and thanked everyone. Her father gave her a big hug afterward.

"I pray you have peace, honey," he said in her ear. "Your mother prays for it too."

After they'd all sat back down, her mother patted her knee, but her eyes never left Pastor Walters.

The moment church let out, she hightailed her butt out of there and headed for the diner.

Keaton was already in a booth when she arrived, a coffee with a creamer packet waiting for her. He took his black now, she noticed. When they were teens, he and Summer had loaded theirs with enough cream and sugar that it no longer qualified as coffee.

"How was church?" he asked, a mischievousness in his eyes. "Do you feel full of the spirit and all that?"

"Well, I didn't catch fire, so I consider that a win."

He laughed. "I wonder what your parents would do if they knew you used to whip rich and powerful men for money."

"I guarantee more than a few men at that church would pay to be whipped."

"What about Pastor Walters? What would be his kink?"

She grinned. "Foot fetish. One hundred percent. He always went on and on about Mary Magdalene bathing Jesus's feet and drying them with her beautiful, flowing hair."

He laughed again, the carefree sound making her heart skip. "I kinda like this irreverent version of you." He smiled. "You know, I haven't felt like myself in a long time." His gaze moved over her face. "But I always feel like myself around you. You're the only person who's ever made me feel that way."

Heat traveled from her belly up to her head, warming her cheeks at his sudden candidness. She felt the same way with him, but there was so much guilt intertwined with those feelings.

Apparently sensing her unease, Keaton looked away from her and jerked his head in the direction of Jackie, who was behind the counter pouring coffee for a customer. "She's been avoiding me like the plague."

"Join the club." She stirred the creamer into her coffee and took a cautious sip. "We need to catch her before this place gets too busy."

Keaton looked past her and stood up from the booth. "Like now. She just stepped out."

She got up and followed him through the entrance. She didn't see Jackie. "Let's check the back by the big dumpster. I've seen workers take their breaks there."

Sure enough, Jackie was vaping behind the diner, and from the scent of the smoke, she didn't mind getting high during work. She didn't seem surprised to see them. "So, now you're dragging him into your delusions? You really do have something wrong with you, don't you?"

"We just want to talk," Keaton said.

Jackie blew smoke in his direction. "You mean you want to accuse."

"Do you have something to be accused of?" Devon asked, unable to conceal the disdain in her tone.

Jackie's dark eyes fell on her like a thousand poisoned darts. "You should be asking yourself that."

Devon stepped forward, invading Jackie's space. "What is your fucking problem with me? You've always acted like a bitch toward me, and I've done nothing to you."

"The problem I have with you," Jackie said, getting close to her face, "is that you act like a mouse when you're really a snake."

"What the fuck does that mean?"

Keaton pulled Devon back. "Listen, Jackie. Devon found a note from my sister. It was written sometime shortly before she died, and she was clearly scared of something or someone. And, yes, she called you a liar in her yearbook, but I'm not saying you have anything to do with her death." His hands were out like he was pleading with her. "We're just trying to find answers here because her death doesn't appear to be by suicide. So, if you can think of anything that might help us, I'd be grateful to you."

"A note?" Jackie looked at the vape pen in her hand as if she couldn't remember why she was holding it. "But she killed herself. Everyone knows that. Why would you think it wasn't suicide?"

Devon and Keaton exchanged a look, and she knew what he was about to say. She shook her head at him.

"Because the toxicology report didn't show anything but weed in her system," Keaton said. "The sheriff's office fucked up. That or they misread the report. Either way, something's off about her death."

Jackie's face hardened. "Then you should talk to Sheriff Wright about it."

"I did," Devon said. "And he patted my head and sent me on my way like I was a dumb kid."

Jackie tucked her vape pen in her back jean pocket. She kept her eyes on Keaton. "All I know is that she was seeing someone. I don't know who it was, but they texted her all the time. When they'd message her, she'd act strange, like she had to drop everything to be with them."

Devon thought of the rapid-fire texting she had seen after Summer had waxed her all those years ago: i want to lick every part of your sweet cunt. i know you want it too. meet me now. And then the mystery person who showed up to Holly's house during her party, how Summer had taunted them outside, Devon unable to see or hear who it was. Could it have been the same person?

A heavyset man cracked the back door. "Break's over, Jackie. We're getting backed up."

Jackie glanced at Keaton. "I've gotta go."

"Thanks," he said. "I appreciate what you've told us."

After Jackie had gone back inside the diner, Devon leaned against the brick exterior, arms crossed. "Why did you tell her about the report?"

"She was Summer's friend too. Just because you two never got along doesn't mean she's hiding something." He held her upper arms. "Interrogating her like she's a criminal would've gotten us nowhere, and now we at least have something to go on."

She knew he was right, but she'd also sensed Jackie holding something back. "We need Summer's cell phone. Maybe the police can pull the text messages. Find out who kept contacting her. And, Keat, there's something I forgot to tell you."

He let go of her and listened as she told him about both Holly's party and the text messages she had seen. He appeared disturbed, and she couldn't tell what he was thinking.

"After what Jackie just told us, I'm not sure the person who showed up at Holly's party was the same person texting her," she said.

"Why?" he asked.

"I don't know. Something about the text I read felt like a demand. And how Summer spoke to the person at the party was taunting, like she didn't care about hurting them. What Jackie said about Summer dropping everything for the person texting her . . . I didn't get the impression that she'd drop anything for the person she spoke with at the party."

Keaton rubbed his face. "Who the hell was texting her?"

She almost brought up Mason as a possibility, but Keaton had been best friends with him throughout high school. Even now, they were friends, from what she could make of their Facebook interactions.

Keaton leaned against the building next to her. "Wasn't Sheriff Wright going to check the autopsy report again?"

"Yeah." She let out an exasperated breath. "He said he found nothing suggesting any other cause of death. I don't think they're going to budge on it being a suicide."

Keaton shook his head. "Lazy bastard. He hates getting off his ass. We reported a stolen baler two years ago, and he never did a damn thing about it." He paused. "As for Summer's phone, the police station has it. Or they did."

"Why?"

"They said it was normal to take it as evidence anytime there's a suicide, which I always thought was weird. We wanted to have it so we could look through it." He rubbed his jaw. "Wanted to see if she left any clues for why she did it, but they never gave it back to us."

"They should now. It's been thirteen years. I'll go check tomorrow."

"Let me do it, Dev. You've been showing your face there too much. People will talk."

She smiled at him. "Now you sound like my mother."

"Fuck. I sure hope not."

That old playfulness entered his eyes again, and she imagined his arms around her, her face pressed to his chest so she could hear the steady thrum of his heart, his hands lowering to her waist, pulling her closer. But then Summer's low-pitched crying drifted into her mind like a warm breeze, and she shuttered the thought.

CHAPTER 30

DEVON

June 2012

Devon showed up at the Harrison house wearing her navy blue one-piece bathing suit under her T-shirt and shorts. She'd been nervous since she woke up that morning. It was the day of Ryan Nelson's party, and she'd spent an hour trying to put her hair up into the perfect high ponytail, the kind girls at school wore with no bumps or baby hairs flying all over the place.

When Summer opened the door, she took one look at Devon's outfit and balked.

"You can't go to Ryan's party like that," she said, pulling Devon into the living room. "And where's your bathing suit?"

"I'm wearing it." Devon lifted her T-shirt.

"Oh, hell no! The granny suit?"

Her heart sagged a little when Keaton walked by and stopped, a water bottle in his hand. "It's a pool party, not a fashion show."

"*You* can say that because you're a guy," Summer said. "You wear this, Dev, and they'll crucify you. It's fine to wear it around Keat and me, but not around the popular kids from school."

Keaton snorted. "Since when do you care so much about what they think?"

Summer glared at him. "I don't give a shit what they think, but I don't want them trashing on my best friend."

Devon hated how they were talking about her like she wasn't there. "Well, this is what I have, so I guess I won't go. I'd hate to embarrass you." She hoped they heard the annoyance in her voice.

"You're not going to embarrass us," Keaton said before taking a drink of his water.

"I have something you can wear." Summer tugged on her hand. "No arguing!"

Devon changed into Summer's bright-green string bikini and immediately wanted to take it off. It was way too small on her body. If her parents saw her in this bathing suit, they'd never let her leave the house again. She was lucky they allowed her to go to Ryan's party during her punishment, but they were only letting her because of his family's standing within the church.

Summer let out a whistle when she saw her. "Damn, boobalicious! Just try not to move too much so you don't pop a tit. Let's go."

Devon slipped on her shorts and started to put her T-shirt back on when Summer told her to keep it off. Then she pulled the elastic band out of Devon's hair, ruining her perfect ponytail.

They hurried down the stairs to where Keaton was waiting for them, holding their towels. When he saw her, his mouth parted and his eyes dropped to her chest before he quickly averted them, his face reddening. In that moment, with her long hair flowing down her back and her breasts pushing against the tiny green fabric of her borrowed suit, she felt powerful, though she couldn't say why exactly.

Maybe this party would be a new beginning for her like she had hoped. If she could pretend to feel as confident as Summer and Keaton, then perhaps others would see her differently.

They got into Keaton's truck, a blue 1999 Ford F-150 with a small dent on the passenger-side door. She still couldn't believe he'd finally saved up enough to get a vehicle of his own, and she'd felt his excitement when he purchased it earlier in the week. She was proud of him. Summer acted like it was her truck, too, though she hadn't contributed anything to getting it, and she got mad at Keaton for refusing to make a duplicate key to put on the key chain Devon had made her, the rainbow one with their saying—FAMF.

"You get the middle," Summer said to her.

She squeezed into the center, her leg jammed against the gear shift and the hot seat searing the backs of her thighs.

Keaton seemed nervous as he started the truck. He gripped the gear shift and put it into drive, his hand grazing her thigh as he did it.

"Sorry," he said, his face getting red again.

She stopped herself from laughing. He was acting so weird, and all because of a bikini. She'd always looked at her full breasts as a curse, same as her mother, so she mostly hid them under shapeless shirts and hoodies, but now she realized they might be her best physical asset.

They pulled up to Ryan's ritzy neighborhood, and vehicles lined his entire street, so Keaton had to park farther down. A knot formed in Devon's stomach, getting larger the closer they walked to the house.

Be confident.

She painted on a smile and hoped the pink lip gloss Summer had given her wasn't smeared on her teeth.

Once they were inside Ryan's house, Devon was overwhelmed by the number of people there. This wasn't only the juniors. There were a lot of seniors who'd just graduated there as well, and many were drinking alcohol. After having to be nearly carried home by Keaton the last time she'd drunk, Devon decided to stick with water. Summer immediately went for the vodka, mixing it with some orange juice sitting out among a bunch of other mixers. Keaton was drinking from his water bottle, and Devon was thankful he was staying sober.

"Let's go out to the pool before someone pukes in it," Summer said, linking her arm with hers. "Time to show you off."

Devon was trying not to stare at the huge amount of skin around her as they made their way through the open French doors leading to the large backyard, but she noticed the boys made no attempt at hiding their leers. She felt naked as eyes landed on her body, most hovering around her chest, and she no longer felt powerful.

She watched Summer saunter over to the edge of the pool, then set her drink and cell down by a large planter overflowing with brightly colored petunias before jumping in without even testing the water first. Keaton followed. Devon toed the water, which was cooler than she expected, given the hot day. She sat down and allowed her legs to dangle in the pool. She didn't see Ryan Nelson anywhere, which she found odd since it was his party.

"Get in!" Summer yelled when she popped up from the water.

"It's too cold." She crossed her arms, shielding her chest so no one would see her hardened nipples. "I just need to get used to it first."

Summer splashed her, laughing. "Don't hide the goods."

Devon tried to smile and relax like everyone else while Summer swam over to Mason, but her body remained stiff, her anxiety ratcheting up as she looked around. A few girls were staring at her and talking, including Holly, her smirk apparent even at a distance. She wondered what they were saying about her. Probably that she looked horrible in Summer's bikini.

She heard Summer's cell phone buzzing behind her. Whoever was trying to reach her was repeatedly texting her, and Devon hoped it wasn't the same person who had texted the lewd words.

"Summer, someone's psycho texting you," Jenna called out.

Summer, who was sitting atop Mason's shoulders about to play chicken with Kinzy and Trevor, stopped laughing. She immediately slid off Mason and got out of the pool, her face strangely serious. Devon twisted around to watch Summer check her phone, the frown on her face growing.

Then Summer squatted next to her. "Hey, I've got to do something really quick. I'll be back. Tell Keat I borrowed the truck, okay?"

Devon didn't want to be left behind. "Want me to come with you?"

"No," Summer said quickly. "I'll be back soon."

"Hey," Keaton said, coming up next to her after Summer had left. "Where'd she go?"

"I don't know." She tightened her arms across her chest. "She said she was borrowing the truck."

"Shit." He sucked his full bottom lip between his teeth. "She better not crash it. She's only driven it a few times with me." He looked at the full sweating vodka cocktail Summer had abandoned by the planter and relaxed a little. He gently tugged on Devon's foot under the water. "Why don't you get in?"

Be confident.

She loved to swim, and she didn't know why she was letting the stares of others prevent her from enjoying it. She didn't have Summer with her, but she had Keaton, who was grinning at her. She could do this. She uncrossed her arms and pushed herself off the cement edge, dropping into the pool. The cold shocked her system, and for a moment she regretted it. Then her limbs loosened as she kicked her feet and floated to the top.

"See?" Keaton said, floating next to her. "It's not so bad once you're in."

Her lips curved. "It's not."

They raced each other back and forth along the long pool, Keaton beating her a few times, but only because he was taller. She was a stronger swimmer, which gave her some confidence as she navigated around the crowds of teens. For a while, she stopped worrying about why Summer had left the party and focused only on how much fun she was having.

When she got tired, she pushed out of the pool and sat on the edge again. She watched Holly hold on to the ledge as she swam over to where Keaton floated while trying and failing to keep her face, which was in full makeup, dry. It was almost comical how she threw herself at him. In a way, Devon felt sorry for her. Holly was pretty; she could have any boy she wanted, yet she went for a person who clearly didn't want her.

Shame bubbled up in her, warming her face. She was no different than Holly. Although she wasn't exactly throwing herself at Summer, sometimes she felt like a leech latched on to Summer's side, sucking on any drop of attention she could get.

"Oh, shit, what do we have here?"

Devon glanced over to the French doors, where Ryan Nelson emerged, looking like a short king flanked by his much taller jock friends. He looked directly at her.

"Did I invite the Jesus freak?" he said, sneering. "I don't remember doing that."

She wanted to remind him they went to the same church, but her heart was racing too fast to speak. It felt like the sun was shining only on her, highlighting every flaw.

Ryan came up to her, his eyes falling on her chest. "Damn. Never would've guessed you had that body under those ugly-ass Walmart fall-apart clothes you wear."

She felt a burning sensation deep in her belly as she heard people laughing with Ryan. Laughing at her.

Keaton swam up closer to her. "Shut your mouth, Ryan."

"She hasn't paid the tax!" Trevor shouted from the other side of the pool.

A wicked grin spread across Ryan's face. "That's right. You need to pay the pool tax."

"The pool tax?" Devon said, the words quivering out of her.

"Don't be an asshole, Ryan!" Holly yelled.

"Shut the fuck up, Holly." Ryan leaned down, getting right next to Devon's face. "You can't use my pool without paying the pool tax."

"What's the po—"

Her question died in the air as Ryan yanked her bikini top hard, her breasts falling free of the thin green material. Time stood still, her body numb as everyone seemed to stop, all eyes on her. Keaton's wide eyes stared at her, her shock reflected on his face.

Then time sped back up, and she frantically grasped for the bathing suit's straps, only to find Ryan had pulled so hard one side was broken. She jumped up from the ledge, trying to shield her breasts with her arms, and did the only thing her brain could think of to do.

She ran.

SUMMER'S JOURNAL

June 2012

I'm going to fucking kill Jackie. I had a plan, a way out of this, but she's ruined everything. No one had to know about it. FUCK! I don't know what to do. Fucking Jackie! She said she doesn't know what I'm talking about, but she does. Fucking liar. I hate her. I HOPE SHE DIES!

CHAPTER 31
DEVON

June 2012

Devon didn't know where to go in Ryan's massive house, but she couldn't just run out the door without a top on. She silently cursed Summer for talking her out of wearing a T-shirt.

Her body was on autopilot as she ignored the many gasps and comments while rushing up the long curved flight of stairs to the second floor. She figured fewer people would be up there, and she could find a shirt to steal. She walked down a long hallway, her eyes darting inside the rooms as she went past, but she was wrong. There were kids upstairs, too; she could hear them through the doors, some of the sounds making her glad she hadn't gone inside without knocking first.

At the end of the hallway, she came to a large office with a library and desk on one side and an ornate marble fireplace and leather couch on the other. She went inside and shut the door. There wasn't a lock, and she hoped no one would burst in.

She sat on the couch, shivering hard, which made it difficult for her to remove the lower straps of the bikini top. She finally steadied her hands enough to undo it and realized quickly there was no way she could temporarily fix the broken strap. Embarrassment crashed down on her, and she sobbed into her hands.

She wasn't sure how long she sat there crying. She knew she couldn't hide in the office forever, but she didn't want to leave the room half-naked. Every time she replayed what Ryan had done, another wave of humiliation tightened her throat, making it hard for her to catch a breath.

A soft knock came at the door. When she said nothing, the door opened and shut, and she scrambled to cover her breasts.

"Someone's in here!" she half cried.

"It's me, Dev."

Keaton's voice. Oh, God, this couldn't get any worse.

"Someone took our towels," he said, "but I found a blanket downstairs." She heard him walk closer to the couch. "Want me to throw it to you?"

She nodded, but he must not have seen her, because she felt the air shift around her and knew he was behind the couch. He draped the blanket across her bare back, and she wrapped it around herself, thankful for the warmth.

"Is it okay if I sit down?"

"Yeah." Her voice sounded raw and raspy.

He sat at the other end of the couch, giving her plenty of space. They were both quiet for several moments before he spoke again. "I don't know what to say. That was really fucked up, what he did."

She finally looked over at him. He had so much concern in his eyes, and a swell of gratitude for him filled her lungs. "Thank you for the blanket."

A shiver ran through her body again, and Keaton motioned to the fancy fireplace. "Want me to turn it on?"

"No, it's okay." She stared down at her lap, her eyes feeling puffy. "Everyone saw me. Didn't they?"

She looked at him, and his mouth was slightly parted like he was going to say something, but she didn't need him to say it. She knew they'd all seen her breasts, these same kids who would be at church the next day, singing hymns and acting so pure.

"Fuck them," he said. "Most of them won't even make it to college, but you will. And you'll leave this place behind and never see them again."

Devon held his gaze. "What about you? Summer said you're not going to apply."

His jaw tightened. "I don't have the same choices as you."

"Yes, you do. You could leave if you wanted to, so why aren't you?"

The muscles in his face twitched. "I just . . . I need to be here."

She didn't understand. Why could Summer leave but he couldn't? The thought of Summer going to live with her aunt in Austin and Keaton staying in Arkana, leaving her alone while she attended college in the city, hit her again, forcing more sobs to erupt. She couldn't stop them.

Strong arms wrapped around her, holding her tight. "It's okay. It's going to be okay," Keaton whispered into her hair.

She held on to him like he was a tree during a flash flood, his naked back under her hands. She hugged him tighter, her mouth near his neck. He smelled so good, like sweat and sunshine and traces of tropical sunscreen. Carefree things. She had an insane urge to lick his chlorine-scented skin, so she did. He tasted like salt, and her mouth watered, craving more of him.

Keaton froze, his hand no longer caressing her hair.

Why had she done it? She was so, so stupid, her emotions all over the place. And he'd tell Summer. Oh, God, he'd tell her, and then Summer would think she was disgusting, going around licking her brother like a Popsicle.

Keaton pulled back from her, and she was afraid to look at him. When she forced herself to find his face, she couldn't read his expression. His eyes looked like the nebula photos she'd once looked up on NASA's website for a science project, the blues, browns, and golds swirling into impossible beauty.

"I—I'm sorry," she said.

She almost flinched when he touched her cheek. His hand was so warm against her skin, and she leaned into it. How he was looking at her now made her feel incandescent, like if someone cut her open, liquid light would pour out. He ran his thumb over her lower lip, his full mouth curving up slightly when she remained still, captivated by the raw anticipation like warm coals nestled at the center of her breastbone.

He leaned forward, his hand moving into her damp hair, and he pressed his lips to hers. She'd never kissed anyone before, and she didn't know what to do, but he did, and his mouth parted hers, deepening the kiss. Her body was on fire as his tongue dipped inside her mouth, and she found herself digging her fingers into his back, wanting him closer. He lowered his head and kissed her neck, and a small moan left her. Everything in her felt open to him, to whatever he wanted to do.

One side of the throw blanket draped over her slipped from her shoulder, but she didn't try to replace it. Keaton stopped kissing her for a moment, noticing, his eyes lowering to her exposed breast, and she wanted him to see her, to touch her. He searched her eyes as if asking for permission and tentatively placed a hand on her breast. Her breathing hitched as he gently caressed and squeezed her breast, his wide eyes on hers in wonder like he couldn't believe this was happening. It didn't feel real to her either, and maybe it wasn't. Maybe she had cried herself to sleep and was dreaming this, but then he pushed her back onto the leather couch, his body over hers. He took the hard peak of her breast in his mouth, sucking, and the sensation went straight between her legs. The other side of the blanket fell from her, and the only thing left on her body was the flimsy bikini bottom.

Keaton explored her other breast, his mouth in turns tender and rough, his teeth tightening around her nipple. The pain went through her, and she wanted more. She was nervous, but she reached for his swim shorts and the obvious hardness there, her pulse so rapid and hot she thought she might catch fire.

He groaned deep when she touched him through the damp fabric, and she wanted to hear the sound forever.

"Dev," he breathed out, placing his hand over hers.

The old embarrassment streaked through her chest. She must be doing something wrong. "I'm sorry, I—I don't know how . . ." Her words trailed off as she turned her face away from him.

"No," he said, holding her chin and forcing her to look at him. "It feels good. Really good, but I . . . I don't have a condom."

Oh. He thought she wanted to have sex. She felt so stupid and then angry at her parents for not teaching her about these things.

Keaton seemed to see something on her face. "We can stop. Whatever you want to do."

"I'm not ready for . . . for that," she said. "But I like what we were doing." She smiled, and his face lit up.

He joined his lips with hers again, his hands roving over her chest and stroking her hair. She ran her hands through his short waves, wanting to touch him through his bathing suit again, but she didn't. His mouth found her breasts once more, his circling tongue making the ache between her legs blossom and pulse until she wanted his tongue there, at the center of her.

She was falling into the pleasure he was giving her, her head back, eyes closed, when a sharp gasp came from behind them. They both stopped, frozen. Then the loud clicking of the door being shut told them that whoever had seen them had left.

The moment between them died; she could see it on Keaton's face.

"Uh . . . we should get you home." He was clearly flustered as he stood up. "I'll steal you a T-shirt to wear."

She got up, too, draping the throw blanket around her. Her eyes went to the bulge in his bathing suit, and the overwhelming need flared in her again. "Okay."

If someone from church had seen her with Keaton and told her parents, life as she knew it would be over. Her heart, which had soared outside her body only minutes before, crashed to the Persian rug beneath her feet.

CHAPTER 32

DEVON

2025

Devon had spent the Monday morning helping her mother harvest and pickle okra. She was exhausted from being out in the heat for so long, and when she made it back to the Harrisons' place, all she wanted to do was sleep. She took a shower and lay in Summer's bed on top of the green comforter, the afternoon sun diffusing soft light across the room.

She hoped Keaton had luck with Sheriff Wright about Summer's cell phone. He was supposed to go by the police station after he'd finished with some work at the farm. When he finally called her, she instantly knew whatever he was about to say wouldn't be good news.

"So, did the sheriff release Summer's phone?" she asked.

He let out a heavy breath. "No. He said it was lost after the tornado that hit ten years ago."

She caught something in his tone. "You don't believe him?"

"I'm not saying that, but after the toxicology report, I can't say I have a lot of faith in Arkana's finest."

She wanted to punch a wall. Yet another roadblock. "Now what?"

"I don't know." He sounded as frustrated as she was.

"We have to find out what happened between Summer and Jackie."

Keaton sighed. "We did everything we could. She obviously isn't going to talk."

"No. We did it the nice way. It's time to be rough about it."

"Dev."

"I'll see you later." She hung up.

She didn't have much leverage over Jackie, but what she did have, she'd use to the fullest extent. Whatever had happened between Summer and Jackie ended badly, she knew that much. In her gut, she had always known Jackie had feelings for Summer. She didn't think Jackie sent the text messages, but she didn't mind using the possibility against her to see what else she'd admit. Devon threw on a tank top and shorts, grabbed her purse, and headed for the diner.

When she got there, one of the servers said Jackie had gone home ill after the morning rush. Devon asked for Jackie's address, said she had to get something to her, and the young server offered it up without a fight.

Jackie still lived out at the same trailer park she'd lived at as a teen. The sprawling park backed into a thick wooded area with even more woods across from it. It took Devon a few drives around the park to find Jackie's place, which was tucked behind a dying pine tree missing more than half its needles. Her trailer had a big rainbow flag hanging from it and two pink flamingos poked into the scant grass out front.

She climbed the three steps to knock on the narrow door. A large-sounding dog barked like mad, and she heard a woman coughing up a lung as she tried to quiet it. Jackie answered the door, her mouth dropping open in surprise. The huge muzzle of what looked like a pit bull mix pushed past Jackie's legs, almost bowling her over. Devon stepped back, trying not to fall off the tiny landing in front of the trailer.

"She won't bite unless I tell her to," Jackie said, pulling the dog back by her thick leather collar. She glared at Devon. "So, give me a reason why I shouldn't tell her to tear you apart."

Devon backed up even more, moving down the steps until she was back on the ground. "Put her away, and I'll talk. You'll want to hear what I have to say."

Jackie's lips curled into a smirk. "You're lucky she's already had dinner." She pushed the dog back into the house and stepped outside, shutting the door behind her. A woman yelled something, and Jackie shouted back, "I'll do it in a minute, Ishki!"

"Is that your mother?" Devon asked.

"Yeah."

"Why aren't you working? You don't look sick."

"My mom is, but they don't let people off for that. She has emphysema and caught RSV." Jackie propped her hands on her narrow hips. "What do you want?"

"I ran into Shrader Thompson the other day." She couldn't tell if it was irritation or anger skittering across Jackie's face.

"So."

"So, he mentioned you and Summer had a falling-out."

"Oh, yeah? And I bet this just magically came up in conversation."

"It was something he noticed," Devon said, "the same way I noticed it. I'm not crazy. Something happened between you and Summer, something that made her call you a liar. And if you don't want people pointing a finger at you once it's been determined she didn't die by suicide, then you need to tell me what happened."

Jackie laughed. "You are fucking insane."

"I saw one of the text messages sent to her. Want to know what it said? 'I want to lick every part of your sweet cunt. I know you want it too.'" She had memorized those words, replayed them a thousand times over the years. "Sound familiar?"

"Are you for fucking real?"

"I know you had a thing for her. Maybe you were obsessed with her."

At this, Jackie outright laughed. "You of all people saying this to me." She shook her head. "Yeah, the big, bad lesbian murdered her.

Sure." Her face turned serious again. "I wasn't the psycho person texting her. You think I was lying about that?"

"Then tell me why she would call you a liar. Why did you two stop being friends?"

Jackie sat down on the top step, her slender arms draped over her knees. "She's the one who stopped speaking to me."

"Why?" Devon repeated.

Jackie sucked in a long breath, her thumb kneading her clasped hands. "She thought I said something about something she did, but I didn't."

Devon's heart began to race. "What did she do?"

Jackie shook her head. "It wasn't a bad thing. Just something she didn't want anyone to know about."

Devon waited, her heartbeat in her ears.

"I saw it in her backpack when she was getting something, so I asked her about it." She looked down at her hands. "She made me promise not to tell anyone, and I never did. But someone found out, I guess, and she thought it was me."

"What was it?"

Jackie looked up at her, her face drawn and shadowed under the shade of the trees. "A pregnancy test."

CHAPTER 33
DEVON

June 2012

Sometimes Devon was glad her parents wouldn't let her have a cell phone. Otherwise, she would've been staring at a phone for the last two days, hoping to get a text from Keaton. Her mind was like the fluff of dandelion seeds blowing in the wind, scattered in every direction.

She didn't know how she felt about what had happened with him. Part of her had loved it and wanted it to happen again, but another part wished she could take it all back. The worst was that it didn't change her feelings for Summer, which only confused her more.

After Keaton had found her a T-shirt to wear, they left Ryan's party, Keaton with his phone out, ready to call Summer as they walked toward the end of Ryan's block. But Summer was already there, sitting in the truck, her eyes red as if she'd been crying. When she and Keaton asked her what was wrong, Summer said it was nothing, that she swallowed some water the wrong way. She didn't even ask why they were leaving early, and Devon wouldn't have told her the reason if it weren't for the broken bikini top.

"I'm going to kill that motherfucker!" Summer said.

Devon talked Summer down after she yelled, saying she was going to run back to the party and strangle Ryan with the bikini strings. They had driven home in near silence, Summer taking the middle seat on the way back.

And here Devon was now, sitting in her room on the late Tuesday morning, finally ungrounded and free to leave the house but with no invite to go anywhere. She climbed down the stairs to the kitchen, feeling restless in the empty house with her parents at work. She was getting a mozzarella stick when the doorbell rang.

She cracked the door open, and Summer stood on the porch wearing a backpack, grinning from ear to ear.

"Hey," Devon said, surprised.

"Look what I have." Summer held up a plastic bag of slender, shriveled-up grayish-brown bits with what looked like little hats on them.

"Are those . . . the mushrooms?"

"Shrooms, Dev." She wiggled the bag in her face. "We need to grab a few things first." Summer stepped inside the house, something she would never do if Devon's parents were home.

Devon didn't know what to say. She had promised to take shrooms with Summer, but that was before what happened at Ryan's party. How could she act normal around her best friend after what she'd done with Keaton?

Summer went straight for the kitchen and opened the fridge. "We need orange juice. Trey's cousin says citric acid helps break down the chemicals or whatever so the trip lasts longer. Also, do you have any chocolate? He says it makes it easier to get the shrooms down since they taste like shit, I guess."

The frantic energy coming off Summer made Devon nervous. "Um, I think we have some Kisses." She went to the pantry and pulled out the nearly empty bag of chocolate, feeling a bit dazed.

Summer snatched the bag from her, a half-empty bottle of orange juice in her other hand. "Great! Let's go."

"Let me write a note for my parents." She wrote a quick message on the dry-erase board they kept in the kitchen for grocery list items and notes to each other. "Should I get a blanket or something?"

Summer giggled, placing the chocolate and orange juice in her backpack. "No. The earth is going to be our blanket. Come on."

She followed Summer out the door and along the road near the Harrison farm. They went down the dirt path leading toward the woods and Chullusa Pond, Devon's mind going back to the scattered state it'd been in since the party. Maybe it would be good to be out of her head for a while, to forget how good it'd felt kissing Keaton with his warm hands on her body.

The June day was clear and pleasantly warm, the sky cornflower blue against the lush green grass they were walking on. In less than a month, the sun would start to bake everything brown and brittle as the temperatures swelled to over one hundred degrees.

They reached the part of the woods they called the grove, where there was little undergrowth and tiny blue wildflowers blanketed the ground, surrounded by taller milkweed laden with butterflies and hovering bees. Around the clearing, there were several redbud trees, which bloomed pink each spring. Even during this time of year, the place looked magical, as if fairies might appear at any moment.

Summer looked up at the bit of sky peeking through the woods surrounding them and let out a huge sigh. "This is perfect." She sat on the ground and patted next to her. "Time to let Mother Nature take us on a journey."

Devon sat down, her nerves turning into excitement. Summer handed her four pieces of the shriveled mushrooms and two unwrapped Kisses.

"Let's eat them as fast as we can and drink it down with the juice, okay?" She held up her own shrooms and chocolate. "Cheers!"

"Cheers." Devon shoved it all into her mouth and immediately wanted to spit it out. The earthy bitterness of it made her stomach clench, but she chewed as fast as she could. She saw Summer's face twist with disgust as well.

Once they'd swallowed, they each chugged the orange juice until it was nearly gone.

"Fuck!" Summer gagged. "That was the nastiest thing I've ever put in my mouth."

"Now what?"

Summer smiled. "Now, we wait."

They both lay back on the cushion of flowers and grass, the rhythmic ticking of the cicadas lulling Devon.

After a long time of peaceful quiescence, Summer said, "I read that Neruda book you gave me. I really like it."

Devon turned to face her, but Summer remained on her back. "Which poem was your favorite?"

"The one you read to me." She closed her eyes, smiling.

They talked about the book for a while, and a small thrill shivered down Devon's spine. She'd never had this long of a conversation about books with Summer. Keaton, yes, since they liked a lot of the same books and were in the same AP Language class, but not Summer. Devon loved hearing Summer's perspective, which was both thoughtful and insightful, and she ached for more times like this where Summer could be open.

Summer grew quiet again before turning onto her side to face Devon. "I think I'm feeling it. I feel all tingly."

"I think I'm feeling it too." Devon felt tingly as well, but also a little nauseated as her heart rate picked up. She looked around, and the leaves on the trees seemed to be breathing in and out in time with her. She trained her gaze back on Summer. "Your face . . . it's all shimmery. Like the blacktop when it's really hot outside."

Summer smiled. "Yours is too." She reached her hand out and touched Devon's cheek. "You're so beautiful. It's like I can see your soul or something."

Devon touched Summer's face, and her skin felt charged, as if she could caress every electron in every atom she made contact with. "You're beautiful too. Like you're not real."

They both continued to run their fingertips across the curves and dips of their faces, marveling at the sensations. Then Summer moved closer and pressed her lips to Devon's. The shock of it vibrated throughout her body. Summer was kissing her. This was happening. It was too surreal, but it felt so good, so natural with them lying on flowers, nature inhaling them in and out, and she kissed her back, savoring the softness of Summer's lips, the sweet taste of her tongue.

When Summer lowered her hands to Devon's chest, she couldn't stop the thoughts of Keaton flitting across her mind. Guilt warmed her face, but she had wanted this for so long, this pleasure with Summer. This thing she'd been taught all her life was a sin.

This isn't right.

But her body ignored her reservations, and she slipped her hand under Summer's tank top. She wasn't wearing a bra because she never needed one like Devon did. Her breasts were small and perfect in Devon's hands, so soft and supple. So different from the hardness of Keaton's chest, but she loved the feel of them both. A crazy, sick thought of Keaton joining them entered her mind, both caressing her body, their mouths on her, fingers sliding inside her wetness, and she realized Summer's hand was down her shorts, in her underwear, on her. Her muscles stiffened.

Summer whispered something to her, but all she could focus on was the sensation growing between her legs. She whispered again, right in her ear, and this time Devon heard her.

"Don't think, Dev. Just relax."

She closed her eyes, inhaling Summer's sweet perfume, her hips grinding against Summer's hand, and let go.

CHAPTER 34

DEVON

2025

Devon couldn't believe it. Summer had a pregnancy test. It had to have been for herself, but what was the result? Had she been pregnant when she died?

Her immediate thought was to call Keaton and meet up, but she didn't want to throw this information at him if it turned out to be nothing. So, she called Dayton, hoping his connections could once again help her find out the truth.

"To what do I owe this pleasure?" Dayton said when he answered.

"I need your help again with my friend."

"I'm not sure what else I can tell you. She died from a hypoxic brain injury, which could be from a number of things, but it wasn't from a drug overdose. At least not illegal drugs."

"That's not why I'm calling." She paused, knowing she was about to ask a lot of him. "I just learned she possibly took a pregnancy test shortly before she died. Is there any way you can check to see if she was pregnant?"

Dayton sighed heavily. "Are you doing okay, Dev? Rae said you haven't been responding to her text messages. We're worried about you. You've been through a lot in the last year, and now you seem a bit obsessed with your friend's death. I hope you're talking to a professional."

She knew she was being a horrible friend to so many people right now, but all she could focus on was the friend she had hurt. She had to know once and for all if she was the reason for Summer's death. Everything she'd gone through at the Coulter mansion the year before was there just beneath her skin, waiting to claw out again if she wasn't careful, but those emotions would have to wait.

"I'm okay, Dayton. Really. And please tell Rae I'll call her soon. I just really need to know this. Can you please find out?"

He was silent for a few seconds. "This is the last thing I'm looking up on this. People could notice and ask questions I don't want to have to answer. Okay?"

"Okay. Thank you so much. For real, I owe you all the beers when I get back."

"I'll hold you to it."

By the time she pulled onto the Harrisons' property, the sun had nearly dipped below the tree line, but she knew Keaton would still be working. She hadn't seen him out in the fields she'd driven past, so she tried the barn. He was leaning over a large wooden table, carefully cutting a piece of black leather with what looked like a box cutter. He was wearing low-slung jeans and no shirt, his well-defined muscles working as he cut, and she imagined reaching out to touch him, her hands caressing his chest and down his flat abs, lowering past the trail of hair to his belt buckle. In a way, it was a relief to know she could still desire a man after what she'd been through, but the thought of having sex still sparked fear in her.

When she got closer, he glanced up, a little flash of surprise on his face.

"Hey," she said, shaking herself out of her lustful fantasy.

"Hey." He stopped cutting the leather. "I see you survived talking to Jackie."

As much as she wanted to tell him about what she had learned, she couldn't yet. Not until she heard back from Dayton, so she shifted him away from the topic. "Is this what I think it is?" She motioned to the leather bands and what appeared to be the base for a handle.

"What do you think it is?"

She smirked. "A flogger."

He grinned. "Then you'd be right."

She thought back to the burlesque show and their talk about how he'd gotten into kink. "Are you making this for yourself or someone else?"

"Someone else." He paused, massaging his right shoulder. "The set I'm making will cover an entire month of my mom's medication cost. Thank God for kinksters, right?" He gazed at her, and heat traveled over her body.

She remembered how Kingston Allen, the BDSM club owner of Subspace, was one of his customers. "I take it you've been to Subspace." Picturing him at the popular club was jarring but also alluring as hell.

"Yeah, of course." He set the cutting tool down and flexed his hands. "It's not really my scene now."

"It's not mine either," she said, leaning against the worktable. "But I had clients who paid me well to top them in public, and they enjoyed going there." She touched the leather, appreciating the softness and quality of it. "Why did you go there? To play? Or to watch?"

He rubbed the stubble on his jaw, his mouth quirking. "To play, but I guess you could also say marketing. People would ask me where I got my implements, and I'd direct them to my online store."

She smiled. "Don't tell me you're on Etsy."

He laughed. "Actually, I am. Even posted an artist statement."

She shook her head. "I still can't believe you're into kink."

"Is it any stranger than you being into it?" he asked.

"I guess not." Her imagination used to go wild with fantasies of him dominating her, but it was hard for her to picture it in real life. "So, what type of top are you? Not a sadist. Daddy Dom? Or maybe . . . sensual?" He was always sensual in her fantasies, giving intense pleasure with pain.

He gave her a wry smile. "So curious, huh? How curious are you?"

A spark of warmth breathed to life in her chest as his eyes held her captive. How easy it would be to move closer, to touch him, to let him show her this unfamiliar part of him and find out if she was ready.

The old guilt breathed to life, too, and she crossed her arms over her chest. Whatever this was between them couldn't grow. It just couldn't. Not without being absolutely truthful with him, and that wasn't possible.

Keaton seemed to sense the shift in her. "Are we ever going to talk about it, Dev? Or are we going to pretend nothing happened between us? If you want me to do that, I will, but I want to hear you say it."

She stared at the box knife on the worktable and imagined all the truths she could tell him that would cut him deep. "I don't want to pretend. But . . ."

"But what?"

"It's complicated, Keat."

He shook his head a little. "Then help me understand because all I know is that we had these moments where I thought you felt a certain way about me, but then it all changed. And don't say it was because of Summer's death because it changed before then."

She didn't know what to say to him. She had felt strongly for him, but she'd been too confused and torn about her feelings for Summer. How fucked up would it be for him to learn his biggest competition had been his twin sister?

She could tell him everything right now and watch his world burn, or she could continue to stay safe within the lies she'd told herself. Perhaps it would be for the best to rip the Band-Aid off. She'd come back to Arkana to exorcise her demons and heal, and what had occurred with Keaton was one of her biggest mistakes.

She stared at his expectant face, and she knew she was too selfish, too cowardly, to tell him the truth. Not yet anyway.

Her phone vibrated in the back pocket of her shorts, saving her from Keaton. It was Dayton.

"Sorry, I have to take this," she said and took a few steps away from him. "Hey, Dayton. What did you find out?"

"Well, I checked the autopsy report, and they had done what's called a human chorionic gonadotropin blood test. It's normal to do one in people of childbearing age."

"And?" She tried not to look at Keaton, whose concerned expression was trained on her as he grabbed his T-shirt.

"It was positive."

Fuck.

CHAPTER 35
DEVON

June 2012

Devon had sinned. And she had loved every moment of it, yet she avoided Summer for the rest of the week. When Summer came by the house the day after what they had done in the grove, Devon ignored the doorbell, glad her parents were at work and wouldn't wonder at her odd behavior. She was scared to talk to Summer, to know how she felt about what they'd done. Maybe it was only the shrooms that had made Summer want to be with her, and maybe she wasn't really into girls at all.

But now she had to act normal around Pastor Carter. Even though she was done with her punishment, he wanted to meet with her for one last counseling session. Would he be able to look at her and know what she'd done with Summer? He'd read her so well before, alluding to her having desires she'd need to hide.

She walked down the dimly lit basement hallway to his office. His door was cracked, so she went in and saw him with his white button-down shirt pulled up, his stomach exposed and a syringe in his hand.

"Oh," he said with a start. He quickly smoothed his shirt back down and placed some kind of protective cap over the syringe. A little vial sat on his desk. "Go ahead and sit down, Devon."

She sat, her eyes glued to the vial, trying to read it.

He placed the vial in a minifridge behind his desk. "I bet you thought I kept soda in this thing." He smiled. "Between you and me, I'm glad Obamacare passed. I hope it helps my insulin costs."

Devon didn't follow politics, but she most definitely knew how most people in town felt about the first Black president. She remembered when Maynard Cashman had hung a straw man by the neck off his big elm tree, an Obama mask on its face. Later, Maynard and a few other men had set the straw man on fire in his backyard as they drank beer, the embers sparking flames in the nearby brush, causing Maynard to lose most of his farmland.

"So, Devon," Pastor Carter said. "Even though this is our last session, you're always welcome to speak with me anytime." He paused. "I spoke with your parents earlier. They said you seem to be doing better at home. Do you feel you're doing okay?"

Her parents saying that she seemed better made her feel a little empty. If they bothered looking at her, they'd see the pain and confusion in her heart.

"No, sir."

His expression grew concerned. "I want to ask you something, and you can choose to answer or not."

She stopped twisting the bottom of her shirt.

"Do you feel attraction toward other girls?"

It was like he'd punched her as hard as he could in her stomach. She wanted to throw up. She wanted to run from the office and keep running until she made it to her bed, under the covers and safe. Why would he ask her this if he didn't suspect it?

"This is a safe space," he said.

She searched his kind face. Could she trust him? She knew she didn't trust Pastor Walters, with his anti-LGBTQ rants every other

Sunday, but she had never heard Pastor Carter talk that way. Still, he was with the church. He might be trying to trap her into admitting she was queer so he could tell her parents. She recalled talks of conversion camps and rumors that the church had tried to talk Jackie's mom into sending her daughter to one. She knew Calvary Baptist had sent Lindsay Dolson's brother to one years before, and he had committed suicide. There was no way she'd ever let them send her to one.

"No, sir. I don't feel that way about girls."

He nodded slightly. "Okay. Because if you did, it doesn't mean God doesn't love you." He tapped his fingers on the desk a few times. "How about this—I'd like for you to explain First John, chapter four, verse sixteen."

Devon swallowed over the lump in her throat. "It states that God is love, and whoever lives in love lives in God, and God in them."

"Very good. I trust you'll always remember that." He adjusted his thick-rimmed glasses, which kept sliding down his nose. "Unless you have anything you'd like to discuss, our session is over."

Over? The abruptness made her uneasy. She was so used to their hour-long talks, and she couldn't help thinking he knew she was lying about liking girls.

She stood up. "Thank you, sir. I . . . I appreciate you helping me."

"Like I said, Devon, I'm always here if you need to talk."

She left the church in a daze, the June day overcast and muggy. There would be rain soon, so she picked up her pace walking home. Within a few minutes, a downpour started, and her church clothes were soaked. As she trudged home, a blue truck drove past her and pulled over on the side of the road a few yards ahead of her. It was Keaton's truck.

He lowered his window. "It's about to get bad. Get in."

Just after he'd said it, the hail started. It was small, only dime size, but it still hurt pinging off her skin. She rushed to the passenger side and got into the truck. He had the A/C blasting but quickly switched it to heat when he saw her shivering.

"You should take off your shirt," he said. "I have something you can wear." He pulled a gray hoodie from behind her seat and handed it to her.

She stared at him, the awkwardness between them thick in the small space. She hadn't heard from him at all in the week since Ryan's party, which felt like a lifetime ago. She wondered if she would've allowed herself to be with Summer if he had tried to contact her, but she knew that wasn't fair to think since her parents would've been a barrier for him.

"Thanks," she said. When she began to unbutton her blouse, his eyes were still on her for a moment before he turned his head. She almost wanted him to look at her, to acknowledge what they had done before.

"Dev . . . about the party." He was still looking out the driver's side window. "I—I feel like I sort of took advantage of you after what Ryan did. And I'm sorry."

Whatever she expected him to say, this was not it. He was her first kiss, her first real experience of pleasure with someone. She had wanted it. "I'm not sorry about it."

He faced her again, and she shielded herself with the hoodie in her hands, her wet bra clinging to her cold skin. "You're not?"

She knew she shouldn't say this to him, but the memories of being in the library on that leather couch, of his mouth on her, made her say, "No."

He smiled a little. "Okay. Because I felt weird about how it happened, but I—I wanted it to happen."

His face was full of anticipation, and she felt it in herself, too, this pull to him. "I wanted it to happen too." A buzz went through her at the thought of doing more with him, to know what it felt like compared to what she'd done with Summer. To feel him inside her, filling the empty ache at her center. She could lean in now and kiss him, but she stopped herself. "But my parents . . ." She let her words trail off.

He slowly nodded as if he understood, but she saw his disappointment. "I get it."

"You're still my friend, though?" she quickly asked, scared at how his body deflated, his eyes looking away.

He dipped his head and looked at her. "Of course."

The storm was getting worse, the hail turning larger with the lashing rain, and she needed to get home before her parents got worried. "We should probably go."

"Right."

On the drive to her house, her mind was ablaze. She thought about Maynard Cashman again, accidentally setting his fields on fire and changing the course of his life, all because of one stupid decision. She looked over at Keaton, his concentration on the hail-covered road, and she knew somewhere in the recesses of her heart he could be hers.

CHAPTER 36
DEVON

2025

Devon stared down at her phone, wishing she could erase what Dayton had just told her. Summer was pregnant when she died. And she wasn't sure if Keaton or his family knew about it. With how the rumor mill worked in Arkana, everyone would've gobbled up that kind of gossip. Devon would've heard about it before now.

She looked at Keaton, his eyes fixed on her.

"Why do you look like you just received horrible news?" he asked.

She sucked in her bottom lip and chewed, a habit she'd tried to kick for the sake of her career. Clients didn't like seeing the nervous tics of their therapist. "It was my friend Dayton. The homicide detective. I . . . I need to tell you something, Keat." She told him what Jackie had said about Summer having a pregnancy test and how she'd asked Dayton to check the autopsy report. Then she steeled herself for his reaction to the news.

He stood there next to his workbench, completely still. After what seemed like forever, he finally said, "How? How would I not know this?"

"I don't know," she said. "I should've told you about the pregnancy test before, but I wanted to check with Dayton first."

His head dropped, his hand going to his forehead. "This isn't happening." Then his head shot back up and he charged out of the barn like he was on a mission.

She followed him all the way back to his mother's house. He busted through the front door and went straight to the kitchen, where Annie was peeling potatoes for dinner. She smiled when she saw the two of them, but the smile fell when she noticed Keaton's steely demeanor.

"What's wrong, son?"

"Summer was pregnant?"

Annie's blue eyes widened. "What?"

"Summer was pregnant when she died, Mom. Did you know?" His voice was growing lower, like the rumblings of an earthquake about to split open the earth.

Annie closed her eyes, her mouth a grimace.

"You did, didn't you?" he said, his voice exploding. "You knew this whole time?"

"Honey, please calm down."

"No, Mom, I'm not going to fucking calm down! Why didn't you and Dad tell me? Why?"

Devon had never seen Keaton angry like this. She placed her hands on his shoulders and kept her voice calm and level, a grounding technique she'd learned from her therapy training. "Keat, why don't you sit down so your mom can explain, okay? And I'll make us some tea. Is that all right, Annie?"

Annie nodded, her eyes tearing up. She sat at the small table in the eat-in kitchen, her hands visibly shaking. Devon felt horrible for her, but she felt worse for Keaton.

Keaton refused to sit, but at least he wasn't yelling. He stood, arms crossed, glaring at his mom as Devon filled the teakettle with water at the sink.

"I . . . I don't know how you found out," Annie said.

"Doesn't matter, Mom."

Devon was oddly thankful he didn't tell Annie it was she who had dug up the painful secret.

"Your father and I, we . . . we thought it was best you didn't know. You'd been through so much already, and we didn't want to put more pain on you." Annie's tears streaked down her face. "The sheriff suggested we keep it quiet and out of the paper for your sake, and we agreed it was best."

Devon stopped searching for the tea bags at hearing Annie's words.

"You know how this town is, son. If people had found out, they would've made life hell for you."

Keaton's face was pale. "It already was."

Another reminder of what Devon had left behind when she ran from Arkana. Keaton, alone to bear everything. They barely spoke during their senior year, both in their own private perdition after Summer's death, and it had been safer that way for her. At the time, she hadn't trusted herself not to expose every lie she'd told and open new wounds in him. So, she'd simply kept her distance until she could escape to college.

"Honey," Annie said, reaching up to touch Keaton's arm, but he jerked away from her. "Please sit. Let's talk about this."

"I think you've said enough." He left the kitchen, and the sound of the front door slamming soon followed.

Annie started to get up, but Devon held out her hand. "Let me go to him. You stay and have some tea." She placed her hand on Annie's shoulder. "It'll be okay."

She rushed out the door and found Keaton about to get into his truck.

"Keat!" she called to him, and he stopped. "We need to talk about this."

"Why? Haven't you done enough already?" He hit the side of his truck. "Fuck! We were all doing fine before you came back here. I didn't have to know any of this! And now what? What am I supposed to do with this information, huh? Go down more rabbit holes? For what purpose? It won't change anything. She's still fucking dead!"

Devon couldn't fault him for his anger at her, but it still crushed her to hear it. He was right. She brought this mess to their doorstep without any real plan for what to do next. "You don't have to do anything, Keat, but I do. I need to find the truth, and my gut tells me someone didn't want her pregnancy to get out. My gut says someone killed her." Summer had been buried thirteen years ago. There probably wasn't anything left of her body to test for fetal matter, which might've helped determine who the father was.

Keaton pinched the bridge of his nose. "Fine. I'll go down one more hole with you," he said, his voice eerily calm. "Who do you think knocked her up?"

The way he said it with contempt made her want to slap him, but she focused on his question. Since she'd learned about the pregnancy, one name kept infiltrating her mind. "Mason Turner."

"Mason?"

"I saw something at Trey's bonfire party junior year."

"Dev, you were completely out of your mind that night."

"I wasn't out of it at the time." She told him about what she'd seen between Summer and Mason in the woods, how she'd been certain she heard Summer saying no to him.

A nasty gleam entered Keaton's eyes, the muscles in his arms twitching. "Let's get a drink."

"A drink?" She wasn't sure if he wanted only to blow off some steam after everything he'd learned, but she didn't trust the unstable energy rolling off him. She could only imagine what he was thinking after hearing about Summer's pregnancy and then her theory about Mason, one of his closest friends growing up. She couldn't let him be alone. "Okay."

He drove them to Lucky's, the parking lot packed with the happy hour crowd. They ordered a couple of draft beers, and then Devon sat on one of the barstools while Keaton leaned against the bar, his eyes scanning the crowd as he sipped his drink. His body became rigid, and

Devon saw why. Mason Turner was in the back of the bar playing darts with a few other men, and she realized why Keaton had wanted to go there.

He stepped away from the bar, and Devon grabbed his arm. "Keat, no. This isn't the time or place."

He shook her off and went straight for Mason.

"Oh, shit, Keaton!" Mason said, arms raised in the air, clearly feeling his drink. "Haven't seen you in a while, man. Come play darts with us." His eyes landed on Devon, and his expression turned wary.

Keaton stood there, a six-foot-two statue of silent fury holding a mug of beer. "No, man, let's go outside for a minute."

Mason's ruddy face grew redder. "What? Nah, man, we're in the middle of a game here."

Keaton grabbed Mason's arm. "Let's go."

Mason looked around at his group of friends, seemingly searching for help. "Man, you drunk or something?"

"Let's do this here then." He had that unpleasant grin on his face again. "You slept with my sister. Did you rape her?"

Mason pushed away from him. "What?"

"Did you rape her?" Keaton repeated, stabbing each word.

Mason laughed. "I never touched your nasty sister. Everyone knows she was a fucking dyke!"

The hateful word was a bullet ripping directly through Devon's heart.

It all seemed to happen in slow motion, how the glass mug in Keaton's hand smashed over Mason's head. Blood poured from a cut on Mason's forehead. Instead of cowering, Mason immediately tackled Keaton, who had a good six inches on Mason. The men started throwing punches back and forth, Keaton's fists connecting more often than not.

"I will fucking kill you!" Keaton kept yelling, his punches coming harder and harder, and Devon couldn't find a way to safely intervene to stop them.

She heard the bartender yell, "Get their asses out of here!"

A barrel-chested man with hands the size of dinner plates separated Keaton and Mason before dragging them out of the bar, Devon rushing to follow them.

"Don't even think about comin' back in, or I'll kick your asses so hard you'll see tomorrow today," the bouncer said before going back inside the bar.

Both men were out of breath and bleeding, but she could see Keaton ramping up to beat on Mason again. He lunged forward, and she held him back, having to use her full weight like he was a hungry rottweiler on a leash. "Stop it!" Then she turned her glare on Mason. "You, piece of shit, are going to answer some questions. And if you don't, I just might kill you myself."

SUMMER'S JOURNAL

June 2012

He knows I'm pregnant. I told him about my plan to go to my aunt's house in Austin to take care of it. I just haven't talked to my aunt yet, and he said that's good, that I shouldn't talk to her or anyone else about it because it could hurt a lot of people if it gets out. He said he'll help me, but I don't know if I believe him. He says if I tell anyone about the baby my life will be ruined, and I know he's right.

I can't stop thinking about Dev. I think he knows. The way he looks when I mention her name. He's so good at reading people. God, I want to tell Dev everything. I want her to tell me I'm not a piece of shit for the things I've done. The things I've let happen. But I am, and nothing will change that.

CHAPTER 37
DEVON

June 2012

Devon was at the kitchen's small wooden prep table mixing the dough for the dumplings while her mother worked on cutting up the vegetables she'd add to the chicken stock simmering on the gas stove. The rain and lightning hadn't let up one bit, but Devon was glad the storm hadn't turned into the kind forcing them into the spider-infested shelter. With how dark and gloomy it was in the house, it felt more like a fall evening than the middle of June. Perfect weather for her mother's chicken and dumplings.

"That Harrison girl came by while you were still at church," her mother said. "She seemed real anxious to see you."

Devon stopped adding melted butter to the dough and looked at her mother, who was staring at her. "What did she say?"

"Nothing, really. Just how she keeps missing you when she comes by." Her mother paused. "Where have you been off to during the week if not hanging out with her?"

Devon bit her bottom lip almost hard enough to break skin. She hated herself for ignoring Summer, but everything was so complicated now. She knew she'd have to talk to Summer eventually and find out how she really felt. "I've just been here. I must've had my headphones on or something when she came by."

"You sure you weren't out with someone else?"

Her heart clenched in her chest. "No, ma'am."

Her mother examined her. "I saw that boy drop you off." She turned back to the vegetables and began chopping them again. "You haven't asked permission to date him. He doesn't even attend church. Your father wouldn't approve."

"I'm not dating him." She added a hasty "ma'am."

"Good. Then I expect next time you won't go riding in cars with a boy by yourself. You might give him the wrong impression, especially being soaked through, with your bra showing clear as day."

"Yes, ma'am." She was thankful her mother didn't catch her changing out of Keaton's hoodie.

After dinner, Devon hid in her bedroom, the empty feeling in her growing. She went to her backpack and pulled out her latest haul from the library earlier in the week. When she had found herself hovering in the poetry section, thinking of what Summer might like while also replaying what had happened with Keaton, Mrs. Sturgis, the librarian, sidled up to her, her gardenia-sweet, old lady perfume reaching her first. Mrs. Sturgis told her she looked troubled and suggested a collection of poems by Anne Sexton, who she said knew a thing or two about trouble.

Lying on her bed, gusts of wind rattling the windowpanes, Devon flipped through the pages and started reading the first poem that caught her eye. She continued reading, not fully understanding the poem, but her eyes kept snagging on the phrase "violent heart." Regardless of what the Bible stated, she never thought of a heart as being violent or wicked, only acts people committed, which she always associated with the mind and all its endless fallacies. But a heart was supposed to be pure, whatever it felt, or was that only the dozens of Disney movies she'd watched growing up? A princess listening to her heart and finding true love. But her heart wasn't pure. It *was* violent, constantly pulling her in opposite directions until one day she'd rip down the center.

Like she had so many nights before, she cried into her pillow, wishing she could be like other girls.

◆　◆　◆

Monday brought better weather, blue skies spotted with marshmallow clouds. After reading the tormented poetry of Anne Sexton half the night, Devon felt a bit better about her life. Yes, she had done something she shouldn't have with both Summer and Keaton, but she could still fix it. But first, she needed to know if Summer truly liked her. Nothing Summer had ever said or done led Devon to believe she was attracted to girls, yet when they were in the grove together, every soft, secret place in them pressing, she seemed to know exactly how to pleasure her.

Skipping breakfast, she threw on a T-shirt and shorts and rode her bike over to the Harrison farm. As she leaned her bike against the side of the house, she saw Keaton scattering feed for the chickens they kept out back by their vegetable garden. He glanced over at her, and she had the desire to go talk to him, but she was there for Summer.

Annie answered when she rang the doorbell.

"Oh, Devon," she said with delight. "Summer will be so glad to see you. She's been missing you."

Devon's chest tightened. "She awake?"

"This early, there's no telling, but go on up."

Devon climbed the stairs and gently knocked on Summer's bedroom door. When Summer didn't answer, Devon opened the door and stepped inside. Summer was on her side, facing away from her.

"Why are you here?" Summer asked, her voice raspy as if she were sick.

Devon closed the door behind her and sat on the edge of the bed. Summer jerked when Devon placed her hand on her arm. "Summer, I . . . I'm sorry."

Summer turned over to face her, and she saw that her eyes were puffy from crying. Devon had done this to her, and she knew saying sorry wasn't enough.

"After what we did in the grove, I was confused." Devon swallowed over the emotions trying to choke her words. "I loved what we did, but I'm also scared you only did those things because of the drug."

Summer stared at her. "It wasn't the shrooms."

"So, you do like girls?"

Summer nodded.

It was a relief to know, but there was also a bitterness in knowing. "Why didn't you tell me before? I came out to you, and I don't understand why you kept it from me when we're supposed to be best friends."

Summer's pretty face contorted. "How can I be out in this fucking place, Dev? It's not like you are either." She sat up in her bed, her face drawn, and her roasted-pecan hair mussed from sleep. "I didn't think you liked me like that, and then you . . ."

"Then I what?"

"Nothing. Just, what we did . . . I don't think I'd be good for you. I'll just mess things up."

Devon was so confused. She'd come here to say she was sorry, to find out how Summer felt, and to say she knew what she wanted and what she wanted was Summer. "I don't understand. We did those things with each other." The memory of Summer's fingers circling between her legs, the pulsing heat that had exploded throughout her body, made her breath catch. "Do you not like me back?"

Summer touched her hand. "It's not like that."

Devon could see her own confusion reflected on Summer's face. All she wanted was a straight answer from her. "What is it like, then, because I've had these feelings for you for a long time, and the day in the grove was the best day of my life because . . . because I love you and it felt so right being with you, but then I was so scared, and now I know why. It's because you don't feel the same way about me, do you?"

Summer looked stunned, her eyes wide. "You love me?"

"Yes," Devon whispered, not understanding Summer's surprise. "I have since I met you. When I'm with you, I just feel . . . I feel alive." She had no other words for how she felt, but it scared her to admit it.

The old bed creaked as Summer moved forward, pressing her forehead against Devon's for a moment before kissing her. It was such a tender kiss, and Devon melted into it, opening her mouth and allowing Summer's tongue to find hers, their hands tangled in the other's hair. When she placed her hand on Summer's breast, Summer murmured, "Not here."

Kissing must've been okay, though, because Summer continued making out with her. The longer they kissed, the more she wanted them to run back to the grove, to roll in the flowers naked under the dappled sun again, sending each other into that blissful state she had dreamed about so many times.

"Did you fucking drive my truck last night?" Keaton's voice boomed as he opened Summer's door without knocking.

Summer and Devon scrambled away from each other and sat up on the bed. Keaton looked between the two of them, fleeting puzzlement crossing his face.

"No, I didn't drive your truck, asshole," Summer said, completely cool, as if she and Devon hadn't just been kissing so heavily that Devon grew slick from it. "Now, get out!"

"I know you did because you never move the seat back," he said, his jaw tense. "Do it again and I'll tell Mom and Dad about you running off in the middle of the night. Don't think I don't know." Then he slammed the door.

Before Devon could ask Summer what Keaton was talking about, Summer said, "You should go. I have chores to do."

The sudden flatness in Summer's voice made Devon want to shake her.

"Okay."

As she pedaled home, she realized something that made her chest burn and her throat feel thick. She'd admitted to being in love with Summer, had said *I love you*, even though it terrified her to say it, but Summer didn't say it back.

CHAPTER 38

DEVON

2025

Mason took off his T-shirt and held it to his forehead where he was bleeding. Devon was amazed he was still able to stand after taking a mug to the head, but then Mason had been on the football team and was probably used to taking hits. Keaton had a cut above his left eyebrow, which he kept wiping at with the heel of his hand.

"Trey's bonfire party junior year," Devon said to Mason. "I saw you pushing Summer against a tree. I heard her saying no to you. Did you rape her?"

He glared at her.

"Did you know she was pregnant when she died?"

Mason's hardened face fell. "She was pregnant?"

The shock in his voice surprised her. "Yes. Answer my question. Did you rape her that night?"

"No." He shook his head harder as he glanced at Keaton. "No, I swear I didn't."

"But you had sex with her that night?" Devon continued.

"We, uh, we were kinda fucked up, but she wanted to. Like she was on me all night, and I didn't know why because I heard she was fucking with girls. But, yeah, it happened, but I swear she was the one who wanted it."

"If she was so into it, why did she keep saying no?" Keaton said, the sharp edge in his voice making Mason flinch.

Mason spit on the ground, and Devon saw it was blood tinged. "She didn't want me to use a condom. She kept saying no when I was trying to put one on."

Keaton's hands balled up again. "You think I'm a fucking idiot, man?"

Devon touched his shoulder, a warning to stay calm, lest the cops get called on them. "For real, you expect us to believe that?"

"I'm telling y'all the truth. She kept saying no when I got out the condom, and then she got pissed, and I couldn't . . ." He paused, shaking his head again. "Shit. I couldn't get hard again, okay."

Something in his tone made Devon believe him, at least the part about him not getting it up. But then his reaction to hearing about Summer's pregnancy bothered her.

"You had sex with her some other time, didn't you?" she asked.

Mason's eyes wouldn't connect with hers.

"When?"

He rubbed the back of his neck and sighed. "Shit. It was during school, after lunch one day. We skipped class and went out under the bleachers."

Devon recalled the day Summer whispered something to Mason at her locker, how she had given him a flirtatious smile. That had been well after Trey's party. Did they have sex that day, and Summer lied to her about not liking him? She didn't understand why Summer would have sex with him. Everyone knew Mason was the school man whore.

"Did you use a condom that time?"

Mason looked down at his feet. "I didn't have one. And then she acted like it never happened anyway." He looked up at Devon. "Was she really pregnant?"

His reaction was either the best acting Devon had seen in a long time, or he was telling the truth. "Yeah."

"Well, it couldn't have been mine." But he didn't sound so sure. "I had to have a surgery to get my wife pregnant." He shook his head. "There's no way it was mine."

Without saying a word, Keaton turned and went back to his truck.

"You should get that head wound checked out," Devon said to Mason before following Keaton.

The silence as Keaton drove them was killing her. Finally, she couldn't take it anymore. "Do you believe what Mason said?"

"I know you do."

"I never said that, but I do remember looking at his Facebook page and seeing a post about his first kid being a miracle child. So, I don't know. Maybe he's telling the truth."

He glanced at her. "I don't want to talk about this right now."

"Well, too bad. It was stupid going after him, Keat. He could've had a gun and—"

"He didn't have a gun, and I said I don't want to talk about it."

She let out a burst of frustration. "Fine. But we should get you checked out. You're cut."

"It's not bad," he said.

"At least let me help you clean it."

He said nothing and kept driving. He went past the road leading to his mother's place, and she realized he was going to his house, which she knew wasn't too far from the Harrison farm. His place was a small white bungalow with a covered porch big enough for two wooden rocking chairs and a tiny table. She stood next to him as he unlocked the front door, the tension in his body palpable.

"You have a first aid kit?" she asked once they were inside.

"Bathroom down the hall."

She noted the place had two bedrooms, one across from the single bathroom and one at the end of the short hallway, which she assumed was his bedroom since it seemed larger. After she found the kit in the medicine cabinet, she went back toward the front of the house to the U-shaped kitchen with a retro dinette for two.

Keaton pulled a beer from his fridge and turned to her. "You want one?"

"Sure."

He popped the tops and handed her a bottle before taking a long pull. Then he sat at the table, pressing the cold bottle to his head where he was cut.

Devon grabbed a paper towel from the kitchen counter and ran it under water so she could clean his wound. She stood over him, dabbing at the small cut as gently as she could.

Keaton grabbed her hand, surprising her. At first, she thought she might've pressed down too hard while tending to him, but then he said, "I didn't mean what I said earlier. None of this is your fault."

Oh, but it is, Summer's voice sang in her head.

Then he turned her hand palm up and ran his thumb over the frog tattoo on her inner wrist. "I used to imagine what it would be like to be an uncle." His voice was barely above a whisper. "She wanted kids, you know. She talked about it. And I wanted to have a family too. I had this dream that we'd always live near each other and have family gatherings, our kids growing up together . . . and we'd grow old together." He looked in her eyes, and she saw all the years of his grief etched in them. "When I dreamed about this, it was always with you."

Her lungs swelled with the words she wanted to say to him, that she wasn't worthy of his dream, but her mouth betrayed her and remained silent. Keaton pressed his lips to her palm right where her line of destiny met her heart line, and she closed her eyes, willing herself to be strong and not encourage him. But when he stood up and cupped her face, she opened her eyes and welcomed his lips on hers.

Any resolve she had left evaporated as he buried his hands in the back of her hair, pulling her against his body. He kissed her like he was starved and she was his only source of nourishment, his tongue caressing hers as his hands traveled down to her ass. He lifted her up, setting her on the table, his lips never leaving hers as he moved between her legs. His large hands ran up to her jean shorts, his thumbs then pressing at the apex of her inner thighs, and a sharp breath escaped her, the ache for his touch crashing through her body. When he gripped her hips and tugged her closer to him, grinding into her, she felt his need was as great as her own, the erection through his jeans the proof. God, she wanted him to take her right there on the table, but fear started scratching at her mind, distracting her.

He pulled back from her for a moment, his thumb grazing her cheek as his gaze skated over her face. "You're so beautiful. Like you're not real."

The words, almost identical to the ones she'd said to Summer in the grove before their first time, her head spinning from the effects of the psychedelic mushrooms. *You're beautiful too. Like you're not real.*

He believed she was someone she wasn't, someone good, someone who wasn't selfish and damaged. Letting him get close like this was the most selfish thing she could do, and she refused to let herself hurt him more than she already had.

"Keat," she said, gently pushing him away. "I can't do this. I'm sorry."

He stared at her as if he was waiting for her to say she was joking. When she said nothing, disbelief twisted his face.

Then his lips curved into a sad smile. "I never stood a chance with you, did I?"

"Keat."

He moved away from her, his mouth a tight line. "I'm going to bed. You can let yourself out."

Then he walked out of the kitchen, leaving her there on the dining table, wishing she could take it all back.

SUMMER'S JOURNAL

July 2012

God, I want to keep Dev for myself forever. I want to lock her away from the bad things she knows nothing about, the things I carry inside me. I want to dig a hole in the ground for us to hide in like bunnies where I can hold her and kiss her soft lips without worrying about this horrible fucking place destroying us.

I don't want to hurt her, but I know I will. I'm poison.

It was a mistake, the day in the grove. I don't deserve her. I don't deserve anything good.

CHAPTER 39

DEVON

July 2012

Devon returned the book of Anne Sexton's poetry to the library after reading it twice. There was something about the constant mood shifts in the poems that reminded her of Summer, and it made her curious enough to look up the poet on one of the library's computers. What she learned about the woman's life and tragic suicide disturbed her, how the poet's bipolar disorder had led her to put on her mother's old fur coat, lock herself in her garage, and start the engine of her car. She read the description for bipolar disorder again, and her stomach turned nauseated at the number of symptoms that seemed to fit Summer, like how she'd have boundless, restless energy for days, her speech so rapid and frenzied it was hard for Devon to keep up with her, and then how Summer would grow despondent, losing interest in doing anything but sleep.

She closed out of her searches, chiding herself for trying to diagnose her friend's mood swings. Her mother always told her teenagers have no control over their emotions, which was why they were easy prey for Satan. Sometimes she worried her mother was right and that Satan had stolen into the night and possessed her, making her have these desires for Summer and Keaton she couldn't restrain.

The July afternoon sun burned the back of her neck as she walked past Calvary Baptist. When she glanced over to the chapel doors, something caught her eye, and she stopped. It was Summer. Devon recognized her confident gait as she walked away from the church in the opposite direction from where Devon stood under the shade of a dogwood tree. Summer didn't see her, or if she did, she didn't act like it. She couldn't imagine why Summer would be at the church unless she had gone there to see Pastor Carter as Devon had once suggested.

She wanted to go to Summer, but she'd promised her mother she would stop by Bill's Pharmacy to pick up her dad's blood pressure pills. The pharmacy's chime went off when she stepped inside, the air-conditioning feeling delicious against her hot skin.

"Hi, Mrs. Johnson," she called to the curvy older lady behind the register.

Mrs. Johnson grinned up from her *People* magazine. "It's hotter than the devil's armpit today, ain't it?"

"Yes, ma'am."

"Your mama making her famous deviled eggs for the Fourth of July potluck?"

Devon hadn't even thought about the Fourth of July celebration the next day. "Yes, ma'am, I think she is."

"The potluck wouldn't be the same without 'em. You ask her to make some without bacon for me, all right? Dr. Cooper says my cholesterol's high enough to reach heaven." Mrs. Johnson chuckled.

"I'll tell her, ma'am."

She collected her dad's medication from Bill Johnson, the pharmacist, and slowly walked down the feminine-products aisle. Her mother bought her bulky pads that made her feel like she was wearing a diaper because she said nice girls didn't use tampons. Her eyes landed on the napkin-size section for condoms at the end of the aisle. Her mind went back to being on the soft leather couch at Ryan Nelson's house, the low groan Keaton had made when she touched the front of his bathing suit, and how he said he didn't have a condom. She didn't know how people put on condoms. She'd heard some of the schools in the bigger cities taught kids how to use them, but that would never happen in Arkana.

The only things she knew about sex were the things she had done with Summer, and they had felt so natural and familiar, almost like being with herself. Those brief moments with Keaton had been both electrifying and terrifying because she hadn't known what to expect, hadn't even known what men's parts looked like in the nude. But she had felt it, and it seemed impossible for it to fit inside her.

There were only two kinds of condoms in the tiny section: lubricated and another kind with something called spermicide. Without thinking, she snatched a package of the lubricated kind and stuffed it into her backpack along with her dad's medication. Her heart pounded as she looked back at the pharmacy counter and thankfully saw that Mr. Johnson had stepped away. She raced to the front of the store.

"See ya tomorrow, hon!" Mrs. Johnson said as Devon dashed out the door.

Her pulse thundered in her ears. She'd stolen something. She couldn't believe she'd done it. Now what? There was no way she could bring condoms into her house, not with how her mother went through her room.

She jogged over to the school since she knew no one would be around with the campus closed for the summer and went under the bleachers. After she sat down, she pulled the box of condoms from her backpack and opened it. She didn't expect the little squares of shiny wrapping, almost like they were some kind of fancy gum. When she tore open one of the squares and dug her finger into the wrapper, it felt as slimy as the slugs she and her mother killed in the vegetable garden. She removed the slick latex and imagined how a boy would put it on. She held up two fingers on her left hand and placed the condom on top like it was a tiny beanie and used her other hand to roll it down. She pictured Keaton sliding it on and pushing inside her, and the thought sent a throb of need so strong to her pelvis it trapped her breath.

"What are you doing?"

Oh God, oh God, oh God.

Jackie was by the bleachers, stooping down, her dark eyes glued to the condom on Devon's hand.

"Oh, this is good," Jackie said with a horrible sneer. "This is so fucking good. Little Miss Bible Thumper practicing for some deep dicking?"

"Shut up!"

"Aw, I know. It's Keaton, isn't it? Does Summer know you're fucking her brother?"

"I . . . I—I didn't . . ." Sweat ran down her back, her throat closing in on her, like she had a Ping-Pong ball lodged in her windpipe. Oh, God, why would Jackie say that? People must know about what had happened at Ryan's party. And now Jackie knew, and she would for sure tell Summer. Tears sprang into her eyes, her protestations still stuck in her throat, asphyxiating her.

Jackie's smirk dropped. "Jesus Christ. Calm down before you bust a vein. Here." She threw a half-empty bottle of water on the ground, which rolled next to Devon.

Then Jackie left her under the bleachers, frozen in absolute panic.

CHAPTER 40
DEVON

2025

Devon woke up to a call from her supervisor. Paulette didn't hold back on her frustration, especially since Devon was dodging her calls and barely acknowledging her text messages. Whether or not Devon had her shit figured out, Paulette wanted her back to work the following week, or she would be on probation and risk losing her practicum hours and, thus, lose her ability to practice therapy in the state. She needed to go back anyway since she was running out of her small savings.

Whatever truth she was going to learn about Summer's death, she needed to do it fast, but now she was unsure if Keaton was still on board to help her. It didn't matter. This was her cross to bear, and she had a new direction to go in.

During the night, she'd had a horrible dream, in which hands were coming down hard on her head like mallets. People were chanting over her, praying so loudly they sounded like a swarm of locusts; her mother's face, angry and red; her father's, passive in the background; and Pastor Carter, his eyes kind as he told her over and over how God still loved her.

And she'd woken up remembering the day she'd seen Summer exiting Calvary Baptist. Had she been there to see Pastor Carter? If so, Devon had to know why Summer was seeing him.

She drank some of the coffee Annie had left in the pot for her and headed for the church. The place was empty when she arrived, but she saw Pastor Carter's car in the parking lot. Walking down the stairs to the basement where Pastor Carter's office was made her feel like an anxious teenager again, like she was in trouble and about to be punished.

He wasn't in his office, but she heard the sound of a Keurig coffee maker farther down the hallway and found him in a small break room.

He looked up, a momentary expression of surprise on his face. "Devon. I was hoping you'd stop by while you're in town. You're coming to the ice cream social tomorrow, aren't you?"

Unfortunately, she had promised her parents she would make an appearance at the church's annual event. "Yeah, I'll be there. How are your wife and kids?"

"They're doing great. William's fourteen and trying out for football next year, and Charlotte just turned ten. She's a little spitfire for sure."

"Oh, wow. They're growing up so fast." She looked at his crisp button-up shirt and pressed slacks and felt awkward being around him in her tank top and jean shorts. "I, uh, wanted to talk to you about something."

"Of course." He motioned to the coffee maker. "Would you like a cup?"

"I'm good, thank you."

He stirred in some powder creamer and walked with her back to his office. His old swivel chair squeaked when he sat in it. Devon sat across from him, those old memories of talking with him every Sunday during her punishment coming back to her.

"So, are you wanting counsel regarding the client you lost?" he asked bluntly.

"Um, no. This is about Summer."

"Oh, I see." His brow furrowed in concern. "Has this recent loss of your client brought up feelings about Summer's suicide?"

"Uh, actually that's the thing. I'm questioning if it really was a suicide." She watched his calm expression shift into confusion.

"Questioning? Why?"

She rolled the hem of her tank top, thinking of the best way to say it before deciding there was no best way. "She was pregnant when she died. I confirmed it with a contact I have at the OKCPD."

There was no shock on his face, which confirmed the answer to one of her questions.

"So, you knew about it?"

He let out a loud exhale and braided his hands on his desk. "I did."

"Did anyone else know besides her parents and the sheriff's office?"

He paused too long before saying, "Not that I know of."

Her instincts said he was lying, but she couldn't tell for sure. Maybe he was protecting someone. The father, perhaps. "Is that why she came to you? Because she needed help?"

"Devon, I don't feel comfortable discussing private meetings I've had with someone seeking counsel. You of all people should understand that."

"Summer's dead. I don't think she'll mind."

Pastor Carter narrowed his eyes at her words. "Well, I do."

She stared at him, weighing how much to trust him. He knew about her lie to the congregation all those years ago and never told anyone, and he never outed her when he could've easily had her sent off to a conversion camp. "There were other findings on her autopsy report that don't add up. She didn't die from a heroin overdose or any other illegal drug, but something caused a hypoxic brain injury in her, and poison can cause that. Everyone just assumed what the sheriff's office said was true, but it's not. They messed up, and they don't want to admit they didn't do their jobs."

Pastor Carter pushed his glasses up and looked down at his clasped hands, his body rigid for a long time before he looked back up at her.

"Devon, I'm going to tell you something, but I ask that you keep it between us." He paused. "Yes, Summer did come to me seeking counsel. And, yes, later on, she did tell me about her pregnancy. But even before the pregnancy, she voiced suicidal ideation. She, in fact, had a history of at least one attempt when she lived in Oklahoma City. She told me about it."

Devon tried to keep the shock from her face. She never knew this, and it hurt to know Summer didn't trust her enough to tell her.

"After one of my meetings with her, I noticed I was missing a couple of insulin vials from my office fridge. At the time, I thought I had forgotten them at home, but later . . ." He seemed lost in thought for a moment. "Later, after Summer died, I wondered."

She couldn't believe what she was hearing. "And you never told the sheriff?"

"Why would I? The sheriff's office confirmed she died from a heroin overdose. And, besides, I'm not telling you this because I believe she killed herself with my insulin. I knew there was a simple explanation for my missing insulin, but my feelings of guilt for not doing enough to help Summer clouded my judgment and made me believe something that wasn't real. And now I think whatever guilt you're feeling about your client is clouding your judgment about Summer's death. I trust our sheriff, and you should too." He sighed heavily. "I know you cared about Summer very much, but she died from suicide, Devon. This I absolutely believe."

How could he be so dismissive after everything she'd told him? She expected more from him, but he was like everyone else in this damn town. She stood up and slapped her hand on his desk. "My judgment is not clouded. But I see yours is."

As she hurried out of the church, she got out her cell phone and called Keaton.

"We need to meet. Now."

CHAPTER 41

DEVON

July 2012

Devon stood under a sugar maple tree, trying not to die from the Fourth of July heat. She breathed in the intoxicating scent coming from the charcoal grills lined up and watched her mother fawn over Holly Lynch's lily-white dress when she'd said nothing about Devon's appearance, even though she'd painstakingly done her hair in Dutch braids, weaving red, white, and blue ribbons in it for the holiday.

She scanned the crowd of townsfolk for Summer, but she didn't see her. Surely, the Harrisons were going to come. They did the year before.

"Looking for someone?"

Devon jumped a little. Coach Thompson was next to her, holding two cups of Deedra Turner's punch, the kind with Sprite and orange sherbet she used to love as a little kid.

"Yes," she said, "but I don't think she's here." Her heart squeezed with disappointment. "How's Braden, sir?"

"Oh, he's great. Starting to walk a little now, so you'll have your work cut out for you next time you watch him."

"That's if Summer lets me have a turn," she said with a weak smile.

He chuckled. "Oh, he's enough for three people. Now, don't be slacking off during break, okay? I need you girls in tip-top shape."

"I won't, sir."

He went back over to his wife and baby boy, and she was left alone again, wishing for Summer and Keaton to show up with their parents. She glanced over to a group of kids from school, Ryan Nelson laughing at the center, and a few of them looked her way with knowing grins on their faces.

She turned away from them, tears burning in her eyes.

"Don't let them bother you."

She wiped her eyes, looking up to see Keaton getting some water from the cooling station near her. "Easy for you to say. The whole school didn't see you naked."

He came up next to her, so close his hand grazed hers. "They'll forget. Their tiny brains will find something else to focus on, and it'll be like it never happened."

She thought about what Jackie had said to her when she'd caught her with the condoms. Devon had buried the box under the bleachers, too embarrassed to sneak them into a trash can somewhere.

"I think some people know about what happened at Ryan's party," she said in a lowered voice. "In the office."

His mouth grew tight as he looked toward the group of teens. "Your parents don't know, though, right?"

"No." If they had, she would've been locked in her room for the next decade.

"Then don't worry about it."

She looked into his eyes, which appeared darker under the shade. "Does Summer know?"

He sucked in his bottom lip, his expression suddenly guarded. "I don't think so."

Devon looked over at the long tables set up for food and saw Summer holding a plate, staring at them.

"I've got to go," she said.

Keaton touched her arm as she was about to walk away. "Can we talk later?"

"Yeah, sure."

She walked over to Summer, who was picking at some macaroni salad on her plate, removing all the black olives.

"Want them?" Summer asked her, pointing to the olives.

"Thanks." Devon popped one into her mouth and chewed.

"Your hair looks cute." Summer paused. "Sorry I haven't been around." Her lips curved into a little smile. "My period was crazy. Like the worst cramps ever."

That was strange. She and Summer had been synced with their periods for nearly two years, like clockwork every month, and they weren't due for another week.

"That sucks," Devon said. She looked around, making sure no one was near them. "I missed you. I've been thinking about you."

Summer eyed her untouched plate of food. "Really?"

Her heart clenched at the uncertainty in Summer's question. "All the time." She wanted to touch her hand, to reassure her, but she couldn't. Not with her parents and everyone from church around them.

Summer gazed at her for a moment with an intensity that made her nervous. "I have to tell you something."

"What?" She hoped it wasn't about Ryan's party.

Summer's eyes shifted away from her, and Devon turned around to see what she was looking at. Pastor Carter was standing next to Coach Thompson and Summer's mom, all of them laughing about something.

"Coach said Braden's walking now," Devon said, turning back to face Summer. "I need to do more babysitting jobs so I can help cover gas for when we go to Lake Murray." She, Keaton, and Summer had talked about camping at the lake. Of course, it would entail lying to her parents.

Summer's expression went blank for a second before her face brightened. "We should go this weekend."

"Um, okay." She'd have to lay the groundwork for her lie fast, but she could do it. It was strange how the more she lied, the easier it was to do. "What do you want to tell me?"

"It's nothing." She threw away her paper plate full of food in the trash can at the end of the table, bees and flies buzzing above it. "It's too hot, and I'm tired. I think I'm going to head home. Tell my parents, okay?"

Devon wanted to go with her, but there was no way she could without others noticing. "Okay. Talk to you later."

For the next three hours, she tried to stay in the background, but her mother kept finding her and dragging her over to church elders to talk. Her long white dress stuck to her skin, wet with her sweat, and all she wanted to do was go home and take a shower, but she was trapped there until after the fireworks show.

After night fell and the first stars could be seen, she was finally able to hide. Keaton found her sitting on a park bench at the edge of town center, her feet aching from standing for so long. He handed her a sparkler and touched his to hers to light his own.

"I've been waiting to talk to you forever. Can we go for a walk?" he asked. "Away from here?"

"Sure." Her parents were busy watching the fireworks that had just started.

They walked toward the end of the empty Main Street, the sparklers lighting their way past the businesses closed for the holiday. Once Keaton stopped at the alleyway by Mable's Antiques, she felt his nervousness even before he spoke.

"Dev." He stared at her, his dying sparkler lighting his face. "I've been thinking a lot about this, and I . . . I don't think I can be friends with you anymore."

Her heart seized. "Why?"

His sparkler finally went out, but the lights from the fireworks in the distance streaked across his face. "Because I really like you. I thought we could go back to how we were before, but . . . I want more." He swallowed. "I don't know what else to do. It's too hard to be around you."

She couldn't breathe. She didn't want to lose him, and it wasn't fair to him after what had happened between them to pretend she wasn't attracted to him, but she also didn't want to hurt Summer. The way Keaton was looking at her, the vulnerability in his eyes, it made her wrap her arms around him tight. She held on to him, not wanting to let him go.

Why did she have to have feelings for him too? Why?

He pulled back from her, his hand going to her cheek.

"I . . . I really like you, too, Keat."

She saw his eyes brighten with her words, an elation she had desperately wanted to see on Summer's face after she'd admitted her love for her, and she didn't want to think about right or wrong in that moment. She wanted to be encased in his hope, to feel his desire, but it didn't stop her from hating her stupid, careless heart as she lifted her head and kissed his lips.

CHAPTER 42
DEVON

2025

The early-Tuesday evening was cotton thick with humidity as she drove to Keaton's place, but Devon knew any rain would stay north of Arkana, leaving the surrounding farmlands to crack and crumble into dust. The longer she was in town, the more she noticed how run down it had become, with more businesses closed and "for lease" signs popping up along the brittle fields. She didn't see how the Harrison farm would survive if the droughts continued. Not even the recent rains had helped.

Keaton was sitting on his front porch drinking a beer when she pulled up to his house. In the better light, she could see how much work he'd put into the place, with its fresh coat of white paint on the wood siding, the shutters painted a moss green, and the tidy flower bed filled with marigolds and a blooming red rosebush. She wondered if he'd ever leave this place if the family business died. She remembered being so scared when she left Arkana, not knowing how she'd learn to adjust to city life. But Keaton had grown up in the city, and he was still young. He could rebuild his life there if he wanted.

When she stepped up onto his porch, he didn't invite her inside, but he handed her a cold beer from the cooler at his feet.

"Thanks," she said and took a drink. She sat in the other rocking chair, next to him, the tiny table between them.

"So, what do you want to tell me that you couldn't just say over the phone?"

She sucked in a breath and relayed her meeting with Pastor Carter and everything he'd told her about Summer and his missing insulin vials.

"Was he right?" she asked. "Summer attempted suicide?"

Keaton ran a hand over his face, his thumb and forefinger pressed against his eyes for a moment before his gaze locked on her. "Yeah. She did before we moved here. Took an entire bottle of Tylenol and had to drink a ton of liquid charcoal to counteract it." He huffed out a humorless laugh. "She was making jokes the whole time with the nurses. Like it was no big deal."

"Was she on medication?"

"They tried her on several over the years. I think the last one was called risperdine."

"Risperidone," she corrected. An antipsychotic commonly used for conditions like bipolar disorder. A disorder she was now certain Summer had suffered from.

Keaton leaned forward in the rocking chair, his hands on his knees. "So, what are you thinking?"

She set her beer down on the table and tried to rub some warmth into her arms, the evening turning cooler and chilling her. "I looked into it, and insulin overdoses can cause the type of brain injury Summer suffered from. But I think insulin would be a weird way for someone to kill themselves, especially if they don't have access to a syringe."

"She did, though."

"What?"

"My uncle has diabetes," he said. "Type two, but he was insulin dependent at that time. Not anymore, though."

Shit. Everything was pointing back to suicide, but she kept returning to the note and everything else. "Still, if you were a teen girl wanting to commit suicide, is that how you would do it?"

Keaton rubbed his chin. "No. But if she did steal insulin, why steal it from Carter? Why not my uncle? It would've been easier, but a lot of methods would've been easier for her."

"I don't know. Maybe it was because she knew Carter was rich and could afford to replace it."

"So, now you think she did kill herself?" he asked.

"No, I don't." Her voice was too loud, too emphatic as she said it, like she was trying to convince herself again, which she was. "Her note, the pregnancy, the text messages she was getting from someone. None of it feels right."

His heavy gaze penetrated her. "But feelings are not the same thing as facts."

The sharpness in his tone let her know he was still upset after she had rejected him. "Keat, about the other night . . . I wish I could explain to you."

He set his beer down on the table and stood up from the rocking chair. He moved to the other side of the small porch, his back to her as he gripped the wood railing. "Did Summer know you were in love with her?"

She was glad he couldn't see how her mouth dropped open in surprise. This was the moment she could tell him the truth. All of it. But then the fragile thread between them would die. The moment she had rejected him the other night, she regretted it. She had wanted to be in his arms, to feel desired by him. To feel anything but this guilt and fear eating her inside.

"No," she said, the lie rolling easily from her lips. "I've never been out to anyone here. Especially not to my parents."

He turned to her, his eyes weighted with a question she was afraid to hear. "Are you still in love with her?"

Her feelings toward Summer had gone through so many seasons, so many shifts from love to pain to lust and regret. But now? "Not anymore."

Keaton crossed his arms, his muscles taut with the movement. "Why did you start something with me back then if you were in love with my sister?"

She stood up and walked over to him. "Because I was attracted to you, but I was also so confused at that age." The truth slipped out, but she held herself back from saying more.

"Are you still attracted to me?"

"Yes," she whispered.

His eyes traveled to her lips. "Then what's holding you back?"

She wanted to touch his cheek, to run her hands through his hair and taste his mouth again. But then she recalled Summer's face, the torment in her eyes so immense, so fathomless, she would never be able to erase the image from her memory. *You don't deserve happiness.* The words hummed in her mind, stirring along with the fear of being intimate again, and she couldn't tell anymore if it was Summer's voice or her own. "I don't know, Keat."

He shook his head. "I always feel like I'm missing a puzzle piece with you." He hesitantly reached out and cupped her cheek with his warm hand. "If you ever want to have anything with me, it has to be all of you. Your mind. Your heart. Your body. All of you. I won't take anything less."

She placed her hand over his, the fluttering in her chest making it difficult for her to catch her breath. "I wish I could give that to you." She pulled away from him. "I'm just . . . I'm not ready."

Although her body yearned for his, painfully so, her heart wasn't in alignment, and she knew why. There were too many layers of lies for him to reach her, and she was too much of a coward to tell him the truth and risk losing him altogether.

Keaton sucked in his lips and blew out a breath. "What *do* you feel ready for?"

She searched his face and smiled a little. "I don't know. Talking? I miss that, how we'd talk about books and films."

"Okay." He returned her smile and sat in one of the rocking chairs, then motioned to the other one for her to sit. "Let's start with books. Tell me about the last one that tore your heart out."

She was relieved by the shift in their conversation, her tense body relaxing as she sat in the chair. They sipped their beers, rocking slightly as they discussed their favorite reads until the night got too chilly for them to be outside. When they hugged goodbye, Keaton's arms lingered tight around her, and the intense buzzing in her body made her want to pull his shirt over his head and run her hands over his chest, to bury her face in his scent.

You don't deserve happiness, the voice in her mind taunted again.

She tempered her desire and broke from the hug. Then she reminded Keaton about the ice cream social the next day and got in her car. On her drive back to the farm, she could barely see through her tears because she knew the voice was right. She didn't deserve him.

SUMMER'S JOURNAL

July 2012

The way he's been looking at me, it's like he wants me to disappear. He knows so much about me, even the time I was in the hospital. It scares me how much I've told him. But what scares me more is myself. I've always thought of this part of me as a dark cloud trying to swallow me up. When I was seeing Dr. Elizabeth, I lied to her so I wouldn't have to see her anymore. I thanked her for helping me and told her the cloud was gone, but it never left. It's bigger than me now.

The other day, I broke into the cabinet where they keep my pills. It was easy to do. And I opened one bottle and poured the pills out on the kitchen counter. No one was home, and I thought how easy it would be to take them all and crawl into my bed, hold Sir Croaks-a-lot, and go to sleep forever. And then it wouldn't matter, this thing I let him do, this thing growing in me.

Then I thought of Dev, and I couldn't do it.

Keat came home and caught me putting my pills up. I made him promise not to tell Mom and Dad, and then he hugged me for a long time. I thought about how he had looked at Dev during the Fourth of July and I wanted to punch his face, but I let him hold me. I want to tell him that Dev loves me, that she's not into him, but I can't out her like that.

It doesn't matter. This will all end eventually. It has to.

CHAPTER 43
DEVON

July 2012

The day after the Fourth, Devon lay in bed for a long time replaying her kiss with Keaton. It was only one kiss, but there was a promise in it, one she knew she wouldn't be able to keep. Already, she felt sick at what she'd done. She loved Summer; she knew this with every part of her. But she was learning that she didn't always love herself when she was with her. Every time she went along with something Summer wanted to do instead of standing up for herself, she felt like little pieces were being torn from her. And with Keaton . . . with him, it was the opposite. When she was with him, it was like she was expanding, her mind free to express whatever she wanted without fear that he'd reject her. She didn't feel on edge with him like she did with Summer, not knowing which version of her she would get each day.

Devon threw on a tank top and cutoff shorts and went downstairs to grab a banana before she headed to the library to return books. Her heart skipped when she saw her mother in the kitchen getting a cup of coffee.

"You're off work today?"

"I lost a shift," her mother said with a hint of irritation as she stirred in some cream. She scanned Devon's outfit. "Modesty is a virtue. Go change into one of the summer dresses I got you."

"Yes, ma'am."

She went back to her room and changed into a long blue cotton dress with cap sleeves and an empire waist. When she came back down to the kitchen, her mother simply said, "Better."

Now she wouldn't be able to ride her bike into town. The heat was stifling, her dress sticking to her legs as she walked, her backpack filled with books slung over her shoulder.

After she dropped the books off, she went by Dotty's Ice Cream to grab a soda for herself and to get a Dr. Pepper–ice cream float to bring to Summer. Thankfully, Jackie wasn't working at the counter, but Holly was there paying for ice cream ahead of her. She knew she couldn't keep avoiding people who'd been at Ryan's party, that she'd have to face them every day once summer break was over, but she didn't want to see Holly's arrogant face, so she started to leave.

"Devon!" Holly's voice sang behind her. "Hey, wait up."

She kept going for the door, but Holly caught up to her outside, an ice cream cone in her hand.

"Hey, didn't you hear me?" Holly asked, her tan face scrunching up as the sun hit her.

"What do you want?" Devon crossed her arms. "To laugh at me some more?"

Holly blinked at her. "It was really shitty what Ryan did. He did it to me too. Sophomore year."

"And yet you still hang out with him."

Holly shrugged, her dark waves perfectly in place as always. "Guys are assholes. You get used to it."

She thought of Keaton. "Not all guys are like that."

Holly stared at her with knowing eyes. "You know, I saw you." She sucked in her lips like she was weighing what to say next. "I was trying to find you, to check on you after what Ryan did, and . . ." She blushed hard. "I wasn't like creeping on you guys or anything."

So, it was Holly she had heard gasp before shutting the door to the office. "You told people about it."

"Only Jenna, I promise."

Jenna, the school's biggest gossip. Summer would definitely find out now.

"You know, you should be careful with Keaton," Holly said, a note of jealousy in her voice. "He's just using you because you're naive and will do anything he wants. I mean, look at you and look at him. No offense, but he's way out of your league."

Before she could stop herself, Devon blurted out, "If he's out of mine, then he's light-years out of yours."

As she walked away, she heard Holly yell, "I was just trying to help you!"

Devon stopped by the drugstore for sodas and a package of mini Snickers, not wanting to go to Summer's empty handed. Her hair was plastered to her sweaty face when she made it to the Harrisons'. Keaton answered the door with only a pair of lounge shorts on, the sharp lines of his muscles distracting her for a second.

"Hey," she said, skirting past him to reach the cool air inside.

He eyed the Dr. Pepper and Snickers in her hand. "Summer's out in the barn. She's been going out there a lot."

"Oh." She couldn't imagine what could be so interesting in the old barn where they stored ancient-looking farm equipment and furniture Summer once said belonged to their great-grandparents. She needed a few minutes in the air-conditioning before she could even consider going outside again.

"Want something to drink?" he asked, seeing she had emptied the soda she'd bought for herself on her way there.

"Uh, sure."

They went to the kitchen, and he pulled a cold bottle of water from the fridge for her.

She leaned against the counter, holding the bottle to the back of her neck to cool herself before opening it and drinking half of it down.

"You look beautiful," he said.

"You mean sweaty?" She smiled, his compliment giving her a small boost of confidence after what Holly had said to her earlier. "I almost had a heatstroke getting here."

He moved closer until he was standing right in front of her. "I keep thinking about last night and . . . what we did before." He leaned into her, his hands gripping the countertop on either side of her. "I dreamed about you."

"Oh, yeah? What was it about?"

He suppressed a grin, his eyes bright with that mischievous look he sometimes got, a look she hadn't seen from him in a long time.

"Tell me," she said, nudging his chest.

"I'd rather show you."

Something in his tone shot sparks to her pelvis, and her legs turned weak. He kissed her, pressing her into the kitchen counter as his hands tugged her hips flush to him. He sucked her bottom lip, lightly pulling the skin with his teeth, and she melted into him, her body fully aware of the hardness through his shorts and the growing slickness between her legs.

"I want to taste you." His whispered words were warm against her lips, making her shiver. "Do you want to go to my room?"

Her stomach tightened. Was he asking her to have sex with him? The way he spoke so confidently, it was like he'd said these words before. Holly's stupid taunting from earlier snaked inside her head, poisoning the pleasure of Keaton's hands on her. "Do you think I'm naive?"

Keaton leaned back from her, confusion in his eyes. "What?"

"Do you think I'm a naive person?"

"No."

She chewed the inside of her bottom lip. "How many people have you had sex with?"

The confusion on his face grew. "One. Why?"

"How old were you?"

"Fifteen, and before you ask, it wasn't with anyone here."

"Why would you be into someone like me?"

"What do you mean?"

"Is it because you think I'm easy? That I'll have sex with you because I don't know any better?"

He shook his head, his eyes wide. "I don't understand where this is coming from, Dev. We've been friends for like two years, and I've always liked you. I just never thought you were into me, but I'm into you because I like talking to you. I can be however I want to be around you, and you don't care. You don't judge me. You're the only person who doesn't expect anything from me. I can just . . . be with you." He paused, the confusion in his eyes softening. "And I don't think you're easy. Yeah, of course I want to have sex with you, but we don't have to do anything you don't want to do."

His confession made her feel lightheaded. She'd allowed Holly to seed doubt in her, and now she felt embarrassed for questioning him. The truth was she felt the same way with him, and she wanted nothing more than to go up to his room and have him show her what he had dreamed about, but she was still in love with Summer, and she could walk into the house at any minute. She placed her hand on the center of his bare chest.

"Can you keep this a secret?" she said. "Us?"

His mouth tensed. "Why? Because of your parents?"

"Yes," she lied.

She felt his chest lift with his breath. "I don't like secrets."

"Please, Keat." She kissed him and felt tension enter his body again, his muscles tightening under her hands, and she hated being the one who put it there. "Please."

He searched her eyes before finally saying, "Okay. For now."

"Thank you." She kissed him again and slipped from his arms, grabbing the Dr. Pepper and bag of Snickers. "See you later."

As she walked toward the barn, she told herself what she was doing wasn't so bad. Summer had been with someone else, too, was probably still with them. The mystery texter and whoever she'd spoken with at Holly's party, maybe different people or the same, she wasn't sure. And Mason Turner. She'd been with him.

She told herself this was only a small secret, but she knew deep down she was setting a land mine, and one day she'd step on it.

CHAPTER 44
DEVON

2025

Before the early-evening ice cream social, Devon sat at the diner eating a meat loaf sandwich for dinner. She wished they served alcohol, because her nerves were shot after a night of tossing and turning, everything Keaton had said racing through her thoughts. She'd been so close to telling him why he sensed her withholding from him, but she allowed her fear to take over again.

Speaking the truth to him would mean admitting to herself not only how much she had hurt him but how much of herself she'd lost in the process. For now, she wanted the illusion that she could make it right, and finding out what had happened with Summer was the beginning and the end of any redemption she could hope for with him. Whatever happened afterward she would face head-on. She had no other choice.

"Can I get you anything else?" Jackie asked her.

"No, thanks."

Jackie leaned down, placing the tab in front of her. "After you pay, come out back. I have to tell you something."

Devon paid and left the diner. She found Jackie by the big dumpster behind the building, her mouth on her vape pen.

She held it out to Devon. "Care for some stress relief?"

"Actually, yeah. Thanks." She took a hit and handed it back.

"So, the sheriff was in here earlier, during the lunch shift. He was talking to Boyd Harrison."

Keaton's uncle chatting with the sheriff? As far as she knew, Boyd had few friends in town, and the sheriff certainly wasn't one of them.

"What about?" she asked, taking the vape pen from Jackie again and hitting it.

"I heard the sheriff telling Boyd about you going around asking questions about Summer, how you're saying her death seems suspicious. Boyd looked really upset, and then they were whispering something to each other I couldn't hear. Looked like they were arguing." She took the vape from Devon and took another hit. "I just thought you should know people are starting to talk about you like you're crazy."

"And what do you care what they say about me?"

Jackie smirked. "Well, it's certainly not because I like you."

"You've still never told me why you've hated me all these years." She took the pen back from Jackie and sucked, enjoying the buzz she was getting.

Jackie's dark eyes leveled her. "Because you didn't deserve her."

"Yet she never chose you." As soon as she said it and saw the look of pain on Jackie's face, she regretted it. Back in the day, she had guessed Jackie's feelings for Summer, but she was never sure. She was now.

"*I* was a good friend." Jackie spit on the ground, almost hitting Devon's sandals. "I wasn't the one fucking her twin brother behind her back."

"I never fucked him." Not technically, like it made a difference.

"Doesn't matter. You still get to go around town pretending you don't eat pussy, and no one's the wiser. You still get to be the good little Christian girl." She grabbed the vape pen back from Devon and put it in her waist apron. "But you'll never be free. Me, though? I've always been free in this fucking town, even when I was face down in the mud with a boot on the back of my neck getting the shit kicked out of me, so you can go fuck yourself in your safe little closet."

Jackie turned to go back inside the diner.

"She was pregnant," Devon said. "My friend at the OKCPD confirmed it."

Jackie stopped dead for a moment, not turning around, her shoulders lifting slightly before she opened the heavy back door and disappeared inside.

People were walking by, moving toward the front of Calvary Baptist, where the ice cream social was already underway. She followed them, her head fuzzy from the weed and what Jackie had said to her.

Jackie was right, and she hated it. She wasn't free, not as long as her parents thought she was straight. But Summer hadn't been out either, not within the community anyway. And if her family knew, Summer never talked about it. She always assumed Summer had to hide like her, that she was as scared as Devon was after seeing how everyone treated Jackie.

She glanced around, looking for Keaton. He probably wouldn't show. She noticed Shrader Thompson looking her way, and she went over to him.

"Hey, Devon," he said. "You doing okay?"

"Not really."

He appeared concerned and moved closer to her. "I've heard some things around town." He lowered his voice. "So, you don't think Summer died by suicide?"

Devon suppressed a sigh. The rumor mill never took a day off in Arkana. "No, I don't."

"Why?"

Devon looked around to make sure no one could overhear. "I have a police contact in the city. There were no hard drugs in her system." She paused a beat. "And she was pregnant."

Shrader looked shocked. "Pregnant?" He stared at the ground as he appeared to process the information. "But maybe that's why she committed suicide. Maybe she took something that doesn't show up on tests."

"There are other strange things that don't add up."

"Like what?" he asked.

More people gathered near them, and she didn't need anyone over-hearing their conversation. "I'm sorry, but I need to find my parents before my mother sends out a search party for me."

"Sure thing," he said. "We can talk later if you want."

Devon made her way over to the tent where the ice cream bar was set up.

"Devon!" her mother said, coming up to her. "Been looking all over for you." She nodded toward the various tubs of ice cream. "I made sure they had some buttered pecan for you."

Her favorite flavor. Her heart squeezed a little at her mother's thoughtfulness. "Thanks, Mama."

She got a couple of scoops in a disposable bowl and let her mother drag her over to where Holly stood with her husband, their chocolate-smeared toddler twins running circles around them like tiny maniacs. Holly's husband, a man Devon vaguely recognized as someone who'd graduated a few years ahead of them, openly stared at her chest as they greeted each other.

"I told Devon about your business," her mother said, touching Holly's arm. "How you have the cutest clothes."

Holly gave Devon an uncomfortable smile. "It's just for fun, really, to get the girls together and chat. Mike is the COO of the Pepsi plant, so it's not like I do it for money, but I've helped a lot of ladies here get into it. You know, so they can be their own boss."

More like so they could give Holly more earning power without her having to work. "Wasn't there a documentary about LuLaRoe and how a ton of people lost thousands of dollars?" Devon said. "But I'm sure it's no longer a pyramid scheme. Right?"

Holly looked like she'd swallowed a bullfrog. "My business *empowers* women in need." She glared at her. "Speaking of women in need, I heard you've been chatting it up with Jackie Byrd." A nasty grin spread on her face. "Makes sense you'd take an interest in each other since you have *so* much in common."

Devon's eyes narrowed. "How so?"

"Oh, you know."

Heat ran up Devon's body to the back of her neck. If Holly was trying to out her in front of her mother, she was about to get a fist to her face. She didn't know how Holly knew, and her mind frantically tried to remember if she had accidentally made a Pride post public on her Facebook page. She glanced at her mother, who looked confused as hell.

"What does she mean, Devon?" her mother said, her face flushed from the heat. "You and Jackie Byrd. You have nothing in common with that woman. You're not . . ." She let the unspoken word dangle in the air along with her unsure smile.

Holly's pouty mouth twisted in an attempt to hide her grin, and the heat in Devon's neck traveled to her head, boiling into a horrible mixture of shame and rage. She looked at her mother again, and her mind flashed on all the ignorant, hateful Facebook posts she had made over the years, posts that had made Devon want to crawl deeper within herself when all she truly wanted to do was beat her chest and scream the truth about who she was. She felt the words burning their way up her throat, wanting to spew from her lips, words she had suppressed for decades, and she couldn't stop herself from opening her mouth. "Queer," she blurted, loud enough for anyone around to hear. "Is that the word you're so afraid to say, Mother? Then let me help you out—I'm *fucking queer*! Bisexual, to be exact. And, no, Holly, I'm not interested in Jackie, and I'm sure as hell not interested in eating a nasty, rotten pussy like yours!"

Without thinking, she threw her bowl of half-melted ice cream at Holly, luxuriating in her anger as she watched it slide down her white dress. It wasn't just Holly who had backed her into a corner, it was everything about Arkana, the entire culture to suppress and squeeze the uniqueness out of people until they fit into neat little boxes. She was done with contorting herself to fit in—for the town, for her mother, for anyone.

Her eyes darted to her mother again, hoping to see some kind of reaction other than the horrified shock on her face. She didn't know what she expected—for her mother to pull her into an embrace? Tears pooled in Devon's eyes, but she didn't want to blink, didn't want to give anyone—least of all her mother—the satisfaction of seeing them fall down her cheeks. She stared at her mother, willing her to speak, to do anything but stand there. Her heartbeat pulsed behind her eyes, an excruciating jolt with each thrum, but her mother didn't move. Devon slowly turned to walk away. That's when she heard her mother's gasping cry, the others around her mother comforting her, driving Devon to keep walking without turning around. As she hurried toward the diner where her car was parked, the tears she now so desperately wanted to release stubbornly suspended in her eyes, she saw Jackie leaning against a tree, an ice cream cone in her hand. Her mouth was parted, eyes wide as quarters, and Devon realized she had witnessed the scene, or at least heard what she'd yelled out.

Then Jackie raised her ice cream cone in salute, a huge smile on her face.

CHAPTER 45
DEVON

July 2012

After leaving Keaton in the kitchen, Devon walked over to the barn with the soda and bag of Snickers, the long summer dress her mother had made her wear still sticking to her legs with every step. She found Summer huddled in a corner next to some of the antique furniture Mrs. Harrison had once said she was going to restore someday. She was sitting at an old desk. When Devon stepped closer, Summer startled and tucked something into the desk drawer before she stood up.

"What are you doing?" Devon asked, wondering why Summer looked so flustered.

"Nothing." She motioned to the soda and candy and smiled. "That for me?"

"Yeah." She placed them on the desk where Summer had been sitting. "I felt bad about you having to leave the Fourth of July celebration early."

"Were the fireworks good?"

She'd missed the fireworks when she was with Keaton. "They were okay. You feeling better today?"

"Yeah. It was just the heat." Summer opened the soda and drank down a few swigs. Her eyes scanned down Devon's body. "Is that dress for me too?"

Devon grinned. "You like it?"

Summer moved closer to her and ran her hands over the dress's cap sleeves before pushing them down her shoulders. "You should wear it like this."

Then Summer leaned in and kissed her shoulder, then her neck, sending a rush of warmth between her legs. The guilt of having kissed Keaton only minutes before was immediate, the nausea making her draw back from Summer's touch.

"You okay?" Summer said.

"I guess the heat's getting to me too."

"We should go swimming at the pond. You can wear one of my suits. Come on."

When Summer commanded her like she did now, it was like Devon's brain shut off, and all she could do was follow her. They went back to the house to change, Summer handing her one of the dozen bikinis she seemed to own, this time a lilac-colored one. She couldn't help watching as Summer shed her clothes with no sense of shyness, her body appearing softer and curvier, like she had gained a little weight. Devon wished she could be that confident to undress without a thought, but she found herself trying to shield her nakedness as she quickly changed.

They ran into Keaton in the hallway.

"Where are y'all going?" he asked.

"Chullusa."

"Wait up. I want to come."

But Summer kept moving down the hallway and to the stairs, Devon hovering there for a moment before following her out of the house. They were at the end of the long driveway when Devon heard Keaton running up behind them.

"Why don't you go hang out with Mason and them?" Summer said as she marched on through the tall grass toward the woods. "You have a truck now. You can do whatever you want."

Devon glanced at Keaton, who was staring at the back of Summer's head, his jaw tight.

"You don't own the pond," he muttered. "Hey, did you tell Dev you're quitting track?"

"What?" Devon jogged to catch up to Summer. "Are you really quitting?"

Summer slowed down some. "Thanks a lot, Keat."

"So, you are?" she asked again, trying to read Summer's face.

"I don't know. Probably."

"Why?"

"I'm just done with it and all the bitches on the team." She looked at Devon. "Not you, of course."

If Summer was going to quit the team, Devon didn't know if she wanted to stay on, although she wasn't sure how she'd tell Coach Thompson. But she didn't want to be stuck at practice with people like Holly Lynch. As they walked along the path in the woods to the pond, she tried to shake off the sense that everything in her life was being swept away, as if by a tornado thrashing through a town, leaving nothing but destruction in its wake.

Thankfully, no one else was at the pond when they arrived. After Ryan's party, she couldn't imagine being around others in a bathing suit without the fear of someone targeting her again. She noticed Keaton's gaze traveling along her body before she began wading into the water. Summer was already up to her neck, her eyes on Keaton.

"God, you're such a perve!" she hollered. "Stop eye-fucking Dev!"

His face turned a deep red.

Devon heard Summer mumble, "So gross," before ducking under the water. When she popped back up, she was next to her. She splashed Devon, giggling. Under the water, Summer's hand went to Devon's breast, causing her to gasp in surprise. She looked across the water at

Keaton, his eyes glued on them for a second before he floated onto his back.

"He can't see us," Summer whispered.

She let Summer shift the bikini top aside, her fingers running across her hardened nipples. Her sudden thoughts disturbed her, of enjoying what Summer was doing and being equally aroused by Keaton not knowing. She could tell it was hard for Summer to keep afloat while touching her, so she submerged herself and tugged on Summer's hand to come under too.

She couldn't see a thing in the murky water, but she felt Summer's lips press to hers in a kiss, their hands quickly touching each other's breasts before they had to come up for air. They sucked in a breath and went back under again and again, seeing how far they could go, sucking and nibbling, before their lungs burned for oxygen.

"What are you doing?" Keaton called out to them when they came back up a fourth time.

Devon half laughed. "Seeing who can hold their breath the longest." Summer burst out laughing.

Keaton swam closer to them, and she knew that was the end of their game. She sensed the tension in him, the frustration in his eyes, and she wished he weren't with them. She ducked under the water a little to adjust her bikini top back over her chest.

Keaton splashed Summer. "I forgot to tell you. Jackie came by earlier, but you were still in bed, so I told her to come by later." He glanced at Devon and back to Summer. "She said you're not answering your phone and she really needs to talk to you."

Devon's eyes shot to Summer, whose face gave no clue as to what she was thinking.

"You should've told her to fuck off," Summer said. Then she swam back to the shore.

Devon watched as Summer grabbed her towel and slipped on her flip-flops.

"Hey!" Devon yelled. "Are you leaving?"

"Yeah, I'm tired. See you later."

It seemed like Summer was always tired now, but she knew there was more to it, something heavier under the surface she didn't understand.

"Okay," she said. "See you later."

She no longer wanted to be in the water, so she swam to the shoreline, lay out under the sun, and closed her eyes. When she felt Keaton's shadow over her, she squinted up at him, at the strange satisfaction in his eyes, and she didn't know why, but she wanted to kick him.

CHAPTER 46
DEVON

2025

I'm out. The words circled in Devon's mind, surreal and exhilarating and utterly terrifying. Everyone knew now. It wouldn't take long for the gossip to travel. She imagined the church elders huddled together, the whispers of how sorry they felt for her parents for their only child being queer. An abomination in the eyes of God.

She sat in her car outside Keaton's house, her eyes puffy from crying and her throat scratchy from her feverish laughter as she had driven down the darkened roads. There was no taking it back, and she felt giddy but also untethered. Her first thought was to see Keaton, to hold on to someone who wouldn't judge her. She looked up at his house, the glow through his windows evidence of him being awake. Just as she was exiting her car, his front door opened and he appeared on the porch, his arms crossed.

"I was wondering how long you were going to stay out here," he said. As she got closer to him, concern etched his forehead. "What's wrong?"

"I, uh, I came out at the ice cream social." Every emotion clenched her chest in a vise grip, and the sobs broke free in her again. "Fucking Holly . . . she pushed me, and I . . . it came out. Oh, God, everyone knows . . . everyone . . . my mother . . ."

She couldn't catch a breath, her chest too tight and her face going numb as she felt herself disassociating from her surroundings. Keaton took her in his arms, and she collapsed against his strong body.

"It's going to be okay." He stroked her hair as he whispered more reassurances to her. When her crying slowed down, he said, "Let's go inside."

She followed him into his home in a daze, her mind barely registering her body's movements. He took her to his living room and sat her down on his deep leather couch, one that appeared secondhand, and it was so comfortable she sank back and closed her eyes with a sudden desire to fall asleep.

Keaton touched her knee, and she opened her eyes to see him offering her a tumbler of amber liquid, the honey fragrance floating up to her, inviting her to drink it all. The bourbon went down with a searing burn, the vanilla-spice warmth flowing through her limbs.

"Thank you," she said.

He motioned to the bottle of Woodford on his coffee table. "You want another? I busted out the good stuff." He smiled a little. "Seemed an appropriate occasion."

"Yeah." She wanted anything to quell the grief in her, of knowing she would likely no longer have a family.

He poured her another and one for himself. Then he raised his glass. "Here's to saying fuck them all."

She smiled with tears heavy in her eyes and raised her glass. "Fuck them all."

He sat next to her on the couch, his woodsy, citrusy scent making her want to press her face to his chest again and inhale.

"I wish I could've seen it," he said. "At the risk of sounding cheesy, I'm proud of you."

"Thanks." She sipped the bourbon, trying to ignore how Keaton's hand was resting near her leg and how much she wanted him to touch her. "Jackie witnessed it. We, uh, talked before it happened. She told me your uncle was talking to Sheriff Wright about me looking into Summer's death. Jackie couldn't hear what else they were talking about, but she said it looked like they were arguing."

Keaton crossed his arms, his expression contemplative. "My uncle hates the sheriff. I can't imagine why he'd give him the time of day."

"Maybe you could talk to him and find out."

He gave a short jerk of his head. "Talking to my uncle is like trying to give a cat a bath. If he doesn't want to talk, he won't, especially when it comes to me."

She leaned forward, resting the glass of bourbon on her knees. "Why?"

"He doesn't like change, and he sees me and the ideas I have for the farm as a threat instead of the truth, which is to save what we have left. If we even can. He fights me on everything and spends money on things we don't need, like new equipment." He drank the rest of his bourbon in one go.

Devon touched his forearm. "You can leave this place, you know? Move to the city and go to school, get your engineering degree. Do something you want to do."

"I'm almost thirty-one years old, Dev. You think it's that easy to start over somewhere else? Everything I have is tied to here, in this land. I have people who rely on me. Not just my mom but the migrant workers. They have families to feed, too, and they have a hard enough time between the mayor and the sheriff giving them trouble."

Devon had never thought of that, but she knew how unhappy he was in this life he was forced to live with. She didn't want him to be trapped here, suffocating like she had for so many years. Like Summer had. "You could sell your house and go to school with the money. And you could live with me. If you wanted, until you find work. Your uncle can hire someone to help out here."

He stared at her for a long time, a cascade of emotions flowing across his face. "Live with you? Do you really want that?"

She took his hand and squeezed it. "I want you to be happy."

His gaze turned hopeful. "I . . . I want to ask you something, but I'm afraid of your answer. I'm afraid it might break me."

Her heart sped up. She couldn't handle whatever was brewing inside him. Not right then. "Then don't ask it."

His lips tightened. "Why are you so afraid? I know you want this as much as I do." His eyes implored her as his hand went to her thigh. "I feel it."

She felt it, too, but she wasn't prepared to lose him now by telling him the truth she'd been holding on to for thirteen years. But she knew those old secrets weren't the only thing holding her back from him. The horrible memories of the mansion speared through her, and she wanted to keep them locked tight, but he needed to hear it so he could understand how much she had changed from the girl he used to know. "Keat . . . I need to tell you something. Something bad that happened to me last year."

Worry entered his face. "Okay."

She couldn't look at him as she told him about being held captive and sexually assaulted. She even told him about getting an IUD because she feared being raped again and not having access to legal abortion services. After a few moments of silence, she looked up at him. "I haven't been with a man since then. I haven't been with anyone. I'm . . . scared of how it might be. How I might react."

Keaton took her hand. "Shit. I'm so sorry you went through that."

"My parents don't know. Most people don't. My name and the other survivors were kept out of the news, but that might change. The court date to prosecute the perpetrators keeps getting delayed, so it's not over yet."

He shook his head. "I shouldn't have pushed you. You told me you weren't ready, and I . . . fuck. I'm sorry."

"It's okay," she said, feeling relief wash over her from sharing this part of her with him. It was one less thing she had to keep hidden from him. She took the bottle of bourbon and raised it. "Wanna play really loud music and get drunk with me?"

A slight smile raised his lips. "Absolutely."

SUMMER'S JOURNAL

July 2012

I finally saw Jackie but only because Keat's dumb ass let her in the house. She was so desperate for me to believe her, but I know she told someone about the test because why else would he ask me if I took one? Who did she tell? She doesn't know about him, but she told someone, and he found out. How could it not be her? She was literally the only person who knew. She asked me if it was positive, and I lied.

I still can't believe Jackie fucking gave me away like that when I defended her after she was kicked off the team. I knew those bitches set her up. I thought we were like this secret queer sisterhood, having each other's backs. And I really tried to like her like that, but I couldn't because of Dev, and she got all crazy. And then she does this to me.

I swear if I die, it's because of her.

CHAPTER 47
DEVON

July 2012

Summer was acting strange, like she was tunneling further into a place Devon couldn't reach her. Whether they were in Summer's room listening to music or hanging out at the pond trying to stay cool, Summer's mind seemed to be somewhere else. And she didn't want to go anywhere now, not even to Lake Murray to camp like they had planned.

"Let's go to town and get some drinks," Devon suggested, feeling restless lying on Summer's bed. She had tried to kiss Summer, to touch her, but Summer didn't seem interested in doing anything but watching TV.

"It's too hot."

"It'll be good to get out. You haven't been on your bike in forever. Plus, you're out of Dr. Pepper." She playfully nudged Summer. "Please."

"Fine."

They rode their bikes over to Main Street, the heat radiating off the asphalt, making everything in the distance appear as a mirage. Bill's Pharmacy, with its air-conditioning on full blast, felt like heaven when they stepped inside.

"Hi, Mrs. Johnson," Devon said.

Mrs. Johnson greeted her, but her smile faded when she saw Summer. "You, Harrison girl, are no longer welcome in here."

Devon looked at Summer, whose sweaty face went red.

"Why not?" Devon asked, completely confused.

"This doesn't concern you, Devon, but your friend needs to wait outside." Mrs. Johnson's eyes stayed on Summer.

Devon didn't know what to say. She'd never seen Mrs. Johnson turn anyone away from the store before.

Summer looked like she was about to cry. "It's okay, Dev. Will you get me a Dr. Pepper?" She handed Devon a few dollar bills.

"Yeah."

Summer left, and Devon walked over to the cooler of cold drinks to get their sodas. When she placed them on the counter for Mrs. Johnson, she did so slowly, still in shock at how Summer had been treated.

Mrs. Johnson offered her a gentle smile as she took the cash Devon handed to her. "You're a good girl. You should mind the company you keep."

"I don't understand what she did," Devon said. "Why can't Summer come in?"

Mrs. Johnson sighed and said in a lowered voice, "Don't be telling anyone this, but she stole something. Mr. Johnson saw it on the security camera. He rarely looks at that thing, but Summer was acting so funny that he checked the footage."

"What did she steal?"

"It doesn't matter, honey. Stealing's stealing. Her parents ain't right for keeping those kids away from church and learning right from wrong, and that's the only reason why we didn't feel the need to press charges. But we can't have someone like that in our shop."

Devon was in a daze as she left the store, the sodas sweating in her hands. Summer was sitting on a bench outside the barbershop under the shade of the awning. She sat next to her and handed her the Dr. Pepper.

"Mrs. Johnson said you stole something." She searched Summer's face and saw tears in her eyes. "Did you really?"

"Yeah." Summer opened the soda and chugged it until half of it was gone. "It was nothing, and it was forever ago."

"When?"

"Like a month ago."

"What did you steal?"

Summer looked at Devon for a long time, her body tense as her hand gripped the soda bottle tight enough to make an indentation in the plastic. "It was just a lip gloss. It wasn't a big deal."

For a second, she thought about admitting to stealing something, too, but she didn't want to explain why she had taken a box of condoms. She now knew it was only luck that had kept her from being caught. Surely, she'd been taped, too, but Mr. Johnson must not have checked.

"Maybe you can give it back and say you're sorry," Devon said. "They're nice people. I'm sure they'll forgive you and forget about it."

Summer jumped up from the bench. "No. Fuck them. I'll go to Git N Split if I want a drink."

Devon stood up, too, and felt the sweat run down her back to her jean shorts. "What do you want to do now?"

A sly grin spread across Summer's face. "I want to go to the grove."

Devon smiled. They hadn't been to the grove since the day they'd taken shrooms. "Let's go."

Even with the heat causing the delicate blue wildflowers to wilt, the grove still looked magical when they parked their bikes against a tree.

Devon kissed Summer's mouth, the salt from her sweat slightly burning her lips.

Summer pulled her to the ground and straddled her waist. She held Devon's hands above her head and leaned in, brushing her lips to hers. "I want to taste you."

Devon flinched at hearing the same words Keaton had said to her when they were in the kitchen, his hardness pressed into her.

"It's okay," Summer said, her lips curling up. "Don't be shy."

Then she tugged Devon's shorts and underwear down and opened her legs. When Summer kissed those tender parts of her, she knew what Keaton had wanted to do with her in his bedroom.

Summer stopped and looked up at her, smiling. "You taste sweet, just like I imagined."

She dipped her head back down between her legs and Devon fell into the sensations of Summer's tongue, her eyes focused on the dark-honey tangle of Summer's hair until the pleasure was too much and she could no longer keep them open.

CHAPTER 48
DEVON

2025

She was in a dream. She could tell because Summer was standing in the grove, a slight glow emanating from her. Macayla was there, too, farther off in the distance, her face blurring into the woods. Summer bent down and plucked out a bundle of the tiny blue wildflowers and held them out to Devon, a beatific smile on her face. It felt like an offering of forgiveness, until Summer yanked her hand back and shoved the flowers into her mouth, gnawing on them with a brutal fire in her eyes.

"I'm sorry," Devon cried, choking on her tears. "I'm so sorry. Please, don't hate me. I'm sorry, I'm sorry, I'm sorry!"

Something touched her shoulder, and she startled awake, her eyes flashing open. A shirtless Keaton stared down at her with damp hair.

"You okay?" he said. "You were yelling."

She swiped a hand under her eyes and felt wetness. She sat up, her head pounding, and realized she was in Keaton's bed. She was fully clothed, her mouth desert dry, and she remembered them drinking the bourbon the night before, her way to escape her memories and her growing desire for him. But there was no escape. She could sense it, this thread in them pulling tighter and tighter until they'd either collide or break. Even now, she wanted to tug him down to the mattress and feel his weight on her, to make her forget the wrongs she had done, and the wrongs done to her.

"Yeah, I'm okay," she said. "Just a bad dream."

His expression turned thoughtful. "Do you get them a lot?"

"Yeah, but this one wasn't about that." She knew he meant her assault. Surprisingly, she hadn't had many flashbacks or dreams about her assault since being in Arkana. That would probably change during the trial whenever it was set. "I think it was the alcohol."

He smiled wryly. "Whiskey will do that. I made some coffee if you want some."

Keaton and his bare chest left the bedroom, and it took her a few moments to shake the lust from her body. When she padded over to his small kitchen, he had a mug waiting for her.

"My hero." She took a grateful sip.

He leaned against the kitchen counter, holding his own mug. "Do you remember what you said last night? About me leaving Arkana and moving in with you?"

"Yeah."

"Did you mean it, or was that the whiskey talking?"

Why had she said it to him? Whiskey was like a goddamn truth serum. "Yeah. I meant it."

He set his mug down on the counter and went over to her. He held her upper arms, and she breathed in the fresh citrus scent of his body-wash. She imagined how horrible she must smell to him after a night of drinking and no shower. "Do you see how confusing that is for me, Dev, inviting me to live with you?"

"I'm not trying to confuse you."

"But you are." He let go of her arms. "You always have. You know I have feelings for you." He huffed out a humorless laugh. "But I have no idea how you feel about me. And then you tell me about what you went through last year, and I feel like a complete asshole for wanting to kiss you, for wanting to . . ." He looked down for a moment before holding her gaze again. "For wanting more than you can give."

"Keat." She wanted to hold him, but she didn't want to keep hurting him, so she squeezed the mug in her hands instead. "Right now, all I can focus on is finding out the truth. We need to know why your uncle was arguing with the sheriff. It might have something to do with Summer."

He let out an exasperated sigh. "I can't do this with you right now. I need to get to the fields." She could tell he was trying to control his frustration, and his expression softened some. "Have more coffee, get something to eat. Stay however long you want."

He left the kitchen, and she heard the front door shut.

She found her shoes and purse in the living room. She went to the bathroom and searched through his medicine cabinet for some toothpaste so she could finger-brush her teeth. She noticed a prescription bottle on the upper shelf of the cabinet, then took it down and read it. Sertraline. An antidepressant, one she had been on herself years ago. She put it back, her mind no longer centered on brushing her teeth.

After she'd left Keaton's house, she drove over to the farm, hoping to catch Keaton's uncle. Boyd was an early riser, like Keaton's father had been, like Keaton was now. She saw Boyd unloading bags of seed from his truck and carrying them inside the house. She remembered all the bags of seed in Keaton's old bedroom, and she supposed that was where he was taking them. When he came back outside again, she was waiting by his truck.

"Good morning," she said.

"Not sure what's good about it, but I'll take your word for it." Boyd wiped sweat from his forehead with a bandanna. "Whatcha doing up so early?"

"Trying to catch you before you get too busy."

"Oh, yeah?" He tucked the bandanna in his back jean pocket. "What for?"

"I, uh, heard you were talking about me to the sheriff, and I'd like to know why."

Nothing in Boyd's expression changed. "Not much to tell. He asked to meet me for lunch, and I wasn't too keen on it, but he said it was important. Basically, he doesn't want you in Arkana, and he doesn't think we should be letting you stay here. He said you've been going around stirring up shit, trying to make up lies about Summer's death. He was worried Annie would find out and it'd put her in a bad way." He shrugged. "He isn't wrong."

"Then why were you arguing with him?"

"Who said I was arguing with him?"

She didn't want to give Jackie away. "People noticed, and it got back to me."

Boyd opened his mouth like he was about to respond, until his eyes strayed past her and stayed there. "Ah, shit."

She turned around to see what he was looking at, and her hands went to her mouth, her shock too great to even gasp.

Someone had taken a key to the passenger side of her car and scratched in all caps: "DIE U FUCKING DYKE!"

SUMMER'S JOURNAL

July 2012

I was riding over to meet Dev at the park by the elementary school, and Sheriff Wright pulled up next to me in his police car, so close that I fell off my bike. He rolled down his window and told me I needed to watch where I was going. I wanted to tell him to fuck off, but I'm not that dumb. Then he said I was lucky the Johnsons didn't press charges against me for stealing. His eyes went to my stomach, and he grinned like a fucking creep. He said I should pray hard that I lose it.

I can't believe it. Jackie was telling the truth about the test. And now I know he wasn't lying when he said he owns the police, even Sheriff Wright. He owns everything.

He tells me he can do anything he wants in this town. He says no one will miss me.

CHAPTER 49
DEVON

August 2012

No matter how hard she tried, Devon couldn't get Summer to leave the house. When she'd come over to the Harrisons', Summer would make excuses not to leave, saying it was too hot or that her bike had a flat or she didn't feel well. It was always something.

School was starting the following week, and Devon didn't want to go the rest of the break sitting on Summer's bed watching TV and eating junk food. She could see Summer gaining weight from it, though she seemed to try to hide it by wearing baggy T-shirts. She'd felt Summer's stomach one time when they were watching a show, and it had grown fuller. She didn't mind her pooch; she had one herself, after all, but it wasn't like Summer. She had always been big on running and biking so she could burn off all the calories from the loads of Dr. Pepper she drank every day. Now, she hardly left her room.

"I'm tired of sitting," Devon said, getting off Summer's bed. "Let's go swim."

"It's going to rain."

She'd seen the clouds gathering, but they'd probably move past Arkana before they released any kind of moisture.

"Then let's go swing in the barn." The week prior, Keaton had been helping his dad and uncle clean up the barn when they found an old rope swing connected to the huge rafters. His dad and uncle apparently had played on it when they were little, and then it had been tucked back up into the loft. "We still haven't tried it out."

Summer turned onto her side and reached for the bowl of popcorn she'd been snacking on. "It's old as hell. The rope will probably snap if someone gets on it."

"Well, it didn't when Keat got on it."

"Then go do it."

"God, Summer, what is wrong with you?" Devon wanted to shake her out of the somber mood entrapping her. "You've been acting weird for weeks, and I can't take it anymore."

Summer sat up in her bed, Sir Croaks-a-lot in her hands. "Sorry I can't be sunshine and rainbows all the fucking time."

Devon sighed. "I don't expect that. It's just . . . we used to talk."

"We still talk."

"Not about meaningful things."

"Oh, you mean like you do with Keat?" Summer mocked.

It felt like a slap because it was true. Conversations with Summer were easy and fun, with only the rare times when Devon felt like she was seeing under the surface. And it frustrated the hell out of her because she knew they could be even closer if Summer opened up more.

"I know something's wrong," Devon said. "Why won't you talk to me about it?"

Summer looked down at her stuffed frog. "I'm fine. Go play in the barn if you want. I don't mind."

Summer's cell phone buzzed with a text, then another. Someone had been texting since Devon arrived, but Summer wouldn't look at her phone.

"Aren't you going to check it?" Devon said, jealousy weaving its way in her mind. She remembered the text she had seen after Summer had waxed her. "It might be someone who wants to lick your *cunt* again."

The foreign word felt wicked on her tongue, but she got an odd joy watching Summer's face light up with anxiety.

"Just go. I'm tired anyway." As if to prove her point, Summer rolled over to face the window, the blinds blocking out most of the sunlight.

"Fine."

She would go to the barn, but not to play on the swing. Keaton had said Summer went out to the barn a lot, and Devon remembered how she'd surprised Summer as she was doing something. She recalled how Summer had tucked something away in a desk drawer. If she could find whatever it was, maybe it would offer a clue to Summer's strange behavior.

The heavy clouds, dark as graphite, shaded a menacing gray across the afternoon sky as she walked to the barn. She stepped inside and went to the corner that held the desk, but she found nothing in the top drawer or in the other drawers running down the right side of it. She carefully maneuvered herself between the pieces of furniture and checked anything else with drawers or nooks. Nothing.

"What are you doing back there?"

She about jumped out of her skin at hearing Keaton's voice. He was standing at the other end of the barn. "Uh, I was looking for the swing."

"You mean this one?" He grabbed the rope swing that was in clear view.

She let out a nervous laugh as he walked over to her, color rushing to her face. "You caught me."

He crossed his arms. "I've tried to find whatever she's hiding in here too."

She wiggled out from the maze of furniture and went to him. "So, you haven't found anything?"

"No." He reached out and brushed something from the front of her shirt, causing her to startle. "You had a spider on you. It was just a wolf spider, but we've found fiddlebacks in here before."

"Thanks," she said, suppressing a shudder. "So, you've noticed her acting weird too?"

"Yeah." Keaton walked back over to the swing, Devon following him, and then he took hold of the thick rope with both hands. "I've tried to talk to her, but she won't even let me in her room." He leaned into the swing a little. "She gets like this sometimes. My parents say she'll come out of it, but . . ."

Devon grabbed the rope, her fingers grazing his. "But what?"

"This feels different." He lowered his hands so that his covered her own. "I guess everyone gets like that."

"Have you?"

He looked into her eyes, a weight in them she recognized because it was the same kind she often saw in Summer's. "Sometimes, but not like her. She feels so . . . distant, you know? Like she'll never come back to herself, and I don't know how to reach her."

She was strangely relieved she wasn't the only one affected by Summer, though it hurt to see Keaton so troubled.

Keaton suddenly closed his eyes, and Devon thought he might start crying, but he raised his head toward the rafters. "Listen."

Summer had been right. It was raining, the soft tap-tap-tap on the barn roof growing louder until it was a full downpour.

"Do you want to swing?" he asked.

"No." She looked out toward the open barn door and sucked in a deep breath of the earthy air rushing inside. "Petrichor. Remember that word from the ACT prep test?"

He smiled. "It's my favorite scent. Besides you."

He leaned in and gently kissed her mouth, his hands squeezing hers into the scratchiness of the rope. She tried hard not to think of Summer closed off in her dark bedroom as Keaton's lips teasingly grazed her neck. This was what she wanted with Summer, to feel connected and desired, and her heart tightened in her chest when she realized it would likely never happen—not how she wanted it, but she didn't know how to shut off her love for Summer. She knew whatever darkness swallowing Summer would engulf her, too, if she allowed it.

Keaton was safe. She wouldn't have to hide with him. She could get her parents' approval to date him and hold hands with him in public and kiss him without worrying if someone would hurt her. But did she love him? She didn't know if a person could be in love with two people at once. All she knew was that being with him would mean never having Summer in her life again.

She pulled away from Keaton's kisses, her heart and body warring inside her, churning her stomach and making her want to puke.

"You okay?" he asked.

She didn't want to make a choice. She couldn't.

She ran from him, from the barn and out into the rain.

SUMMER'S JOURNAL

August 2012

I keep thinking about the first time. What I said and how I looked that night, and I still don't know how it happened. I was just there on the couch watching TV while the baby was sleeping, and he came back to the house alone. He said his wife wanted to stay out with her friends for a while. Then he made himself a drink and asked me if I wanted one too. Of course I wanted one. There was so much going on at home with Mom and Dad and with Jackie, and it kinda felt like I deserved one. And he had some good shit too. Like rich people stuff. I always forget how rich he is, but his house is bigger than Ryan's. Bigger than any house I've ever been in.

So, I had a couple of drinks with him, and we talked like we have before. Just normal stuff. He was so easy to talk to. I felt like I could tell him things I couldn't tell anyone else, not even Dev. Stuff about Mom and Dad. He seemed to really understand what I was going through at home. When he kissed me, it didn't feel weird, exactly, but I didn't know what to do. I felt frozen. Then he got on top of me, and it just sort of happened. And I said nothing. It didn't feel real, like I was outside of my body looking down at myself. Then it was over, and I went home. I thought it couldn't have been real. Like I imagined it all.

Everything he said was a lie. There is no farm loan. I don't know what made me say something, but I asked Mom about it the other day, and she looked at me like I was crazy. I wanted to die because I did it all for nothing.

I just want this thing out of me. I think about how everyone was treating Jackie like shit for being out, and I started hooking up with Mason so they wouldn't come at me like they did her. But then he took off the condom that first time at Trey's party, and I was so scared he wouldn't stop when I told him to, but he did. And I thought maybe it could be his, but I knew it wasn't because he was so drunk his dick went all limp. I was so fucking stupid when I kept messing with him, wanting everyone to see us together and prove to them I was straight.

And Dev saw it all, and I feel like shit for it, for not being brave enough to be with her. She doesn't know how much I love her, but how could she when I can't even say it?

I wish I could take everything back, but he knows I have proof of what he's done inside me. I don't know what he's going to do to me. I don't trust anyone here except for Dev. God, why can't I just tell her?

CHAPTER 50
DEVON

2025

"DIE U FUCKING DYKE!" The jolt of seeing those words gouged into the passenger side of her car sent waves of fear through Devon. This was why she'd never come out when she was younger. Hell, she was still careful in Oklahoma City, where there was a thriving gay community, a haven she hadn't fully appreciated until seeing those hateful words.

She wanted to believe Holly was behind it, but the truth was it could've been anyone, even the sheriff. Someone could've easily followed her to Keaton's house and done it. She was more concerned about what Boyd had said to her, that the sheriff didn't want her in Arkana. He knew his lazy-ass police department had fucked up Summer's case, and he also knew she would keep looking to find answers. The only question was whether she could find them before someone in Arkana did something even worse to get her to leave town.

When Annie saw her car, she helped her cover the words with paper bags and painter's tape. It was a temporary fix that would have to last a while since she had no money to fix it. As a thank-you to Annie, Devon spent the day helping her in the garden, weeding and harvesting ripe tomatoes and cucumbers Annie would sell at the farmers' market.

After about three hours, the heat got to them, and they went inside. Devon rested on Summer's bed, the weight of coming out to her mother hitting her again. Her father would know, every church member too. She would be ostracized by everyone.

She checked her phone; still no call attempts or text messages from her parents. Her heart sat heavy as a stone in her chest, sinking her deeper into Summer's mattress.

Somehow, she fell asleep with no dreams of her mother's disappointed face and no ghosts of Summer or Macayla haunting her. When she dragged herself from the bed, it was dusk, the sun only a gleaming blade on the horizon.

Annie was cooking when Devon went to the kitchen for a drink of water.

"Hey, hon," Annie said. "You get some rest?"

"Yeah. That heat zapped me good."

"Can you do me a favor and take this out to Keaton?" She held out a plate loaded with fried chicken. "He's in the barn doing his thing."

"Sure."

"Take some for yourself too."

As she walked over to the barn, the buttery light glowing from the open door, Devon munched on a chicken leg, the skin perfectly seasoned and crispy. She hadn't realized how hungry she was, and the chicken felt like a big hug from Annie.

"Your mom asked me to bring this to you."

Keaton looked up from his workbench and eyed the plate. "She cooks like there are five of me."

She smiled. "Moms always think we're going to starve to death, don't they?" She licked the grease from her fingers, her chest tightening with thoughts of her own mother and the possibility of never tasting her food again. "You better hurry because I just might eat all of this."

He took a piece of breast. "I heard about your car. I'm sorry. That's really messed up."

"People don't want me here. That's obvious enough," she said before taking another bite of her chicken leg.

"Not all people." He pulled a couple of beers from a cooler and handed her one.

"Well, the sheriff certainly doesn't. Your uncle said so."

"Maybe that only confirms he screwed up Summer's case. He doesn't want you digging because he knows he'll be fucked if it's exposed."

She took a long drink of the beer. "Or maybe he's covering up for someone."

"I've thought of that too." He looked at the bottle in his hand. "I've thought of too many things lately."

She gazed at him, at his golden sun-kissed skin, the lights catching the cinnamon threads in his dark-caramel hair. Earlier in the day when she was in the garden, all she could think about was what Keaton had said to her that morning, how she confused him. He was right. The same as when she'd be onstage doing burlesque, she had always teased him with the idea of something more happening between them. She knew to have a real relationship with him would require her to come clean, but she couldn't. How he'd held her the night prior, comforting her after she'd come out to her mother and told him about her assault, she wanted more than anything for him to know all the parts of her, even her most abhorrent secret. But she realized she would never be brave enough to see him hate her, so that part of her would always have to be closed to him. However wrong it was, she had to keep this one lie because she didn't want to resist her feelings for him anymore.

Nervousness tried to swallow her as she went over to his workbench and studied the crops he had made. His work was impeccable, the kind of work people paid a lot of money for. She'd found his Etsy store online, not shocked to see his flogger sets going for $400 or more.

She sensed his eyes on her as she stroked one of the crops and turned to face him, warmth pooling low in her belly. She needed to tell him how she felt about him, but she didn't know where to begin, the fluttering in her chest making it difficult to get the words out. "I have a confession." She smiled a little at him, losing her nerve even as she spoke. "When we were younger, I used to fantasize about you dominating me." She paused, willing herself to say what she really meant, which was that he made her feel whole and accepted as she was, and she wanted nothing more than to make him feel the same way, but fear tightened her throat, and all she could get out was "I still do."

He stared at her for what seemed like an eternity, his expression impenetrable, before he left the barn without a word. His reaction hit her square in the chest, and she followed him outside. He stood with his arms crossed, his back to her, looking out toward the woods in the distance, flashes of fireflies dotting the air like drops of neon.

"I can't tell if you're purposefully trying to torture me or not," he said. "Saying things like that to me . . ."

His words lingered in the warm evening air like the dying light of dusk around them.

There was no turning back now; she felt it. If she didn't admit her feelings for him, she knew he would withdraw from her, probably forever. And she wouldn't blame him.

When she went behind him and wrapped her arms around his waist, he didn't pull away. "I'm so sorry, Keat. For confusing you and not telling you how much you mean to me. How much you've always meant to me." She pressed her head against his back and squeezed him harder. "I want to be with you—I do, so much—but I don't know how to explain why I've never felt like I deserve to be happy. With you. With anyone, really."

He turned around, and she couldn't see his features well, but her heart lifted when he held her face. "Of course you deserve to be happy. But I do too. If you're not ready . . ."

She reached up and placed her hand over his. "I want to be." She pushed up on her feet and kissed him softly. He kissed her back, and they savored each other's mouths, warmth settling in her chest at being held by him.

"I have a confession too," he said, a sexy huskiness entering his voice. "I knew you were going to perform at Ponyboy."

She grinned, though she knew he couldn't see it. "Oh, yeah?"

"That wax routine you did . . . the things I've wanted to do to you."

When he kissed her hard, she felt it all the way to her toes, to the top of her head, through every inch of her. She suddenly thought of the leather crops inside the barn, of what Keaton would look like wielding one, and a wave of heat went through the center of her.

"What things would you do to me?" she whispered in his ear.

"Anything you want."

What she wanted at that moment was not to think but to feel, to take the pain and confusion she had caused him, the pain others had inflicted upon her, too, and take command of it, to transform it into something new, something healing that would bond them. He could give this to her, this exchange of power and trust, if she allowed him. "I . . . I want you to punish me."

Keaton pulled back from her. "Punish you?"

"Yes. I want you to use one of your crops on me . . . and I want you to fuck me. Hard, from behind."

His breath stuttered at her words. "Are you sure?"

Uncertainty tried to spike in her, but she was too emboldened in her desire. "Yes. This is what I want from you."

He was quiet for so long she thought her bold request might've weirded him out too much, but then his hand went to the back of her hair, gripping a fistful and tugging hard enough to bring tears to her eyes as he brought his mouth down upon hers again, deepening his kisses until she felt breathless and dizzy from the taste of his tongue.

"Go inside the barn," he commanded, his deep voice authoritative, sending a spasm of need between her thighs.

She did as he said, her mind hyperconscious of his eyes on her. She went to the center of the barn and watched as he closed the large doors on either side, her pulse singing faster, causing her to become lightheaded. Was she really ready for this? Her body screamed yes, and her mind told her Keaton would stop the second she asked him to. Yes. She was ready.

Then Keaton stood in front of her, his height intimidating, face composed but with intense desire lighting up his eyes. "You know how this works. How far do you want me to go?"

Right then, she didn't care what he did to her. She trusted him with her body, with her heart, trust and desire she feared she had lost after everything she'd been through. She looked him in the eye. "As far as you want."

An amused smile crossed his face. "Remember that later."

CHAPTER 51

DEVON

August 2012

Devon was drenched from the downpour, but she kept running far from the Harrison farm, her lungs and legs on fire as she entered the woods. She slowed to a jog and then to a walk the closer she got to the grove, to the place where she and Summer had blissed out on shrooms, their hands stroking pleasure in each other.

The rain stopped, the air cooler but heavy with the humidity. She dropped to the ground and lay flat on her back, exhaustion and confusion overtaking her. She covered her face with her hands and let the tears come fast and hard, her body shaking with sobs.

The air shifted next to her, and a hand touched her shoulder. For a moment, she imagined it was Summer's, and her breath caught, but the hand was too big, too strong as it pulled her fingers away from her face.

Keaton was propped up on one arm lying next to her, his hair and clothes wet from the rain and worry on his face. "What's wrong? Did I do something?"

She swallowed back more tears. "No. It's me. It's all me. I'm a horrible person."

"No, you aren't." He pushed a strand of wet hair from her face. "Why are you saying that?"

"I don't want to hurt you, Keat."

His warm hand cupped her cheek, and he smiled. "Then don't."

I already have.

She could've said those words, but she didn't. Instead, she pushed herself up and kissed him. He cradled her head as his urgent lips met hers, her mouth opening, eager to taste him as she ran her hands through his wet hair. Their kisses deepened, the ache in her growing, the need for him to touch her, to feel the warmth of his body against her chilled skin almost unendurable. She didn't know how to ask for what she wanted, so she found the bottom of his T-shirt and started pulling it up. He stopped kissing her for a second to remove it, and then his hands went to the edge of her shirt and paused. She nodded, and he pulled it off, the sudden exposure causing her to shiver. Shaking with nerves, she unclasped her bra, impatient to remove more of her wet clothes and feel the warming air around them.

His hand went to one of her breasts as her lips found his again. When he squeezed her nipple hard, pleasure gasped through her, and her mind no longer felt like it was within her control.

He moved on top of her, his mouth traveling down her body to her breasts, the dampness of his shorts freezing against her thighs. He was too tall for her to reach his waist to tug them down when she tried, but he noticed and paused to remove them. Her eyes went to the length of hardness in his boxer briefs, this part so foreign from her own body, and she reached out a tentative hand to touch it. The chest-deep moan he made, the same sound he'd made when she'd touched him at Ryan's party, amplified the ache between her legs, her thighs trembling from it.

She didn't know what to do, so she continued moving her hand up and down, his hand over hers, through his boxer briefs while he seemed frozen with pleasure, his ragged breathing getting faster until he stopped her.

"Fuck," he breathed out. "I want to be inside you so bad."

A zap of anxiety speared through the back of her head.

He must've seen it on her face because he immediately said, "We can wait."

She took his hand, pulling him back closer to her. "I . . . I want you to show me your dream."

His lips pricked up. "Are you sure?"

"Yeah."

She unbuttoned her jean shorts and kicked them off, but then she suddenly felt too naked, too curvy for someone like him to want, and shame burrowed in her. Then he gazed at her body, his eyes lit with wonderment, and she no longer felt any of those things. She felt like a beautiful painting, like something to be admired and appreciated. No one had looked at her body like that before, not even Summer.

He slid down her underwear, and his head went between her legs, kissing her inner thighs, kissing her everywhere but where she expected. Her stomach muscles tightened, anticipating. He ran his fingers on either side of her slickness, so tenderly, before dipping two fingers inside her, hooking them up and pressing, and she moaned deep in the back of her throat, her hips arching up. When his tongue joined his fingers, she almost laughed at how good it felt. Then his tongue circled over the most sensitive part of her, and all she could do was anchor herself by gripping his hair and closing her eyes, the intensity so great she could barely breathe.

The loud hum of the insects around them seemed to intensify, the pulse between her legs like a ticklish beating heart about to explode. She fell into the thrum-thrum beat of it, the rhythm of her increased breath, the sounds of Keaton's breathing with her legs spread wide, and heat burst through her pelvis and quaked up her body, the release causing her to groan with each spasm of pleasure.

She opened her eyes and caught a flash of peach among the green of the trees, and her head went electric cold.

There, standing drenched next to a thin pine tree, was Summer, her eyes wide and mouth set in horror like she had just witnessed a murder.

SUMMER'S JOURNAL

August 2012

This is a fucking nightmare. I keep thinking I'll wake up and then I'll laugh about it, how impossible it was for her to be with him in the grove, doing the same thing we did together, but I know it's real and I want to burn my eyes out. WHY?! Why Dev? Why Keat? Why our place?

I thought about getting my pills again. I really want to. Maybe if I did it in the grove, then Dev would know I did it because of her. I want to hurt her. I want to scar her for life. But it'd also kill Keat. I want to hate him so much, but I can't. I've never told him I like girls, but sometimes I thought he knew and that maybe he knew I liked Dev, but I never told him, so I don't know how to hate him for it.

But I knew. I knew how much he liked her, and I told him she'd never like him back, that he wasn't her type, and he shouldn't even try. I just wanted one thing of my own, one thing, but he took it from me, and he doesn't even know.

Nothing will ever be the same.

CHAPTER 52
DEVON

2025

Devon waited at the center of the barn, her body vibrating with need. Keaton commanded her to undress, closely watching her every move like an animal eager to devour its prey. He removed his shirt, his cut muscles proving he was no longer the sweet teenage boy she once knew; he was a man who could do damage if he chose to. Then he took off his belt and bound her wrists with it, pausing to make sure she was okay, before tugging her hard into his body and claiming her mouth, his tongue sliding against hers, causing the vibrations in her to quake further.

He threw a wool blanket over his workbench and bent her over it, her arms above her head, the scent of leather and wood filling her lungs. He kissed the base of her neck and ran his hand up and down her spine, causing goose bumps to trail his long fingers to her backside and upper thighs, his hand teasing higher between her legs, grazing the edge of her wetness before stopping.

"No words," he said and kissed below her ear. "I want you to be . . . silent."

The first strike knocked the breath from her, but she didn't cry out, however much she wanted to. He tap-tap-tapped the crop lightly against her skin before bringing it down hard on her ass and upper thighs, over and over. For every hit he made with the crop, he caressed where he'd struck, guiding her further into the still place in her mind where only pain could take her. Time didn't exist in that serene place, so she had no way of telling how long or how hard he was owning her. All she knew was suspense and the small release she'd get from his hits, the only sounds Keaton's heavy, sharp breath and the crop hitting flesh. She was only half-aware when he stopped striking her, his hand trailing down her back again as he ran the crop up between her legs, bringing her back fully into her body, her need slick against the leather teasing her. She was so desperate for something to fill her that she pushed back against the crop, wanting the tip inside her, but Keaton pulled the crop away, preventing her, and cupped her from behind, the heat from his hand driving her need to an unbearable level.

At the back of her mind, she knew he was edging her, denying her orgasm, and all she could focus on was his palm against her, so close to her swollen clit. She tried rearing back to increase the pressure he was refusing her. When she couldn't take it any longer and a whimper broke free from her, he dipped his fingers inside her and out again, eliciting a deep groan from the back of her throat.

"Silent," he reminded her with a swat to her ass with his hand.

He pulled on the loose tail of the leather belt binding her wrists, forcing her to stand up and face him. She kept her eyes on his bare chest, sweat glistening in the light dusting of golden hair.

"Look at me," he said, a new rawness to his voice. When she looked into his eyes, the impossible beauty of them filled with lust, with the power she had offered up to him, she felt flayed open and completely exposed.

Pulled close to his body, his eyes searing hers, his hand caressed over her breasts before moving between her thighs again, his other hand bracing her back. She closed her eyes at his touch.

"No," he said, stopping the movement of his hand. "Keep looking at me."

It seemed like a simple command, but it made her feel even more vulnerable, allowing him to see her in complete surrender. At first, he moved his fingers on her like he was gently rolling a marble in lazy circles, but then the circles he made grew wider over her wetness, driving the ache through her center until she bucked her hips forward, trying to push his fingertips inside her again. He seemed to find this amusing, because his lips quirked ever so slightly. He remained elusive, only giving enough pleasure to make her greedy for more as he kissed the tops of her shoulders and up along the side of her neck, building the ache as he drew the circles tighter and tighter over her clit, bringing her so close tears sprang into her eyes from trying to stay quiet while also not losing eye contact with him. She couldn't stand it one second longer, her breath too trapped to beg even if he allowed her to.

Then he suddenly stopped, releasing her, and she nearly crumpled to the ground without his strength holding her up. He removed his jeans and boxer briefs, the sound of his zipper making her center spasm in anticipation. His naked body was beautiful. All muscle and power and gorgeous desire. He turned her back around, bending her over the workbench again, and raked his fingertips over the sensitive welts he'd made on her body, causing her to gasp. She let out another shuddering breath as he pressed his warm, naked skin to hers, his hard length against the wetness creeping down her upper thighs as he fisted her hair and bit down on the flesh between her neck and shoulder, ruthlessly marking her. He slid inside her just enough to tease her. "Tell me what you want," he growled into her ear as he slowly dipped the thick head of his erection in and out of her, "or I won't give it to you."

"I," she gasped out. "I want you inside me. Please." She sounded like some wanton creature she didn't recognize as herself. "Please."

His large hand gripped the back of her neck, holding her down. "Now you can be as loud as you want." As the words left his lips, he drove into her, the fullness of him overwhelming, and there was no shape to her thoughts, only guttural sounds and muscles clenching hard and endless around him, her orgasm slamming into her, making her body tighten and then go slack as he continued to thrust until he came.

Afterward, he removed the belt binding her wrists and held her to his chest, stroking her hair and whispering praise into her ear for how much she had taken and how good she had felt. It was all like a dream, how he'd thrust in her, relentless in his strength with the side of her face pressed against the workbench, and how impossibly tender he turned after he'd finished. Then he led her up to the loft and took her again, this time slower and gentler, kissing her deeply and sucking the hard peaks of her breasts as he moved inside her. Her release creeped along her body, like a brush fire slowly burning through every part of her, laying waste to all her past reservations, her fears and shame, and she held on to him while he came deep in her, his sharp groan spurring even more ripples in her.

She watched him as he fell asleep next to her, listening to the soft purr of his breathing. She'd never fully realized how much tension he carried within his limbs, his face, until she studied him now in satisfied repose. He had so much responsibility on his shoulders, so much grief, and she wished she could remove it all from him.

She wanted to give him everything he deserved and so much more. He'd given her exactly what she wanted, what she needed after years filled with self-loathing and barriers built so thick she never thought anyone could break through to reach her, but he had. He understood her fears of intimacy after her assault, and he had eased her into it on her own terms, and her body had responded because she knew she was safe. And she now accepted what she'd always known but hadn't allowed herself to admit before.

She was in love with him.

She gently kissed his cheek, and he stirred a little, his eyes opening enough for him to smile and wrap his arm around her, tucking her against his body again. Eventually, she allowed herself to drift off with him.

◆ ◆ ◆

Wake up, Dev! Summer's voice, loud and urgent, but she didn't want to open her eyes. *Fucking wake up now!*

Devon coughed awake, her lungs on fire. There was smoke, so thick she could hardly see in front of her. She felt dazed and sluggish, like she was still in a dream. She looked next to her, and Keaton was asleep.

"Keat!" She looked around, trying to orient herself as another coughing fit hit her. "Keat! Get up!" She shook him hard until he roused, and he started coughing too.

His eyes widened, and she knew he was seeing the same thing she did: an ominous orange light from below, the smoke billowing up around them like a deathly robe.

"Fuck!" he yelled, struggling to free himself from the tangle of the wool blanket they were lying on. He took her arm, lifting her up with him.

"Help!" she screamed as loud as she could. "Fire!"

Keaton joined her in hollering, then his eyes searched around them. "How in the hell?" He grabbed the wool blanket, draping it around her nakedness and making sure it covered her head. He looked over the edge of the loft. "I think it's on the other side, but it's getting closer." He held her arms, his fingers digging hard. "Listen, we've got to get down before it reaches the ladder, okay?"

She nodded, adrenaline coursing through her blood.

Sweat ran down Keaton's face, hers, too, as he looked over the edge again. He turned toward her, and she saw the fear in his eyes. "I'll go down first, and you come right behind me," he commanded.

He began climbing down the ladder, and she forced her legs over the edge to follow him, her mind racing with fear as her feet hit the first wooden rung. She remembered how the barn doors were closed, and she didn't know how they'd get out if the fire blocked them on either side. Once they were down the ladder, she saw that the opposite side of the barn was completely ablaze. Her eyes darted to the exit closest

290

to them, and fire was licking up one side of the wide double doors and quickly spreading.

Keaton doubled over coughing, and she pulled him to her, placing the blanket over them both as she carefully steered them toward the door that wasn't yet fully engulfed. Heat seared her face, but she forced them forward, ducking low to avoid the smoke as much as possible. They made it to the exit, or she thought they did, the smoke so black and thick she wasn't sure, but Keaton apparently saw the door. He used their blanket as a shield as he fought to slide the door open without burning himself.

They tumbled through the small crack he'd made and staggered several feet before they fell to the ground, gasping for fresh air.

"Are you okay?" Keaton said once he'd caught his breath.

"Yeah. You?"

He nodded.

Naked, they crawled farther away, dragging the blanket with them until they found a safe distance.

Stunned and grasping each other close, they watched the barn torch the night, too exhausted to move.

Annie rushed out of the house in her robe, her voice frantic when she saw them on the grass. She dropped her cell phone as she knelt on the ground to look them over. When she saw they were naked under the blanket barely covering them, she averted her eyes.

"Fire department's on their way," she said. She looked on with them at the barn. "Good God. How did this happen?"

That was a damn good question, one Devon didn't have the energy to think about right then.

Boyd stumbled out of the garage apartment looking half-drunk. His face went white when he saw them under the blanket.

She glanced at Keaton and knew he was still in shock, his face pale. Not only was he losing everything for his side business, but he was also losing part of his family history, the barn his grandfather had built going up in flames. She squeezed his hand tight and tried not to imagine what would've happened if she hadn't woken up.

◆　◆　◆

The fire department came quick enough that the structure of the barn still stood, but the interior was badly damaged. They had received the okay to check for anything salvageable, though Devon doubted they'd find anything.

"I'm going to check over there," she said to Keaton, who was seeing if any of his tools were still good.

She stepped over pieces of wet, burnt debris as she walked to the corner of the barn where they kept the pieces of antique family furniture. From what she could tell, some could perhaps be sanded down to remove the smoke-and-water damage. She went to the desk she remembered Summer sitting at once. One corner had suffered a lot of fire damage, the wood blackened. She levered the top drawer open to see the extent of it and noticed the base of the drawer had bent and lifted. At first, she wasn't sure what she was seeing, but then she realized there was a hidden drawer within it. She saw something inside—something covered in frog stickers—and she suddenly felt lightheaded.

Using all her strength, she pried the wood up enough to pull the item out. It was damp and badly damaged, but she knew exactly what it was.

Summer's journal.

CHAPTER 53

DEVON

August 2012

The first day of senior year was one of the hottest of the summer, and the tepid air the school's vents were blowing was doing nothing to cool Devon down, her restlessness like fire ants crawling under her skin. Everyone in the school seemed on edge, the heat driving away any excitement about the first day. The only thing cold in the school was the way Summer had looked at her when they passed in the hallway. As for Keaton, Devon didn't know how to be around him now.

After what they had done in the grove, she quickly dressed and ran back home, leaving him half-naked and baffled in the woods. For the rest of the week, she'd mostly stayed in her room, knowing he wouldn't risk coming to her house to see her. She couldn't tell him she was disgusted with herself, with her betrayal of both Summer and him. If he found out about Summer . . .

In her morning classes, she sat as far away from him as she could, but she knew he would eventually corner her and want to talk. Same as with Summer, but she wasn't prepared to confront either of them. She didn't think she ever would be.

This is what sin does, a voice in her mind whispered. *You have fallen.*

When her last morning class ended, she didn't go to the cafeteria with the rest of the students. She couldn't stand the giggles and side glances from the people who had attended Ryan's party, the same people who'd said nothing when he removed her bathing suit top. It drove anger and shame through her body all over again knowing he'd gotten away with it while facing zero consequences.

She rushed outside and went to the back of the school by the huge, loud air-conditioning units working overtime. The old granola bar she had dug out of her backpack would have to suffice for lunch.

"Did you think you could hide from me forever?"

Devon spun around, almost choking on her bite of granola. It was Summer, her arms crossed. She was wearing shorts and an uncharacteristically baggy T-shirt, the scowl on her beautiful face making Devon's stomach roil.

"So, how long have you been fucking my brother?"

"I—we—we didn't."

Summer laughed, shaking her head in mock disbelief. "What do you think eating pussy is, Dev? It's sex. It's all fucking sex!"

She knew she had no right to cry, but she couldn't help it. She was losing Summer, and she didn't know how to stop it. "I'm sorry. I didn't mean for anything to happen with him. I promise, I didn't."

Tears were in Summer's eyes now, too, and it killed Devon to see them. "Out of anyone in the whole world, why him? My *fucking twin brother?* Why? Did you have some sick fantasy of banging both of us at the same time?"

"No!" But she did have that fantasy once or twice, and it shamed her to think of it now. It was like Summer could peer inside her thoughts.

"Then what?" Summer got right in her face. "Was I some kind of experiment for you to see if you really liked girls?"

"No, it wasn't like that." Devon squeezed her eyes tight for a moment, her lungs feeling too big for her chest. She would take it all back if it meant not seeing the pain in Summer's face.

Tears rolled down Summer's cheeks, and Devon wanted to hold her and wipe them away. "God, I've been so fucking jealous of him, and I didn't know why. But I knew I wasn't crazy. I knew it, and then I saw him follow you into the woods." Her lips curled back from her teeth, and she looked like she was going to scream, be sick, or both. She stared at Devon, and there was so much hurt in her eyes. "Do you love him more than me?"

"No," she quickly said, but she knew she sounded unsure, and she hated herself for it.

Summer closed her eyes. When she opened them again, her gaze was cold and empty. "Don't worry. I won't tell him about us. There *is* no us."

No. She couldn't let this happen. She couldn't lose her like this. She latched on to Summer, trying to hold her tight, to show her she did love her, only her, but Summer shoved her away. "Please, Summer, please forgive me! I'm so sorry!"

Summer gave her one last glare. "I'm glad I never trusted you." Then she walked away, and Devon collapsed to the ground, her heart feeling like a million bees were stinging it at once.

The bell rang, signaling the end of lunch, and it took everything in her to pull herself together enough to go to her AP Lit class. She was late, and the only free desk was next to Keaton. She knew he must've saved it for her, which crushed her even more. After she sat down, he reached over and touched her arm. She glanced at him and saw the concern on his face.

"Hey," he said. "I missed you at lunch."

She attempted a smile and failed. "Sorry."

He was about to say something else to her, but the teacher started talking, and she was thankful for it. She kept her focus straight ahead on the teacher, though she couldn't process a single word the woman said. When the period ended, she tried to hurry from the classroom, but Keaton caught up to her.

"Dev." He held her upper arm. "What's wrong?"

"Nothing."

"You've been avoiding me since last week when we . . . you know."

"I'm just not feeling well, okay? I think I caught a cold from being out in the rain." She could tell he didn't believe her as his eyes narrowed.

"Sure." He continued to stare at her for a few beats. "I hope you feel better. See you later." He slung his backpack over his shoulder and continued down the hallway to his next class.

Her stomach cramped so bad she almost bent over from the pain. She didn't think she'd ever feel better again. Not for as long as she lived.

SUMMER'S JOURNAL

August 2012

I don't want to think about Dev with Keat anymore. I can't. I have to think about myself and take care of this before he tries to get rid of me.

I know in my gut I wasn't the first one. I texted Jackie and told her I believe her about the test now, but she didn't text back. I think I ruined things with her. I wish I could talk to her because I think she's the only person who might understand what I'm going through. Everyone thinks he's this perfect Christian, including Dev. Why would they believe a queer, atheist girl like me?

But he won't touch me or anyone else ever again because I know something he doesn't, and no amount of money will protect him now.

I think I know where he keeps the photos he took of me, and I bet he took some of other girls too. I just need to find a way to get to them and take them to my parents. Then we can call the FBI or something. Get his ass locked up. If I tell my parents now, they'll report him, and he'll have time to destroy the evidence. It'll be my word against his, and I know how that would go.

I don't have a choice. I have to get them, but I need Dev's help.

CHAPTER 54

DEVON

2025

Devon stared down at the charred pages of Summer's journal in her hands. She was scared to handle it too much since it was damp from the firefighters' work, but she had opened it enough to see the familiar loopy handwriting, her heart seizing in her chest.

"Keat!" Her strangled voice didn't carry enough for him to hear her. "Keat!" she said louder, and he made his way through the debris to her.

"What is it?"

"A journal. It's Summer's. It was in a hidden drawer in the desk." She held it out to him, but she was reluctant to let it go.

He took it from her like it was a priceless relic. "Jesus. I can't believe you found this." He tried to open it and stopped. "We need to dry it out. Do you have a hair dryer?"

"Yeah, at your mom's."

As they walked out of the barn, Boyd was talking to the insurance adjustor who'd been assessing the damage. Devon overheard Boyd saying the fire had been caused by a trash burn that got out of control, and she noticed Keaton stopped to listen, Boyd darting wary-eyed glances at him.

Keaton handed the journal to her and went to the other side of the barn, Devon following, and stood where a metal burn barrel sat about twenty feet away from the structure.

"That bastard," he whispered under his breath.

"What?"

"He moved it."

"The barrel?"

"Yeah." He shook his head. "We don't burn trash anywhere near the house or barn, and we damn sure don't burn without someone watching it."

Devon was starting to understand his anger because she was now feeling it herself. "Do you think he got drunk and forgot to put it out?"

"No. That fire didn't start from this barrel."

His long legs stormed to the house, Devon struggling to keep up with him. Once they were inside, he went straight up the stairs to his old bedroom. He threw open the door, and harsh laughter escaped him when he saw the huge bags of wheat seed piled up to the height of the ceiling.

"My mom said you were staying in Summer's room because Boyd was storing things in mine." He punched one of the bags. "Yeah, a whole fucking year's worth of seed that should've been in that barn."

"What are you saying?" she said, her stomach going queasy. "That he set the fire on purpose?"

"Yes."

Her face went numb. "That's crazy, Keat. He had to have seen the light on in the barn. He *had* to know we were in there."

He moved past her and descended the stairs way faster than her own legs could carry her. When she caught up to him, he was standing outside by the porch, watching his uncle finish up with the adjustor. She could feel the rage stored in his body wanting to unleash, but he stayed put. Annie was pulling items out of the barn, leaving Boyd to handle the insurance claim.

After a while, the adjustor shook Boyd's hand and drove off in his car. Keaton immediately rushed over to his uncle.

"How much did you get for almost killing us?"

Boyd tucked a business card in his back pocket and crossed his arms. "You both look fine to me."

"You fucking bastard!" Keaton said, shoving Boyd hard. "For fucking insurance money? Tell me I'm wrong. Tell me!"

Boyd glanced at Devon. "I checked the barn, and I didn't see y'all in there. How was I supposed to know you were in the loft? Someone's got to take care of this business, and you sure as shit ain't. The payout on that useless old barn is going to cover our back taxes and then some."

"It's fraud! We could all go to prison!"

Boyd shook his head. "We won't. You're just too dumb to see what needed to be done. You think the IRS was just going to wait? It had to be done."

"We could've died!"

"But you didn't, so stop fucking crying about it!"

Keaton let out an animal howl as he tackled Boyd to the ground and started punching him, but his uncle was strong, too, and got in a good hit to Keaton's jaw, knocking him backward. Boyd climbed on top of him and started throwing punches. When Devon tried to pull Boyd off, he shoved her back, giving Keaton an opportunity to land a jab at Boyd's face, narrowly missing his nose and hitting his cheek. She looked around for Annie but didn't see her. She had to do something before they ended up killing each other.

"I'm calling the cops if y'all don't stop right now!" she screamed, but they kept fighting.

An eardrum-bursting bang went off, and they all froze as birds in the fields scattered into the cloudless blue sky. Devon's eyes darted over to where Annie stood, a shotgun gripped in her hands, her face still as stone.

"Y'all get the hell away from each other right now," she said in that stern, scary-calm voice only mothers had.

Keaton got up and brushed grass and dirt from his jeans. "Did you hear what he said, Mom?"

"Yeah, I heard him." She turned to Boyd, who was now standing. "Is that why you met up with the sheriff? You try to sweet-talk him again into chatting with his brother-in-law at the bank? As if Starling Thompson would ever give us a loan."

"At least I fucking tried!"

"Get your shit, and get the hell out of my house."

"That's my house, too, Annie," Boyd said.

"The land, yes, but that house is mine and Keaton's. It was left to John. Not you. Now, don't make me tell you again." She pointed the shotgun at him.

"After everything I've done for this family?" He spit blood on the ground. "Fuck you, Annie. And you." He looked at Keaton. "Ungrateful shit. Let's see how you do on your own."

Keaton rubbed his jaw where he'd been hit and grinned. "You can have it all. I never wanted it. I'm out." He looked over at his mom. "I'm done."

"Son," Annie said, moving toward him. "Let's talk about—"

"I'm done, Mom!" He started walking to his truck, but he stopped and looked back at Devon. "You coming?"

She gave Annie a sympathetic glance before running to catch up to Keaton.

As he drove them to his house, his knuckles white from gripping the steering wheel, he had the anxious energy of someone who'd just quit their job with nothing lined up. In a way, she supposed he had.

"Looks like I might be taking you up on your offer," he said with a nervous smile, his eyes not leaving the gravel road.

You'll have to tell him the truth eventually, Summer taunted her.

CHAPTER 55

DEVON

August 2012

College applications had opened, but Devon could only motivate herself long enough to complete one before she went back to lying in her bed. The first week of school had been the longest of her life, as she avoided Summer and Keaton and then heard the new rumor that she had gotten drunk and flashed everyone at Ryan's party. Now it was finally Saturday, and here she was at home when all the other seniors were going to the senior bash in Sweet Water Hollow.

She was on her way downstairs to get a snack when the doorbell rang. Her mother got to the door before she could.

"Hi, Mrs. Mayes, is Dev home?"

It was Keaton, and her stomach did a little somersault.

"Yes, Devon's here." Her mother pretended she wasn't standing only feet away from her on the staircase. "What do you want, Keaton?"

"Well, ma'am, I'm picking her up for the senior bash. Is she ready?"

"Oh." She turned around to look at Devon, her expression as sour as if she'd eaten a hundred lemons, rinds and all, before she faced Keaton again. "I guess she forgot to tell us. Her father wouldn't approve of her attending a party. Or going on a date without permission."

"It's not a party, ma'am. Or a date," Keaton said from the doorway. "It's a rite of passage for the seniors, and it's chaperoned."

"Who's chaperoning?"

"Holly Lynch's parents. And it won't last past midnight."

Devon knew that was a big, fat lie, and she marveled at how easily Keaton had said it.

Her mother faced her again. "Well. Go get your shoes on, girl."

It would've been easy for her to say she wasn't feeling well, but she didn't want to spend the rest of her senior year hiding in her room like Summer had half the break. And the truth was she missed Keaton. If Summer hated her now, what did it matter if she went to the bash with him?

She ran back upstairs and threw on her shoes. She thought about changing out of her T-shirt and shorts and into a dress but opted to keep them on since Keaton was waiting on her.

"I'll have her back by midnight, ma'am," Keaton said to her mother when he saw her coming down the stairs.

"I expect you will."

She hugged her mother goodbye, a newfound excitement lifting her spirits.

"I can't believe you lied to my mother," she said with a laugh as they walked down the long driveway to his truck.

He smirked at her. "I figured it'd be harder for you to avoid me if you were entrusted to my care."

"Keat, I—"

"It's okay, I understand why you got weirded out. We kinda went a little fast before, and I didn't think about it being your first time doing something like that. I guess I should've told you what I was going to do."

She blushed at the memory of her actual first time with oral sex, Summer's head between her legs, her tongue running inside her, and how unsure Devon had been when Summer guided her on what to do to her, how Summer had tasted slightly salty. She had known exactly what Keaton was going to do that day in the grove.

"It's all right," she said. "I liked it."

He smiled and took hold of her hand, and she almost yanked it away from him when she saw Summer in the passenger seat of his truck, her stare piercing right through her.

She felt like throwing up. "I told you we needed to keep us a secret."

"From your parents, yeah, but not other people. Summer won't say anything to them. I'm kinda surprised you didn't tell her about us."

Before she could respond, Summer popped out of the truck. "Hey, bestie. You get the middle so you can be next to your man."

She didn't know if Keaton had caught the sarcasm in Summer's voice, but she sure had.

When she got into the truck, Summer squeezed in next to her, her candy-scented perfume filling her head. On the other side of her, Keaton's scent of citrus and cedar battled with her senses, and she wished she'd never left the house.

As Keaton drove, he placed his hand on her upper thigh, and she could feel Summer's eyes on her leg.

Sweet Water Hollow was on the outskirts of town in the piney woods near the trailer park where Jackie Byrd lived. It was the place where people went to do bad things without prying eyes, but kids went there to party.

When they pulled onto the shoulder of the road, there were already a couple of dozen cars and trucks parked along the woods. They got out of the truck and strolled the path leading to the hollow about half a football field's length into the thick trees. Hip-hop music was blasting, and a couple of kegs were set up, with kids surrounding a small bonfire shooting sparks into the sky. Given how dry and hot it had been, Devon knew there was currently a burn ban, and she thought of the trailer park community. If a fire caught, these kids, many of them rich, knew their nice houses were a safe distance away.

Summer complained about beer being her only alcohol option, but she still lined up at the nearest keg with Keaton and Devon.

Devon didn't want to drink, so she pretended to sip the beer. Keaton draped his arm around her, and she saw Summer eyeing them.

"Let's go to the Witch's Lair," Devon said to him, wanting to get away from Summer. The Witch's Lair was what they called the giant pine with the hollowed-out base that looked like it led to a hidden underground world.

They walked for a bit until they reached the tree, the moon lighting their path.

Keaton leaned against the tree and drank from his Solo cup. "You and Summer are acting weird. Are you fighting again?"

"No."

He was quiet for a moment. "I think I might apply for college."

"So, you're not going to stay at the farm?" Hope filled her chest.

"My dad wants me to, but I don't want to do this for the rest of my life, you know? I want to travel. I want to see things, but . . . I don't want my mom to be alone."

"She wouldn't be alone. She has your dad."

"Yeah." Keaton took another sip of his beer and went quiet again. She saw his body tense up, and she didn't understand why he was letting the idea of college stress him out so much. With his mom being a former teacher, Devon figured she would support him in getting a degree.

Her own parents had always encouraged her to go to college since neither of them had, but they also expected her to come back and start her life in Arkana, to get married and have kids. But she wasn't even sure if she wanted those things.

"You should go to college, Keat. With your grades, you can get so many scholarships." She herself was banking on her good grades getting her some aid so she wouldn't have to take out a bunch of student loans. "You've always talked about being an engineer. You should do what you want and not care about your dad."

"I wish it was that simple." He set his cup down on the ground and pulled her to him. "What do you want for your life, Dev?"

Now, her mind brimming with guilt, she didn't feel like she had a right to want anything, but she eventually whispered, "To get out of here." She dipped her head. "To be happy."

Keaton wrapped his arms around her and lifted her chin. He pressed his lips to hers so softly her entire body burned for him.

"I want to make you happy." He kissed the words into her skin just below her ear, his hands going to her hair, and in that moment, she believed him and almost forgot about how she'd betrayed Summer. She believed she could be happy with him if she allowed herself.

"Yo, Keaton!" a voice called their way. It sounded like Mason, but she couldn't see the person through the darkness. "You've gotta come quick. It's your sister, man. I don't know what she took, but something's wrong with her."

Devon and Keaton raced down the path back to the hollow. A group of kids hovered around Summer, who was on the ground moaning, her mouth hanging open and skin so pale it seemed to glow. Devon stood frozen at the sight of her, but Keaton immediately dropped to the ground to cradle her head.

Jackie Byrd broke through the crowd of kids, cussing about the bonfire, which had grown larger. When she saw Summer, her eyes went straight to Devon and then back to the kids around her.

"What the fuck did you assholes give her?"

CHAPTER 56
DEVON

2025

Devon made Keaton go back to the farmhouse so she could grab some clean clothes and her hair dryer. She knew the best way to dry out a damp book was to air-dry it, but that could take days, and she didn't want to wait that long to see what Summer had written. When they made it back to Keaton's house, she asked to take a shower to wash off the smoke permeating her. She wasn't surprised when he joined her, gathering her soap-slick skin against him and holding her like she'd slip down the drain. After almost dying, it was like lust and fear possessed them, and she clung to him too. Once they were clean, they fell, wet haired, onto his bed, the sex urgent and primal.

She didn't know if it was because of how physically and emotionally exhausted they were, but they both fell asleep with the late-afternoon sun spilling gold across his bedroom walls.

The next morning, they spent a good hour sitting on Keaton's couch, carefully fanning the journal pages while running her hair dryer, the scent of smoke giving her a headache. Her heart sank when she saw just how badly the journal had been damaged. Most of the ink was smeared and unreadable, with other parts charred from the fire, the paper so fragile it crumbled away in her hands. But the parts she could make out created a lot of questions, some she was terrified Keaton would ask her about.

It was clear someone was abusing Summer, but she didn't name the person in the journal, at least not in the parts they could read. One entry in particular stirred nausea in her: *He took pictures of me with a Polaroid camera and some with one of those old flip phones. He said if I don't go to him whenever he tells me to, he won't help my family and he'll post the pictures online and everyone at school will see them.*

It had to be the mysterious texter. It hadn't been someone Summer was seeing because she wanted to; this person had manipulated her to his will. And Devon had been so jealous of him, taunting Summer about it. She had misjudged everything. Summer's depression, her isolation. She had been scared.

Devon tried to decipher other parts of the entry, but the paper was too smoke-damaged to make out the words.

An earlier journal entry mentioning Pastor Carter jarred her, and she tried to sort out her thoughts as Keaton read through the entries as well.

After he read them, he looked at her, a horrible understanding dawning on his face. "This fucker . . . he raped her." His eyes went back to the journal in his hands. "I didn't protect her. I'm her brother, and I . . . I didn't . . ." He placed the journal on the coffee table, and his face collapsed into his hands.

His body shook as she held him, and she wanted to absorb his guilt. She deserved it all. "You couldn't have done anything." But she could've. If she had known, if Summer had given her the note, she could've helped her. But Summer had decided not to give it to her, and she knew why. *I'm glad I never trusted you.* Summer's words coming back to her.

Keaton lifted his head and wiped the tears from his face, his jaw set. "She talked about Carter. She talks about watching his kid, and there was that part where she said he was going to help her, but he told her not to tell anyone about the pregnancy."

"We don't know for sure if she was talking about him," Devon said, though it was hard to imagine who else Summer could've been referring to. "She didn't name him in that entry. She could've been talking about someone else."

"Are you seriously trying to defend him?"

She knew Keaton was ready to pin blame on the first target he could, but they needed more information. "No, but I've known Carter my entire life."

"Just because you've known him forever doesn't mean he's not a pedophile." He stood up from the couch looking amped to start a fight. "What if he told you about his missing insulin vials on purpose to plant the idea of Summer killing herself that way? To explain away the inconsistencies of her death so you'd stop asking questions."

His theory made her sweat.

"I'm going to talk to him," he said. "See what he has to say for himself."

"No, Keat." She got up and took his arm. "Let me talk to him. You can drive me to the church, but stay in the truck and let me ask the questions. If he sees you looking like you're going to rip his head off, then we'll get nothing from him."

He shook his head, his hands anchored to his waist. "Fine. We're going now."

Devon wanted there to be an easy explanation for why Carter had seemed to be so involved with Summer toward the end of her life. She'd suggested that Summer see him, and if Carter was the one abusing her, forcing her into sex acts with him, then Devon would have a whole new layer of guilt to deal with.

Keaton pulled into the church parking lot under the shade of a tree.

"You should record the conversation with your phone," he said.

"Good idea." It was, though she suspected he wanted her to record it so he could see if she went easy on Carter.

The church was quiet, and she wasn't sure if anyone was there besides Kelli Williams, the church's secretary.

She didn't find Carter in his office, so she went farther down the basement hallway to the room where she used to go for Bible study. Carter was writing notes on the large dry-erase board for the youth group Bible-study meeting. She saw the theme was about making difficult choices, with stories about Rehoboam and Abraham, and she wanted to laugh at the irony. She hit record on her phone and slipped it into her pocket with the mic facing up.

She cleared her throat, and Carter turned around.

"Devon." He capped the dry-erase marker. "I'm surprised to see you again, especially after our last meeting."

The meeting where she had basically blamed him for not helping Summer when he knew she was pregnant. And now she had no idea how to find out if he was the cause of her pregnancy. She looked at him with his thick-rimmed glasses and unassuming smile, and she knew how easy it was to blindly trust him.

"What can I do for you?" he asked.

"I'm not sure if you heard, but there was a fire at the Harrison farm. In the barn."

"No, I didn't hear. Is everyone okay?"

"Yes, but the barn is a total loss. We found something of Summer's, though."

"Here, sit down." He took a seat on one of the plastic chairs, and she sat a couple of chairs down from him.

"It was her journal, and she mentioned you a lot." Although Summer hadn't named Carter in the entry Devon wanted to ask about, she decided to act as if Summer had. "She said you were going to help her with her pregnancy. She said you told her not to tell anyone or it could ruin her life."

His face went oddly blank for a second. He took a long pause, and when he finally spoke, his words were slow and measured. "I think Summer may have misinterpreted what I said to her. It's true I did tell

310

her I would try to help her, and I did suggest that she not say anything about the father to others."

"So, you knew who the father was?"

"No," he quickly said. "But she did say he was older when I pushed her. When I asked her if he was married, she wouldn't say, but I assumed he was. A teen girl getting involved with a married man? You know how the town would look at that. She would be a pariah, not him."

Nothing he was saying necessarily rang false, but something about how strangely calm he was talking about it bothered her. Maybe Keaton was right, and Carter had told her about the insulin vials on purpose. Maybe he was deflecting again, trying to steer her to someone else as the rapist since he now knew about the journal.

She narrowed her eyes at him. "Did you just assume Summer was having consensual sex with this older man she told you about? Did you even ask her when she was coming to you? Because I'll tell you, what we found in that journal says she was being sexually abused."

Carter removed his glasses and rubbed his eyes. He replaced his glasses and stared down at his clasped hands, his expression still calm. "I should've asked her. I regret that now."

"How were you going to help her?" she asked, trying to suppress her anger at him.

He looked at Devon, and she saw the first signs of apprehension in his brown eyes. Then he lowered his voice and said, "I was going to help her access an abortion."

She blinked, not believing what she was hearing. A Calvary Baptist pastor helping with an abortion? It was one of the biggest sins that had been driven into her brain since she was a child. And it was illegal in Oklahoma.

"How?"

He paused again, almost like he was thinking through what he'd tell her. "This was when it was still legal here. I had a friend who worked at a clinic in the city, but Summer wasn't old enough to get one without a parent's knowledge and consent, and I told her this. And if she had waited until she turned eighteen, it would've been too late, but she didn't want her parents to know."

She could tell he was withholding information. She had the same gut feeling she'd get when her clients were evasive. "Her journal entry said you would help, but it might take some time. What was going to take time?" A phone call to his friend wouldn't have taken long at all.

He sat in silence for a long time, his clasped hands motionless on his lap. "My friend at the clinic had connections. She was going to get Summer an abortion pill. But it was coming from another state, and she didn't know how long it would take." He sucked in a harsh breath. "It arrived the week after Summer died."

If what he was saying was true, he had done something highly illegal and, in the eyes of the church, immoral.

"Why would you risk doing that for her?" she said.

He shook his head a little and shrugged. "Because she asked me for help. And I believed God would forgive her. And me."

"Still, that's a lot to do for someone you barely knew." Maybe he'd been helping her only to get rid of the evidence of his abuse, but then he killed her instead for some reason. Perhaps Summer was going to report him. The more she thought about it, the more it seemed plausible, and it made her sick. She was scared to ask it, but she had to. "Did you . . . did you ever have sex with her?"

Carter stiffened, and his expression turned hard as granite. "I think you should leave now, Devon. I have work to do."

Then he walked out of the room, leaving her alone on the uncomfortable plastic chair, her question unanswered.

CHAPTER 57
DEVON

August 2012

Summer had a bad acid trip, or that's what everyone was saying at school the Monday after the senior bash. Whatever drug it was, it had taken a long time to leave Summer's system. Devon and Keaton had held Summer for several hours as she mumbled incoherently, her arms occasionally thrashing wildly at nothing.

Keaton drove Devon home by midnight as he had promised her mother, Summer still in her own terrifying world next to Devon, the flashes of the red dirt road from the headlights the only color she could see in the pitch-black night.

Devon's mind was still stuck on that night when she saw Summer hovering near her locker after the last morning class. Her stomach dropped at seeing how bad she looked. Her hair was unkempt and greasy, her body lost in the baggy sweatshirt she wore with shorts, and she wasn't even wearing lip gloss.

"Hey. How are you feeling?" Devon asked when she reached her locker.

Summer shrugged, not looking at her. "Fine." She seemed anxious, her fingers fiddling with the silver frog on her rainbow key chain, and Devon noticed her fingernails were bitten down to the quick.

Summer opened her mouth like she was about to say something more, but Keaton came up to them.

"You doing okay?" he said to Summer. "Jenna said you weren't in class this morning."

"Jenna should mind her own fucking business." Her face was an inscrutable mask. "I'm fine."

He didn't look like he believed her either. "Okay."

He took Devon's hand, and she saw the pain brewing in Summer's eyes at seeing them so close together. She wanted to go somewhere private so Summer wouldn't have to see it. She couldn't enjoy Keaton's touch around Summer, and she wasn't sure how to handle it without making things worse.

"Do you want to eat outside?" he asked her as he squeezed her hand.

She nodded, eager to get away from the torment on Summer's face.

After they'd gotten lunch from the cafeteria, they walked over to the bleachers, ducking underneath them to get out of the sun. She thought back to the day when Jackie had caught her with the condoms she had stolen, and heat rushed to her face.

Keaton took a bite of his ham-and-cheese sandwich, and she saw the unease in his eyes.

"Summer doesn't look good," she said.

He swallowed his bite. "I know. I can't keep covering for her when she does dumb shit like she did at the bash."

"Then don't. Tell your parents. She obviously needs help."

"You don't understand how it is having a sibling, especially a twin," he said. "It's like there's a code of ethics, and you can't break it no matter what."

"And what if she accidentally overdoses one day and dies? Wouldn't it be worth breaking a stupid code to save her life?"

Keaton's piercing gaze went straight to her heart. He had thought of it; she could tell.

"I don't need a lecture. I know my sister a thousand times better than you do, and I know whatever's going on with her will pass and everything will go back to normal."

Her impulse to argue with him further died when she saw the doubt on his face. He didn't believe his own words, and he didn't need her reprimanding him. Besides, she was sure she was the cause of Summer's recent behavior.

She moved closer and hugged him. "Hey, I'm sorry." Then she held out a peace offering. "You want my chocolate milk?"

He smiled a little. "I'd rather have you."

When he pulled her onto his lap, her pelvis grinding into him as they kissed, her mind wandered back to her locker, where Summer had stood waiting for her.

Summer was going to say something to her, and now Devon feared she'd never know what.

SUMMER'S JOURNAL

August 2012

I was going to leave the note in Dev's locker, but I couldn't. I just stood there. Then I went home and put the note in the Neruda book she gave me. I don't know why. Maybe my subconscious wants me to change my mind.

I thought about it so much, but I can't ask her to do something so dangerous. I can't drag her into this.

But it's not like I can get inside his house now. I wish I could tell his wife I forgot something, but he told her bad things about me, saying I was doing drugs, so I know she won't let me in. I'll have to do it when they're not home. She's going to visit her family in Lawton on Friday. I saw it on her Facebook page. And I know when he won't be there. I know their alarm code. I just hope they didn't change it. I'm scared he'll show up and try to hurt me, but I have a plan if he does. One time, Uncle Boyd took too much of his insulin and he got really sick. I don't want to take any from him, not when I know how much it costs, but I know exactly where I can get some.

If he shows up, I'll be ready. I'll fucking stab his ass with that shit and watch him die.

CHAPTER 58

DEVON

2025

Keaton held Devon's cell phone, his eyes closed as he listened to her conversation with Carter on speakerphone. He had turned down the A/C in his truck so he could hear better, and she was already sweating again. When the recording ended, he opened his eyes and looked at her.

"He didn't answer the question," he said.

"I think he was offended that I asked him."

"Offended?" He let out an incredulous laugh. "How hard is it to answer a simple question like that? He either did or didn't have sex with her."

It bothered her too. She knew Carter was hiding something, but she didn't know what.

"I don't know what to believe, but I don't trust what he's saying," she said. "But if it's not Carter, I think he knows something and he's not disclosing it, that he might know who the abuser was."

"And what? He's just going to protect him?" He slammed his steering wheel. "God, this fucking town!"

She touched his arm, wanting to calm him, but he pulled away from her.

He stared out the windshield at the church, his hands gripping the wheel. "When you were in there, I read the journal again, trying to find any clues, and what I kept finding was you." He looked dead-on at her.

She had deciphered those entries, too, the parts that weren't too smudged from the water damage to read, and she knew the question was coming. She'd been expecting it, but she didn't want to hear it.

"Did you . . . did you have sex with her?"

She wanted to lie, to tell him everything Summer had written about them was fiction, but she couldn't dishonor Summer like that. Not anymore. "Yes."

His head dropped. "Before or after you and me?"

She sucked in a quivering breath, her pulse quickening so much it made her dizzy. Telling him the truth would change everything between them, and she knew they wouldn't survive it. "During."

He lifted his head, but he wouldn't look at her.

"I'm sorry, Keat."

He got out of the truck and slammed the door shut, leaving the engine running.

When she saw him walking away, she turned off the ignition and pulled out his keys. By the time she got out of the truck, he was already halfway down Main Street, and she ran to catch up to him.

"Keat, please stop!"

He kept charging forward, passing a few teenagers hanging outside Dotty's Ice Cream.

"Please! Let's talk about this!"

He abruptly stopped and whipped around to face her. "She saw us, Dev! She saw us in the grove! Where you two . . . fucking hell!"

"I know. I'm sorry."

"Do you understand how completely fucked up that is?"

"Yes!"

His eyes shifted to the ground. "That's why she wouldn't talk to me. I could've helped her, but she didn't trust me. And you." He looked at her again, disbelief on his face. "You were her best friend. How could you do that to her?"

Tears came, and she couldn't stop them. "I don't know. I was young and confused, but I know that's not an excuse for what I did to you and her. I can't take it back. I wish I could, but I can't, and I'm so sorry."

Keaton had tears in his eyes now, too, and it nearly broke her to see them. "I knew. On some level, I think I knew, but I ignored it because . . ." He squeezed his eyes shut for a moment before opening them again, and the amount of anguish in them killed her. "But Summer . . . she always knew how I felt about you, and she still . . ." He shook his head and looked like he was going to be sick.

So many words choked her throat. She'd never considered that Summer might have betrayed him, too, by being with her. "Keat, plea—"

"I fucking loved you, Dev!"

She swallowed back her tears, the words she'd always wanted to hear hitting her like a grenade. "I loved you too. I still do, but I was too young to understand it then. I never wanted to hurt you. I really need you to believe that."

For the longest time, he seemed to be on the edge of a precipice, his face searching hers like he was looking for a safety net, and for a moment her ignorant heart thought he might sweep her into his arms, whispering his forgiveness.

"I don't *need* to believe anything you say." He held out his hand. "Give me my keys."

As soon as she gave them to him, sobs ripped through her. This couldn't be how things ended with them—it couldn't—but there was nothing else she could say. She had fucked everything up.

He remained there in front of her for several seconds as she cried, but then he turned and walked back in the direction of the church's parking lot.

In her mind, she heard Summer crying with her, or maybe it wasn't Summer at all. Maybe the voice had been her own all along.

It didn't matter now.

CHAPTER 59

DEVON

August 2012

Devon hadn't seen Summer all day at school that Friday, but she kept a lookout for her, wanting to see if she appeared any better than she had during the rest of the week. During lunch, she asked Keaton about her. When he said Summer had stayed home sick, an uneasiness clung to her for the rest of the school day.

It was strange not having Summer warming up next to her during the first cross-country practice after school, and she felt especially vulnerable standing off to the side by the bleachers while Holly and her minions looked her way, their fits of laughter making her want to run off the field.

Holly grinned at her just as Coach Thompson was walking onto the track field. "Hey, Devon, wouldn't you be more comfortable topless?"

The other girls laughed, and her face burned, but she refused to feed into Holly's taunting.

Coach Thompson looked between the two of them. "That's enough out of you, Holly." He turned to the others gathered around.

"Okay, girls, I can already see some of you got lazy over break. Don't let me see you slacking today, or I'll add weekend practice. Get to it—eight laps."

With the heat, she had hoped he would go easy on them, and she heard the other girls groaning about the number of laps he wanted them to do.

"Do you want ten?" he yelled.

That got the girls moving. Devon paced herself, feeling every bit of the junk food she'd eaten over the summer and the endless hours of TV. She made it around the track three times when she noticed Coach was looking at his cell phone, his face serious.

"Hey, girls!" he called to them. "Finish out your laps. Neighbor said my dog got loose."

She loved his little dog, Nova. "Hope you find her!" she said, but he was jogging toward his truck, and she didn't think he heard her.

With Coach out of sight, everyone stopped running. The anxiety Devon had been having all day increased. Summer never stayed home from school, but then she never really got sick, at least not in the two years Devon had known her. But Summer had looked so disheveled the last time she saw her, and she kept thinking about what Keaton had said, how she'd have low moods but would always come out of them. What if she didn't this time and it was because of Devon? The look of devastation on Summer's face when she'd seen her with Keaton in the grove—it was something she couldn't erase from her memory.

She hurried inside the school to grab her things. When she opened her locker, something fell out. She looked down and saw Summer's key chain, the one Devon had made for Summer with the silver frog charm, their saying—FAMF—surrounded by rainbow beads. She'd made it at the beginning of sophomore year, not long after she'd been at Summer's house one night, eating popcorn on her bed and laughing at YouTube videos Devon's parents would never have allowed her to watch, and Summer had hugged her so hard out of nowhere.

You're my fam now.

Her stomach lurched as she picked up the key chain from the linoleum floor.

Fam forever.

CHAPTER 60
DEVON

2025

After Keaton had left her on the sidewalk in tears, Devon felt disconnected from her body. She'd gone from feeling like she could have a real life with Keaton, that they could finally love each other equally, to having nothing.

With her car at Annie's house, she walked aimlessly for a while in town and eventually found her way to the diner. She heard people whispering about her when she entered the diner, but she didn't care. She wouldn't be in Arkana for much longer. She was at a dead end, and she didn't know what else she could do to find out who had abused Summer, gotten her pregnant, and likely wanted her gone.

Two older men behind her were talking about a business-alliance meeting scheduled for Monday and how high their bank loan rates were, and she thought about the Harrison farm and what Annie had said to Boyd about him trying to get a loan to help with the taxes they owed. She couldn't help imagining the entire town slowly shuttering and dying, Keaton along with it, and her heart ached for them all, even the people whispering about her.

Jackie was working, and Devon recalled some of the entries she'd been able to read from Summer's journal. She used to think Jackie's attraction to Summer went one way, but it was clear Summer had been with her.

"You look like shit," Jackie said, setting a full steaming mug and two creamers in front of her without asking first if she wanted coffee.

"Thanks."

Jackie sat across from her in the booth, apparently not caring if her boss noticed. "That was pretty badass, what you did to Holly at the ice cream social."

"Tell that to my mother."

Jackie smirked. "You talk to your parents yet?"

"No." They still hadn't texted or called her, and she was too numb from everything else to dive back into that black hole.

"Yeah, well, we're not all lucky," Jackie said. "My mom's always been cool with it, but the rest of my family . . ." Jackie shook her head. "Not so much. But you make your own family."

It was weird how nice Jackie was being to her. She really must look like shit.

"I found something of Summer's," Devon said. "A journal. It was damaged in a fire, but I could read some of it."

Jackie's eyes widened.

"She wrote about you. About the two of you." She thought back to Holly's party, to the night Summer spoke to someone outside, mocking their desire for her. "You went to Holly's house when she had her party. You talked to Summer."

She saw the naked shock on Jackie's face. "She wrote about that?"

"No," Devon said, knowing she had guessed correctly. "I overheard you two that night." She paused, trying to get a hold of the emotions pushing back up. "She also wrote about someone abusing her." She cleared her throat. "They were raping her."

Jackie sat there frozen, her eyes on the tabletop between them.

"She talked about Pastor Carter. And I don't know what to believe, but he knew about her being pregnant, and I think he's lying about some things."

As soon as she said his name, Jackie looked up. "Carter's not like that."

"How do you know?"

"Because he's . . . because I just know."

Devon stared at her. "Sorry, but I'm not simply going to take your word for it."

Jackie's mouth tightened, and she leaned forward. "Listen," she said in a lowered voice, "he, uh, he helped me when Pastor Walters wanted to send me to that conversion camp after they caught me making out with Holly."

"Holly?" Devon couldn't believe it. She'd heard all about it when Jackie was caught messing around with a girl, but she never heard anything about the other girl. Of course, Pastor Walters would protect his niece from town scrutiny.

"Yeah. We were just teenagers messing around, and Pastor Walters made it sound like I forced myself on her. Naturally, Holly said nothing to back me up. And then my mom and I ended up leaving the church."

Devon didn't know what to make of what Jackie was telling her. She wanted to believe Carter was the kind person she had known growing up, but he was still a Stinchcomb, one of the most powerful families in Arkana, like the Thompsons. He could do whatever he wanted in this town and probably easily get away with it.

"I hope you're right about Carter," Devon said.

Jackie left her to drink the coffee she never asked for, and something in one of Summer's journal entries began to nag at her after hearing the old men talking in the diner. It was something about a farm loan. She thought again about what Annie had said during the fight with Boyd. She needed to read the entry again to be sure, but that would mean going to Keaton's house, the one place she knew she wasn't welcome.

CHAPTER 61
DEVON

August 2012

Devon had to get to the Harrison house, the fear washing over her in bigger waves now. As she pedaled down the road on her bike as fast as she could, she saw Keaton's truck coming toward her, and she slowed down. He pulled to a stop on the shoulder, worry apparent on his face when he lowered his window.

"Have you seen Summer?" he asked.

"No. I was on my way to your house to check on her."

The concern in his eyes grew. "She's not there, and she's not answering her phone."

She rested her bike on the ground and moved closer to his truck, her heart speeding up. "What do your parents say?"

"I haven't seen my dad, but my mom's pissed. She thinks Summer was faking being sick so she could run off with someone."

She saw his doubt. She pulled the key chain from her back pocket and held it out. "I don't know when she did it, but she put this in my locker."

Keaton knew as well as she did how much Summer loved that key chain, how she'd fidget with it when she got excited or nervous about something, and she watched his face drop.

"I need to get back to my house," he said.

"Can I come with you?"

"Yeah."

He got out and helped her put her bike in the truck bed.

As he sped down the gravel road leading to his house, Devon's stomach coiled tighter. "You feel it, too, don't you? Something's not right."

He glanced at her. "My mom's probably right. She ditched, and . . . and maybe her phone is dead."

"You don't believe that."

"Stop making it a big deal, Dev. She's fine."

She scooted down in the passenger seat, hugging herself. Keaton did feel it, too, the sense of dread, but she couldn't change his mind if he wanted to pretend otherwise.

Keaton's mom was sitting at the eat-in kitchen table on her cell phone when they got to his house. His dad was brewing coffee and getting down two mugs from the cabinet. Annie gave her a tiny smile, but Devon saw the worry creases between her eyes.

"Okay, thank you, sheriff," Annie said and ended the call.

Keaton's dad came up behind Annie's chair, placing his hands on her shoulders, and Devon noticed her flinch. "What did he say?"

"That she's probably with friends and will be home before it gets too dark. He says it's too early to suggest she's missing."

"Too early?" his dad spit out. "So, he's just going to ignore what Faye Sturgis told us?"

"What did Mrs. Sturgis say?" Devon said, wondering what the old librarian had to do with Summer.

Annie's mouth tensed. "She called me a bit ago and said Summer was outside the library earlier today crying. When Mrs. Sturgis asked her if she was okay, Summer rode away on her bike. It bothered her, so she thought we should know about it."

"Did you check her stuff?" Keaton asked, obvious fear in his voice.

Annie's eyes widened, and she darted a glance at Devon. "Yes. She hasn't been in there."

Been in where? Keaton looked relieved, which confused her. How could he feel relief about anything with Summer missing?

"Her bike's still gone," he said. "I'm going to drive around some more to look for her."

"I'm coming with you," Devon said, not caring that her parents would be expecting her home. She'd call them later with Keaton's cell phone and explain.

"I don't want you all going out into the woods," Annie said to them. "We can wait until the morning, when there's better light. Your dad and I will check on the south side of town."

The south side, where Sweet Water Hollow was, where Jackie Byrd lived. The place where people hid their bad deeds in the thick pines.

If they found Summer there . . .

Devon refused to think of it. If she did, if she allowed herself to imagine all the horrible possibilities, she would crumple into a ball on the floor, useless. She had to stay strong for Keaton, for his parents. She had to help them locate Summer.

We'll find you, she chanted to herself. *We'll find you safe.*

CHAPTER 62

DEVON

2025

Keaton's truck was in the driveway, so she knew he was home. She'd walked all the way to his place in the heat. As she watched the early-evening sunset splash orange across his windows, she did a quick deep-breathing exercise, one she'd taught many of her clients suffering from chronic anxiety, one she used herself when flashbacks hit her out of nowhere. Before she could even knock on his door, Keaton opened it, his mouth set in a hard line.

"What are you doing here?"

Her heart was in her throat at hearing the coldness in his voice. "I—I need to see the journal. There's something I need to check."

"Is that the only reason you're here?"

"No." She wanted to hold him and tell him again how sorry she was, but the rigidness of his body told her to keep her distance.

His gaze was as heavy as a weighted blanket, but there was comfort in it. He opened the door fully and walked away. She took that to mean *come inside*, so she shut the door behind her and followed him to his living room. The journal was open on his coffee table.

She sat on his couch and glanced at him sitting on the opposite end from her, holding a tumbler of whiskey, anger emanating from him. "Thank you for letting me see it."

He shook his head. "I can't believe you had the nerve to come here."

"Keat, I—"

"No. I don't want to hear more apologies from you." His tone was harsh, and she deserved it. "You lied this entire time. You could've told me the truth back then, but you were too fucking selfish. You made me believe you gave a shit about me, and I'm sure you made Summer feel the same way while you thought only about yourself. Tell me why."

She looked down at her lap, gathering herself so she wouldn't cry. She owed him an explanation, but how? When she looked at him, there was so much expectation on his face, as if everything depended on what she was about to say. "Every day I lived in Arkana meant hiding myself, hiding the fact that I was queer so I could stay safe. I got so used to lying that I didn't think about how it would hurt others. But you . . . how I felt about you was never a lie. But neither was how I felt about Summer. I just didn't know how to ignore my attraction to you both. I was selfish, and then when Summer died and they said she killed herself, I knew I was the one who caused it." Her words broke as she uttered them, the guilt washing over her again as it always did. "I carry that every single day."

Keaton's hard demeanor softened some. "You didn't cause her death. You know that. You don't have to carry it anymore."

She was thankful for his words even though she didn't deserve them. "I carry a lot for you too. I wanted to be there for you, but I didn't want to hurt you more, so I stayed away." She swallowed back tears. "I wish I could change that. I wish . . . we could have a chance."

He sucked in his lips and looked away from her. "Check the journal. It's why you're here. I can't look at it anymore."

As she carefully opened the pages of the journal, trying to find the entry she wanted to reread, she fought the urge to stretch out her arm to touch him.

When she got to the entry, the ink was badly smudged, but she could make out enough to guess the meaning: *Everything he said . . . a lie. There is no farm loan . . . but I asked Mom about it the other day, and she looked at me like I was crazy. I wanted . . . I did it all for nothing.*

Devon looked at Keaton, and he was staring at her, some warring emotions stirring in his eyes. "She asked your mom about a farm loan." She remembered what Annie had said earlier to Boyd, about Starling Thompson not giving them a loan. Starling Thompson, who owned the bank in town.

She stood up, taking her cell phone from her back pocket, and dialed Annie's number, putting the call on speaker. Keaton looked more curious than annoyed now.

"Devon?" Annie said. "Are you okay? Is Keaton?"

"Yes, we're fine." She peeked at Keaton. "We found Summer's journal in the barn yesterday."

Annie let out a gasp.

"It's pretty damaged, but I read an entry where she said she asked you about a farm loan. Do you remember anything about that?"

Annie was silent for a few moments. "She, uh, she asked me one day why we rented our land from the bank. At the time, I thought it was a strange question because the land's never been rented. It's always belonged to the Harrison family, and I thought she knew that. For some reason, she was worried we could lose the land and our house, but I told her there was nothing to fret over."

"Thank you, Annie."

"Is Keaton really okay?"

"I hope so," she said, her eyes on him. "Try to get some rest, okay? I'll see you later."

After she hung up, she remained standing, the few threads she had collected weaving together in her mind.

"What are you thinking?" Keaton finally said after a long silence.

"I think the man who abused her has a connection to the bank."

"It'd have to have been someone high up," he said. "Someone who had the power to make big decisions on loans so Summer would believe it."

"Or someone who knows someone high up." That could be so many people, including Carter. His family was so entwined with the Thompsons. Summer would've believed him if he had said he could make a call to Starling Thompson. And the abuser had a baby. Summer had watched Carter's baby boy several times. She had written about it. She had babysat many kids, though, same as Devon, but only a few families had kids as young as Carter's at the time of Summer's death. There was the Tates' baby, and the Chandlers' baby girl . . . and Shrader Thompson's son.

Shrader Thompson, whose uncle owned the bank.

"Fuck."

"What?" Keaton said, standing up and coming closer to her.

"I think I need a drink."

CHAPTER 63

DEVON

August 2012

Devon's parents were about to ground her for being late until she explained about Summer having gone missing. Her mother surprised her by making her a cup of chamomile tea to help calm her.

"You know that girl's wild," her mother said, patting Devon's hand as they sat at the dining table. "I'm sure she'll come back home soon safe and sound. Let's pray about it."

But Summer didn't come back, not that Saturday morning or afternoon, and the Arkana police had no choice but to take it seriously. They pulled together a large search party and began combing the areas where Summer had last been seen in town. When they found nothing, they started searching closer to the Harrison farm, and a heavy dread laid claim to Devon, steadily growing and squeezing her head like a vise.

She was searching with Keaton and a few others in the northern part of the woods by the Harrisons' house, finding no evidence of Summer, though Devon wasn't even sure what to look for. She took out the rainbow key chain from her shorts pocket, squeezing it and praying hard to find something, anything, that would help them find Summer.

The August sun bore down on her, but she continued to move through the tall grass next to Keaton, his forehead fixed in a determined furrow, sweat soaking through his T-shirt. Devon only paused once to pull a fat tick from her ankle. They were turning back south when they heard frantic shouting.

Keaton's body stiffened for a second, his eyes widening, before he ran toward the shouts coming from the pond, Devon chasing after him through the thick brush.

There was a large crowd of volunteers forming by Chullusa Pond, some people yelling, others crying. Devon didn't want to know, didn't want to see whatever they were seeing.

Keaton fought through the crowd, Devon numbly following behind in his wake.

As soon as she saw Summer's parents jump up from where they were crouching, their faces pale as fresh milk, she knew. She was completely outside her body as she watched Keaton slowly go to his parents like he was walking toward his death. When he tried to turn his head to where everyone was looking, his parents quickly pulled him into their arms, preventing him from seeing, and they all collapsed to the ground, his parents grasping at him as if he'd slip away, their cries spreading throughout the woods like some dreadful song that even the birds stopped chirping to listen to it.

Devon forced her eyes to move to the place everyone was looking, the place where Keaton's parents had been crouching: a flash of freckled skin once golden but now drained of color, the caramel locks fanned across the ground with her bike close by, the hazel eyes that had mesmerized her from the first moment she saw them now open and staring at nothing.

You did this to me, Summer's voice rasped. *You did.*

She leaned over and threw up, heaving until there was nothing left.

Her legs barely carried her, but she made them move and ran, ran, ran all the way back to her house, pain and horror sluicing through her veins. Her mother was sitting in the living room, folding laundry, but she stopped when she saw Devon and rushed to her.

"Mama . . . Mama . . ."

She couldn't feel her mother's arms tightening around her. She couldn't feel anything at all.

"It's my fault," she heard herself chant, over and over. "It's my fault."

"No." Her mother squeezed her tighter, like she was trying to force the shock from her body. "No, it's not." She placed a hand on Devon's head, her other raised in the air. "Lord, please fill this child with Your Holy Presence. Please let her find refuge and strength in You, oh Lord. In Jesus's name."

Her mother prodded her, and she mumbled out, "In Jesus's name."

"Amen."

She let her mother press her face to her breast, but there was no refuge for her, not with God, not with her family.

Not anywhere.

◆ ◆ ◆

When people die on TV shows or movies, the funeral is always in the rain, the crying loved ones hidden beneath black umbrellas. But for Summer's, it was a blinding blue day and over one hundred degrees. Devon's long black dress glued to her back, her hair limp with sweat like everyone else's.

It seemed appropriate to suffer under the sun as Summer's body was lowered into the red earth. She tortured herself more by stealing a glance at Keaton, at his broken, empty expression as his mother held him close to her side like she would lose him too. She'd seen him cry during the church service, but he must've run out of tears like she had. It was like everything had been pulled out of her, a stuffed animal with its fluff removed. The thought made her think about Sir Croaks-a-lot. She hoped he was in the casket; Summer would've wanted that.

After the graveside service was complete, Devon shifted along with her parents in line to pay their respects to Summer's family. There were only a few dozen people who attended the service, and they were mostly school friends. People in Arkana didn't like attending funerals for someone who'd committed suicide. It was an affront to God, as Devon's mother had reminded her that morning. Pastor Carter, not Pastor Walters, had led the service.

Devon's father shook hands with Summer's dad, saying how sorry he was for his loss, and her mother told Annie she would keep them in her prayers. No one said anything to Keaton, to the twin who had lost his other half.

This is your fault, Summer's voice hissed. *You did this to him.*

She was right there, in front of him, but no words would come to her mouth.

His eyes connected with hers, and the ache in them filled her chest. If she spoke to him, if she held him, she would only hurt him more. She was tainted. Cursed. He could never know what she'd done, what she'd caused. All she could do now was let him go. Let him be free from her forever.

So, she said nothing to him.

Back at her house, curled in her bed with her black dress still on, she held Summer's key chain and pressed it to her lips.

Her parting gift.

Her severance.

CHAPTER 64
DEVON

2025

"So, you think it could be Shrader Thompson?" Keaton asked.

"I don't know." She sat on his couch, her head pounding. "I babysat for him and his wife at least a dozen times, and I never got any bad vibes from him. I mean, he was my track coach for six years. He had so many opportunities to abuse girls, but if he had, no one reported him." She leaned forward, pressing her fingers to her temples. "But with the work I do and the abused girls I've seen, that's not uncommon. Survivors stay quiet for a lot of reasons. And we already know the abuser was blackmailing Summer."

Keaton got up and went to his kitchen, soon returning with another glass tumbler. He poured her a finger of bourbon, and she was grateful. He didn't owe her anything, and he could've kicked her out of his home, but instead he seemed open to her ideas. She couldn't hope for more than that.

"Her journal," he said, "it's not enough to pin anything on him or Carter or anyone else. We need hard evidence."

"The abuser took pictures of her. He might've kept them someplace hidden. Someplace close to home so he could look at them whenever he wanted. Like a keepsake."

"Fucking sick." Keaton could barely disguise the revulsion and rage on his face as he took another sip of whiskey. "What are you suggesting then? Break into Shrader's house and try to find them?"

She straightened with an idea, a sudden buzzing going through her head and traveling down to her fingers, like the time she'd accidentally touched the frayed wiring of an extension cord and got shocked. "Maybe that's exactly what Summer tried to do." She thought back to the day when Summer had gone missing, the first cross-country practice of senior year and how Shrader abruptly left because his dog had gotten loose. She never thought of how strange it was then, but she did now. The Thompson house had a high, almost impenetrable fence, one their tiny dog would never have been able to breach. And the Thompsons had an alarm system with an easy code even Devon had known since she'd watched Shrader enter it many times. Summer had to have known practice was that day, and maybe Shrader's wife and baby weren't home. Summer might've stayed home from school so she could wait for them to be gone. It would've been a perfect time to search for the photos without getting caught. But perhaps Shrader got an alert that the alarm had been triggered and turned off, and he went to his house to check.

She relayed her thoughts to Keaton, and he sat quietly, taking in her every word.

"I'll go to his house," she said. "I'll chat with his wife, catch up. Do some snooping," She could see Keaton's skepticism. "There's a business-alliance meeting at town hall Monday afternoon." She remembered people talking about it when she was at the diner. "He's on the board, so he'll be there."

Keaton shook his head. "No, you can't risk that. If it was him, then he's really fucking dangerous. Only a psychopath could kill someone and then go about town like a normal person."

"I have to, Keat. For her. And people need to know if there's a killer among them who could do this to another girl." He was right, though; it would be a huge risk. She took a long sip of bourbon. "I'll be careful."

He held eye contact with her, his gaze softening. "I don't want anything to happen to you."

Her heart skipped at his words. "I meant what I said before. I know you may not believe it and that you'll probably never forgive me, but I—I'm in love with you. No matter what happens, I wanted you to know that's the one truth I have in my life right now." She couldn't tell what he was thinking as he stared at her, but the silence was becoming too awkward, so she stood up. "I'm, uh, I'm going to go. Maybe hit up some of your mom's good cooking." She tried to smile, but the attempt failed. She didn't have the nerve to ask him to drive her back to his mom's place.

As she reached his front door, a hand clasped her arm, forcing her to turn around. Keaton's eyes were full of every emotion, the gold and copper bleeding into the blue, sucking her into a familiar trance.

He cupped her face with both hands, the citrus-cedar scent intoxicating her as it always had. "I don't want to be in love with you, Dev." With her back against the door, he pressed his forehead to hers. "I want to hate you for what you did." His thumbs dug into her skin as his cheek brushed against hers, his stubble scratching her. "So much." His whispered words tickled her ear. "But I can't." He pulled back, his eyes glinting. There was resolve in his expression as he stroked her jawline with his thumb. "I can't."

Wetness dampened her cheeks as his lips found hers, and she opened herself to him, relishing his love, their kisses deepening, tongues caressing as hands glided across clothes, quickly unbuckling and unbuttoning, pulling off shirts and sliding down the last barriers to reach skin, fingers entering slick warmth and stroking hardness, their need too great for words, and when he lifted her there against the door and filled her completely, thrusting into her as she cried grateful tears and held on to his neck, she knew.

She was forgiven.

CHAPTER 65
DEVON

2025

As they lay in bed most of Sunday, Devon's head nestled against Keaton's chest while they talked and momentarily lost themselves with each other, she understood she had more work to do to earn back his trust. He may have forgiven her, but she knew him well enough to know he wouldn't forget. He had slowly stroked her hair as he made her promise not to go to the Thompsons' house the next day.

It was her last lie to him.

Miranda Thompson, with her fake-bake tan, blond highlights, and Pilates body, was exactly the same as Devon remembered her when she used to babysit as a teenager. Miranda was surprised to see Devon at her doorstep, but southern etiquette dictated that she invite her inside and offer food and drink.

"It's too bad Shrader isn't here," Miranda said, offering a tall glass of sweet tea after they'd gathered in the living room. "I'm sure he'd love to catch up with you, too, and hear about what you've been doing in the city. Are you dating anyone there?"

The way she asked it, with slight distaste, let her know Miranda knew all about what had happened at the ice cream social. All it took was one person in town knowing about something for it to spread like wildfire.

"Actually, I just started seeing someone," Devon said with a small smile. "And Shrader and I caught up a bit before."

"Well, you know he's pretty busy these days." Miranda sipped her tea. "Between his family's businesses and church duties and, of course, coaching."

Nausea hit her stomach at the reminder. "I'm surprised he has time to coach still."

Miranda's thin face tensed, her smile tight as a gnat's ass. "Oh, he always makes time to coach the girls. He's so good at it."

Devon couldn't deny it. For a rural town, the girls' team had won a record number of division medals during state track meets over the years. "He is. Tough but good."

They chatted for a bit about Braden and how he was doing in school and about Devon preparing to have her own clients soon. She thought about Paulette, how unbelievably patient she had been with her, even when she asked for a couple of more days before returning to work.

After they'd finished their tea and some pecan shortbread cookies, Devon knew she needed to make a move before she ran out of time. "This tea is going right through me. You mind if I use your powder room before I go?"

"Of course not. I'm sure you remember where it is." Miranda got up from the couch. "I'm just going to clean up in the kitchen. Got some dishes to do."

Devon hurried down the long hallway in the massive house to the powder room, turning on the light and shutting the door before going to Shrader's office, the first place she thought of for him to hide something private. It was a hypermasculine space with dark wood paneling, a heavy desk that appeared to be an antique, and two green leather club chairs in front of a fireplace. God, it was like every rich person in Arkana had a fireplace in every room. She quickly went to his desk and began opening drawers, searching as fast as she could. She was coming up empty until she found a small brass key tucked at the very back of the bottom drawer. None of the desk drawers had a lock, but a cabinet to the left of her did. She tried it, but the key was too tiny. She looked behind her at the small library, her eyes scanning for anything unusual looking that might take a key, like a fake book to conceal something, but nothing stood out.

She looked through the desk drawers again. Nothing. Then she noticed a wooden box on top of the mantel. Her pulse raced when she saw that it took a key. She pulled the box down and tested the key, but no matter which way she turned it, the box wouldn't open.

"Fuck," she huffed out.

She was ready to give up on the whole thing when her eyes fell to the hardwood floor and traveled over the stupidly ornate rug at the center of the room. There was a slight bump in the rug, as if it had been disturbed and not properly replaced.

She crouched on the floor and lifted the edge of the rug, and one slat of the wood flooring was missing about a half inch of its edge. It appeared loose, and her pulse spiked as she pried it up. Hidden in the tiny area, there was a metal case the size of a paperback novel. She pulled it out and saw it opened with a key, a tiny one like the one in her sweating hand. She wanted to open it right then, but she heard Miranda knocking on the powder room's door, asking if she was okay.

She'd taken way too long.

Her heart pounded in her chest as she tucked the metal case into her waistband, hoping her flowy top would conceal it. She put the key in her pocket and replaced the wood slat and the rug.

"What are you doing in here?"

Devon popped up from the floor so fast, she got lightheaded. "I, uh . . . I was just admiring the book collection. And this beautiful rug. Was it imported?"

Miranda stared at her like there were ants crawling out of her mouth. "It's a family heirloom." Her blue eyes drilled through Devon. "I need you to go. I need to pick up Braden from football camp."

"Oh, sure. I didn't mean to impose."

Miranda said nothing, her mouth tight, but she moved away from the doorframe of the office as if to say *get the fuck out of my house.*

"Thank you for the tea and cookies."

Devon left and rushed to her car parked next to the driveway. As soon as she got inside her car and turned on the engine, she pulled the metal case from her waistband. Once she opened it with the key and saw what was inside, her stomach recoiled, and she almost vomited right there in her car.

So many photos.

So many girls.

Summer was in several, her face vacant in each photograph. In one, Shrader's left hand gripped the back of her head as he forced himself into her mouth, his thick signet wedding ring glinting from the Polaroid camera's light.

She made herself look at them all. There was only one other girl she thought she recognized. The girl's face wasn't shown in the photo, but Devon was 90 percent sure she knew the girl from her body alone. All the track practices they'd had together—it had to be her.

Jackie Byrd.

She heard a vehicle and quickly tucked the metal case under her shirt. Shrader's large black monster of a truck pulled up next to her.

For a split second, their eyes met.

And then she drove off, trying not to speed, trying not to give herself away, but the inquisitive look in his eyes chased her.

CHAPTER 66
DEVON

2025

Devon needed to get to Jackie. She needed answers. She drove to the diner, which was nearly empty, hoping to find Jackie at work, but she had the day off. As Devon left the diner, she saw Sheriff Wright squatting behind her car.

He slowly stood when he saw her approaching. "Your tags are almost expired."

"I'll make sure to get on that, sir," she spit out, hurrying into her vehicle.

As she sped along the road heading south toward Jackie's trailer park and the part of town where Sweet Water Hollow lay, she called Keaton.

"It's Shrader," she said when he picked up.

"How do you know for sure?"

She paused. "I, uh, I went to his house."

"Dammit, Dev."

"I found the pictures he hid . . . pictures of Summer and other girls." Her voice caught, her words becoming strangled as she fought back tears. "It's so horrible, Keat."

"Jesus." He exhaled loudly. "Come back to my house. We'll figure out what to do next. Who to call."

"I will. But I . . . I need to see Jackie Byrd first. I'm going to go to her place."

"Why?" But then he seemed to quickly realize. "The police can talk to her later. Just come here."

Her mind was all over the place, the only thought strong enough to stick was seeing Jackie and confirming what she was almost certain of. If it was true, she didn't want Jackie to hear it first from some detective showing up at her trailer. She wanted it to come from someone Jackie knew, someone who cared. "I'll be right over after I see her."

"Dev, don—"

She hated hanging up on him, but she knew he wouldn't understand. She thought back to the time after her own sexual trauma, how she'd been in a room full of male investigators asking her question after question, some making her feel like everything had been her fault because of the sex work she'd done. Whatever was going to happen, she needed Jackie to know someone had her back.

She was nearing the turnoff to Jackie's trailer park when her car began to slow down as if her tires were melting into the asphalt. Her flat-tire light turned on.

"Fucking hell," she said under her breath as she got out to check her tires. Sure enough, both of her back tires were flat. When she inspected them closer, she saw clear puncture holes, and her mind immediately went to the sheriff. Maybe he was the one who'd marked up her car and left her that threatening note.

She heard the rumble of a large vehicle and turned around to see Shrader's truck parking behind her.

"Got a flat, huh?" he said, getting out of his truck and walking toward her. "Need some help?"

Her heart hammered in her head, making it hard to focus. Seeing him in front of her, knowing what he'd done, what he was capable of, made it damn near impossible for her to control her breathing.

"No, I'm fine, thanks. I was just about to call roadside assistance." She got out her cell phone and pulled up the number keypad, ready to dial 911.

"I'd put that away, Devon."

That's when she noticed the gun in his waistband and the black gloves he was wearing. *Breathe,* she told herself, but all she could think was *oh shit, oh shit, oh shit.*

"I think you have something of mine, and I'd like it back."

"I don't know what you mean," she said, trying to make her tone convincing, but her voice was strained and too high.

"Come on, Devon."

He took a step forward, and she backed away from him, her fear making her fumble over her own feet.

"You've always been a smart girl. Don't be dumb now. We both know what I'm talking about."

She thought of Summer, of all the other girls in those pictures, how scared they must've been, and her fear turned to rage. "Fuck you! I know what you did to Summer. To those other girls."

He smiled at her. "Everything was consensual. They all made their own choices."

"Blackmail is not a choice, you fucking monster!"

He came closer to her, pulling out his gun and pointing it at her. "Get it."

She tried to thumb 911 without him seeing, but he rushed to her, grabbed her phone, and smashed it on the ground. He kicked the pieces onto the grassy ditch by the road.

"Get it now."

She opened her car door and got the metal case she had placed in the middle console storage.

He yanked it from her hands, and a look of pity crossed his face. "I've always liked you, Devon. I'm sorry it needs to be this way."

"Fire!" she screamed as loud as her lungs could manage, knowing someone was more likely to come than if she'd screamed for help. "There's a fi—"

Pain shot through her head, bursting stars into black nothingness.

◆ ◆ ◆

When she came to, her head felt like a huge watermelon that had rolled off a table, splitting open into a hundred pieces. She tried to keep her eyes open, but they wanted to close again. *Stay awake,* a voice told her.

The ground was hard beneath her, dried pine needles poking the backs of her thighs. She realized she was in Sweet Water Hollow. Her hands were bound in front of her with a plastic zip tie, her feet, too, and her back was against the rough bark of a tree, and there was something stuffed into her mouth—a dirty rag, maybe something used on his truck, the overwhelming scent of oil making her nauseated. Her eyes focused enough to see Shrader a few feet away from her. He had a shovel in his hands, and he was digging.

She began to moan, in part from the tremendous pain in her head but mostly because she knew she was likely going to die and all she could do was watch her killer dig her grave right in front of her.

After everything she'd been through, she couldn't let this mother-fucker kill her. She shoved her fear down and used her tongue to push the rag from her mouth.

"Fire!" she screamed before Shrader stopped digging and took out his gun.

"Scream again and I'll put a bullet through your head."

Her thoughts were a jumbled mess, but she fought through the pain. She held her bound hands up. "You don't have to do this, Shrader. Please. You've known me for more than half my life. Let's talk this through. I know you're not a bad person. You just need help. I know you don't really want to do this."

"Shut your mouth," he said, not even breaking from shoveling the dirt. "I don't need your therapist psychobabble."

She grunted, twisting her hands, but there was no breaking the zip tie. "Others know about you. They know I went to your house. They're going to know you did something to me."

He raised the gun, pointing it at her head. "No more talking." Shrader tucked the gun back into the waistband of his jeans and looked at her, his face filled with that placating, pitying expression again. "You know, Devon, I never meant to hurt Summer. She was very special to me." He smiled to himself for a moment, like he was remembering something pleasant. "But she was a liar. She hid things from me." The quick shift to anger in his sharp blue eyes made her sick. "She tried to hurt me and my family. Did you know that? She broke into my home, and she had a syringe full of poison. And I . . . I couldn't allow her to hurt us. I had no choice, you understand. I *had* to protect my family."

Hearing him admit it brought her no closure. She would take the truth of Summer's murder to the grave he'd started digging again. She would join Summer in having failed at bringing him to justice. And she would take her last breath without Keaton by her side. He would have to find a way now. He would have to avenge them both.

She wasn't sure how much time had passed when Shrader stopped digging. He came over to her and grabbed her by her bound feet, dragging her over to the shallow grave as she kicked as much as she could.

He raised the shovel in his hands above his head. "I'm truly sorry for this." Then he brought it down upon her. She instinctively moved her arms in front of her, trying to shield the blow as much as she could as she kicked her feet out, hitting one of his shins hard. But it didn't deter him, and he landed another blow, narrowly missing her head when she tried to block him and hitting her shoulder. She kicked out again, her feet connecting with his knee this time. He growled like an animal, his face contorting with anger and pain.

"Fucking bitch!"

She knew he was going to beat her to death rather than use his gun and risk alerting the people who lived nearby. Eventually, he would win—her mind acknowledged this with cold detachment—but she would fight like hell. She would hurt him as much as she could, until the very end. She would do the thing Summer never had a chance to do.

He held the shovel high again, a renewed determination in his cold eyes, and she tried to ignore the shattering pain in her head, arms, and shoulder so she could prepare. She attempted to scoot back from him, trying to gain purchase, but her feet only slid along the pine needles, and she barely moved, so she quickly pushed onto her side, the blinding pain in her body knocking the breath from her as she rolled away from him. The shovel hit the ground next to her head, and she screamed as loud as her vocal cords would allow her and kicked her legs as he stalked toward her again.

Her vision blackened around her, and she knew she probably had a concussion.

Shrader straddled her, pinning her down with his weight, rage distorting the sharp angles of his face, making him look like an actual monster come to life. He wrapped his hands around her throat and squeezed, his body heavy on top of her useless bound hands, her heels digging into the ground as she tried to rear up. But her legs grew too tired, and she could no longer move.

There was nothing else she could do. This was the end. Shrader would kill her and destroy the evidence, and it would be Keaton's word against his.

Her vision blurred, but then she saw Summer standing behind Shrader. She looked so beautiful, so young and carefree. She smiled at Devon, and there was no anger, no pain in her expression. Devon wanted to hold her so bad.

I'm sorry I didn't get him, Summer.

She closed her eyes, and Shrader squeezed her neck tighter.

A loud blast rang out, and Shrader let go of her throat. Her eyes watered as she coughed, fighting to suck in whatever air she could.

She cracked her eyes open enough to watch him grab the gun from his waistband and stand up. She followed his movement, grateful to have his weight off her chest.

Then she saw her.

Jackie, holding a rifle in her hands several yards away, her tan skin looking ashen with fear.

Shrader held his handgun level with Jackie's head. "Put it down."

Jackie lifted the rifle higher. "I'll blow your fucking head off!"

Shrader laughed, shaking his head. "You always were a spitfire. I think that's why I loved watching you cry so much. You remember that, don't you? How you'd cry when I knew how much you wanted it. How much you wanted to escape that disgusting, abnormal part of you. You were so tough. So tough with everyone, but you weren't tough with me. Were you? No, with me you were soft. So very soft."

Devon saw the raw emotions playing out on Jackie's face, the immensity Devon felt in her bones.

"Put it down, Jackie, and then walk away." A strained smile spread on Shrader's face. "I'll forget you were ever here."

Jackie slowly shook her head. "Not a chance, motherfucker."

"Too bad." Shrader fired his gun.

Jackie hit the ground hard, and Devon thought for sure she'd been hit. Shrader apparently thought so, too, because he turned to face Devon again. But then she saw Jackie pull herself to her knees, her rifle high in her grip as she fired.

A short stunned grunt left Shrader's mouth. Devon watched blood bloom on his lower chest like flower petals stretching out under the sun's rays. He tried to take a few steps, but he stumbled onto the ground, his hand pressed to his wound.

Jackie struggled to her feet, and Devon now saw that she had in fact been hit in her shoulder, or at least grazed, since there was blood. She walked over to Shrader, the rifle still in her hands, and kicked his gun away from him. She looked down at his crumpled form as he stared up at her, terrified and whimpering, and she leaned down, getting right in his face, and laughed like no other laugh Devon had heard in her life. The chatter of animals stopped, insects hushed their buzzing, and the birds flew from the surrounding branches into the sky because of the terrible, loud beauty of that laugh. For a moment, she looked like she was going to shoot him, her rifle held up to his forehead, but then she took the butt of her gun and hit the side of his head, knocking him out.

When her wild, dark eyes fell on Devon, she grinned so wide and pure, like a child before anything bad in the world touches them.

From a distance, the faint sound of sirens reached them, and Devon grinned too.

CHAPTER 67
DEVON

2025—Four Days Later

Devon looked at Keaton's bathroom mirror and didn't recognize the woman staring back for a second. For one, her hair was greasy as shit since it hurt too much to wash it with her head wound. Twelve stitches and a bad concussion, along with an arm sling for her injured left shoulder, which had been knocked out of socket and reset. But despite her gross hair and the multiple bruises on her body from having been repeatedly pommeled by a shovel and choked, there was a new pride and calmness in her green eyes, something she hadn't seen in thirteen years. Maybe because she no longer had anything to hide, no secrets and lies to keep tucked away from others. She could look in her own eyes again; she could finally forgive herself.

She dabbed on a little lip gloss and pulled her hair back into a low ponytail. It was as good as it was going to get.

She entered Keaton's bedroom, and he was stretched out on his bed. Her chest felt full every time she saw him, knowing she was safe. He'd been like a mother hen the last four days, constantly tending to her, bringing her tea and whipping up meals for her even when she could do things for herself. He even made her chocolate chip cookies using his mom's recipe. She guessed it was easier for him to be in motion than focus on everything that had happened. When he learned what Shrader had said, she thought it would bring him some closure—Annie, too—but the only words he spoke after he'd cried in her arms for a long time were "I wish I didn't know."

He still had her old clothes in the large plastic bag the hospital had provided on his bedroom floor, as if she'd want to keep her bloodstained top and jean shorts. Perhaps she would frame them as a reminder of what she had survived. A reminder of Shrader Thompson finally being brought to justice. Jackie might've felt differently, but Devon was glad Shrader didn't die from his gunshot wound. She wanted to see him stand trial for Summer's murder and for the multiple sexual assaults he had inflicted upon so many girls. She wanted to see him put away for life. And he would if she had any say in it.

"You ready?" Keaton asked, getting up from the bed to help her put on the shirt she was struggling with.

"Yeah. Ready as I'll ever be."

He held her by her waist, careful not to touch her injured shoulder, which was still sore as hell. "Do you need another pain pill? You haven't had one since last night."

"No. I need to be clearheaded." She smirked, motioning to her stitches. "Well, as much as I can be."

He ran his thumb along her cheek. "You've already told them so much, and you're still recovering. They can wait if you need more time to rest."

"I think they just want to make sure my story doesn't change. And I'd rather get it over with."

The Arkana police department wasn't in charge of Shrader's case, not with almost a dozen girls involved over who knows how many years. The FBI had taken over, and they already had Summer's journal in their possession. Apparently, their forensics team had the ability to chemically remove the smoke damage so they could possibly find more evidence tying Shrader to Summer's murder. While she was still being looked at in the hospital, Devon had told them to make sure they checked his home alarm system from the day Summer had gone missing, if it was possible. She had a strong feeling it would tell them a lot. If they could pinpoint when his alarm went off, which Devon suspected would have been the same time she recalled him running from track practice to go to his house, then maybe it would align with Summer's estimated time of death. And there was also her pregnancy and the clear-as-day photo evidence of Shrader abusing her.

There had to be enough to convict him of her murder. As it was, she knew the FBI was trying to identify the girls in the photos. They had already spoken with Jackie and probably would again.

She wanted to believe Jackie hadn't made the connection of her own abuse to Summer's until after she'd found Shrader in the woods. Jackie had heard the scream of fire, and when she went to investigate, she found Devon's car with flat tires and a broken phone nearby. Then she went back to her trailer to grab her rifle and searched the area, seeing Shrader's truck tucked into the woods. She'd called 911, something Keaton had already done when Devon failed to answer her phone after he attempted to reach her several times. Then Jackie followed Shrader's tracks deep into Sweet Water Hollow, finding Devon just in time.

She would likely never learn the extent of what Jackie knew unless she chose to talk about it. But Devon knew one thing for sure: few people in Arkana had suffered as much as Jackie had, and she wouldn't allow herself to be upset at her.

Not for anything.

◆ ◆ ◆

After the meeting with the FBI agents and everything she'd learned from them, she finally took one of her pain pills. She didn't want to think anymore. All this time, she had thought Sheriff Wright and his department had fucked up Summer's case by ignoring important information, but it was so much worse.

Right around Summer's death, Sheriff Wright received a large transfer into his account, money the FBI determined to be from Shrader Thompson's son's savings account. Wright was in custody for questioning, so they didn't have much information yet. If he had helped to stage Summer's body with the drug paraphernalia found near her, it would've been easy for him, given his access to confiscated drugs. Since there were no hard substances in Summer's system, the agents agreed her death was likely a murder. With the evidence investigators had, they figured the sheriff had at least some type of involvement, including most likely covering up the murder for Shrader. Either way, they immediately found the sheriff's negligence in the case suspicious, which led to further investigation.

Devon didn't want to point any fingers at Carter since she now knew he had nothing to do with the abuse, but she did tell the agents what he had said to her about missing vials of his insulin around the time of Summer's death. She could've stolen it like he had initially thought. The "poison" Shrader had described Summer having in a syringe could've been a lethal amount of insulin. It was easy to imagine Shrader finding Summer searching through his place and then taking the syringe from her, injecting her with it. She might've lived if he had brought her to a hospital in time. But instead, she likely went into a coma until her organs shut down.

Carter may have helped Jackie when the town shunned her, but he had failed Summer. Instead of asking more questions and urging Summer to tell her parents about her pregnancy, he had told her to keep it a secret. Devon couldn't help but wonder what might've happened if he had done the right thing. She hoped he'd learned from this tragedy as much as she had.

Macayla's fairylike features still haunted her, as well as all the signs she hadn't acknowledged when she pushed the girl to speak against her rapist at trial. Macayla would never have justice. But Summer would, one way or another, and Devon hoped it would mean an end to at least one ghost crying in her dreams each night.

CHAPTER 68
DEVON

2025—Three Weeks Later

Oklahoma in August was dreadful unless you were indoors with the air conditioner blasting or lounging by a pool with a glass of iced tea. Or, in Devon's case, skinny-dipping in a cold pond with an impossibly hot man.

After three weeks, her head wound was healed up and her deep bruising had faded to being barely noticeable. The psychological wounds were another story. Shrader had betrayed her trust, had made her and everyone else believe he was an honorable person, and he'd almost succeeded in killing her, but it was nothing compared to what the girls he'd repeatedly abused had endured.

Once Paulette had learned about her attack, she told Devon to take her time and that she and some of the other psychologists in the office had pooled funds together to help cover her rent and bills. Even though she appreciated the offer, she ended up going back to work a week after her attack. She needed the distraction, although she was missing Arkana, something she never thought she'd say. Really, she missed Keaton—the way he got so ticklish when she danced her fingertips over his chest and down the ripples of his abs, and the way his tongue tasted sweet as caramel when she kissed him after they'd shared a drink of bourbon, and how he whispered *I love you* when he thought she was asleep.

She also missed her parents, but she wasn't willing to compromise her mental health by trying to get them to understand her sexuality or how much their brand of religion had harmed her. As soon as she got a new phone, since Shrader had destroyed her other one, she saw a single text from her mother asking if she was okay. If her parents really cared to know, they could've called or, better yet, gotten off their butts to check on her in person. The rumors were already out about Keaton and her being together, and she knew her parents were probably confused. She didn't owe anyone an explanation about how her sexual attractions didn't change just because her partners did. If her parents wanted to have any kind of relationship with her, it was their responsibility to take ownership of the pain they'd caused her. She wasn't sure if it was partially out of spite, but she had texted her parents a link to Free Mom Hugs, an LGBTQIA+ organization started by an Oklahoma Christian mom who'd spent years rejecting her gay son before changing and starting a national movement of support and celebration of the community. They didn't text her back, and she was trying to be at peace with it, but sometimes the loss of their love felt like a phantom limb, begging to be touched and feeling only air and ache.

All she could focus on now was healing and her growing relationship with Keaton. Until his house sold, they would have to take turns driving to each other on the weekends. He applied to a few engineering programs in the city with a plan to work part time while in school so he could graduate faster. The thought of him finally moving in with her filled her with a hope for a future she'd never dreamed of having in her life.

Annie and Boyd were dealing with their own life changes by figuring out what to do with the land and property since they finally agreed they couldn't continue in the farming business. Keaton might've told them he was giving up his rights to his inheritance, but Annie wouldn't hear of it. Devon knew whatever money he might get would go toward his education and the new life he would build with her in the city.

Chullusa Pond was pleasantly cool when she ducked under the water again, coming back up to splash Keaton in the face. He stopped her, cuffing her wrists with his hands.

"You're lucky I love you. You're being so naughty today." He tugged her closer, until her captured hands touched his chest. "It's almost like you want to be punished."

A quiver of excitement went to her hips. "And what if I do?"

His lips quirked. "That can be arranged."

She was thankful he appreciated that part of her sexuality, how he shared her desire to bond on a deeper level than simply their bodies. After what she'd gone through the year before, it felt like another way to heal by reclaiming what others had tried to take.

She kissed him, and his hands released hers so he could hold her, both kicking their legs to stay afloat. When they got too tired, they swam back to the shoreline. As much as she wanted to push him back onto a towel and ride him right there, teenagers could show up, with it being a Saturday, so they grabbed their things and walked into the woods.

They both knew the perfect spot to stretch out and pleasure each other, but they went along a different path. The grove wasn't for them; it was Summer's place.

Going to the pond had been difficult for her, but it'd been a happy place for them all once upon a time, and she wanted to honor those memories. And she wanted to create new ones with Keaton.

When they found a grassy area nestled among the trees, Devon dropped her tote bag and helped Keaton spread out their towels. As she straddled him, sinking herself onto him, his eyes staring up at her with pure adoration, she made a promise to herself to always savor this, to never take for granted this love she had with him. They held eye contact the entire time their bodies joined, something she knew Keaton enjoyed, and the intensity of it made her feel so vulnerable, but not in a bad way. She was safe. She had always been safe with him, and it made it easier for her to lose herself as she slid up and down him, circling her hips and grinding, watching his pleasure mount alongside hers. The moment she came, her muscles pulsing around him, he gripped her hips hard, thrusting up until he came, too, filling her.

After they lazed for a while, their bodies spent, they forced themselves to move out of hunger. It was getting near dusk, the cicadas' song growing louder. They pulled on their clothes and shoes and walked back through the woods along the path they had taken so many times as teenagers.

They came to a fork, one path leading back toward the area where Keaton's truck was parked, the other to the grove.

As they passed it by, Devon stopped. There was something she needed to do, something she had discussed with Keaton before she drove up to Arkana for the weekend.

Keaton squeezed her hand. "Do you want me to come with you?"

She adjusted the bag slung over her shoulder and kissed him. "No. But thank you."

She walked down the trail to where the trees thinned out and the ground turned from tall grass to a thick bed of delicate blue flowers. It truly was a fairyland. A sacred place.

Devon felt Summer all around her as if her friend's soul had fused with nature. She opened her tote bag and pulled out the small hammer and long nail she'd packed. She walked over to one of the redbud trees lining the clearing. Summer had loved the redbuds when they bloomed in spring, their magenta flowers vibrant against the viridescent woods.

Devon took the nail, placing it at eye level, and hammered it into the bark. Then she dug into her bag and pulled out the gift she'd made Summer all those years ago, the gift Summer had returned before she left the world: the rainbow key chain, the beads scratched with age, the frog charm tarnished.

She placed the key chain on the nail and then hammered the head upward so it would hopefully stay on through wind and rain.

Devon held the key chain, caressing it as she whispered her own kind of prayer, tears spilling down her cheeks. "I'm sorry I didn't love you the way you deserved to be loved." She twisted the white beads until the letters aligned: FAMF. "But I did always love you. And I'll always be your fam." She swallowed, the fullness in her throat as thick as the flowers beneath her feet.

A lightness came over her as she left the grove and made her way back to Keaton. When she saw him leaning against a tree, his gaze catching her, she realized she no longer felt guilty for loving him. Maybe it was because she had forgiven herself, and maybe Summer had forgiven her too.

She turned back one last time toward the grove, a tug in her chest tightening before expanding her lungs, filling her with immense gratitude.

Forever.

ACKNOWLEDGMENTS

Thank you to my family and friends who made it easier for me to be an out and proud bisexual person. Since I grew up in a highly conservative state, it took me a long time to feel safe to live my truest self, and I'm grateful for my local vibrant, supportive LGBTQ+ community.

As always, I'm forever thankful to you, the reader, for allowing me to share stories important to me, which I hope will resonate with you. Sharing this writing journey with you and hearing your thoughts is one of the greatest joys of my life.

Endless thanks to the beautiful bookstagram community, who spread the word about my work and offer so much love, humor, and support to me and other authors. I've loved getting to know so many of you, and I look forward to meeting more of you in person someday. You are a gift!

Eternal thanks to my wonderful agent, Sandy Lu, who has been such a huge support. Thank you for believing in me even when I'm unsure of myself (and for helping my insomnia!).

Huge thank-yous to Anh Schluep, Alison Dasho, and the rest of the amazing team at Amazon Publishing. Everyone knows editing is where the magic happens, and I don't have enough words to express my gratitude for the incomparable Charlotte Herscher. This is my second time working with Charlotte, and she always seems to know exactly how to push me to make the story stronger and richer. Big thank-you as well to Alicia and Rachel for their extraordinary copyediting skills—you catch everything!

Writing is a lonely endeavor, but it's made less so by the outstanding writers I get to call friends: S. A. Cosby, Paulette Kennedy, Samantha Bailey, Christa Faust, Mer Whinery, Suzanne Miller, James Queally, Mark Westmoreland, and Amina Akhtar, just to name a few. You all inspire me, and I love you to pieces!

Last but never least, thank you to my husband—the best partner, father, and friend—for always accepting every part of me and showing me the true meaning of unconditional love. I lovers you, Bambi.

ABOUT THE AUTHOR

Photo © 2021 David Bricquet

Heather Levy is a born-and-bred Oklahoman and graduate of Oklahoma City University's Red Earth MFA program for creative writing. The *New York Times* called her Anthony-nominated debut *Walking Through Needles* "a spellbinding novel at the nexus of power, desire, and abuse that portends a bright future"; and the *LA Times* called it "a standout for its frank but sensitive exploration of trauma and desire." *Publishers Weekly* said her thriller *Hurt for Me* "delivers both heat and heart."

Her novels focus on kink-positive stories centered on complex women. She lives in Oklahoma with her husband, two kids, and three murderous cats. Readers can follow her on X and IG @heatherllevy or on her website at www.heatherlevywriter.com.